Sweet Dreams Publishing
of Massachusetts

HOA
GOLD

I0617792

STEVEN I. DAHL, M.D.
A NOVEL

Other books by
STEVEN I. DAHL, M·D·

Chicken Fried Steak, Action-Adventure
Picasso's Zipline, Adventure/Medical Mystery
Kick the Can, Murder-Mystery
Rattlesnake, Wait and "See"

HOA GOLD

STEVEN I. DAHL, M.D.

A Novel

Sweet Dreams Publishing
of Massachusetts

HOA Gold!
Published by Sweet Dreams Publishing of Massachusetts, December, 2010

Cover Design: Susan Veach
Interior Design & Layout: Lisa Akoury-Ross
Photo credits: Front cover: *bulldozer,* iStockphoto.com; *cactus and city,* iStockphoto.com; Back cover: *shovels,* IStockphoto.com; *neighborhood on shovel blade,* IStockphoto.com

For more information about this book contact Sweet Dreams Publishing of MA by email at info@PublishAtSweetDreams.com

Library of Congress Control Number: 2010931120

ISBN-10: 0-9824461-6-0
ISBN-13: 978-0-9824461-6-4

Printed in the United States of America

"The stories of gold buried in the hills around Phoenix have lit a fire of yearning in the dreams of young and old for years. *HOA Gold* fans the embers into a brush fire. Steve Dahl's narrative is so down to earth, so real you begin to think Hidden Canyon is your neighborhood, your neighbors; and together you are about to unearth lost treasure. This is a clever story with many twists, interesting characters, and striking metaphor. A great read!"

Julie Schenk Lassetter, Author of
Scripture Symbol Stories for Children

Other books published by
Sweet Dreams Publishing of Massachusetts

Chicken Fried Steak, Action-Adventure
  by Steven I. Dahl, M.D.

*One on One: My Journey with Hall of Famers, Fan
    Favorites and Rising Stars*, Sports Memoir
  by Jane Mitchell, TV Sports Show Host,
  San Diego, CA

New American Cuisine for Today's Family, Mediterranean
Cookbook
  by Lisa Akoury-Ross

A Wayward Oath, Crime/Detective Novella
  by Bill Jacques, Writer, Actor

Oodle Van Boodle and The Great Cake Adventure,
A Children's Story
  by Kim Shanley-Peretti, Olivia and Luke's Mom

The Emperor's New Throne, A Children's Story
  by Julia Broomall

Visit us at:
www.PublishAtSweetDreams.com
or
Contact us at:
info@PublishAtSweetDreams.com

To my brothers, Doug and Carl, who encouraged me to create a work that would outlive my mortal being.

I

ATTACKED

Brighton Dunn adjusted his magnifying glasses to a higher power and squinted, trying to visualize the miniscule fragments of gold scattered into the corners of the workbench. Using tiny tweezers with ultra-fine tips, he carefully plucked each fragment from its resting place and dropped it into a small glass beaker. The cleanup work was tedious and, in his mind, a waste of time following the grinding, shaping, and polishing of the third molar gold crown. The work had drained his energy. It was beginning to look as though his day would never end.

"Don't forget to clean up after yourself this time, Dr. Dunn. Your mother still doesn't work here," Margo, the resident witch and manager of the dental lab, yelled at him as she slammed the door to leave for the night. She was down his throat if she found even the slightest particle of wasted gold dust. The last time he used the lab, Margo had ranted on about how he left a toothpick lying on the bench.

As he exited the dental lab that night, he resolved to start his own lab, but in reality, it wasn't worth the effort.

Renting time at the dental lab had been a big help to his fledgling dental practice. Buying materials only as he needed them these last twenty months had saved tons of money, as the startup expenses of his dental practice had been astonishing. That was something for which he had been unprepared. The dental school faculty had lectured students on the fine points of every tooth anomaly with the arrogance of rock stars. He had been promised that his training would prepare him for every possible dental situation. The problem was that the professors didn't have a clue when it came to the business of the practice of dentistry.

Brighton had to learn about the business by trial and error. He learned new ways of doing almost everything, and was feeling comfortable in the management of his practice. His business was flourishing, and the long-awaited reward for his years of schooling and huge student loan debt was starting to pay off.

Using a camel hairbrush and a miniature dustpan, he gleaned the last visible particles of dental-grade gold from the workbench, adding them to the crucible for weighing. Holding the finished molar crown up to the light, he smiled and took a deep breath. It was a work of art, and would be a perfect fit for the patient.

He stretched his muscular, six-foot-tall body, making a few twists and shoulder rotations to get the blood circulating. He hung his tattered blue lab coat on a hook and headed toward the parking lot. Eight hours working in the office, another two in the lab, and now the commute home to the rental. What a day, what a week, what a crazy life. On occasion he looked back on his school years with a wish to return to that uncomplicated life of a newlywed student.

Calculating the few minutes of remaining daylight, he smiled at his watch, then diverted from his usual route home. Within ten minutes he wheeled his faded silver Honda to a stop in front of the large, bronze-colored gates of Hidden Canyon. It was the newest and, he and Gina felt certain, the finest residential area in the entire desert valley. Putting his life savings on the table, they signed away what seemed like any future earnings to buy the building lot for a new home. Only time would tell if they had been wise, crazy, or just infatuated. Maybe it was all three.

Gina had insisted on using a special code to open the ornately designed security gate. It was the only entrance into the newest private neighborhood in the East Valley.

"No brainless and meaningless number for the Dunn family," she had insisted. The number "1776" was the code she wanted. "It will remind us each time we enter that the pleasures, luxuries, and freedoms of our lives should not be taken for granted."

Lot #37 was up a twisty, long, sloping hill toward the last cul-de-sac in the development. Rustic street lamps lined the new, smooth roadway with its dedicated biking and hiking paths. An ornate street sign near their building lot read, "CACTUS WREN CIRCLE."

Brighton stopped his car in front of a small, carved wooden SOLD sign nailed below Lot #37. The little wooden sign made Brighton grin.

When they initially viewed the lot, the first thing that caught the Dunns' attention was a giant saguaro cactus with its three upward-reaching arms. The Dunns were told that a cactus like theirs was over 150 years old. When the building plans for the house were drawn up, the cactus became the focal point of the entire project.

The large lot bordered on undeveloped virgin desert with rock-strewn hills, scattered native trees, and more towering cacti. They were promised that there would never be any development behind their property line, since it had been designated a protected environment. The sprawling valley stretched to the horizon with the early evening lights of Scottsdale, Mesa, and far beyond the skyline of downtown Phoenix all outlined by the setting sun. He loved this lot. He loved the view. He couldn't wait for his own home to be built, so he and his wife could sit on the porches and soak in the views.

Jumping out of the car with a renewed level of energy, Brighton walked up the freshly graded driveway where just days before the natural desert plants and rocks first had been assaulted with Caterpillar tractors and giant backhoes. Having picked his way up to the leveled house site, he turned to face the west and the setting sun. His lot sat far enough above the surrounding houses; once darkness settled over the valley he knew the entire horizon would be a jubilee of lights. His giant saguaro cactus stood in the foreground of the sunset, giving a postcard-perfect image to the scene.

"And thus ends the life and beauty of hundreds of God's masterful botanical creations!" a woman's voice thundered through the cool, still air.

Startled, Brighton froze in place.

"I would suppose that this rape of the desert is your idea of the good life?" she continued. "Why, I'll bet you've probably never even ventured off that paved street down there until the tractors cleared away the nasty, sharp cactus. Bare dirt covered with concrete and artificial turf, that's what your kind wants. Isn't it?"

He turned toward the voice and saw the outline of a woman standing a couple feet away. Stepping backward, he was barely able to maintain his balance on the uneven ground. His smooth, leather-soled shoes skidded on the loose dirt, scraping his ankle against a large, uprooted chunk of granite, slicing through his sock and into his flesh.

The woman carried a tall, oak-colored walking stick in one hand and an apple-sized rock in the other. In the diminishing light, her long gray hair appeared streaked with blonde. It was braided and tied at the end with a piece of what looked like packing twine. She wore leather sandals with soles made from discarded auto tires, just like ones he had in his college days. The woman's loose-fitting cotton dress had a scooped neck and long sleeves and hung just above her ankles. Later that night, when Gina would ask him to describe the woman, he would only remember that the dress looked like the flour sacks his grandmother used to keep around the house for cleaning rags.

"You spooked me," Brighton said to the woman in a voice that didn't even sound like his own. He waited for a response or apology but received only a vicious glare.

"I'm Brighton Dunn. I'm building a home here," he continued in a cautious voice. He extended his hand toward the woman, but she didn't even look at it, let alone take it.

"You rich people send your tractors up my mountain to rip everything to pieces just so you can prove to your city friends that you can build a bigger, fancier house and look down your noses at them. This land doesn't belong to you. It belongs to the animals and birds and the few who appreciate it. Not to you," she said in a hateful voice.

He stared at the hardwood walking stick and wondered if she might use it on his head if he didn't say the right thing. He dropped his hand and cleared his throat. He was sure he could cajole this woman; after all, he talked people into root canals, didn't he?

"My wife and I come from hard-working families. We have been starving students for years. We just want to live up here to enjoy the view and the fresh air. We love the birds and the wild animals, too."

She dropped the rock in her hand and continued to glare at him.

"It seems the air at this altitude is much cleaner and clearer. Wouldn't you agree?" he asked, trying to get her to warm up to him a little. "Are the stars a lot brighter here at night?" She didn't answer.

"We haven't had the chance to be up here late at night." He continued, still trying to pry a little humanity out of this woman, whom he was beginning to think was a complete nutcase, or maybe just a bit slow.

"Is your tractor finished ripping out the plants yet, or are you going to keep scraping until nothing is left alive?" Her voice was cold and flat.

"I'm sure this is all they are going to do. They just need to level it and bring in some fill dirt for the base of the house. When the house is completed, we will replace all the plants and trees with natural desert landscaping." He could feel himself beginning to get angry. His ankle was throbbing, but he hadn't looked down to see if it was bleeding. The conversation with her was pointless, just like trying to talk sense to his patients who thought fluoride toothpaste was lethal.

"Your idea of natural landscaping is a joke. You can't scrape off the surface vegetation that's been here for hundreds of years and then replace it in two weeks with a bunch of nursery-grown plants and call that natural. Are you stupid?"

He turned away from her and took a deep breath. He just wanted to view the sunset and regain the sense of calm he had driven up here to enjoy. He took another deep breath and started to walk away when the walking stick smashed into his right knee. Before he could put out his hands to catch his fall, his knee collapsed, and with a gruesome thud his shoulder and the side of his face hit the uneven ground. His mouth was bleeding where it had hit the solid ground. He could taste the blood mixed with bits of gravel. He swore to himself, trying to get to his feet when a blaze of pain shot through the back of his head. His face smashed back into the ground, the glancing blow stunning him. Afraid to move again, he laid motionless, awaiting yet another blow.

A deathly silence followed, disturbed only by the distant whine of a jet on its approach to Sky Harbor airport. A few minutes passed, and he could hear the faint howl of a dog or maybe a coyote in the distance. He wanted to get up and run from the crazy woman, but the pain in his leg was so intense he wasn't sure he could stand, let alone run.

As Brighton waited for more strikes of the wooden stick he realized he was feeling a different kind of pain. His hand was resting on the branch of a cholla cactus. This and the fear of scorpions and snakes brought him quickly to his feet. He was unsteady and stumbling in the dark as he made his way toward his car. He looked over his shoulders for the insane woman, but she was gone.

When he got into his car, trying to collect his senses, he began to doubt the reality of the whole scene, but the cactus thorns in his hand, knee, and ankle still throbbed. When he rubbed the back of his head, his matted hair was sticky from the drying blood. He looked at his watch and realized an hour had gone by.

***

Gina Dunn was in her tiny kitchen finishing up the dishes when Brighton came through the apartment door. She felt a strong sense of aggravation at his tardiness. His table setting remained, the serving dishes and Gina's plates having long since been cleared. Only when Gina saw the pallor of his face and the crimson matting of hair and blood over his right ear did she change her posture, rushing to his side. Her first action was to call 911, but Brighton put his hand on hers and asked her to wait.

Rehashing the episode took some time. He couldn't get the exact sequence of the events straight. He also couldn't remember how he had made it to his car, nor could he remember driving home.

As she accessed her husband's wounds Gina grew frantic. She again insisted on calling the police, but as she picked up the phone to punch in 911, it dawned on her that the disjointed story Brighton told was too incredulous to be explained secondhand. He was already sitting at the dining table digging into a plate of cold enchiladas and refried beans while mindlessly picking cactus spines out of his hands. She cradled the phone and retrieved her scanty first-aid supplies, most of which consisted of expired drug samples given to Brighton by pharmaceutical reps during his dental school days. The matted blood would require a shower to clear the clots and scuffed skin fragments. She hiked up his pant leg and gasped when she saw the apple-sized hematoma on the side of his knee. When she touched the bruise, he yelped, then returned to eating.

"I'm driving you to the ER," she insisted. "You probably need stitches in your head and an X-ray of that leg. You probably have a concussion too. You are acting pretty goofy."

"Who, me? Go to the ER? Sit there for six hours? I'll go take a shower, and then you can check me over," he said, scooping up the last bit of beans with a corn chip as he stood up from the table. He exited the room wobbling, trying not to limp.

Gina helped him undress then slipped off her own clothes to join him in the shower. Gently she rinsed his head, being careful not to restart any bleeding. She was amazed at how tiny the laceration was that had produced all the matted blood. Underneath it was a big, fat goose egg. Once he was shampooed and scrubbed, she helped him dry off and led him to the bedroom. Lying naked on the bed with a towel draped over the pillowcase, they talked again about the event, while Gina dressed the cuts, scrapes, and bruises. His thoughts seemed to be clearing, and the reality of the assault was setting in.

"What set her off like that?" Gina asked. "I heard some of the girls at the gym talking about the resistance to the development of Hidden Canyon from some of the old local residents, but I thought it was settled. What a freak that woman must be to attack you like that! Maybe we should sue her. Are you sure you don't want to call the police?"

Her question went unanswered. Brighton was already asleep.

She lay awake for hours thinking about the mysterious "gray-haired lady" with her walking stick. Then her ruminations turned to their new house. Many of the lower sites were developed during the previous year. The new neighbors-to-be had seemed friendly and complimentary when the Dunns' house plans had been presented to the architectural review committee. The neighbors Gina had spoken to all agreed it was a wonderful place to live. Privacy seemed to be the element that drove the market.

"We hardly know one another except to wave as we pass on the street," she had heard someone say. Gina was determined to be more of a good neighbor than that and to make new friends. The rental unit she and Brighton had been living in for the last eighteen months was in an anonymous older townhome project where people also didn't wave.

She pictured her new house sitting on the lot with its view out of the master bedroom window. There were no houses in that direction, just the giant rocks and the distant red mountains—more like monuments than mountains. Maybe she wouldn't even need drapes. One thing was for sure, they had waited a long time for this. They had endured many hard times during school to be in the position to build a dream house. Even now, it was going to be a financial struggle. They didn't need the interference of some old eco-witch. Gina wanted her dream house, the cactus huggers be damned.

2

NEIGHBORS

Charley Banks sat on a dirty plastic chair in the JFK airport terminal in New York. The best chairs were all occupied, not that they were all that much better or more comfortable or clean. He was tired and his butt hurt from sitting all day in a continuing education law course at NYU Law School.

His flight was delayed due to a stubborn woman who refused to take off her spiked heels for the security screening. When asked a second time to comply with the standard federal rules, she started screaming at the TSA screener that she didn't want to remove her shoes and walk barefoot on the filthy cement floor. In the confusion, the woman's Gucci tote bag rolled through the X-ray machine. Right in front of everyone, the bag had been snatched up by a shifty-eyed teen, who hurried off down the jet way. Spiky Heels bolted, now barefoot, through the scanner, shoes in hand, elbowing the obese federal agent out of the way. She caught up with the purse snatcher fifty yards down the corridor where she tackled the teen, bludgeoning the kid with her spike-heeled shoes. Alarms sounded, lights flashed, and the entire air terminal was closed down. Charley had witnessed the event, but like everyone else, when it came time to give evidence to the cops, he had turned away. After all, it was New York, and he had a plane to catch.

Charley's boss had chosen him as the lucky one allowed to attend an updated course on the intricacies of society's most annoying governing body—the neighborhood homeowners' association. Though HOAs, as they were increasingly known to thousands of suburbanites, were not particularly new, the case law regarding them was evolving at an exponential rate, as developers and residents abandoned the "Old West" method of settling property disputes in favor of courts, torts, and arbitrating judges. Charley was now officially the firm's HOA expert.

He had learned a great deal about HOA law at the meeting and was glad he had attended. It was a gray area of the law that opened a whole new arena of legal opportunity. Charley thought this would be a lot better than defending scumbag drug dealers and car thieves that had wasted the first four years out of law school.

He had finished law school in the middle of his class when the economy had been in the dumps, thus only the best law firms had been hiring. The county prosecutor's and defender's offices had provided a quick start on courtroom experience and a steady income, meager as it was. Four long years later, the firm of Fuller and Fuller, Esq. had opened the door into the world of mahogany boardrooms and spinach salad lunches. Soon, he would be in line for a partnership, if he behaved. Getting most of the HOA clients would be a big feather in his cap. The extra hassle of travel and taking the classes would be worth it.

***

Kara Banks, Charley's wife, had proven to be a powerful force behind his success. She had met Charley during his third year of law school while she was working at her dad's laundry business. Charley had finally broken down and taken a white shirt to be pressed at the laundry, but only after scorching his only other white dress shirt with a Salvation Army iron. He had a mock trial the next day and was desperate for help. Kara promised to have his shirt ready in just twenty-four hours. When he cried out in frustration, she agreed to do it herself and bring it by his apartment that night.

Their first date had been to a lecture at the law school library by Peter Benchley, the author of *Jaws*. She had told Charley she would have out-swum the shark. That bragging led to months of swim races at the university's gym, and Kara metamorphosed from a muscular size ten to a svelte size six. She set her heart on winning the hand of the handsome law student, but knew that her forty hours of community college general education classes wouldn't keep her in the running. She signed up for an online business course followed by months of studying the ways of the professional class. By the time their romance had solidified and they made it to the altar, Kara had molded herself into the perfect business-oriented socialite. Six years later, the Banks' new luxury home in the desert foothills was a gigantic charm on her bracelet of conquest. Hidden Canyon would be the perfect site to raise their perfect twin daughters and launch the rest of their perfect life.

***

The first four bars of the Beach Boys' "Little Deuce Coupe" chorus rang out over and over from Charley's briefcase. Only when a young girl pointed at the case and started to dance to the tune did he realize it was his cell phone emitting the music. He fumbled with the latch on the briefcase, finally snapping the phone open.

"Hello, hello," Charley answered with his usual upbeat tone. Unlike his wife and most of his legal buddies, he never looked at the caller I.D. before answering. He enjoyed the surprise of hearing the voice first and then the challenge of getting out of an unwanted conversation.

"Mr. Banks its Emi. I know you checked in before the office closed, but I wanted to give you a heads-up on a call that came in. Some dentist's wife from the east valley called claiming that an old woman attacked her husband while he was inspecting his lot in Hidden Canyon. Mr. Fuller told me that since the firm had spent big bucks on you and your trip to New York, you are the new official HOA point-man and should handle it."

"What do you mean, she attacked him?"

"While the dentist was standing on his own property, the unknown woman snuck up on him and clubbed him on the head and leg with a walking stick. He now has a serious staph infection in his leg. It's so bad that he can't go to work. Like I said, he's a dentist and has to stand on his feet all day but can't. Sounds like a good lawsuit to me."

"Did they call the cops?" Charley asked, paying more attention to the airport cop and the spiky-heeled woman.

"The wife tried that, but they told her since it was on private property, they wanted it handled through the Hidden Canyon HOA—something about there being no witnesses and no identification of the attacker," Emily said.

"Okay. Thanks for the info. Go ahead and make an appointment with her. You know, Emily, that's my new neighborhood—Hidden Canyon. You need to see this place; it's like living in a heaven on earth. Maybe I'll load up my six-gun and wander through the cactus and Palo Verde trees on Sunday to see if I can find the old lady, fill her full o' lead with my .45. That would solve the problem once and for all," Charley Banks said in a joking, Southwestern drawl.

A giggle came over the cell phone. Emily's "See you Monday" was drowned out by the overhead boarding instructions for Charley's long-overdue flight. He packed up his briefcase, laptop, and a Toys "R" Us shopping bag, full of treats for his twin daughters, most of which they would probably find too childish. Dads are lousy shoppers.

✳✳✳

Roy Richards was a single white male. His broad muscular shoulders hinted of a history of football or wrestling, but Roy was an outdoorsman. His Mediterranean ancestry endowed him with skin that tanned, not burned, and thick dark hair that had a natural wave, usually raising eyebrows from the ladies. He had always been single and was beginning to think that he always would be. It wasn't that he disliked women. He loved his mom and sisters and he got along great with his female coworkers at Sky Harbor Airport's air-traffic control. He joked with them and went out on TGIF with the gang from work when his schedule permitted. On rare occasions he had been lined up for dates with friends of friends. His situation, and he didn't consider it a problem, was that his lifestyle did not fit in with a permanent female relationship. When he wasn't working his stress-filled job, trying to keep the passenger jets of the friendly skies from smashing into one another, he was exploring the vast wonders of nature. Roy was an outdoor freak!

Roy's life as an air-traffic controller started straight out of UC San Francisco. He was a city kid but longed for a life as an outdoorsman. He had done all the necessary training and then landed a job in Twin Falls, Idaho. The airport was small, handling primarily private flights and a few commuter landings each day. A busy day for Roy was when he had to interrupt reading an article in *Field & Stream* magazine to give takeoff or landing clearance to a private jet that couldn't make it into Sun Valley because of bad weather. His job in Twin Falls had been the perfect combination of good pay, a pleasant community, and plenty of time off for his passions. During those years he had hiked, skied, canoed, rappelled, fished, and hunted every river, mountain, canyon, trail, and cliff within two hundred miles of the town. Only the mandatory transfer policy of some pinhead Washington FAA bureau chief had ended his personal nirvana.

Each subsequent transfer however, brought new regions to explore and exciting trails to blaze. He had been smart with his money, investing in a house in each of his assigned towns. With each move, Roy had built up an increasingly healthy home equity balance, allowing him to buy a bigger and nicer home each time he moved. In addition, his stock portfolio seemed to avoid the dips and catch the upsides of the markets. He drove a used pickup truck and did most of his clothes shopping online at Cabala's and REI.

He was a true mountain man of sorts but didn't buy into the yuppie party line of all organic foods, natural healing and Hybrids. He watched his diet but still loved a Big Mac, fries and trucks with a lot of horsepower. Some of his friends suggested that he was born a hundred years too late, that he should have been hanging out with Lewis or Clark or even Daniel Boone. He thought he had been born just right; he loved a hot bath and a soft mattress.

Roy was on a morning mountain bike ride, armed with only a trail map and his two-quart water bottle, when he rode over a steep rise. While he stopped to catch his breath, he looked out and was amazed by the beauty of Hidden Canyon. It was an area of pure natural desert with cactus and Palo Verde trees and gigantic rock formations all sitting high above the populated valley. The surrounding towns viewed from this lofty perch seemed close enough to commute to, but far enough away that it was perfectly quiet. Most spectacular was the clear view of Red Mountain, a two-thousand-foot-high granite and red sandstone rock that looked like a god had set it down in the middle of the desert as a milepost for future travelers.

There were home lots being cleared in the little valley in front of him. Some houses had been started, and the infrastructure of sewer, water, and underground power was being installed. He realized that as the houses were built on all the lots, the feeling of openness and solitude would decrease. However, as a place to come home to each night, it had an allure that he couldn't get out of his head.

He spent the next several weeks researching the area, finally picking out a building lot he knew would be perfect. He lay awake for weeks formulating the ideal floor plan. He wanted a layout that would give him the maximum views from his living areas and still give him plenty of room for his hunting trophies and exercise equipment. He also needed a separate room for his dog, Chad, who snored at night.

Within nine months of first seeing Hidden Canyon, Roy had moved his belongings into the new house. It was on a Sunday evening in the new house that he first saw the gray-haired woman.

He and Chad had taken a short hike to the top of one of the hills to watch the sunset. The old woman was walking down a steep trail outside the property stakes of the development. She stopped to stare at him and then made a slow motioning with her arms, shaking a large stick at him. No sounds came from her lips, but her intention was clear. She wanted him gone, and she wanted him to know it. From the moment they first made eye contact she didn't move, holding her ground until Roy walked away.

That night, he couldn't get her out of his mind. Her darkly tanned face was long with high cheekbones and a nose that accentuated her large brown eyes. She was pretty in a strange sort of way, but her eyes had the crazed look of fanatics he had seen picketing the airport. At first, he thought she might be a Native American. He could only guess her age, but thought she looked too young for the silver hair.

✳✳✳

It took eight days for the swelling and pain in Brighton's leg to improve enough for him to return to a full day's work. Antibiotics had cured the infection, but the whole area around the original strike was still inflamed, swollen, and tender. He and Gina had decided to drop any legal pursuit of the attacker. They just plain didn't have the time. They needed to get back to their life. One Sunday morning after church, Gina offered to drive him out to see what the site looked like. It had been over two weeks since the attack. To his amazement, the retaining walls were finished and the concrete footings had been poured. As she walked up the graded drive, Gina insisted on a complete, on-site, blow-by-blow description of Brighton's altercation with "the desert witch."

"This place looks so different," he said. The bigger trees and cactus had been dug up and boxed for later replanting. Some of the bigger boulders had been pushed to the downhill corner of the lot, and at the back a huge notch had been carved into the hill where his swimming pool and future child's play area would be located.

He had left his sunglasses in his car and was squinting when he caught a flash of something in his peripheral vision. Curious, he walked to the very back of the excavation and kicked around in the dirt and small rocks, trying to find whatever it was that had glittered. Looking straight at the area, he found a tiny fleck of metal imbedded in a rock. When he picked up the stone and rocked it back and forth in his hand, the reflection was enhanced. *Interesting*, he was thinking, when he tripped on a surveyor's corner stake and lost his balance. Catching himself with his hands to keep from falling, his right palm landed on a broken piece of granite, gouging the skin, pain shooting up his arm.

"Crap! This place is nothing but an accident waiting for a time to happen," he said, pressing his handkerchief onto the bleeding hand. Dabbing at the cut, he noticed his handkerchief didn't just turn red but had a strange orange color. This he soon forgot, having to concentrate on walking without tripping.

"The whole place is so awesome Brighton! I can't wait to see how it looks when the actual house is finished." Gina chattered the whole drive back to their apartment, describing every detail of the decorating she planned. It made Brighton smile. He truly believed that his wife deserved everything the good life could provide.

***

Brighton and Gina's stroll around their newly cleared lot had not gone unnoticed. Through the lenses of a pair of old Army surplus binoculars, Alma Ziegler was watching. The childhood nickname Azi had evolved into "Crazy Azi" by the time she had graduated from ASU with a major in philosophy and minors in geology and zoology. She was standing in the shade of one of the numerous giant boulders east of Hidden Canyon. The trails made by the coyotes and javalina made easy walking for Azi. Rare was the day that she didn't meet one of the rocky hill's unique residents. Rabbits, fox, coyote, javalina, bobcats, skunks, lizards, and snakes could be seen with regularity. Occasionally, she could even see a mountain lion or black bear. Now, new animals had arrived for her to watch.

The builders of the new development invaded the desert eighteen months earlier. Their tractors and trucks had invaded the pristine desert, belching diesel fumes and spewing up clouds of dust bigger than the worst summer storms. Soon to follow were the lumber and cement trucks with their tall stacks of boards and grinding, churning tanks of concrete. The worst day was when the framers arrived. This group of rude and crude men brought electrical generators to power their nail guns, power saws, and blaring boom box radios. After the framers, came the roofers and stucco men, favoring Mexican music played from cheap radios, often accompanied by the workman singing along off key and at maximum volume. Eventually the workmen went inside, but the muffled sound of construction continued. The project was a big blight.

Alma's disgust grew daily. At night she would lie awake, fantasizing about ways to stop the building. Her encounters with the desert's wildlife became less frequent, and it seemed the animals were putting distance between themselves and the construction noise. The plants were covered with smothering layers of construction dust, which even the occasional rain didn't wash clean. As she watched each new building lot cleared of the centuries-old cacti and plants, she grew more frustrated and angry at the intrusion of her solitude.

*****

It wasn't the first time in her life that Alma Ziegler had become distraught. During her college days at Arizona State University, she had wanted to belong to the coed elite. She had pledged the Chi Omega sorority and was readily accepted, especially when one of the senior girls read an article in *Forbes* magazine about Azi's dad. His rare metal refining company had grown exponentially during the previous twenty years with the increased need for exotic metals in semiconductor and computer chip manufacturing. The magazine article had called Mr. Ziegler one of the bright new stars of *Forbes'* "500 Richest Americans."

The article was a surprise to her. Her father had never disclosed his wealth, continuing to live in the house Alma was born in and sending his kids to public schools. After the article, Azi was whisked into a new world of parties, social climbing, and pressures previously unknown in her girlhood town of Steamboat Springs, Colorado. The East Coast sorority gals brought their version of sophistication and propriety to the organization, and at first, Azi learned a great deal. Later, she was to learn the other side of the social coin.

It was mid-semester of her senior year when her dad's airplane crashed. Her mom, dad, and both younger brothers were killed in the accident. The twin-engine airplane crashed somewhere on the remote Navajo reservation after its fuel had all leaked out through a faulty fuel sump valve. The family had flown down to Phoenix for a spring break from the Colorado cold. Alma had loved the time spent with them, and cried when her dad's King Air taxied out to the runway at Falcon Field. It was the last glimpse she would ever have of her living family. Just before departure, her dad had handed her an envelope, telling her it was a graduation gift. "Open it later," he said, giving her a long, tight hug and a kiss.

Over the next eighteen months, her dad's $900 million company was neatly picked clean by the lawyers, financial advisors, and the Denver IRS agents. What little that wasn't stolen was tied up in court for the next five years. Azi had turned to her sorority friends for comfort, but after a couple months of sharing her depression and the state of her financial chaos, the friends all but vanished. Within a year she had depleted her savings and was desperate to find a teaching job. With her snobbish friends long gone, her only contacts were her dad's personal lawyers. As her frustration grew, a new feeling welled up in her heart. She could see it visually in the mirror. The pain of losing her family was being replaced by a cold apathy for everyone and almost everything.

It was nearly three years after the plane crash, while teaching at a small community college, that Alma came across the envelope her dad had given her. It was a Merrill Lynch account statement addressed to Azi Ziegler, rather than Alma. She caught a flight to Denver to visit the stockbroker whose name was on the account summary. She had no idea what the stock symbols meant or what the value represented.

After hours of discussions and multiple phone calls to verify her identity, the broker told her that what her dad had started as a modest gift account, invested primarily in a Seattle-based software company, was now a portfolio worth over 6.5 million dollars.

She flew back to Phoenix, quit her job, and after a month-long search, bought a large but very inexpensive piece of virgin desert land, accessed at the time only by a rutted Jeep trail. At first it had no water, power, or phone lines. It was arid, natural desert strewn with boulders too big to move and soil too sandy to grow anything but cacti. She loved it.

Over the next couple years, she had replaced her tiny Airstream travel trailer with a frame house complete with indoor plumbing, electricity, and eventually a phone. Quite quickly, she abandoned her fellow teacher acquaintances and settled into the lifestyle of a hermit. She had no close neighbors and made no effort to make new friends or contact the old ones. She developed mundane routines of hiking and reading. Within a year, the desert vegetation had grown up around her house and solitude had enveloped her life.

3

FRIENDSHIPS

Gina Dunn was a woman whom when judged by her peers in an honest and non-jealous manner, was found to be just plain awesome. As a child, Gina Dunn had all the qualities any parent could ever hope for in a daughter. She had always giggled when she was fed and only threw food on the floor when she was entertaining her family. She even smiled when she had her diaper changed. Only when her dad nailed her with diaper pins—those were the pre-Pamper years—did she let out bloodcurdling screams. Gina smiled at the camera in the family pictures and cuddled with the aunts, uncles, and grandparents without begging. School had been a cakewalk for her and her parents, with accolades enough to be nearly embarrassing.

Every girl wanted to be her best friend, and every boy craved her attention. The high school boys lined up to take her on dates, but she had a strict rule about extended dating and never fell in love.

On the physical side, Gina was a "ten," not just in looks, but she had a regal grace that would part the sea of guys lining the school corridors. She had made the pom-pom squad, the school's varsity choir, the volleyball squad, national honor society, and student counsel all three years of high school.

At Stanford, Gina's life was similar to high school. She could do little wrong. She did lose her interest in organized social clubs and selected her close circle of friends from roommates and study group partners. She liked living away from home but would never admit it to her family, frequently sending them notes and cards.

It wasn't until her senior year of college after breaking a score of college boy's hearts, that Brighton Dunn fell head over heels for her. They met on a beautiful autumn Palo Alto afternoon with leaves fluttering down from the trees. She was walking past the dental school on her way to the bus stop when she saw him fall. His pant leg had tangled in the chain of his bicycle sprocket and down he went, skidding past her. Dazed, he could lift his face off of the pavement only enough to see her ten perfectly painted toenails, just inches from his bleeding nose.

Gina leaned over him, gently placing a consoling hand on his shoulder. She asked in her soft, yet controlled voice if he felt he could stand up. When he didn't answer immediately, she said, "Maybe you should lie still while I call for the paramedics."

"No, no, please don't do that. I'll be okay," he pleaded. "I don't have any insurance right now. They'll charge me a semester's tuition for a packet of Band-Aids."

He kicked his feet out of the clip-in pedals and rolled onto his back. Blinking to clear his vision, he smiled at her.

"Please stay right where you are while I run to get some wet paper towels. I'll help you clean up those scrapes."

By the time she returned, he had dragged himself over to lean against a stone wall. His road bike was scratched but otherwise looked okay.

"Thank you," he muttered as she dabbed at the abrasions and drying blood streaks on his arms.

"My name is Brighton Dunn, though I'm sure you are questioning the 'bright' part of my name. You must be Florence Nightingale."

"Gina Peterson," she said, offering him her hand.

By the time he was able to stand up and rearrange his clothes, she had retrieved a cell phone from her backpack and dialed "411" to order a taxi. By the end of the cab ride back to Brighton's flat, they had become friends. By the end of the week, they had fallen in love. By the end of the fall semester, she was wearing a simple yet elegant engagement ring.

The next few years of school, interviews, job searches, and romance had flown by. Their wedding had been a small affair in the backyard of her parents' home. The frugal honeymoon was at a B&B in Carmel. Their first apartment was the size of a U-Haul truck. They never went out to eat except for birthdays and anniversaries. The prospect of settling into a new dental practice, earning real money and now owning a new luxury home in the desert foothills, was a constant source of joy for them both.

Gina, still the perfect daughter, had become the perfect wife and homemaker. She made friends everywhere she went, thus allowing Brighton to have a great social life with no particular effort on his part. Once his practice was up and running, his daily social life was an obligatory smile and small talk with patients. Away from the office, Gina took care of everything else. Brighton was a lucky man, and he knew it.

✳✳✳

Charley Banks and Brighton Dunn met for the first time in front of Dunn's new home site. It was a late afternoon with the sun low on the horizon and pink clouds extending across the western sky. Brighton was clasping a heavy padlock into the gate latch of the six-foot high chain-link fence around his construction site.

"Hi neighbor!" Charley shouted, getting out of his new BMW sedan. He walked briskly toward Brighton with his hand extended and a smile on his face. He was still dressed in his business attire.

After introductions and somewhat lame apologies for not taking the time to meet each other sooner, Brighton redialed the combination on the lock and led Charley on a tour of the yet-to-be-completed house. As Charley could see, construction was moving at a quick pace.

"I'll bet you can't wait to get moved in and sit out by the pool to watch these awesome sunsets," Charley remarked. "We moved in about six months ago, and except for an occasional scorpion and the ever-threatening, but never seen, diamondback rattlesnake, we couldn't be happier."

"How many of the houses are ready to be occupied?"

"About twenty-five of us have moved in so far, and by the looks of it, you shouldn't be far behind. A few of the neighbors are out in the evenings walking, but I seldom get home in time to eat dinner with Kara and my twin daughters, let alone go for walks. You know the legend, that as lawyers we've got to bill those hours to keep the partners happy and the mortgage paid."

"I read you loud and clear," Brighton said. "I have to stand on my feet, staring into someone's mouth with instruments of torture in my hands, just to make a nickel."

They visited through the remaining daylight minutes, looking at the framed-up house. They compared notes about the construction and discovered a few common acquaintances. Darkness came on quickly, leaving them barely enough light to see their way back to their cars.

Back beside the cars, Charley leaned against his new car. Brighton couldn't help glancing down the road a few paces toward his ten-year-old Honda, making a silent comparison. He had always prided himself in the altruistic aspects of a dental profession, serving the poor and the needy and making the mouth a whiter, better biting, and pain-free place to chew. He often stated to friends, or anyone who would listen, that expensive cars, boats, jewelry, and even houses were society's cancer. It should be knowledge, understanding, and compassion that all should strive for; the real gold of this world was in service to one's fellow man.

It had been such a good speech to preach, and he had gotten a lot of mileage out of it at student parties and dental student dinners. The problem was that since he became able to qualify for a big enough loan to build a nice house, Gina's taste for the other nice things of life was evolving. This evolution was starting to erode into Brighton's convictions and attitudes as well. Like it or not, Brighton knew he was sliding down the same slippery slope of materialism as his predecessors. Hondas were okay for their time and place, but wouldn't it be cool to cruise into the driveway in new silver or black Mercedes?

"Well, I'd better head for home or the wife will wonder if I've been abducted or run off with the secretary. It has been a real pleasure meeting you," Charley said, offering his hand. "Please stop in at the house next time you are up here with your wife. We would love to meet her and look forward to getting to know you two."

Charley suddenly pointed at Brighton and asked, "Say, aren't you the guy who was clubbed by some mystery woman out here?"

Brighten nodded, not sure what the rumors about the incident said.

"I was supposed to meet with your wife to hear about it, but she cancelled the appointment. How could I have forgotten about that? Are you okay now?"

"Oh that," Brighton said. "It was really nothing, and I talked Gina out of bothering you. Honestly, we just want to move here and live a peaceful life. The last thing I wanted was to get in the middle of a big controversy. The poor woman is obviously off her rocker. Doing anything about her attack would only bring everyone grief."

"Well, if you have any more problems, just give me a call," Charley said with a big smile. He dug a business card out of his wallet and handed it to Brighton.

They shook hands, and Charley opened the door, sliding onto the rich leather seat. Brighton could smell the newness of the car. "What a wonderful machine," he thought. Charley started the engine and revved it once, sending a throaty seductive rumble into the canyon.

***

"He seemed like a genuinely nice guy. He's very friendly and wants to be a good neighbor; matter of fact, I think he wants us to be close friends," Brighton told Gina later that evening. "Too bad the guy is a darn lawyer. And to make it worse, his law firm represents the HOA for Hidden Canyon."

Gina was standing at the sink finishing the dishes. She had changed out of her workout clothes and was wearing a pink satin robe her sisters had given her years ago as a wedding shower gift. It was on the wrong side of the wear spectrum, one sleeve hem coming loose and with a snag or two. It was now relegated to everyday use. To Brighton, it still looked beautiful on his wife.

"But doesn't that mean he works for us if he works for the HOA?"

"Not until the developer sells all the lots and the project is finished. Until then, anything we do or don't do to the house and yard that a neighbor or developer doesn't like, my new friend, Charley, will write us a warning letter about. One of my new patients told me about being fined by his HOA in Scottsdale because he placed a portable basketball hoop in his driveway for his autistic nine-year-old daughter. It was one of the only things the kid would respond to, and he refused to take it down, so they fined him. When he refused to pay, they filed a lien against his house. When he found a better house and sold the old one, he discovered that a six thousand dollar lien had been subtracted from the closing money. He said he talked to an attorney and the guy charged him three hundred bucks to tell him he was toast. The good news was that in the meantime his daughter made the junior high basketball team, came out of her shell, and is now taking mostly regular classes at school. He says the six grand was worth it and a lot more. I wouldn't want to see him stranded on a desert island with a lawyer though. He hates them with a passion."

"You'll have to admit that that was very nice of Mr. Banks to offer the use of his house. What's his wife's name?"

Brighton shrugged. "I didn't get into the family history. It seems like he said something about Terra or Kara, and he mentioned twins girls. Maybe you'd better let me get their phone number, and then you can call to be sure someone is home before you pop in for a pit stop. Who knows; maybe he's a serial killer in hiding and loves to murder dentists' wives with over-distended bladders."

Gina wadded up a sloppy, wet dishcloth and threw it across the room at Brighton. His peripheral vision caught the motion, and he grabbed the cloth in midflight, splattering soapy water across the kitchen. He faked a return throw at her but instead did a nifty behind-the-back toss landing the cloth in the sink. With the same motion, he took two big strides toward her, grabbing her in a bear hug. He planted a hard kiss on her forehead. She giggled, hugged him, and then slipped out of his grasp.

"The truth of the matter is," Gina said, wiping her hands as she turned out the kitchen light, "it sounds like Mr. Lawyer Charley is eager to have good neighbors and he's likely to become your new best friend."

4

FOOL'S GOLD?

Roy Richard's eyes caught sight of the glitter as he hiked down the narrow, dusty trail one Sunday afternoon. He was looking for the shortest way back to his new house when his attention was immediately refocused on something that caught his eye.

He was just now getting familiar with the hills and canyons around this area of the valley, having spent his free time the last several months seeing to the details of his house. Now that it was complete and he was settled in, he could get back to the reason he had moved to the desert.

Several times that day, he had assured himself that he was on an established trail only to have it come to a boxed-in canyon, thus forcing him to turn back. This time, he came over a small hill, and there, thank goodness, Hidden Canyon sprawled out in front of him. He was standing on the literal edge of the National Forest. Behind him lay tens of thousands of acres of primitive desert land.

Looking east from the development, he noticed a private piece of property. There were old barbed-wire fences in terrible repair stretching for several hundred yards between the National Forest and what he thought was the border of Hidden Canyon. At the far end of the broken-down fence, he could see the outline of a wooden shack. Trees and desert plants hid most of it from view.

About three hundred yards in the other direction, a huge, yellow backhoe had cut into a hill. Not far beyond the cut were concrete footings of another new house. His own rooftop was just another two hundred yards beyond. It was at the base of the newest excavation that Roy caught the glitter of an unusual rock formation. Chad had already made a beeline for the house, and although Roy was hot and thirsty, he instead moved toward the unusual stone.

He wasn't a geologist, but he had years of experience wandering on foot and exploring thousands of miles of primitive country. What he saw glittering at the base of the newly disturbed earth in the excavation area was different from the usual fool's gold, mica, or quartz. Approaching the sun's reflection off of the stone, a six-foot chain-link construction fence blocked his way. Red-and-white NO TRESPASSING signs were in place every fifty feet along the fence. He chuckled to himself. He respected most posted signs but still knew he wouldn't be content until he could see the glittering rock up close. A sign wasn't going to slow him down. What did slow him down was the chained gate with its big, shiny combination lock.

Roy walked around to the side of the lot. He had started to pull up the bottom of the wire high enough to crawl under it when he heard a truck approaching. Jumping to his feet, he quickly made his way up the hill onto National Forest property. "I'll come back later," he vowed to himself, making a firm mental note of the exact location of the light-refracting area, knowing that it would be harder to find in the dark.

Back at his house he let the thirsty dog in for a drink. Fifteen-month-old Chad was getting smarter every day. The first few weeks after the two of them moved into Hidden Canyon had been hard on the dog. The prowling coyotes, fox, bobcats, and occasional mountain lion all had caused Chad to have nervous fits of howling and barking, which in turn were followed by Roy having to get out of bed to pet and talk Chad out of his canine hysteria. Roy poured the dry food into Chad's bowl and cut up a couple of hot dogs to add to the mix.

"Hey Chad, your breeder said you weren't supposed to have any of these yummy hot dogs, but what the heck, my Mom raised me on hot dogs and bologna sandwiches. Look how big, strong, and smart I grew up to be. Did I mention handsome?" He popped a couple of the cold hot dog chunks into his own mouth.

Chad looked at him with a twinkle in his eyes and a wagging tail that nearly knocked over a barstool. The dog was undoubtedly thinking, "So what, Roy? Just put the bowl on the floor."

Roy took a long, hot shower and then settled down behind his computer keyboard to Google some information about desert rock formation and content, unable to get the uniqueness of the glittering rocks out of his mind. Volumes of information were at his fingertips, but after reading until his eyes were sore, he still didn't have much of an answer. What he needed was a sample of the rock and a trained eye, or even an assay of some sort. It was still two hours until sundown. Maybe he still had time to sneak back before dark.

***

Kara Banks loved her new house. Like most young professionals' wives, she had sacrificed a great deal more than people realized to get to this station in life. She had worked hard putting Charley through school, dealing with a difficult twin pregnancy and never enough money. She had dreamed almost as hard as she had worked. Her new home was more than she had ever imagined, especially after the years they were first married. They had lived in a subsidized student housing project and had driven old clunker cars. Some days they walked or rode the city bus when the cars wouldn't run at all.

The girls arrived looking curious and healthy; for Kara, however, the ordeal wasn't over. She started bleeding two hours post-op, and in spite of timely and medically correct treatment, her body would not respond. The placenta had grown into the wall of the uterus, and all the blood vessels around it were torn. Kara's life was spared only after a hysterectomy and multiple blood transfusions. She recovered quickly but left a part of her life's plans for a big family in the hospital operating room.

The girls had grown into sweet and competent preteens. They were their mom's buddies and their dad's pals. They were model students and required little outside the norm. They were not big fans of the move to Hidden Canyon, away from their old neighborhood and friends, but didn't complain much as long as they could go back to visit and have friends over to the new house.

Nowadays, for Charley and Kara, the income had a few more zeros behind the numbers on their paychecks. But as life would have it, the bills and obligations also had their share of extra zeros as well. New furniture, appliances, decorating accessories, and picture frames all were unplanned expenses of her new house. Now, a new promotion and the probability of full partnership created a sense of excitement for Kara. She was the family banker. It would be great to finally get rid of the student loans, to have a positive balance in the checking account at the end of the month. Maybe they could even take an extended vacation with the girls—or maybe without the girls.

Charley was oblivious to the extent of debt lurking over them. Ever since the day he was accepted into the law firm, he had confidence in his future and had long since decided that if he always worked hard, the money would always be there. On occasion, he had to remind himself and his wife and daughters that money doesn't grow on trees, but since those early lean years, Kara had usually managed the money with a maestro's touch. The new house was a whole new symphony.

***

Like salesmen the world over, the real estate salespeople at Hidden Canyon had embellished the qualities and minimized the costs of the building sites that were available for Charley and Kara. They weren't the first, nor would they be the last, to be told that their views would be forever unobstructed only to later find that the house being framed up on the next lot had obliterated part of the city lights. The salesman also had explained that although every building site was unique, the variations in grade and shape of the lots would not present a construction problem.

The promised view of the Scottsdale city lights, which Kara and Charley had fallen in love with, all but disappeared when the twin two-story villa to the west of them was framed. The new owners of the two homes were apparently brothers from Germany. Charley had received a panicked phone call at his office from Kara, insisting that he come home immediately and stop the workman from nailing another board in place.

"The salesman promised that the view of saddleback ridge would always be there," Kara moaned, knowing in her heart that she had ignored the reality of the situation. To comfort her, Charley had agreed to add on a workout room off the master bedroom with a big window looking out at Red Mountain, in another direction.

Kara knew very well how their debt was growing with each addition and change order on the house. Each month when the "big three" arrived—the house payment, the home equity credit line bill, and the American Express Platinum Card bill—she would break into a cold sweat and start looking through her closet for clothes she could take back to Nordstrom's. If she only knew that most of her neighbors had the same anxieties, maybe she would have been more at ease.

***

The first residents of Cactus Wren Circle to move into their home were Kashmir Patel and his wife. Natives of New Delhi, the Patels had two American-born sons, both of whom were usually away at boarding school. Bavana Patel was a beautiful woman with a kind, soft voice. Though she stood only four foot eleven inches, she had a magnetic presence that drew attention wherever she went, dressing in the traditional saris of her homeland with elaborate bracelets, filigreed rings, earrings, and broaches. She was a system's engineer with a Ph.D. from MIT, employed at Intel and known around the computer industry as a diagnostic genius. Kashmir was of average height and build with a very strong Indian accent. He was a neurologist and practiced at the Mayo Clinic.

Of all the new neighbors, the Patels seemed to have had the least amount of problems building their house. Their view of the city and the surrounding mountains was unequaled in the development. The yard lighting was dramatic, giving their house a mystic appearance, sitting on the slope at the end of a winding stone driveway. Rumor had it that the Patels had the best lot and the lesser problems building because they knew how to treat people. Really "treat" people, that is. The origin of their wealth and subsequent education was said to come from a family fortune in precious gemstones. Friends wondered if they didn't return from family visits to India with the seams of their clothing lined with high-grade rubies and diamonds.

Now that they had neighbors, the couple had made a habit of asking Charley and Kara to keep an eye on the house when they were gone. Watching Harley, the Patels' Great Dane, was relegated to a "cousin" who lived in town. The Patels employed a full complement of caretakers to clean, cook, and keep the rocks in the large yard beautifully raked and arranged. When they left the country, they would lock up their doors and gates and allow the help to have time off.

It was during one of their extended trips to India that Roy Richards initiated his plan to search the neighborhood for the unusual glittering rocks.

***

It was amazing to Brighton how quickly a house could be built once the actual construction finally started. The planning, building permits, and architectural approvals from the HOA committee and the county had taken months. Once ground was broken, however, things moved. Trenches were dug, the plumbing was placed, and the cement floor poured. Next, it was ready for the framers. Huge stacks of newly milled lumber were delivered. Brighton was surprised how good the wood smelled when it came straight from the planning mill. The day after the wood arrived, a swarm of workmen invaded with hammers, saws, and nail guns. Within hours, the walls rose above the horizon.

Gina had called Brighton at his office, insisting that he meet her at the building site immediately. He had rushed through his last three patients, all kids with cavities from too much fruit leather. His office staff said they would lock up so he could leave early.

Driving into Hidden Canyon and up the road to their lot, he could see Gina's Toyota sitting at an odd angle to the road. He had just gone through the gate and couldn't understand why she would park so far from the homesite. The next thing he saw was a huge black Hummer, immediately facing the Toyota. He panicked when he realized that the front end of the Camry was flattened, its airbags deployed and the pavement around it strewn with glass.

Gina had just met the developer of Hidden Canyon, Dean Shutter. But not the way one would desire. She had met him head-on at thirty miles per hour.

***

Dean Shutter was used to driving the newly paved streets of Hidden Canyon with wild abandon. The few residents who had moved in during the past year never seemed to be at home, let alone on the streets. He never slowed for the intersections and their miniature yield signs and never stopped for the few stop signs in the development. As he drove through the neighborhood, he was usually trying to multitask, talking on the phone, looking at plans or building bids, and occasionally steering the Hummer. The first time he saw the Toyota, it was less than twenty feet in front of him. Even with his athlete-quick reflexes, he had smashed into the right front quarter panel of the car before he could move his foot to the brake pedal.

Gina had already driven by her beautiful lot and was thrilled that walls were being erected. Her cell phone was in a low-signal area, so she had driven to the closest gas station to call Brighton asking him to meet her at the lot to inspect the progress. With a large Diet Coke cup in her hand, she reentered the gate to Hidden Canyon then turned toward Cactus Wren Circle.

She saw the black bumper flying toward her just as she felt the crush and heard the gunshot-loud sound of the airbag bursting into her chest and face. Stunned by the deceleration and the airbag noise, she sank back into her seat. Cold liquid was everywhere, dripping from her hair, clothes, and the entire interior of the Toyota. After a moment of head clearing, she felt reassured that the liquid was Diet Coke, not blood.

Dean Shutter jumped out of his Hummer and ran around the car to her driver-side door. The windshield was shattered but in one piece, the safety glass having done its job. He was careful opening the door. The airbag was now flaccid, so he pushed it out of the way and reached across the seat, unlatching her seatbelt. Dean spoke to her in a soft Southern drawl. "Are you hurting anywhere? We need to get you out of the car little lady. My gosh! What are you covered with? If that's blood, you must be a witch cause its ice cold."

"I think I'm okay. I don't feel any pain; it's just that my ears keep ringing."

"Do you want me to call an ambulance for you?" Dean asked, helping her toward his vehicle while hoping she would say no. He was assessing the damage to the vehicles, knowing he would be blamed for the wreck and also remembering he had just finished a can of Coors with the boys at the sales office. Calling an ambulance would bring the deputy sheriff, a breath alcohol test, and a boatload of trouble.

"Could I just sit down for a few minutes and catch my breath? I think I'm all right, I just need to sit down for a minute," Gina said and pointed toward a cement curb.

Dean led her to the raised curb and steadied her as she sat down. He quickly walked back to his Hummer to grab an un-opened bottle of water for her. He also grabbed the clean towel he kept in the back of his truck, just in case he ever he decided to take a dip in the clubhouse pool. He offered her the water and began gently blotting the Diet Coke from her hair and face with the towel. He couldn't find any sign of bleeding. At that moment, Brighton drove around the corner.

He was hyperventilating by the time he reached the crash site. Gina's car was obviously badly wrecked. He could see a man lean-ing over someone but couldn't for sure see Gina. This sent an-other visceral jolt through his system.

"Gina, Gina! Where is my wife?" he screamed at the tall man standing on the other side of the car.

"I'm right here!" yelled Gina.

The reunion changed quickly from Brighton's panic to relief and joy that she was not dead or seriously injured; then in the next instant it turned to hostility when Brighton asked how long until the ambulance should be there, only to be told that one had not been called.

"Why the hell not?" Brighton shouted into the man's vaguely familiar face. It was all he could do to restrain himself from tak-ing a swing at the guy.

"I told him not to call anyone," Gina answered quickly, trying to diffuse her husband, who was usually very slow to anger.

The answer only made him angrier. Gina begged him to settle down. Slowly, he quieted enough to have a more objective con-versation.

"Listen to me for a minute," insisted Dean. "This accident was entirely my fault. I just didn't stop to look for a car. I drive these streets a hundred times a day, and there isn't much traffic, espe-cially now that the workmen have gone home. If you are not se-riously hurt, we could go to the sales office where you can freshen up. I'll call a tow truck and have your car towed to the dealer. I'll take responsibility for fixing or replacing your car."

Brighton couldn't believe his ears. The guy would buy him another car? Finally, it dawned on him who this man was. Dean Shutter, the king of the hill in Hidden Canyon. Shutter was the most admired developer in town. It had been months since Brighton and Mr. Shutter had met or even spoken on the phone, as Brighton had elected to use a different builder and had purchased his lot as a resale.

"I just need to go straight home," Gina stated, leaving no alternative to be considered. She was tired and shaken. "Thank you for helping me out of the car and for the water. I'm sure you didn't plan on an accident to end your day either. I'm grateful you weren't hurt, and I'm sure I'll be fine." She offered one scuff-knuckled hand to the man and the other to her husband to help her to her feet and then nodded for Brighton to move toward the Honda.

More apologies were extended and accepted. Brighton and Dean agreed to meet the next morning at his lot to discuss the accident further. "The car will be towed to the closest Toyota dealer," Dean assured them both.

"I'm taking you to the hospital," Brighton stated after helping Gina get comfortable in the backseat of his Accord. By the time they were out of the development gate, Gina was arguing against going to the hospital with such conviction that Brighton agreed to take her straight home.

✳✳✳

Dean Shutter had other things on his mind. He had just dodged a huge bullet. "More like a stinger missile," he thought, as he struggled to keep the Hummer on the road. He couldn't believe how flimsy his macho SUV was—nearly disabled by a Camry? His mind wandered. Close calls did strange things to one's thinking. He couldn't get his mind off the look on the woman's face as his truck plowed into her helpless little car. Thank goodness there was no ambulance, no police, and no sobriety test, not that it would have been positive. One beer probably wouldn't have been a problem, but who could know? The planets must be aligned in his favor tonight.

Dean hadn't always had the galaxies on his side. He pulled into the driveway of the sales office and shut off the engine. It had been a long day, and he thought he should just get his briefcase and go home, but he wasn't sure the truck would make it. His office staff had all gone home for the day. He started to use his cell phone to call his wife, but then remembered she was gone. Not off to some decorating market or home to Mother's as in years past. She was gone. "I'm off somewhere to think and reevaluate," she had said. She had even hinted that she might not be back for a while.

"So what else is new?" he said to the evening sky and whoever or whatever else was out the open window. "Just one more rotten piece of Shutter bad luck."

For a college educated and athletically trained redneck, he had had more than most men's share of luck, both bad and good. He had grown up in a modest home with enough love and concern but never enough money to go around. His dad was seldom home, and his mom was always busy with the "little kids." He was expected to take care of himself and stay out of trouble. He was way too smart to just sit around the house, so he found adventure or it found him.

Dean had been a skinny kid until the seventh grade when his hormones kicked in. He had always been a good athlete but was often overlooked because of his thin, wiry frame. So he got a part-time job working in a cement factory lifting bags of cement. With work, a set of rusty weights, and lots of great home-cooked meals, he became a hulk. The high school football coach invited him to try out for the freshman team. By his sophomore year, he was the starting linebacker, breaking opponents' bones and the hearts of the classiest girls at school. College was no different. He was loved by the coaches and sorority girls and hated by all the men. He was on his way to the NFL when he made the mistake of trying to ride a four-track ATV on a rough mountain trail and lost control. His fractured pelvis put him into a hospital bed for weeks and out of the NFL draft forever.

Dean resolved to make a life for himself in business. He began to make money with his good looks and curious, exploring mind. He had seen opportunities where others had seen nothing. The cycles of business had come and gone, taking their toll, but he had always been able to bounce back. Until lately, that is. He was in over his head in the Hidden Canyon project. He had leveraged himself beyond his comfort zone and had turned in desperation to "hard money" lenders to stay afloat the last few months. Sales had been brisk, but it seemed to take forever to close on the half-million-dollar lots. The interest he owed on the project was a monster that never slept.

His latest holdup had come from the desert witch, as he liked to call her. She was a weirdo who wandered around the fringes of the development, scaring off potential buyers and frightening the owners. Just two days before the car accident, a buyer had stopped the final purchase of a lot because he had found a note nailed to his lot number sign he was about to close on, dictating that the ground was an ancient Indian burial site, and anyone who tried to build on the site would be cursed.

Dean had also heard rumors of Dr. Dunn's attack by the desert woman, but since no police report had been filed, he didn't want to ask about it and stir up a possible lawsuit. He knew that the disturbed woman lived in a shack on a parcel of land in the desert behind Hidden Canyon. She lived like a hermit, but she was rumored to have money. His attorney had advised him to ignore her. Any legal action and the negative publicity from it could be a disaster. His lenders had recently pressured him to close out the project and pay off the existing debt. Just a dozen or so lots to sell and he could be home free with a truckload of money in the bank. Failing to close the project out soon could leave him with nothing to show for all his time and hard work. With the exception of some living expenses, all of his profit remained in the last handful of lots. He really needed some Shutter good luck.

Shutter luck, his childhood friends had called it. Now with the car wreck and his wife leaving and the million-plus-dollar debt the development still carried, he needed more than good luck. He needed a miracle.

Dean's Hidden Canyon development consisted of eighty lots, each well over an acre. There was an additional twenty acres of common land with trails and some limited grassy areas. A private clubhouse and tennis courts added to the attractiveness of the project. Strong deed restrictions and building codes guaranteed the buyers that the neighbors would build quality homes and would maintain them at the highest standard possible. In addition, the homeowners' association would provide around-the-clock security, and maintain all the common places including the pool, clubhouse, tennis courts, and hiking paths. The HOA would collect the annual fees and see that the money was judiciously spent to maintain the development. Until 90 percent of the lots were sold, the HOA was controlled by the developer, Dean Shutter. He couldn't wait to be just one of the neighbors.

5

FORGOTTEN TREASURE

Roy Richards had almost forgotten about the strange rocks he had retrieved from his neighbor's construction site. Always on a busy schedule, he had gone to work the day after finding the rocks. He had thrown them into a shoebox then placed it on the passenger seat of his truck. Over the next two weeks, the box had become just another layer in the pile of coats, papers, and food wrappers on the truck seat. Until the day a panic stop at an intersection, to avoid a traffic photo radar camera, had thrown the rocks and the collection of junk off the seat, scattering the whole mess on the floorboard. When it reminded him of how he finally obtained the rocks, he broke out in beads of sweat.

The evening he had decided to pick up the rocks, there were no workmen on the dentist's lot. The high chain-link fencing and the entrance gate were always locked when the workday was over, and the HOA security guard patrolled the project after work hours.

Roy also had watched the Patels' house to be sure they were not at home. Their backyard had a low fence next to the dentist's building site. Roy planned to walk up the Patels' driveway and go through the side gate into the yard. From there he could jump the fence and spend whatever time it took to study and collect the shiny rocks in the dentist's backyard. He was pretty sure the Patels were out of town; he had heard rumors at the clubhouse that the wife's sister-in-law had died in India, and the family would be flying away to the funeral.

Roy had dressed in a black shirt and jeans. He laughed at himself as he looked in the mirror and added a black Diamondback baseball cap. "A regular James Bond," he thought. It was a three-quarter moon, so he didn't think his flashlight was needed until he had jumped the fence, landing on a board with a protruding nail. When he shined the light at his foot, he could see the nail poking up clear through the top of his sneakers. Suppressing a cry of pain, he found a place to sit and pulled the board away from his foot. With the nail removed, he could feel his blood welling up in his shoe. The sharp pain turned into throbbing, making walking difficult. He decided to go forward with the plan anyway, and soon found six or eight representative samples of apple-sized stones. Lifting two of the rocks, he realized he didn't have anything to carry them in. He scrounged around in a garbage barrel and found a heavy plastic bag.

He hobbled over to the Patel side of the lot and was halfway up the fence when the floodlights in the Patels' yard came on. Their back door swung open, and a huge black-and-white male Great Dane came trotting across the desert yard toward Roy. The bark couldn't be judged against the bite, but the former probably would have won out. To make matters worse, the sound stirred up a few other canines in the canyon. Soon a few coyotes joined in the serenade.

"Quiet, Harley!" yelled a young male voice from the edge of the house. "Do your job, and then get back in here!"

The dog stopped barking as the male voice retreated into the darkened house. Roy, half-straddling the block wall, held his breath another ten seconds and finally jumped back into the dentist's yard, accepting a more difficult route home.

He crept around the corner of the framed building and watched for lights from the security company's vehicle. Dragging his bag of rocks, he proceeded toward the locked gate. The ground was irregular and covered with debris. A pool of mud lay where a water hose had been dripping. He found the padlocked gates. Prying the two gates apart, he squeezed through, scraping his chest and back on the rough chain-link wire in the process.

By the time he was back in his house, Roy was bleeding, scratched, and bruised, but he had his shiny rocks. He took the bag to the bathroom and dumped them into the tub. He filled the tub with water, carefully dumping some shampoo in for good measure. Roy took a shower while the rocks soaked off their layer of crusted dirt. Catching a glimpse of himself in the mirror, he pondered his sanity. His naked body was covered with welts and scratches, and his foot throbbed where the nail had perforated it. He also had picked up some weird kind of orange stain on his hands. "What was I thinking, sneaking around in the dark like some low-class cat burglar?"

He removed each of the rocks from the tub and laid them out on a bath towel to dry. The glitter that had first caught his eye was even more intense. Some rocks were speckled, and some areas had streaked lines diving deep into the rocks, only to emerge on the other side of the stone. They were beautiful, but what other value they had, he could only guess. He placed his treasure in an empty shoebox, and was carrying them to the kitchen when the doorbell rang.

His heart started racing as he grabbed a bathrobe and hobbled to the door. Since he had moved in months ago, no one had ever come to his door at night. He looked through the peephole, and there was his worst nightmare: the security guard holding a flashlight as long as a trombone.

"Sorry to bother you, Mr. Richards," the obese security guard said. "The Patel boys are staying in their house while the parents are out of town and called to report a prowler. It's probably the desert lady. I just wanted to ask if you had seen anything suspicious." The excited young security guard was half-facing the door and half-glancing toward the street, shining his mega-light around the yard as he talked. He acted so nervous that Roy thought he might ask to come in the house just to feel safe.

"Thanks for the warning, Clyde," Roy said, having snuck a look at the guard's name tag. "I was in in the shower and haven't heard or seen a thing, but I'll keep my eyes open."

"I wondered if your dog had barked or had been acting crazy. The Patels' dog went ballistic on them. Have you seen their dog? He's as big as a cow. He's black and white and looks just like one of them Holstein cows."

"Chad was sleeping like a baby until the doorbell rang," Roy said, looking down at his dog. Chad was busy licking the travertine floor, which had faint outlines of Roy's right footprints in dark, dried blood.

"That's a good-looking animal. I'll bet he keeps those frisky coyotes away," Clyde commented as Roy nudged the door closed a bit to obstruct his bloody footprints. "Say, Mr. Richards, how did you get all those scrapes and scratches?"

"Oh, they are nothing. I tripped when I was hiking last weekend. Guess I'll start wearing gloves. Thanks again for the warning. It was probably just a coyote or bobcat that spooked their dog. No one in their right mind would be prowling around this place at night, what with the snakes and scorpions."

Roy almost had the door closed when Chad licked the top of Roy's foot where the nail had come through, and a new flow of blood had erupted.

"Wow, look at your foot. It's bleeding a lot. You ought to have a doctor look at that foot. It looks pretty nasty to me," Clyde said in an authoritative voice and shining the flashlight beam directly on Roy's foot. "Man alive, you're bleeding like a stuck pig, maybe you're one of them hemophiliacs or something".

Roy waved off the comment and closed the door. Sweat beads covered his forehead. His foot was throbbing. *What a buffoon*, he thought, watching Clyde shine his way to his mini pickup truck with its ridiculous little yellow flashing light on top. "Why did I let him agitate me? He is as clueless and stupid as they come," Roy thought, trying to reassure himself that things were okay.

✳✳✳

Two weeks later, Roy dug through the papers he kept in an old cigar box on the dashboard of the truck. He found the address and phone number of the assay company and unclipped his cell phone from his belt. The line was busy, so on a whim, he threw the car in gear and drove off in the direction of the assay office.

Geological Associates Ltd. was in an industrial park wedged between a window manufacturer and a heavy equipment dealer. Roy parked a few stalls down from the entrance then picked up the heavy shoebox. A buzzer rang as he entered the small foyer. He waited several minutes, hearing sounds behind the partition. When someone came out from a back office, Roy was greeted by a tall blonde woman in a tastefully fitted white blouse and indigo blue skirt. A red pencil was wedged behind her ear, giving her a scholarly air.

"Good morning. How can I help you?" she asked.

"Hi, my name is Roy. I have some rock samples I found in the desert and would like to have them assayed. Is there someone here I could talk to about the details?

"I'm Lori Pederson," she said, still shaking his hand. "I'm on my way out the door, but I'll find one of my chemists for you."

"I'd like to speak with the manager or owner if possible. I have several questions," Roy said, starting to feel a little put off.

"I own the place. That is, the bank and I own it. If you can fill out a sample registration form, I'll get Bill. He has lots of experience. He can help answer any questions you might have," she said with a smile. Lori then called out his name, and with a little smirk, simply walked out the front door. She got into a red Mustang GT and drove away.

Bill was a tall, massive man with an unkempt beard. He wore a plaid flannel shirt that had sopped up many coffee spills. On his head was an old sweat-stained John Deere baseball cap with a tuft of a short, greasy ponytail sticking out the back. Roy looked the man over and was about to turn around to leave.

"What can I do for you?" Bill asked, wiping his hands on a blue hand towel.

Roy took a deep breath. "I found some rocks in the desert that caught my eye. They sparkle more than any I've seen."

"Let's take a look at these babies. Just spread them out in this pan. I'll get my magnifying eyes. Where did you pick these up?" he asked, disappearing into the back of the building.

Roy started to answer, but Bill was already behind the partition door.

He returned with a pair of jeweler's magnifying loupes propped on his head. He rotated the individual rocks over a light while studying them closely. Whistling softly, he took them to a small sink in the corner and carefully ran cold water on each of the rocks. He placed them back in the metal pan and looked again using the loupes.

"How interested are you in really finding out what's in these critters? Reason I ask, is you now owe me twenty bucks. To know for sure what they are made of, and how much of each of the contents is there, and what a ton of the stuff would yield, is going to cost a whole lot more than twenty bucks."

Roy shrugged. "What is your best guess, Bill, you know, the twenty-dollar guess?"

"I'd say you probably have some silver and maybe a trace of platinum. If you had a train-car load of the stuff, you might have enough for an earring stud. To know for certain, we'd have to do a full assay. The lady who just left owns the business, and she insists we do a complete assay on our samples. That's going to run about five hundred dollars. It would be nice if we had more of the sample—maybe a hundred pounds or so."

Roy was surprised at the cost estimate and started to dismiss the idea of pursuing it any further when Bill got nosey.

"I'm off this weekend," Bill said with a little more interest than he had shown thus far. "Tell me the area where you found this scrabble, and I'll see if I can pick up a little more of the stuff. The larger the sample, the better."

A sixth sense had been a big help to Roy in the air-traffic control tower, saving airplane collisions and lives. At that moment, his sixth sense was on high alert. Something wasn't right. He had a tiger by the tail. Now he decided he was going to let go.

"I really need to get to the airport," he said, gathering up the rocks and putting them back into their shoebox. He took a twenty dollar bill from his wallet and laid it on the counter. He nodded to Bill, studying his face as he did so. Not another word was spoken as he turned and walked out the door and went around the corner toward his truck.

"Crap!" he exclaimed, colliding into the blonde woman as she came around the corner. She fell backwards, landing hard on the sidewalk with Roy flat on top of her. He hurriedly pushed himself off, jumping to his feet. He looked down at Lori Pederson as she started to laugh.

"I hope you haven't been waiting there just to jump on me," she jested, making no effort to get up let alone straighten her blouse or tug her skirt back down in place.

"I am so sorry," Roy said as he offered her a hand and helped her to her feet. "Are you okay?"

Lori brushed off her skirt as Roy brushed a couple of dead leaves off her shoulder. The shoebox had fallen on the ground, scattering the rocks on the pavement.

"Are you sure you are all right? I am so sorry," he repeated as he bent down and tried to gather his rock samples.

"I'm all right. I grew up with brothers so I'm used to being tackled, but not necessarily in parking lots," Lori said with a smile, her deep double dimples flashing. She then turned and walked away toward her business entrance.

He grabbed a plastic sack from his truck and gathered up the samples. He got into the truck and started backing out of his parking space. Just as he began to pull forward, he heard a banging on the side of his truck. Startled, he glanced in the mirror and saw Lori, holding out a can of Pepsi. He put the truck in park and rolled down the passenger window.

"Since you didn't offer to buy a girl a drink, I brought you one," she said with a smile. "Maybe you thought I was smashed enough for one day? Bill said you didn't leave the samples. He said you thought the cost was a little too much. Let me take a closer look, and we can agree on a smaller charge later."

As though there was nothing more to discuss, she reached through the window, firmly gripping the sack of rocks.

"Give me a call in two days," she said. "And by the way, you still owe me a real drink," Lori concluded, looking over her shoulder at Roy as she walked away, rock samples in hand, hips swaying back and forth.

***

Months that seemed like years went by before the Dunns' dream home was finally ready, and they could move into it. As the day approached, there were phone calls every few minutes, interrupting Brighton's dental procedures. Gina's packing took a backseat to overseeing the details of the new house. Brighton was her sounding board for nearly every decision.

Dean Shutter's daily work also was interrupted with calls and complaints, all in an effort to iron out the final details of completing the Dunns' house. Their general contractor had been on schedule and within budget, until four weeks ago, when the contractor unexpectedly left town. In desperation, Brighton had asked Dean to take over the job of finishing the house. One of the last obstacles to the move in, however, was the driveway. Gina had chosen large cobblestones for the drive, and they could not be placed until the landscapers finished the water-drip lines, and the landscapers couldn't finish until the swimming pool company finished digging the pool.

Dean was working on trying to talk the building inspector into letting the Dunns move in before the driveway was completed. Brighton had forgiven Dean for the auto accident, especially when Dean persuaded his insurance company and the Toyota dealer to give Gina a new Highlander to replace her three-year-old Camry. It hadn't cost Brighton a penny, though he suspected Dean had paid something to seal the deal.

A swimming pool had originally sounded way too extravagant to the Dunns, but business at the office had been brisk and interest rates had come down, making the new estimated mortgage payment seem affordable. And after Gina had seen the lap pool at the Banks' house, she decided they couldn't live without a pool.

Charley's earlier offer to have Gina stop by his house had been accepted. Over the next few months, with frequent short visits to the Banks' home, Gina and Kara had become close friends. Kara had also become a valuable decorating advisor to Gina. Having just finished her own home, she was up to full speed on all the latest in appliances and kitchen décor as well as colors, fabrics, and even silk flowers, and offered tips as where to buy them at the best prices.

The two women often shared lunch and life stories. They even discovered a couple of common acquaintances. The Banks and the Dunns hadn't gotten together as couples, nor had either wife met the other's husband. Kara had helped Gina find a swimming pool company to build the pool. Now unfortunately, the afterthought of adding a swimming pool to the home was holding up the completion of the driveway.

Gina was driving to the lot for her regular daily inspection rounds of the house and backyard. She rounded the corner in her new car, and from the curve in the road could see the huge yellow backhoe leaving her driveway. As her car approached, the backhoe operator waved at her and motioned for her to stop. The driver shut down his tractor and approached her car shaking his fist, obviously eager to speak to her.

"Mrs. Dunn, you didn't tell me you have some of them psychopathic maniacs running around this neighborhood," the dust-covered, scruffy-looking backhoe man said.

"What are you talking about?" Gina asked, suddenly not wanting to hear, yet knowing the answer the man was about to give.

"A freaky woman with long, gray hair stood on the hill behind your house and threw rocks at me while I was trying to finish digging your pool. Her aim improved enough that she hit me with a rock, and that's when I got off my machine and yelled at her. She acted surprised that I even noticed her, and then she turned and walked back over the hill," he said taking a drink from a plastic thermos. "She came back twice, but only shook her fist at me those times. She is as spooky as any Halloween monster. I got your pool dug, but don't expect me to ever come back to this neighborhood again. I wouldn't be surprised to see her come back with a gun the next time she wanders over that hill. You be careful back there!"

Before she could respond, the man returned to his tractor and was gone. Gina parked on the pavement, and then trudged up the dirt drive to where it made a circle in front of the main entrance. She walked through her new house, dodging boxes of light fixtures and scraps of leftover carpet, finally making her way to the back door. She peeked out into the expansive backyard, looking for any sign of the desert witch. The coast appeared clear. She walked to the edge of the freshly dug pool and tried to imagine it full of water. How great it was going to be to walk outside anytime she wanted, day or night, and dive into this cool, clear water. She loved the way they had carved out a special lover's cove where she and Brighton would sit and visit.

No matter how hard Gina tried, she couldn't get that crazy desert woman out of her head. "First Brighton's attack, and now this rock throwing. It's time to do something about it," she thought. She retrieved her hiking shoes out of the back of the car, found a pair of socks in the storage bin, and put on an old Stanford baseball cap. She stuffed a bottle of drinking water in the back pocket of her baggy painter pants and checked the charge on her cell phone. She considered calling Brighton to tell him what she was up to, but decided it would just worry him. Without another thought, she started off hiking over the cactus and boulder-strewn hills.

The sun was bright, and the desert flowers were in a new blooming phase and were beautiful. The heavy rain two weeks before had breathed new life into the desert. It didn't take long before Gina found a beaten-down path that wandered up and over the nearby horizon. She walked along the trail, being quite cautious at first, but then, enjoying the fresh air, she started whistling. From the top of the first hill, she could look back down toward Hidden Canyon and her new house. Gazing off into the opposite direction, she could see the jagged peaks of the distant mountains appearing as overlapping layers of tissue paper on an abstract collage. At what she guessed was about a mile away, sitting on the edge of a steep arroyo, she could see the outline of a building.

Wishing she had a pair of binoculars, she squinted until her eyes watered, but in the midday glare of the sun, she still wasn't positive what it was she was seeing. She could feel the beading of sweat accumulate on her upper lip and another river trickle down between her breasts. The sun was like a giant laser. A couple of jumping cactus thorns had found their way into the cuff of her cotton pants, pricking her leg. These warnings were just enough to discourage her from going any further into the searing desert. She squinted one more time, studying the dirt road leading in the direction of the shack from the opposite direction and then turned back toward the air-conditioned comfort of her car.

Sunlight flashed directly at Gina, who had stopped on the trail to look back one last time before she crossed the ridgeline.

"So, that's the game that woman wants to play?" she said out loud, figuring the old woman must have used a mirror or glass to reflect the light. "Someday soon I will do a little snooping and maybe a bit of harassing of my own."

She unscrewed the lid on her water bottle and took a long pull while continuing to survey the surrounding hills and gullies. "Living here might be more fun than I could have ever imagined," she thought.

✳✳✳

"First, we each need to get a pair of powerful binoculars, maybe even a pair of the night vision kind," Gina told Kara.

They were sitting beside Kara's lap pool, sipping on tall, frosty glasses of Diet Coke with fresh, sliced lemon wedges. Kara was everything Gina had wanted in a close friend. Kara had class and yet a bit of wildness in her attitude and even in her dress. Today it was the yellow toenail polish that made Gina laugh.

She had seen Kara's car in her driveway and decided on a whim to stop in and share her desert woman story. When Kara listened to the tale, she became enthralled, eventually begging to be included in Gina's snooping adventure.

"The last thing we want is to be caught," Kara warned. "I don't even want Charley to know we're checking this woman out. He'll throw a fit and give us a legal lecture about some esoteric binocular law. I'll bet your husband won't be thrilled about you creeping around in the cactus, spying on the witch that beat him with her broom."

"I won't ask permission, just forgiveness," Gina joked. "We need to find a night when both of the guys are occupied. How hard is it for you to find a sitter for the girls?"

Not having any children of her own, Gina could only guess that it must be a hassle having to plan every move and motion based on where the children were and what they were doing. She and Brighton had postponed a family until school was finished, but the now desired pregnancy hadn't happened.

"Babysitters won't be a problem." Kara answered. "There are two older teenage sisters who moved in right next to the clubhouse. Say, I've got an idea. Thursday is the HOA meeting. Charley has to go since he's the attorney for the organization. You just need to be sure that your husband will be there. It will give us a good two hours to see what we can see," Kara said with a smile as she finished her drink.

***

Roy noticed the new nautical blue Highlander pulling into Charley Banks' driveway. He also noticed its driver. He hadn't seen the cute blonde woman in the neighborhood before. Though a confirmed bachelor, he was very much an admirer of beautiful women. "Who knows?" he said to Chad. "Maybe she is a single chick out looking for a husband."

Chad was sitting on the front passenger seat of the pickup truck, drooling a long thin chain of saliva. He had just finished scarfing down a burrito from the gas station.

As the man and dog stared at the woman, she brushed a strand of hair away from her face, and her diamond wedding ring flashed a sparkling "married" sign to Roy.

"Oh Chad, did you see that ring flash? Oh darn, another one got away," Roy laughed, giving the dog's head a vigorous rub. Chad just licked his mouth and put his head down on the seat.

Roy had noticed the huge, yellow backhoe earlier as it slowly moved down the main road, and wondered if there had been a new house started in the neighborhood. He circled through the streets looking for signs of excavation when he saw the sign at the front of the dentist's house.

"Mahi Mahi Pools." Deep tractor tire tracks had compressed the dirt and building materials leading up and into the backyard. No other cars or trucks were on or near the site. Roy saw his opportunity. He pulled his truck to a safe spot across from the house and rolled the windows down a couple of inches. "Stay here, Chad; I'll just be a second."

He walked up the driveway, giving the appearance that he belonged there. Rounding the back corner of the patio, he saw a huge pile of rock and dirt the backhoe had created digging the swimming pool. "Perfect," he thought. There it was again, the reflecting glitter from the newly excavated ground, not far from where he had borrowed the first collection of rocks. The ten-foot pile of dirt glistened in the sunlight. He couldn't believe his eyes. It had to be something better than fool's gold. He bent down and with both hands, scooped up a mass of the crumbled gravel and dirt. Every single stone contained glittering particles.

Roy walked to the edge of the large hole and studied the sheer walls. He could see the same glitter on the north side where the sun was hitting. Looking closely, he could make out striations in the wall, lines indicating layers of different types of stone. He knew that separate layers were usually from sediment laid down at different times over eons. Lake bottoms were the most common sites of sedimentation layers. Looking out over the surrounding hills and the valley below, it was hard to believe that this place could have ever been a lakebed, but that was what he had often been told.

"I can't wait until it's full of water and I can dive in," said a cheerful female voice from behind.

Roy almost fell into the hole, he was so startled. He gathered himself and turned toward the attractive blonde woman. "It's a beautiful spot for a pool. Is this yours?"

"Sure is. Hi, I'm Gina Dunn. Do you live around here?" she asked, extending her slender, manicured hand.

"Roy Richards," he answered, feeling her soft skin but strong grip. He could smell the subtle fragrance of her perfume and noted the lack of flashy jewelry. She wore a red, cotton-knit top with a V neck that accented her muscular shoulders and perfect figure. Her cargo pants had a red tassel tie around her narrow waist. Roy was instantly infatuated. Though her solitaire diamond ring told him she was married, Roy was still appreciative of her beauty. He wanted to find and marry a woman just like her.

"Yes, I do live around here. That's my house right there," he said, pointing to the Tuscan single-story, four houses down and around the circle from the Dunns'. "I moved in six months ago, just when they were starting to scrape the surface of your lot. I saw the backhoe tractor leaving earlier and couldn't contain my curiosity about your pool. I hope you don't mind my snooping."

"Not at all," Gina said with a smile. "Would you like to see the inside of the house?"

"Sure, if you have the time. The house looks awesome from the outside. You did a great job picking the elevation and colors. I could have used your help on mine. I never was sure what would look good, and the design people in the sales office weren't much help. I think they picked out the add-ons with the biggest profit margin." They both laughed and headed for the house.

Gina led him into the foyer and closed the door behind them. He immediately felt a sense of anxiety, with just the two of them being alone inside the house. He could barely concentrate on what she was saying as she showed him the various rooms and features of the house. He felt like a school kid on his first date. Way too soon the tour of the house was over, and they were standing on the patio looking at the hole in the backyard.

"Well, I need to run to the grocery store," she said, offering him her hand. "It was great to meet you. Please stop by again to meet Brighton. We are both eager to get to know the neighbors and get settled in. By the way, I forgot to ask, is there a Mrs. Richards?"

"My dog, Chad, and I are still working on that."

Roy released her hand reluctantly, secretly wishing he could hang on forever. *What the heck is wrong with me?* Had he been thunderstruck by a happily married woman?

"Thank you so much for the tour. You have a wonderful place. It puts mine to shame. If I can do anything to help you get settled in, let me know. Please call me to help you and your husband when you are unloading." Roy took a scrap of paper and a pen from his pocket and wrote down his phone numbers.

He walked her to her car and waved as she drove off. Trying to get his mind back on the rock in the backyard, he walked to the pool and picked up an empty paint can. He scooped up a gallon-sized sample of the most colorful pulverized dirt and rock. Later, when he returned home and washed his hands, there again was a yellow-orange stain on his palms. "Very weird," he told Chad.

✳✳✳

Brighton and Gina had eaten another rushed evening meal. By the time Brighton finished up at the office then picked up the gold crowns at the dental lab, it was too late to go by the new house. They ate their salads and pasta quietly, picking up bits of news from the television. In the past they wouldn't have had the thing on during dinner, but their life was subtly evolving on a new path. Gina had always worked in the past, and now she didn't. Brighton had always gone to school, and now he worked. They used to be dirt poor and now, slowly, they were seeing that proverbial light at the end of the tunnel. The romantic candlelit dinners of tuna casseroles with fun conversations had given way to rushed meals that started too late and conversations trending toward the house and things needed for the money pit. Now, more frequently than not, dinners were lit by the glow of the television instead of candles.

Tonight's big rush was to get Brighton to the HOA meeting at the newly finished Hidden Canyon clubhouse. The clubhouse was the pride and joy of the neighborhood with its 25-meter swimming pool, fitness spa, four lighted tennis courts, and a spacious playground for the little ones. The "Club Home," as Dean Shutter had coined the name, was ready to hold its first official home owners association function. Later in the week there would be a grand opening barbeque party, and everyone would be invited. Tonight's HOA meeting was to be strictly business.

*****

"And just why is it you are sending me to the HOA meeting by myself?" Brighton asked as he rinsed his plate off in the sink. "You are the pulse of the neighborhood affairs. I'm not going to remember all the things you will want to know. You'll have a million questions when I get home, and I won't know the answers to half of them. Sure you don't want to come?"

"I promised Kara Banks that I would go shopping with her. She is embarrassed to be at the meeting since her husband is the attorney for the HOA. Don't forget to reintroduce yourself to him. Charley is his name. He may not remember you unless you mention me." She had met and visited with the attorney several times at his and Kara's home.

Gina finished the last sentence as she picked up her car keys and gave him a hard peck on the cheek. He tried to get a squeeze from her, but she wiggled away and was out the door, leaving him a little dissatisfied and a little curious. She was up to something. He could feel it. *Was there a birthday or anniversary coming up?*

*****

The parking lot at the "Club Home" was nearly full when Brighton pulled in. This surprised him, since he had seen so little activity in the development on his near-daily drives through the new neighborhood. He picked out Charley Bank's BMW parked in a reserved spot near the building's entrance.

The meeting room was packed. Most of the women were middle-aged and overdressed. The men, standing primarily in small groups and trying to look interested, seemed tired from the day's work duties. Drinks and hors d'oeuvres were set up at the back of the room and were being enjoyed by the crowd.

Brighton had just taken a seat when someone tapped him on the shoulder and asked if the chair next to him was taken. He shook his head.

"Hello, my name is Kashmir Patel. Are you possibly the dentist?" the diminutive man asked. He was dressed in an expensive suit and white shirt complete with embroidered initials on the pocket, gold cuff links, and a diamond-studded Rolex. His hair was black as coal, shiny from the hair dressing that obviously held it in rigid place. His nails were manicured and his black mustache was trimmed to perfection.

Brighton took the man's pre-offered hand and nodded. "I'm Brighton Dunn, and yes, I'm a dentist."

"You are going to soon be my new neighbor next to my door," Kashmir stated in a staccato accent and a high voice. He explained that he and his wife, Bivana, and their two teenage sons had moved in several months ago. "We have been traveling much of the time. I apologize for not having met you sooner." They chatted about their houses and about the Patels' dog, Harley.

A gavel banged at the front of the room, interrupting the din of conversations. People found places to sit as Dean Shutter tapped the microphone. He took a sip of his drink and began to address the crowd.

"Good evening, ladies and gentlemen. Welcome to Hidden Canyon. My name is Dean Shutter, and though I have met most of you, I hope to get to know all of you soon. Welcome to the first official meeting of the Hidden Canyon Homeowners' Association. The HOA will become a part of your everyday lexicon.

"Since the Hidden Canyon project is over 90 percent sold out, I have instructed the law firm of Fuller and Fuller to prepare documents to transfer full rights and responsibility of the project to the HOA. This clubhouse, the swimming pool, and all the other common properties will soon belong completely to the association itself. Mr. Fuller has appointed one of our own residents, attorney Charley Bank, to oversee the transition. This is your community. We want you to feel you truly own it and have a direct say in how it is managed. My wife and I have just decided to join you here as permanent residents and will begin construction on Lot #26 next week."

This news was met with a round of applause.

"Pride of ownership will encourage each of us and our families to care for things in our neighborhood and to be involved in the management of the community. Since I am turning things over to you, the new owners, I am going to have Mr. Banks—he likes to be called Charley—preside over the rest of this meeting. Later, I will be available to answer any of your questions." Dean sat down to a scattering of applause as Charley took the podium.

"Greetings from the Banks family," he began. "I'm Charley and I have a wonderful wife, Kara, and twin preteen daughters, Ashlyn and Hailey. We're hoping to keep them preteen as long as possible."

This brought smiles and a lightened mood to the room.

"I hope you will love living in Hidden Canyon as much as we already do. The first order of business is to elect a board of directors. And you wondered why you learned to hold class elections in fifth grade?"

6

SNOOPING

Sitting in Gina's car on the narrow gravel road, the first order of business was to get the flashlights to work. Gina had parked the Toyota along the side of the dusty road about two hundred yards from where they thought the woman's shack was located. A low hill blocked their view. They were quiet as mice getting out of the car, but thanks to the safety features of the new model, the interior lights came on when they exited and wouldn't go off. The headlights also stayed on, outlining their bodies to anyone who might be looking. This panicked the women, but they pushed the doors closed and crept away from the glowing car. Ten seconds later, the lights went off.

Walking in a half-crouch, they moved slowly up the trail. In the darkness, it seemed as though the desert plants were moving closer, and the sounds in the desert at night were impressive—with insects, night birds, and the ever-present howl of the coyote. The ambient starlight produced shadows across the trail, adding to the intrigue. Gina's and Kara's imaginations were on high power.

"Stop!" Gina gasped, grabbing Kara's arm.

She pointed to a stick lying across the trail, but as she squinted to see it more clearly, it moved. Both women gasped again, grabbing one another's arms. Kara clicked on the flashlight, shining it on the trail. Slowly the stick slithered across the trail and down a small hill. Kara had resisted the urge to turn on the flashlight, but now just left it on. Cupping her hand over the lens, she allowed just enough light to shine through to assure them that the snake was gone.

When they cleared the rise, they worked their way to a place on the trail where they could finally see the outline of the shack. Behind the building, they could make out the vague image of a small car. No lights were on.

"Look, can you believe that?" Gina whispered in Kara's ear, pointing to a single tiny building fifty or sixty feet from the shack. "It's an actual outhouse. I just can't believe it. This woman is living in the eighteenth century."

The women's mixed impressions were a cross between derision and sympathy for the person living an existence of apparent abject poverty just a mile from their own magnificent homes. Afraid to move any closer, they continued to survey the surroundings. There were piles of discarded lumber, stacks of gardening tools, and even a small hand push-plow. As their night vision improved, they could see the outline of a few mesh wire cages, none with apparent occupants.

The sudden explosion of sound came with no warning. Both women saw the flash of light then instantly heard the sound that shattered the night's silence. Their bodies even felt the compression of the blast. Moments later, a second blast fractured the silence, and the bushes to their left disintegrated in a shower of flying twigs, rocks, and dust.

"We're being shot at!" screamed Kara.

When they opened their eyes to look at one another, both were crouched near the ground with hands over their ears. The old flashlight lay in the dirt as they scurried toward their car.

No shouts, voices, or footfall sounds were heard. No lights came on nor were they certain from which direction the gunshot sounds had come. Only the ringing in their ears assured them that anything real even had happened. They waited by the side of the car, holding on to each other. For several minutes, they were motionless, afraid to open the doors and turning on the car's interior lights. Finally, they got into the car and backed down the dirt road until Gina found a safe place to turn around. She gunned the engine, spraying gravel from all four of the SUV's tires as they left the scene in a trail of dust. Once they reached paved road, Gina pulled off on the shoulder and killed the engine. They stared at each other in silence hearing only each another's labored breathing and feeling the pounding of their own hearts.

"I think I peed my pants!" declared Kara with a blank look on her face.

"Me too," said Gina, as they both burst into embarrassed laughter.

***

The HOA meeting was well organized with a carefully designed logo gracing the letterhead on which the agenda was printed. The pre-meeting food and drink had been just the right amount for most. The only problem was that there was apparently too much of a good thing for some of the participants. By the second half of the meeting, two of the residents were working themselves well into the high teens on their blood alcohol levels.

The Steiner brothers were retired Pontiac Michigan auto workers. Otto and Heinz claimed to have put in nearly twenty-five years at a GMC plant, assembling truck suspensions. Born in West Germany, they had immigrated to the U.S. with their parents while in their late teens. They had grown up eating high-fat foods and drinking German beer.

When the lottery mania hit the U.S. in the eighties, the Steiners were thrilled. They routinely spent a few bucks a week trying to win the "Big One," but never saw more than an occasional five or ten dollar payoff. One night, the years of playing and paying finally paid off. After a few beers at the local tavern, they had agreed to pool their money to buy forty Power Ball tickets for a chance at the $34 million. Otto had picked numbers that he said came to him in a dream, but wouldn't tell Heinz what the numbers meant. On the following Wednesday night, just before the ten o'clock news, the numbers were announced. Otto couldn't believe his eyes. His exact numbers were on the TV screen—the same numbers he had picked on forty identical tickets.

The Steiners' dream came true; they hit the jackpot. In their excitement to get their hands on the money, they went to the lottery's office and press conference without talking to an attorney or a tax advisor. They showed up at the lottery office only with the liquor store owner who had sold Otto the tickets. The store owner received a check for fifty thousand dollars. When the Steiner brothers were asked how they wanted their money, cash or annuity, they had no idea what the question even meant. They looked at each other, and agreed that the word annuity sounded important. They gave each other high fives and told the manager they'd take the annuity.

The brothers quit their jobs the next day. They didn't even go back to the auto factory to clean out their lockers and say good-bye to their lifelong friends.

Instead of passing out a few favors or buying a round for the boys, they deposited the lottery money in the local bank and went to a travel agency that the giddy bank manager recommended. There, they bought tickets for each other and their wives and flew off to Cancun for two weeks. They dumped their fifty-year-old row houses and left the snow behind for the sunshine of Arizona, purchasing adjoining lots in Hidden Canyon. They had hired and fired three architects and two general contractors before their houses were out of the ground. Now, they were at the HOA meeting drunk and waving a list of demands for ridiculous variances, including a glass-enclosed corridor between their two houses.

Brighton and his new friend, Dr. Patel, gave each other sideways glances as the Steiners went on about how the deed restrictions were prejudicial against foreigners.

Charley took the microphone and announced, "A quick review of the Steiners' requests has found that all are far outside the guidelines. Even a positive vote by this forum wouldn't make them acceptable. The county and the EPA both regulate use of any land outside your individually designated building sites. The area of non-disturb is sacred." Charley expected at least a chuckle from his last statement, but instead heard screaming.

"Just 'cause ve ver born in Germany and have a little accent, you won't let us change a ting around here. Why don't you pick on dose rag-head Indians and the monster dog they keep in the yard? And what about dose beaner wetbacks playing that Mexican music so loud all day?" Heinz said, slurring his words.

"That's enough of that crap you boneheads," came the voice of Clyde. The security guard grabbed Heinz by the arm and tried to escort him from the room. Otto responded by slapping Clyde on the back of the head. Dean and Charley barely had started to react to the ruckus when Otto was suddenly on his face on the floor in a full-Nelson, Roy Richards sitting on Otto's back with a matter-of-fact look on his face. Meanwhile, Clyde had drawn his mace canister and had it pointed at Heinz's face.

"You're living in the Wild West now," Clyde told him. "You have two choices: either leave now and wait for the cops at your place, or I can take you both outside and shoot you." Clyde followed his threat by menacingly shaking the mace can at both of them. The fact that he had no gun to shoot them with went unnoticed.

"Schweine! Sie sind alle Schweine! You are all a bunch of pigs," Heinz screamed at his new neighbors.

Roy pulled Otto to his feet, and Clyde led both drunken men stumbling toward the door. There was dead silence until they were out the door, and then everyone started talking at once. Most of those present had never seen such an altercation in their entire lives.

"Please be seated, and quiet down please!" Charley shouted over the din of the crowd. Once it quieted, Charley continued. "I'm sure we are all embarrassed and sorry about that scene. Looking over the rest of the agenda, I think we can table the remainder of the questions until our meeting next month. If you have individual problems, I'll stay right here until they are all addressed. Incidentally, I'd like to thank Clyde and Mr. . . . sorry; I don't know your name."

Everyone turned toward the corner where Roy had been standing. He was not there. "I think he left," a voice from the audience announced. "His name is Roy Richards."

As the meeting broke up a full hour and a great deal of discussion later, Clyde returned to report that the drunken brothers were home safely. The sheriff had been called but, after hearing the story, had refused to get involved. "What happened in the HOA stays in the HOA," he was quoted as saying.

By the time Charley was turning out the lights, he had met a score or more of new neighbors, but still hadn't met the winner of the night's fight. He made himself a note on his Droid to meet that man, Mr. Richards.

✳✳✳

By the time Brighton arrived home, he was wishing he had taken notes at the meeting so that he didn't forget any details when he told Gina of the night's excitement. He walked into the bathroom of the tiny rental they were soon to vacate and found his wife neck-deep in bubbles. The mirror in the small bathroom was fogged over, and Gina lay motionless with wet strands of her blonde hair draped on her forehead. A ginger-scented candle was burning on the back of the windowsill, and he could hear her softly humming. Brighton stood in silence and watched. He hated to intrude on her meditation and so he tiptoed into the bedroom and waited several minutes. He then slipped off his clothes and walked back into the bathroom. Some of the bubbles had thinned, leaving her nipples emerging from the water like heavenly periscopes.

"So you have any room in there for a tired dentist?" he whispered.

Gina looked up at him and smiled. "There is always room for you in my life and possibly room for you in my tub. Before you get in though, look on the sink countertop."

On the ledge of the sink lay a small, oval plastic test kit. Brighton squinted at it in the dim candlelight and saw a narrow horizontal line. "Is this for real?"

Gina motioned him toward her. He carefully stepped into the tub and slid into the water. He took her face in his hand and, ever so softly, kissed her lips. They could hear the water overflowing the edge of the tub, but it didn't really matter.

***

Alma Ziegler lay in her bed, alone as always, unable to fall asleep. She kept walking to the door, parting the curtains, and looking for the flashing lights of a sheriff's car. She knew she had gone too far this time. Actually shooting at human beings. What in the world was she thinking? Maybe those women were lost or had car trouble or had come to offer friendship or a peace offering. She was pretty sure the car came from the development but wasn't positive. Maybe it was the woman she had seen with the binoculars.

Alma had dreamed up all sorts of scenarios of how she could stop the developers' encroachment into her desert. It was her desert, after all. She had been here years before anyone bothered to pave the roads. Of course, she would never carry out any of her planned scenarios. They were risky and would take time away from the work she had to do each day, tending her garden and native animals. What would her coyotes and the rabbits and the owls do without her?

Her best plan to stop development years ago was spreading the rumor that the ground was full of radon gas. She had written to the newspaper and warned them that any new houses would slowly fill up with radioactive radon gas and cause everyone to get cancer. The newspaper had run its own version in an article citing tests that confirmed the presence of radon gas but also demonstrated the benign nature of it.

Next, she had decided to set one of the new houses in Hidden Canyon on fire while it was in the framing stage. After a few weeks of obsessing about it, she bought a can of lighter fluid. She lay awake at nights, plotting and deciding. Often, she would walk over the hill to the development in the evenings, trying to pick out her victim. Then she found a half-read newspaper on a bench in front of the grocery store that put her plan on hold. The newspaper announced the capture of an arsonist in Phoenix who had torched four houses. The policemen who had captured the guy had taken a detour on the way to the jail driving through the neighborhood where the arsonist had burned the houses. When the locals learned who was in the car, they dragged the man out of the police car and beat him to near death with the garden hoses they had used during the fires. The policemen turned a blind eye.

Alma herself felt beaten. She hadn't felt worse since the weeks following her parents' plane crash. In her mental state, she was even considering moving away from the desert to some tiny mountain town. But she loved the desert and hated the idea of being forced to change her life because of someone else. Now, by firing her shotgun at the women, she was sure she had forced herself into a corner. She had no friends, no family, and no one to counsel her. She felt desperate. There had to be something she could do to stop these intruders.

✳✳✳

Roy's cell phone rang as he was pulling into the industrial park. "Roy here," he answered.

"Hey, Mr. Richards, we need to know where you got the rock samples you brought to us last week."

"Hang on a few minutes; I'm just pulling off the highway. I'll be at your shop in five minutes," Roy said. He had called earlier and left a voice message that he planned to drop by the Geological Associates office, but he guessed that they hadn't received it. He had the paint can full of more samples from the dentist's house but was unsure whether to tell them about it or not. He would just have to see how things went. He left the can in his truck.

"Good morning," Roy said to the accompaniment of a tiny bell attached to the door that jingled as he entered. He had spent the night working the control tower. His clothes were wrinkled, and he had a full day's beard. It had been a long night with an unusual amount of landing and departures. He wasn't in the mood to play verbal games. As before, Bill was dressed in an outfit designed for garbage removal. Lori, on the other hand, could have walked into any business boardroom and been in style.

"Hi there, big guy," said Lori. "How have you been? Attacked any helpless women on the sidewalks lately?" Lori asked in a jesting tone. She was dressed in a navy blue sleeveless dress with a neck cut lower than Roy's eyes could resist. Her dark hair was pulled into a ponytail on one side of her head.

"Where did you get these rock samples?" demanded Bill in a tone Roy hadn't heard since his Marine boot camp days. Annoyed, he glanced at Bill, and then he turned to Lori.

Her greeting had been much friendlier, even a little too social. She gave Roy the feeling of needing to be on his guard. He noticed a stack of computer printouts from an old roller, dot-matrix printer lying on the counter. The last one of those he had seen was at a car rental agency in Guam ten years earlier.

"What have you got for me?" he asked, wanting to get the information and get out of this place. He was beginning to feel like he was the specimen being examined.

"I need to know the location where this stuff came from so I can add it to the National Geological database," said Bill. "It's a way to study the country's makeup, if you know what I mean."

"I found it east of Kingman," Roy lied. "It was on an unmarked trail, and I just picked it up because it looked interesting. What's in the stuff, anyway?"

Lori, feeling that a confrontation was in the making, stepped in front of Big Bill. "You have a very fascinating specimen, Mr.

Richards, or may I call you Roy? It has a significant amount of gold, hence the glitter, but there is something else much more interesting. Did you happen to notice that your hands turned yellow after handling the rocks?" She didn't wait for an answer. "Have you ever heard of rhodium?"

"Can't say as I have. What is it?" asked Roy, keeping the yellow hand-staining fact to himself.

"Rhodium is one of a group of platinum metals. There are five or six of them in the group. They are all valuable and pretty scarce. Rhodium is the most valuable. It doesn't have the luster and workability of gold or platinum, but it has unique properties, especially during chemical reactions that act as a catalyst. You know what a catalyst is, right?"

Roy was all ears and nodded that he was following her explanation.

Bill interrupted Lori. "Just in case you're interested, platinum sells for about eighteen hundred bucks an ounce. Rhodium, however, is scarcer. I looked up the spot price today; it goes up and down with demand. It's around twenty-eight hundred dollars per ounce. Your specimen, Mr. Richards, assays out at over four ounces per ton. That's the way the mining industry values metals," Bill explained. "That comes out to roughly thirteen thousand dollars for every ton of ore. That's not counting the value of the gold and platinum and other trace metals that could be in the ore. Since finding it in its native state in that concentration is most improbable, we have to question where you really obtained the stuff. Or maybe you are with the Feds, and you are testing us in some way." Bill's last statement was posed more as an indictment than as a curious inquiry.

When Roy didn't answer right away, Lori smiled at him and said, "If you aren't testing us, then perhaps you are playing some major hoax on someone, Mr. Richards?"

Again, Roy held his ground. He could barely process what he was hearing from this Ying and Yang pair.

"If this find is legitimate, you could be the luckiest amateur prospector in the history of mining." Bill glared at Roy.

"I'm a Fed, all right, but I have nothing to do with mining or metals," said Roy. "I work for air traffic control at the airport. I'm a control officer. You know, I tell the pilots where and when to land and take off."

Roy was getting nervous. These two were treating him like a thief instead of a valued customer. He didn't believe the precious metal or rhodium story they were telling him anymore than he expected them to believe his bogus location story.

"Well, listen, I've got to get to work. They have us on a short leash at the tower. If I could get a copy of that assay report and a bill, I'll be on my way."

Lori smiled at him as she handed him a plastic folder with his name and the date below the company's letterhead. "Everything is in there. But just so you know, Roy Richards," she said, reading his name from the title page of the report, "Rhodium is on the government's list of strategic metals. We need to send a copy of the report to the Department of Defense. If we don't, there is a huge fine. You know, just like the doctors have to report HIV and all those nasty socially contracted bugs to the health department."

Bill gave a gusty laugh at Lori's analogy and laid an invoice on the counter with numbers on it.

"I sure hope your wallet is a big as your curiosity," Bill said, laughing again.

Roy pulled out his wallet and tossed a Visa card on the counter, looking at the numbers on the statement as the plastic landed. He gave out a faint gasp and then looked up at Lori and Bill.

"Is this right?" he said. "Four hundred and fifty dollars?"

"You bet. We always give new customers a discounted rate," Bill answered with a chuckle.

Lori processed the card and returned it to Roy with a smile. He signed the receipt and picked up the plastic folder. He was almost out the door when he felt something touch his arm. Lori gently gripped his sleeve, startling him. She spoke in a subdued voice. "Wherever you found those rocks, Roy, you'd better get down to the appropriate county recorder's office and file a mining claim. Who knows, maybe it isn't already claimed by someone else. You could be just like Billie Boy said—the luckiest prospector in the world."

Roy's hands were shaking when he tried to put the key in the ignition. Pulling onto the highway, he couldn't concentrate, so he drove through a McDonald's and bought a Coke. Slowly and carefully, he read the computer printout. Sure enough, there were the various metals and the relative quantitative values. His mind was racing.

He had found something very special. Now, he had to figure out a way to get to it. Was his neighbor's backyard loaded with the stuff? What about his own patch of ground? Was it just in the dentist's yard or the entire Hidden Canyon? Each of the lots was only a few hundred feet apart. What about the open land behind the project? It didn't take him long to calculate that a couple of pickup beds full of the precious ore would be worth more than the truck itself. He needed more answers and maybe the help of a partner.

✳✳✳

Dean Shutter sat at a conference table in the Surety Title Company's office. He had spent a lot of time in title company offices over the years, but he never had been there to receive such a big paycheck. He couldn't believe the roller coaster he had been riding these last several months—one day thinking he was broke, then the next, a day like today, feeling on top of the world. There had been calls from the bank as recently as six months before threatening his personal solvency and his state of mind. Now, brisk sales had brought the cream to the top of the milk bucket. All the hard work, the worry, the planning, and the neglect of his family were going to be rewarded.

After all the closings of the Hidden Canyon lots, only one lot remained. Dean had always had his eye on the particular lot, never listing it. With the consent of his financial partners, he had finally decided to keep it in his name—a bonus for a job well done. The checks for the lenders and his previous partner's share were cut separately with everything spelled out in clear legalese. His would be the final Hidden Canyon money.

The starvation-thin, blonde woman at the title company office was way overdressed. She definitely could have gone a size larger with the pink wool skirt and a size smaller with the silicone. She had been handing him document after document to read, sign, and initial for the last forty minutes. At last she opened a separate manila folder that held a single sheet of paper. She withdrew the check, placing it in front of him with an air of formality.

"That's $3,884,207," she said with a smile. "And change," she finished with a bigger grin. "Not that it is any of my business, Mr. Shutter, but every one of my friends says that Hidden Canyon is the most beautiful development in the state. You must be really proud of it. What's next for you, Mr. Shutter?"

"I guess I'll build my wife a house and settle down for a while. I've gotten to know the residents, and I like most of them. Who knows, maybe they won't even mind having me for a neighbor."

Once out of the title office and into the warm morning sunshine, Dean felt so happy he nearly skipped down the sidewalk on his way to his Hummer. He had had no idea that his residual check was going to be so big. He had been overwhelmed with work the last several weeks and hadn't met with the accountants for months. Frankly, he had worried that there might not even be a profit. Maybe the Shutter bad luck was over for good. He turned on his cell phone to call his wife with the good news, but the incoming line rang before he could finish dialing.

"Dean, its Charley Banks. I'm so glad I caught you. There is a problem in the Canyon. Someone just shot the Patels' dog. You know the Great Dane? I think they call him Harley."

"Who would want to shoot a dog? Especially a big, happy fellow like their Harley," Dean said with sadness in his voice. "Is he dead?"

"Dr. Patel called from the vet's office. He was talking a mile a minute, and from what little I could understand, the dog is wounded in the hip. Dean, the poor dog wasn't even out running around. He was in the Patels' backyard, and someone just walked up and shot him. Doc Patel is mad as heck and says if he finds out who did it, he is going to pour gasoline—he calls it petrol—on the person and set him on fire. I guess they have that down to an art form in India."

Dean's mind raced for a minute. He kept seeing the image of the Ziegler lady as he considered the problem. Then again there were the German idiots, Heinz and Otto Steiner. They had threatened retribution after they were thrown out of the homeowners' meeting. Why the Patels' Great Dane? He was the friendliest and most regal animal Dean had ever known.

"You know these people better than I do. Should I call the sheriff, or should we try to handle it in the HOA?" Charley asked.

"I would suggest that we have Clyde check into it," Dean said. "The last time I called the sheriff I spent more time filling out forms than they did investigating. They never did find the thieves."

"Okay. Do you want me to call Clyde, or will you see him?" Charley asked.

"The truth is, Charley, I just left the title office and signed the last of the papers relinquishing my ownership of the project, thus handing it completely over to the HOA. From this moment on, I am just another homeowner in Hidden Canyon. You and the new HOA president, Dr. Cooperman, are the new Kings of the Hill," Dean said with a chuckle. "If you have any questions, I'll be around, but the rest is up to you and your minions." Dean clicked off his phone and redialed his house. He planned to take his wife to Las Vegas for the weekend and buy her the biggest diamond necklace he could find.

***

"Why would someone shoot that poor dog?" Gina squeezed a lemon wedge and dropped it into her drink. They were sitting in the shade of the Banks' patio, looking up the rolling hillside toward the Patel and Dunn homes.

Kara pondered the bottom of her glass and shook her head. "Charley said the dog had been barking and the jerk—whoever it was—was most likely trying to get him to shut up. The poor pup was probably just trying to scare away one of those mangy coyotes."

"Well, we both know who is at the top of our list. If we told our husbands about our little adventure and her shooting at us, they would both have heart attacks. Charley said that the vet had recovered the bullet. Now if they can match it to a gun, they could prove who shot the poor thing. I mean, we know who it has to be. Who else besides the gray phantom lady is going to come in our neighborhood and shoot somebody's poor dog?"

"This is getting spicy," Gina said with a smirk on her face. "It sounds to me like it's time for the real investigators to get back in the loop. We can hardly expect Clyde to solve the mystery. He can barely heft his huge body in and out of the security truck."

"So how about us trying to get her gun and give it to the police so they can test it?" Kara asked, looking over the top of her designer sunglasses.

"Did Charley say it was a single bullet? I'm pretty sure we were shot at with a shotgun the other night. Maybe she doesn't even have a pistol or a rifle."

"How about doing a little better research this time?" suggested Gina. "We really need to know who that woman is and why she is so freaky. When do you have some time?"

***

Dr. and Mrs. Patel had come home after a frantic call from one of their boys. Their dog Harley had been inside the house with the boys when he had suddenly jumped up and ran to the back door and started barking. They told him to be quiet but Harley ignored the boys completely, so they let him out. Outside, the barking continued for several minutes before the boys heard the shots.

The pet hospital had a full-time "on call" veterinarian. With IV fluids, surgery, and a lot of luck, Harley had survived. The bullet had been retrieved, and the sheriff had filled out a report.

7
Moving In

The three huge Allied moving vans rolled through the gates of Hidden Canyon early in the afternoon. The trucks were spattered with mud and road salt, but would not have attracted any particular attention had it not been for their number and the shiny, black, million-dollar Prevost motor home following them. Behind the motor home was a matching shiny black trailer almost as big. Not far behind the black trailer rolled a pearl-black Bentley sedan.

The caravan pulled to a stop in front of the house on Lot #33. Taking turns, each of the vans backed slowly up the newly-paved driveway to the garage where their contents were carefully unloaded. There were so many boxes that even after unwrapping and distributing the furniture and belongings in the house, there was barely room for the Bentley in the six-car garage.

Most all the neighbors were aware of the move-in. It was the big topic of interest at the Club Home. Clyde had driven his security truck by the lot so many times that one of the movers considered asking him to buy pizza for the crew.

The house on Lot #33 was a monster. It was the biggest and fanciest house in Hidden Canyon. No one knew anything about the homeowner. The contractor was a California firm, and there were guards at the chain-link gate around the clock until the fences were removed the same morning that the moving vans arrived. Someone special was joining the neighborhood.

Roy had been on duty the night before and had enjoyed a nap, a vigorous workout, and a steam bath followed by a cold shower. Dripping as he dried off, he parted the shutters for a look. No neighbor that Roy had talked to knew who was moving into the monster house. It appeared to be such a big secret that even Dean Shutter had only met and dealt with a real estate broker and a landscaper. The owner of record was an offshore company with some sort of "eye chart" letters for a name. Maybe they were Greek.

Roy observed that as the rear door of the Bentley opened, a tall, slender but shapely woman with flaming red hair exited the car. She was wearing black, skintight jeans and a powder-blue top that glittered with some kind of stones or sequins. As he squinted to clear his vision, he had the strong feeling that he had seen her before. The woman walked up the stone entrance path, stopping several times to stretch and to look back out over the valley. She examined the abundance of newly planted cacti and desert plants as if it were the first time she had seen them.

Squinting harder into the glare of the sun, Roy noticed a gold-colored logo on the door of the million-dollar motor home. It was a small rocking chair with a name printed above the logo: "RHONDA." That was more than enough for Roy. The woman's face, body, and even her walk were obviously that of Rhonda Tucker. He couldn't believe his eyes. He had followed her career for years. She was a top-ten country singer with Grammys on her shelves and at least two Oscar nominations. She had it all: the silken voice, the teasing body, and the no-nonsense business reputation that stopped competitors and paparazzi in their tracks. For the last ten years she had been the hottest female commodity in Nashville and one of the most sought-after in Hollywood.

He dressed in his usual blue jeans, but left the T-shirt lying on the kitchen counter. Even though he had plenty to do that afternoon, he kept wandering back to the window to check out the progress of his new neighbor's movers. Eventually, he became bored with the move-in show and settled down to pay some bills when he heard the doorbell ring. He slipped his shirt on and peeked out the side panel of the front door only to see the lady herself standing on his doorstep five feet away from his face. Startled, he hesitated before gaining the courage to open the door.

"Hi there," Rhonda said in a lusty voice with just a tinge of Southern drawl. Her smile could have warmed dry ice. "My name is Rhonda Tucker, and I'm your new next-door neighbor. I sure hope I'm not bothering you, but I'm just this minute moving in, and believe it or not, the water has been shut off for a couple of hours while they hook up the ice maker. I hate to be a nuisance, but I'm in desperate need of your bathroom facilities!"

"Come in, come in," Roy said, stepping out of the doorway, allowing her to enter the hall. "The powder room is right here." He directed her and flipped on the light to the powder room.

She went in and closed the door. He didn't hear the door lock but did hear the rustle of clothes. He walked down the hall into the kitchen, not wanting to be found standing in front of the door when she came out. He was embarrassed when he heard the water running. Pacing the floor, he waited.

"All done," she announced, opening the bathroom door. "Where did you go, neighbor?"

"Down here in the kitchen," came Roy's voice. "Can I offer you a cold drink of water or a soda?" he asked, poking his head out from around the corner.

She didn't answer right away but, taking her time, wandered down the hallway toward him, checking out the rooms, the wall hangings, and the framed pictures as she went. "What are these certificates for … 'Valor beyond the Call of Duty' … 'Outstanding Flight Safety Record?' My, my! Here is one for saving the city of Boise from a disaster. It sounds like you are some sort of superhero." She continued walking and talking in her Southern accent until she had walked through the open part of his house into his great room. Occasionally, she reached down to pet Chad, who would not leave her side, apparently as enthralled with the stranger as was his master.

Roy followed at a distance, saying nothing. There was little to say that was better than listening and watching her.

"This is an awesome home, but I sense a lack of feminine touch," Rhonda said.

"I'm sure you are right. I'm not married, so what you see is what my mom taught me. Hey, I'm open for suggestions. How about a cold bottle of water?" Not waiting for an answer this time, he put a chilled Evian bottle in her hand.

"Thanks, you're a lifesaver." She unscrewed the lid, took a healthy swallow, and sighed. "Moving really sucks, if you know what I mean. What do you do for a living, Roy?"

"I'm an air traffic controller at the Phoenix Airport. When I'm not working, I love outdoor sports; maybe that's why I've never landed a decorator. My mom always said, 'No taste is better than poor taste,' so I haven't taken the time to do much in the way of decorating." Roy laughed at his nervousness. Rhonda joined in with him.

"What brings you to Hidden Canyon?" Roy asked, beginning to feel remarkably comfortable talking to this superstar. He owned several of her CDs and had seen her latest movie on the big screen, enjoying the movie more than the popcorn for a change. He also had seen her playing in cameo roles in several of the more popular series on TV. From where he was standing in his great room, he could glimpse her picture on the cover of a recent *People* magazine lying on his coffee table. The headline under her picture was announcing the finalization of her divorce from her stage manager.

Biting on the end of the earpiece of her designer sunglasses, she asked, "I have to guess that you maybe know who I am?"

He gave a slight nod of affirmation.

"I don't mean to be rude and ignore your question. Am I interrupting something important, or have you got a minute to visit? I'm really tired of watching the movers, and by the way, your house smells a lot better than those mover guys. They are getting a little gamey after working all day in this heat." She laughed at her joke, and Roy smiled and motioned her toward the oxblood leather couch.

As she sat down, Rhonda put her half-empty bottle of water directly on top of the People magazine, covering the picture of her face. Roy sat in a recliner across from her and waited for her to begin.

"You were kind enough to ask what brought me to your neighborhood, so here it is. For the last two years, all I have done is work. I did a road tour all across the U.S. and Europe, and then I had a six-month run in Las Vegas, and on my days off, I filmed two movies in Hollywood. My agent has been working me like a trained monkey. When it became obvious that my marriage was finally finished," she said, glancing at the wet magazine, "I made my manager promise to cut me loose for two years. I want to reclaim reality and a sense of how real people live their lives." She finished her sentence staring out the window at the landscaped backyard and the swimming pool. "I just need a rest." She leaned back, sinking into the leather cushions. She sat in silence, rubbing Chad's ears.

Feeling awkward about breaking the mood, Roy said, "Maybe you won't like it … how real people live their lives … I mean … most people would like to be you," Roy stammered, fearing he might have insulted her.

When she didn't answer, he jumped up and went to the nearby wet bar, pulling a couple of Diet Pepsis and a bucket of ice out of the fridge. Popping the top open, he put ice in two glasses and poured the drink. He placed a cork coaster on the table and handed her the drink. The gesture seemed so natural and yet so foreign to her that she paused for a second. In her world, the attention she received made her forget that friends could be just that, just because they were on the same page, rather than one expecting something from the other.

"That Pepsi looks so good! I guess I'm thirstier than I thought. Thank you so much," Rhonda said with the most sincere look she had given anyone in months. She stood up and, with the glass in one hand, took his arm and said, "How about a tour of your pool area?"

The two stood on the patio visiting about the desert, Hidden Canyon, and what little he knew about the neighbors. "Most people here are very private," he said. "With a few exceptions they are busy folks who enjoy their homes, the view of the mountains in the daytime, and the city lights at night. Many of them live here just a few months a year. You'll probably never get a real chance to meet some of them."

"What do you think about my chances of being accepted as a neighbor? I'd like to fit in," she said. Her soft, almost shy, tone of voice left him perplexed and somewhat protective.

"Like I said, I doubt that most of the neighbors will ever know you are here, though I'm sure they all know who you are," Roy answered. "Of course, if you really want to blend in, you could hide some of the million-dollar wagon train out there in the driveway; it might help lower the barrier. After all, there are only eight or ten Bentleys in the neighborhood so far," he joked.

She gave him a friendly slug in the shoulder. Then to his huge surprise, she wrapped her arms around him, trapping his arms against his body, and gave him a hug. He stood still, not knowing quite what to do.

She stepped away, as if embarrassed. "I have been so afraid that I wouldn't find anyone here to be a friend. Thank you." She turned away from him for a couple of minutes then turned back and said, "How about helping me do just that, you know, lowering that wall or barrier? I'll make you a deal. I'd just love it if you would help me buy a pickup. I've always wanted to drive a truck. I've sung songs about them, but quite honestly I don't think I've ever even ridden in one. Maybe if I drove a regular pickup, people would be more accepting of me. Help me buy a pickup, and you can drive the Bentley for the next year."

"I have a pickup. How about I trade you straight across for the Bentley?" he joked.

"I'll have to think about that for a while," she said raising her eyebrow and tilting her head like he had seen her do in her movies. "I haven't even seen your truck."

They both laughed.

✳✳✳

Brighton and Gina loved their new home. When move-in time came, he took a long weekend off, rented a U-Haul truck, and with the help of a couple of the husbands of his office staff, they moved in and unpacked all the heavy items, including the bigger boxes. Brighton's leg was still a source of frequent pain, so he loaded up on enough Advil to get him through the day. Gina had constant morning sickness, usually worse at nighttime. There were still the occasional workmen barging into the house to finish up on the minor details. They came and left without bothering to knock on doors or shout any warning.

The Banks dropped by to help them with some of the putting away. Kara often dropped off something for Brighton to eat at night since Gina couldn't face looking at food, let alone cooking. After Charley and Brighton had been reintroduced at the HOA meeting, the two men had become casual friends. Life was good for the Dunns.

***

The weather had been perfect—if you liked it hot. Brighton was sitting on his back porch on a dusty but new patio chair, studying a proposed plan for the backyard landscaping. He had just gone for his first swim since the pool was filled. Gina was off to her doctor's appointment, leaving the initiation of the pool to him alone.

"Hello!" called out a male voice from around the side of the house. "Mind if I come in?"

Brighton arose and looked around to see who was calling. He recognized the man from the HOA meeting. It was the tough guy who had subdued the drunks and then disappeared.

"Come on in," he said, waving his hand in a gesture of welcome to the man.

"Hi, I'm Roy Richards. I hope I'm not disturbing you. I rang the front doorbell, but when there was no answer I noticed your car outside the garage."

"No, not at all. The car is outside because boxes still fill its spot. Come, pull up a chair. Maybe you can help me with this backyard plan. I'm Brighton Dunn," he said extending his hand to Roy. "Someone said you worked for the government, but I didn't know it was the FBI." Brighton pointed at Roy's hat.

"No, no, I bought the hat at a street kiosk in D.C. like every other tourist. Actually, I'm with the FAA. You're a dentist, if the rumors are true, or are you with the CIA?"

They both laughed. Brighton excused himself and went in the house for bottles of cold Gatorade. They looked over the landscape plans and chatted about the neighborhood and the desert surrounding the project. They made a few connections with old college classmates, and then after a subtle pause, Brighton asked, "Anything I can do for you?"

"I want to share something with you," Roy said, finally getting around to the reason for his visit. "I've recently become interested in geology and have done some studies on some of the mineral formations in the Hidden Canyon area. This land was truly virgin desert. When they excavated the lots to start new houses, new subsurface layers of rock were uncovered. Interesting things have begun to appear. What I've found on some of the lots in the project is very interesting and a little perplexing."

"I'm all ears," Brighton said, having no clue where this conversation was headed.

"Please don't write me off as some sort of head case when you hear what I'm going to tell you. I wouldn't have believed it myself if I had not seen the assay reports."

Brighton gave a shrug, still wondering what Roy was about to say.

"Believe it or not, our homes may be sitting on one of the richest veins of rare platinum-type minerals ever found. At least that's what one assay company has told me. There are gold and silver in the rock as well, but the percentage of the platinum group of precious metals, especially one called rhodium, is off the charts. The stuff is hard to find. It is four to five times more valuable than gold. Have you ever heard of rhodium?"

"Actually, I have. As you probably know, in dentistry we use a lot of metals and create different alloys and amalgams. As I recall, rhodium is a lot like platinum but a little more brittle. It's really in the ground right here?"

"It is. Matter of fact, some of the samples I submitted were from the cut over by the side of your house. I looked up rhodium after I got the assay report. One of the stories about it said that there was a music award prepared for Paul McCartney ... I don't remember which one ... anyway, someone decided that a platinum record was too ordinary for him, so they had a record plaque made out of rhodium."

"Tell me what else you know about it," Brighton said.

"Well, like I was saying, it is used by industry as a catalyst. Apparently the aerospace industry buys everything that's refined. I checked the spot price myself, and just like any commodity it fluctuates, but yesterday the stuff was almost three grand per ounce. If this area were to be mined, it could yield a fortune. Let me show you something. You might want to put on some shoes."

Roy led Brighton out in the yard away from the pool to a stack of rocks awaiting the landscaper's tractor. Roy picked up one of the broken rocks and poured a little of his Gatorade on it to wash off the dust. Immediately, the shining sun lit up the rock, a brilliant glitter reflecting off of the stone. The refraction was remarkable. Brighton took it from Roy and turned it back and forth then removed his sunglasses and looked at it even closer. He bent down and picked up more stones then carried several of them over to the pool edge. Splashing water from the pool, he carefully washed each sample, and without a word carried them to the patio table. Roy followed in anxious expectation.

"I'll be right back," Brighton said, disappearing into the house.

Roy started to get a little anxious, hoping the man wasn't calling the police.

Brighton returned in two or three minutes carrying a large frying pan, an ice pick, and a handheld propane torch that he explained his wife used to caramelize crème brûlée. He set one of the more brilliant samples in the pan and lit the torch. Putting on his sunglasses again, he carefully began heating the rock.

"Dentists use metals every day," Brighton began. "Most people think of the modern dentist as a driller and filler, but the thing most of us do best is sculpture. Recreating a tooth that fits the other teeth and the mouth is a lot more challenging than finding a cavity, removing the dead area, and filling the hole. To make a gold or ceramic crown is an art form."

As he talked, he focused the torch's flame on a single area of the rock—an area on the shiniest side. It only took a couple of minutes before the patch of the stone changed appearance. Then all of a sudden, a tiny teardrop of molten metal appeared on the side of the rock and began to creep downward into the pan.

"Unbelievable," Brighton said. "I just can't believe it. It's got to be nearly pure gold to melt like that. Or maybe it is rhodium or platinum. Son of a gun! You know I saw this stuff—these rocks—glittering months ago, and then I forgot about them. I got distracted by an old witch with a walking stick. Maybe you heard … that's another story for another time."

Roy stood intently watching the process.

Brighton placed the cooking torch on the cement and, picking up the ice pick, stabbed the teardrop of metal then held it up in the sunlight. The tiny sphere shone like an orange diamond in the light. He handed the ice pick to Roy, and they both kept staring at the glob of precious metal. When they looked at each other, grins broke out.

"This is so very cool. I just can't believe it," Brighton said. "Precious metals right here in my backyard. Tell me again how you found the stuff and how the heck you knew what it was."

"Do you have another Gatorade? My throat is suddenly dry," Roy said.

✳✳✳

Gina was sworn to absolute secrecy by her husband. Before he would even say hello or breathe a word of the story, he made her cross her heart and hope to die then give the Girl Scout sign. "But I've never been a Girl Scout," she said.

He laughed at her cute comeback then went on to tell her, nearly out of breath, about meeting Roy and the discovery he had made. To his surprise, she acted like she didn't get it. She had been shopping with Kara and her girls, and was eager to show off the sacks full of towels and dish cloths she had purchased.

Gina agreed, reluctantly, to the secrecy pact, which was great for her because now she could have a secret of her own and not tell the whole truth about her day. She had purchased the towels days ago and had left them in the back of her car as a decoy for today. She had never kept secrets from Brighton, but in this particular situation she reminded herself that he wasn't born stupid.

The truth was that she and Kara had gone for a drive in the desert. The girls had found a forest service dirt road and drove as close to the hill on the back side of Alma Ziegler's house as they could get. Kara brought Charley's high-power binoculars, thinking that they might come in handy. They had watched the weathered old shack for nearly two hours. Absolutely nothing had happened the whole time, even though they were sure that at any moment some new-found mystery would be unearthed. There had been an occasional car driving by on the dusty road and one hungry coyote that sniffed around a rusted barrel where the woman apparently burned her garbage, but no gray-haired woman. Finally, the heat of the sun had made them head back to Hidden Canyon. They had learned little or nothing and had now decided on a new tactic. They contrived a new plan whereby they would stop at the desert lady's house, pretending to be Jehovah Witnesses. Kara even had some proselyte tracts that someone had left on her doorstep. They would try it next week.

✱✱✱

Brighton asked Gina to sit down at the table. He explained to her again, in detail, what their neighbor Roy had shared with Brighton but, more excitingly, what their little experiment had discovered. Gina's reaction was one of patient disbelief. She listened and nodded her head and said, "Hmm," as if she didn't quite believe it. Only when Brighton showed her the tiny ball of melted gold did she start being solicitous.

Roy and Brighton had each agreed to do homework on the various metals. They had set up a time for a brainstorming session the following day. Roy hadn't explained to Brighton exactly how he had obtained the samples. He explained that most likely the entire area was a fractured vein of precious metal that had been pushed to near the surface by earthquakes and volcanoes. Brighton explained to Roy that Gina, his wife, was an impossible person to keep a secret from. She would have to know everything about what was going on, or it just plain wouldn't go on. Roy told Brighton he was fine with that.

✱✱✱

That evening, Gina spent two hours on the Internet searching for information regarding platinum metals and the Arizona desert. It was precious time lost in her quest to get everything put away in the new house. The more she read, the more she began to believe that Brighton and his new best friend hadn't lost their minds.

She searched the website of the Chicago Board of Trade and international commodities markets until she learned that the metals in question were valuable. She checked on current prices of all the metals. Rhodium was by far the most valuable. She learned that prices had been stable for more than twenty years, but with increased demand from China, prices seemed to be going through the roof. Next she read about rhodium. She had never even heard the word before. According to Brighton's and Mr. Richard's story, a dump truck load of the dirt and rocks from their yard could be worth fifty thousand dollars or more.

By the time she finished her research, she was a believer. She also was becoming very anxious. Had she and Brighton thrown the baby out with the bathwater?

She decided to call the guy who dug their swimming pool, the one that had rocks thrown at him by the witch-lady. He greeted her late-night call with suspicion, but in spite of his bad experience with her pool and the neighbor, he agreed to track down the phone number of the man who had hauled off the dirt from the hole. To Gina's surprise, he didn't even ask why she wanted the dirt. Within a few minutes he called back to report that the man was out of town, and they would have to wait until Wednesday to see if the guy had dumped the eight loads of dirt and rock someplace where they could be retrieved.

The two of them had brainstormed for hours about the possibilities of getting the metal out of the ground. They weren't really getting much closer to a solution, but by now, both were full-fledged converts to the idea that they were sitting on a gold mine. All they had to do was find a way to dig it up and get it to a market. It seemed so simple and yet so impossible. "How are we supposed to sleep tonight?" she asked Brighton as they turned back the covers and crawled into bed. Dinner had been all but forgotten, and the unpacking had been put off for the night.

Brighton, ever the optimistic one, rubbed her back and reminded her that they had started the day in a wonderful house, in a wonderful neighborhood, in a town that needed plenty of dentists. He told her that she was beautiful and wonderful and that she was pregnant with a wonderful baby on board. He kissed her softly and promised her that none of these things were going to change whether they found millions of dollars' worth of metal in their yard. Everything would work out well. Gina finally fell sound asleep.

***

Dean Shutter had his Hummer in the shop for some long overdue repair work from the accident with the car belonging to the dentist's wife. He was walking around the dealer's showroom, killing time while the repairs were being completed, when he saw Roy Richards. He was in the brightly lit showroom talking to a salesman and motioning toward a black sports-model truck.

Dean had already seen the truck, which was loaded with every option in the catalogue. Standing beside Roy, looking alternately at him and a salesman, was the most strikingly beautiful red-headed woman Dean had ever seen. He waved at Roy then recognized the salesman as a fellow he had dealt with before.

"Good morning, Tom, Roy. How you boys doing? Is Tom trying to talk you out of your arm and a leg to pay for one of his trucks?" Dean asked Roy with a chuckle. He nodded recognition to the woman.

Roy took control of the situation. "Rhonda, have you met Dean Shutter? He's the man who developed our neighborhood. Dean, allow me to introduce you to Ms. Tucker, our newest Hidden Canyon resident."

"It's a pleasure to meet you, sir." Rhonda said in a cheerful southern accent as she offered her hand to Dean. "I just love my new house, and Roy and the Patels have already made me feel right at home. Do ya'll live in Hidden Canyon, Mr. Shutter?"

As he listened to her voice, the puzzle pieces suddenly fit together. A vivid memory of seeing her just two weeks before on the Tonight Show hit him like a wet sponge. When Dean recovered his senses enough to answer her, he realized he was still shaking her hand. This was amazing. "You are in the house on Lot #33, right?"

He had worked with her manager and realtor and the California contractor who built the house, but at no time would they disclose the name of the home's owner. Even the recorded deed and permits gave no hint as to the actual owner.

"It's an honor to meet you, Ms. Tucker. Now, I finally know who the mystery house belongs to. Your agent did a great job of hiding your identity from me and everyone else."

"Well, I apologize if it caused you any problems. My ex-husband is the original Mr. Mystery. He hides things from people all the time. Why, he hid all three of his girlfriends from me." Rhonda blushed. The men made no comment.

She quickly recovered and put on a new smile. "Roy and Tom are helping me buy a new pickup. Do you have any recommendations?"

Roy was leaning against the hood of a Tahoe, watching the scene play out. Dean's tongue was nearly hanging out of his mouth, and Tom was grinning like the Cheshire cat.

"Mr. Shutter, your truck is ready," a welcomed voice came from the overhead loudspeaker.

"We'd better get a move on," hinted Roy to Rhonda. "I've got to be at the airport in an hour. Tom, why don't you give us the keys to the black SS? She can bring it back in the morning if she doesn't like it."

Rhonda nodded approval to Roy.

"You can bring the paperwork out to her house tomorrow evening, and I can look it over with her. She won't need any finance information." Without waiting for an answer, Roy and Rhonda were heading out the door toward the new truck she had just test driven.

Dean watched the three of them talking in front of the dealership. As he walked toward the cashier's window, he saw the black truck drive out onto the street.

"Man oh man," Tom said, catching up to Dean at the cashier window. "That is one beautiful woman. How that guy hooked up with her I have no idea, but he is a lucky son of a gun. You really didn't know that she was building a house in your development?"

Dean was still in a state of shock. He had never met anyone who was famous. He couldn't believe that the Rhonda Tucker was living in his development on Lot #33. Her house was kitty-corner from the lot he had reserved for himself and his wife Sharron. Not only would his property value skyrocket when the word got out, but it would be just plain cool that he would have a celebrity for a neighbor. Before he picked up his truck, he plucked his cell phone off his hip and speed-dialed his wife. She was not going to believe it.

8

CHURCH LADIES

Alma Ziegler could see the distant cloud of dust long before she could see the white car or hear its tires crunching on the gravel road. It was twisting and turning slowly along the county road, slowing for the dips, and especially for the larger rocks appearing in the middle of the graded road. The car was definitely headed for her house. The postman was the only regular visitor and his truck was gray and blue. It had already gone by for the day, skipping her house as usual. He seldom even slowed down by the entrance to her lane except to drop off the power bill or her bank statement or some third-class trash mail.

Her mailbox was an old milk can nailed to the top of a chopped-off railroad tie. It had been left there by the old man that had originally cleared the lot for his trailer. She hadn't bothered to upgrade the box in spite of warnings from the mailman that he shouldn't leave mail there, since it wasn't an approved box and couldn't be closed. Still, each month when the power bill came and every six months when the tax bill came, he would stop and leave the mail in the can with a warning to fix her mailbox. He never forgot to place a rock on top of the mail. Fourteen years later, it was precisely the same. He would put a big, round rock on the bills so they couldn't blow away.

Alma's senses went on full alert when the car slowed down then turned into the rutted lane leading up a hill to her house. As the car slowed and then stopped behind her old Mustang, a cloud of dust followed the car and settled over the two vehicles. It continued toward the house, adding a new layer to the front porch. Alma stood behind the curtain and watched as two women in their early thirties got out of the car and slowly moved toward the house.

Her concern when she first saw the car had been that they were police or FBI. She knew that she shouldn't have fired a gun at that car the other night. Nor should she have whacked that guy on the shin last fall. Maybe she shouldn't have done any of the other things that seemed to "just happen" since the bulldozers started destroying her desert. She considered herself a pacifist, not a protester or a terrorist, but sometimes she just got so mad she couldn't restrain her actions. All she had ever wanted since her family had been killed was to be left alone, to be at peace with her surroundings. She couldn't imagine what other people wanted or needed from her. She really didn't care.

"Why can't they just leave me alone?" she said out loud to herself and the doorpost as the women got out of the car. She let the curtain fall back in place and waited for the sharp knock at the door.

"Go away. I don't want anything, and I don't need anything. Just go away!" Alma shouted through the door, surprised at the volume and harsh tone of her own voice.

She rarely spoke out loud, and when she did, it was only to her desert friends. Sometimes when she spoke to them, they acted as though they could clearly understand her. At those times she wondered if she really needed to make any sound at all. She was quite sure that the animals could read her mind just like she could read theirs.

✸✸✸

"We need to speak to the lady of the house. It's very important that we talk to you," Kara said from the door stoop. She and Gina were standing less than five feet from the woman.

"We have an important message for you. Please open the door and let us talk to you," Gina added in the sweetest voice she could muster. "Open up or I'll kick the door down!" was what she really wanted to say.

The screen door finally opened a crack. It took several exchanges before Alma allowed the two women to enter the dark room.

While Kara presented Alma with a believable but very bogus religious pitch, Gina was scoping the main room of the house. She was both surprised and disheartened as she noticed the furnishings and wall hangings.

Instead of the cheap discount-quality items she had expected to find, Gina saw a formal dining table of inlaid wood with ten brocade-upholstered, high-back chairs. There was a giant hand-carved Italian china hutch holding Wedgwood china, Waterford crystal goblets, and several large, flower-covered Lladró figurines.

On the walls were signed prints of early contemporary artists with hand-carved gold frames. There was an old, worn, leather chair and ottoman with a standing Tiffany floor lamp surrounded by neatly stacked leather-bound books. Stacks of glossy magazines were in neat piles against the wall, including *Architectural Digest* and *Scientific American*. A large-print family Bible sat alone on a small inlaid cherry coffee table. The cement floor was covered with several small handwoven Turkish silk rugs. Strikingly out of place was a polished slide action shotgun with hand carving on the barrel, a rifle, and a shoulder-height, thick, very worn walking stick. Seeing it gave Gina goose bumps. She could imagine this very piece of solid wood smashing into her husband's leg and head.

The woman was dressed in a cotton housedress with faded print flowers. Her blonde hair was braided, hiding some of the gray. On her feet were ankle-high hiking boots but no socks. She wore no makeup or jewelry with the exception of a fat man's gold and diamond ring on her right middle finger. Gina guessed the stone was at least two carets.

"Do you have anything to add, Sister Gina?" Kara asked in a perfunctory voice, interrupting Gina's uninvited inspection.

"We need to leave," Gina whispered to Kara, staring at the wooden stick as she spoke.

"Sorry to have bothered you. Here are some things to read. We need to get home to her children," Gina said, handing Alma the paper tracts while tugging on Kara's arm and turning toward the door.

They were almost out the door when, to their surprise, Alma asked, "How can I get in touch with you if I want to learn more?"

"We could stop by next week," Gina answered with a loud voice, talking over her shoulder to Alma, having spoken before thinking. The last thing she wanted to do was to ever come back to this strange place with this sad, even pathetic, lonely woman.

Back in the car, Kara asked Gina what the heck was going on. "Why were you in such a hurry to leave?" Kara asked.

"That woman is not the person we imagined she is. She is not some stupid, white, down-and-out, trailer-trash, tree-hugging psycho. That ramshackle shack is full of furniture that neither you nor I could afford to buy. There are stacks of classic books and new textbooks on archeology and geology. That woman is educated. She also is rich, and she is smarter than both of us put together. She is probably laughing her head off at us right now." Gina was talking a mile a minute as they drove down the dusty road.

"I can't believe how stupid it was of us to try to pull that religious act on her," Gina continued. "To make matters worse, much worse, she has guns sitting out in the open by the china hutch. There was a great big Berretta shotgun just like my Dad's trap-shooting gun leaning just inches from her hand. On the kitchen sink I saw another gun, a pistol. She could have killed us both in two seconds, shooting right through the door without even opening it."

"There is no way I'm ever going to go back there. What were we thinking? I'm pregnant. She could have shot my baby. She still may shoot my baby, or Brighton, or your girls, any of us. She may come tonight and kill all of us. How could we be so stupid?"

The more Gina talked, the more frightened Kara became. "This is getting too crazy. We need some help!" Kara said.

They passed by the turnoff to Hidden Canyon, heading instead toward the city. It was time to get some sound legal advice, and Kara didn't want to get it at home in front of the girls. She speed-dialed her husband's office and told Charley's secretary to create fifteen minutes in his schedule.

"Tell Charley that it is urgent!"

✳✳✳

Rhonda Tucker had been living in Arizona just four days when she was discovered by the paparazzi. She had agreed to pick up Roy and Chad and take them to the airport, then the pet hotel. She was excited to have a reason to drive her new truck, but sitting in Rhonda's driveway, blocking her exit, was a Channel 3 News van and crew. Two other cars were parked on the street. She could see two men loitering beside the cars holding cameras with gigantic lenses.

When she spotted the van, she immediately caught on to the

scenario that was playing out. It wasn't anything new to her. If they could cause trouble, so could she. Rhonda simply started honking the horn and wouldn't stop until the driver got back in the van, clearing a path for her to leave.

As Rhonda's truck turned onto the road, one of the photographers stepped in front of her. He held a Nikon camera, on a shoulder mount pointed right at her, set up with a telephoto lens the size of a rocket launcher. She slammed on the brakes, coming to a stop just as her bumper touched the man's leg. It appeared doubtful that he even felt the vehicle touch his leg, but he saw his opportunity and fell to the ground, dropping his camera on the road. He made a dramatic effort to display pain.

By that time, Roy and Chad were twenty feet away, observing the fiasco. "Are you okay?" asked Roy, trying to read the situation clearly before he overreacted.

"Did you see that?" the photographer screamed. "She tried to run me down. I'm lucky to be alive. I'm sure my camera is ruined. You are a witness. I need your name and address."

Roy walked up to the window of the black pickup truck and motioned for Rhonda to roll it down. By this time, the TV crew was out of their truck again and had their camera rolling. Roy could see the look on Rhonda's face and guessed that this wasn't the first time a trick like this had been pulled on her. He gave her a smile and a nod of assurance, then signaled for her to close her tinted window.

Turning to the man who was now standing and brushing the dust off his pants and camera, Roy said, "I was a witness, all right, and what I saw was a trespasser trying to cause an accident on private property. You'd better hope and pray that the lady in the truck is uninjured. You'd also better hope that you can get to your car before my dog decides to have your pant leg for lunch. He's been known to kill big male coyotes with a single bite to the throat."

Just as the man started to protest, Clyde pulled up with yellow lights flashing.

"Arrest this man, Clyde!" Roy barked. "He was trying to attack the lady in the pickup truck. I'm pretty sure he's the guy who broke into the Patels' backyard and shot their dog. There could be a hidden gun in that long camera lens," said Roy with authority. Glaring at the paparazzi, he continued, "Aren't you the guy they just arrested for attacking a junior school high girl?"

The last statement was all Clyde needed to hear. He looked at the man and then at Rhonda and at last saw the news truck and the news team with their camera aimed at him. He pulled his only weapon, a can of mace and pointing it at the paparazzi yelled, "You are under arrest, meathead. Get down on the ground, and put your hands behind your back."

The man looked at Clyde, dumbfounded. He turned, tucking his camera under his arm and ran toward a gray sedan parked up the road.

With that problem resolved, Clyde turned next toward the television crew and yelled, "Do you guys have a permit to be in Hidden Canyon? I saw you blow by the gate behind a cement truck. I'm going to file a complaint with the station. Pack it up and get out of Dodge," Clyde concluded.

"Could you believe the look in that guy's face when you told him he was under arrest?" Rhonda asked Clyde as she laughed. They were standing beside her truck just minutes after the cavalcade of media left the circle. "Thank you so much for coming to my aid. You were like a knight in shining armor riding up on a white stallion."

"More like a fat knight driving up in a white Toyota," said Clyde in a self-deprecating tone.

"Don't you think Clyde has earned the right to know why the cameramen were here in the first place?" Roy said looking at Rhonda for a nonverbal okay.

Rhonda stuck out her hand and took Clyde's hand, gently placing her left on top of his. "I can't thank you enough for helping. This isn't the first time I've have had to deal with these people. You probably don't know who I am, but my name is Rhonda Tucker. I do a little singing and acting, so those men think they can make money by selling pictures of me and telling stories about me. I don't understand why anyone would even care."

Clyde knew good and well who she was. The rumors had spread through the neighborhood like a flash flood.

"You are my knight in shining armor ... Clyde," she said, glancing at his name tag while stretching up on her tiptoes to give him a peck on the cheek. "I'll bet you can keep those nasty wolves away from my door from now on."

Rhonda and Roy then climbed into her truck with Roy behind the wheel. Chad had already jumped into the backseat, where he was sitting with his head half out the window—the happiest dog on earth. Rhonda gave Clyde a little wave as they drove away, leaving him standing by the road, wearing a grin as big as Montana.

***

Emily escorted the women into Charley's office. He gave Kara a warm embrace then offered her and Gina a seat at his conference table. Something about the warmth of Kara's touch diffused his fear.

Charley smiled. "Okay, what have the two of you gotten your-selves into?"

Kara spoke first, giving her version of the events involving the desert lady. They still didn't know her real name. Kara mentioned the attack on Brighton, which was old news to Charley, but as the story developed, Gina added a few new details. Kara reiterated the shooting of Harley the Great Dane. Finally, she got to the meat of the story, explaining how she and Gina had driven out to the desert shack the night of the HOA meeting. They gave all their rationale for going, most of which was sound-ing pretty lame. Then they told about their experience less than an hour before, emphasizing the big gun Gina saw rather than the Jehovah Witness impersonations.

Charley was a very patient and understanding attorney, having learned that just listening to his clients talk often resolved their problems. When he finally spoke, he asked Gina if she was feel-ing okay and then he asked her if she had a dollar bill.

"A dollar bill?" Kara asked.

Charley put his index finger to his lips in a hushing motion and held out his hand while Gina opened her purse and found a folded five-dollar bill in her wallet.

"Will this do?" Gina asked with a questioning look as she handed him the bill.

He reached across the desk, accepted the money and then took a piece of letterhead stationery from a drawer. He neatly printed a receipt for five dollars while the girls watched, trying to figure what the heck he was doing. He handed her the paper and slid the money into the top drawer.

"Mrs. Dunn, I am now your attorney of record. Everything you and Kara have told me is now privileged information. It doesn't go beyond this room. I need to inform you both that you have probably broken several laws, not to mention put your lives and possibly the lives of your families in danger."

He leaned further into his high-backed leather chair and looking over the top of his reading glasses asked them, "What the hell have the two of you been smoking? Do you think Brighton and I want to raise our children by ourselves while you two rot in prison, healing from your gunshot wounds?" He was not joking as he asked the last questions, but when he saw that Gina was about to cry, he backed off a bit, giving them both a smile. "Fortunately for the two of you, I am a very good attorney."

The three of them talked more about the desert lady and their suspicions. He went over some ideas that he had to diffuse the situation, and agreed that the rest of their legal consultations could best be accomplished at home or at the Dunns'. He felt that Brighton needed to be advised of the situation and recommended dinner at a good restaurant for the first meeting.

"That way, we will all have to keep our voices down, and Brighton won't be able to yell when you tell him the story, and he tells the two of you how he really feels about your adolescent antics." Charley's mood had lightened, and he gave them each a reassuring embrace and bid them farewell.

Once they were out the door, he called his secretary on the intercom and asked her to bring in his next appointment. "Also, I need you to phone your friend at the title company and ask her to pull up the ownership records of what few houses there are on Fence Rider Road, to the east of Hidden Canyon."

***

Roy was having a very hard time concentrating at work. For the majority of people, a lack of concentration at work would mean having to redo a job report or correct a calculation mistake. In

Roy's profession, everything was in real time. There was no eraser or spell-check or take it apart and put it back together again.

He couldn't stop thinking about Rhonda Tucker. The two of them had hit it off so well that it seemed like a dream. It had been a long, long time since he had been really interested in a woman for anything but the obvious. His social skills certainly hadn't been sharpened by hiking in the mountains and deserts with good old Chad. He worried at first that Rhonda could be using him, but wasn't that what friends were for?

So far, nothing had warmed up physically between the two of them beyond a peck on the cheek. Her smiles were sincere and were lasting longer each time the two were together—at least that's what he thought. He was infatuated with her and was slowly convincing himself that she was attracted to him as well.

"Concentrate," he commanded his brain while giving a heading to the pilot on an approach to Sky Harbor from Reno.

Rhonda had dropped him off at work, saying she had to take a quick flight to L.A., and would be coming back just when he finished his shift.

"What if you get here early or your flight gets delayed?" he had asked.

"That won't happen," she promised him as he hopped out of the truck, not explaining to him why she was certain her flight would be on time. She had suggested he come over to her place when they got back and that she would fix a light midnight snack.

Beyond Rhonda, the next distraction for Roy was the rhodium, platinum, and gold. He kept wondering what Hidden Canyon really was sitting on. He kept seeing that drop of molten gold being extruded from the fist-sized rock and dropping into Brighton's pan like a drop of precious blood. Were there precious metals in the yards of all his neighbors? The dirt and rock from his yard had been used as fill to build up his driveway; could it be "a road paved in gold?"

He had promised the dentist that he would do more research and maybe even try to get another assay done. He had researched other assay companies on the Internet, all of which were out of town. He could FedEx the samples. He just needed to take the time to do it. The next question on his wandering mind was whether he should he should tell Rhonda about the metals. He tried to put the concerns out of his mind. After his shift, he could speculate about the future.

✳✳✳

Rhonda was precisely on time when she picked him up. This time the peck on the cheek was accompanied with a hug. After she dropped him off, he walked into his house for a quick shower and change of clothes before the promised midnight snack. He saw his answering machine was blinking. He hit the play button and immediately knew something big was about to happen.

"Roy, it's Brighton Dunn. I'm calling to tell you the good news. Gina tracked down the truckloads of dirt and rock that had been excavated from our pool. They are sitting in a vacant lot, and we can pick them up if we want to. The guy is glad to have us move it for him. Let me know what you want me to do with it. I already promised the landscaper to remove it in the next day or two. Give me a call when you get this message."

It was too late to call the Dunn house, so he filed it in his brain's planner along with the rest of the following day's tasks. He had originally scheduled a day of hiking in the desert with Chad; he couldn't remember the last time he had gone hiking.

The getting together with Rhonda turned out to be a bust. He knocked lightly then entered through the mansion's massive ornate glass and steel door. Inside the house he was greeted with the smell of garlic and butter. She hollered for him to come into the kitchen, where she was standing in front of the enormous gas range. She was barefoot, wearing a silk robe and a frilly pink apron.

Just as they were sitting down on the couch to eat the shrimp stir-fry and tossed spinach salad, the telephone rang. The call was from her agent, who was in London and had just awakened. Rhonda waved for Roy to begin eating then went into another room, carrying the telephone. He tried to ignore it but overheard parts of the conversation. It didn't sound like a happy one, her muffled voice sounding strained. He decided to wait for her to begin eating, but he couldn't sit still and was soon pacing the enormous family room.

It was the first time Roy had really examined the inside of the house since things had been arranged and the hundreds of boxes emptied and removed. It made his place look like a camping trailer. From the appliances and countertops to the flooring and electronics, it was a homeowner's dream house. Her furniture was the most beautiful and probably the most expensive he had ever seen in his life. The leather couches gave the feeling of sitting on a cloud. Alongside original paintings and articles of movie memorabilia were framed awards, including eight or ten gold records mounted in elaborate frames. There were tastefully placed photos of Rhonda with famous movie stars and other celebrities, including one of her standing on a stage arm in arm with the previous President.

"I cherish the one with John Wayne the most," Rhonda said, slipping her arm into the crook of his elbow. "I was invited to share the podium to read an award with him. It was the year he passed away. Few people knew that he was gravely ill. He asked me to help hang onto him while we stood. Then afterward he winked at me and said it was just a trick so I would snuggle against him."

Roy looked down at her to see tears in her eyes, but didn't realize they were not from the nostalgia of the moment. They sat back down at the table and began to eat the now lukewarm meal. It tasted great to Roy, but Rhonda tasted some of her shrimp then walked to the counter and scraped her plate of food into the sink. There were red streaks around her eyes, and she was dabbing at her nose with a tissue.

"Please excuse my bad manners. My pigheaded ex-husband is threatening to sue me because I am taking time off and not earning him more money," she said in a sad voice. "He is officially my ex-husband, but still my business manager for another year. I apparently have some stupid clause in my contract with the recording company we both own, which states that I have to produce a new album or do a major concert every twelve months. His lawyer says I have six months to schedule a concert or cut a new album or they will file a motion to reevaluate the divorce agreement. It's a big mess, and no matter how hard I try to please those people, I never seem to do it without hurting myself."

She stood by the sink, leaning on the white granite counter-top, staring out of the window into the dark for several minutes. Roy walked over to her, cautiously placing both hands on her shoulders to comfort her. Slowly, she turned her head toward him, letting her body slide into his encircling arms. After several moments, she looked up at him with apologetic tears in her eyes, which told him it would be best if he went home.

"I love the new truck," she said as he crossed the threshold into the night. "Thanks for being my friend."

9

PHANTOMS

Crashing glass made Brighton and Gina bolt upright in bed. He turned on the bedside light, and they stared at each other. Brighton slipped out of bed, listening for the slightest sound. He wiggled his feet into his slippers—always afraid of stepping on a scorpion if he were to go barefoot—then walked into the main hall, flipping on every light switch he passed. Before he reached the family room, the house was aglow, and there he found a volleyball-sized hole in a section of the sliding glass door. Lying on the travertine floor amid scattered shards of glass was a broken piece of a red brick, much like the ones used to line his fireplace. Threaded through one of the holes in the brick was a piece of copper wire. Twisted at the end of the wire was a round metal tag. Brighton walked closer to the door, crunching pieces of glass underfoot as he walked. He turned on the floodlights to the backyard but could see nothing unusual.

"Brighton, what happened? What's going on?"

When he looked back at Gina, she was bent over inspecting the round metal tag. It looked unfamiliar to her.

"Be careful where you step, and stay back away from the window," he cautioned.

"What is it? Who would do this to us?"

Brighton took the brick from her and held it near a brighter light. "It's the surveyor's tag from the corner of our lot," Brighton finally said. "This is too weird. It's time to call the police."

"Or maybe it's payback time," Gina mumbled aloud.

Kara had called earlier the previous evening to cancel their "tell all" dinner. One of the twins was sick, and Charley had gotten behind at the office. Kara passed along Charley's advice that Gina should go ahead and fill Brighton in on the desert lady affair. She did just that, but only after a candlelight dinner and skinny-dip together under the desert stars. She hated breaking the mood of the late-night date but had gone ahead with her story anyway. They were sitting in the dark, wrapped in beach towels as she began the saga. He had been attentive, not even once interrupting her narrative. When she finished, he asked only a few questions then they had made love on the double chaise lounge at the pool's edge. Nothing else was mentioned until now.

Now the wife and husband stood facing one another, neither eager to raise the obvious question. Should they call the sheriff, or should they clean up the mess and accept the desert lady's doing without calling attention to themselves and Gina's hairbrained visit to the lonely woman?

***

Charley Banks was working his way up the legal ladder much faster than he could ever have imagined. It wasn't just his talent helping. One of the senior partners, the oldest of the Fuller brothers, had announced his intention to retire at the end of the fiscal year. Two weeks after his announcement, still with numerous active cases pending, the sixty-three-year-old attorney was in his backyard pruning some grapefruit trees when a swarm of Africanized killer bees flew into the orchard. He died from an allergic reaction to the numerous bee stings.

The result was that Charley's desk looked like an effort to break the Ripley's "Believe It or Not!" record for the highest stack of active legal files. The last thing he needed was a call from his wife's new best friend and his newest client.

Hearing about the brick through the window, his reflex reaction was to advise Gina to call the sheriff, but then he wisely became rational. He remembered all too vividly the description of his wife gloating about what a good job she had done impersonating an evangelical missionary. The wives were undoubtedly the precipitating cause of the thrown brick. After careful consideration for five or six minutes, he scribbled out a note on a piece of letterhead and told Emily to fax it to Doctor Dunn.

Brighton,
Regarding the brick and the sheriff:
We do not want to go there!

Let sleeping dogs lie?
Charley

The next Hidden Canyon HOA meeting was in five days. Since Charley was the managing counsel, he had decided to consolidate all the Hidden Canyon problems into a single night's meeting and then spread the issues among a few ad hoc committees. "Let the homeowners hash out the problems themselves. Let them fight some of the battles," he told Emily. He had way too many cases to worry about.

"Who knows?" he thought. "Maybe most of the problems, the thrown bricks and the broken gates and the stolen building materials, were the work of pranksters or disgruntled trade laborers." Charley's decision to do nothing was reinforced later when his intercom buzzed.

The producer of the local Channel 3 TV station was on the phone to inform Charley of an assault on one of the investigating news team members. The assault took place in Hidden Canyon by a new resident named Rhonda Tucker—The Rhonda Tucker. Charley knew he needed to look into the incident immediately or Channel 3's account would be publicized, and a would be lawsuit filed.

Charley called Kara and assigned her the task of learning all she could about the new neighbor, Ms. Tucker. He had real work to do. It took seven years to make partnership in the traditional law firms, but like medicine and accounting, the law profession was evolving into a new and different animal. Partnership would mean at least an additional six figures in his annual bonus. He and Kara had paid their dues and were ready and eager to join the elite of the law profession. The next executive partnership meeting for firm planning and expansion was less than three months away. For Charley, Hidden Canyon HOA duties and all other distractions from his real work needed to take a backseat to the accounts he had just inherited.

✸✸✸

Likewise under stress, Brighton sat at his desk biting his fingernails. He was desperate for time. He had three dental patients sitting in exam chairs, each wearing their little plastic bibs to protect their clothes. A fourth patient was getting her teeth cleaned by the hygienist, expecting Dr. Dunn's timely arrival as well.

Brighton was on hold with some guy who owned a front-end loader and dump truck. He was ready to go to work moving the excavation dirt from the Dunns' pool but had no place to unload the eight truckloads that Brighton hoped—and Roy Richards promised—contained a fortune in rhodium, platinum, and gold.

Brighton racked his brain but couldn't think of any farmers or landscapers who would allow dumping multiple truckloads of dirt on their land. He also had an urgent message from Gina that he needed to answer. Apparently, the insurance company would not process the broken window claim without a full explanation of how a two thousand dollar, double pane, tinted glass door had met with a brick at two o'clock in the morning. The insurance company suggested a police report would help speed along the claim.

In a spark of brilliance, he phoned Roy Richards on his cell, and catching him on a mandatory break from his control tower duties, Brighton got right to the point.

"You have been in the neighborhood longer than we have. Please help us find a place for the pool dirt. We'll sit down this weekend and work out a legal partnership agreement. Half of whatever we get is yours."

Roy thought about it for a minute, just long enough for Brighton to come up with his own idea.

"How about using the backyard of someone who isn't close to starting their landscaping yet? What about the new neighbor lady? Gina saw you with her when the news trucks were in the neighborhood. Is she getting close to starting her yard?"

"I can ask her," Roy said. "But, we really need to get that dirt out of town before somebody starts nosing around and picks up on what we're doing. In the meantime, I'll give her a call. Matter of fact, I'm supposed to take her to dinner tonight. Maybe you and your wife could just happen to stop by our table at Cisco's Mexican Grill around eight tonight. I'll introduce you, and we can ask her together. Her backyard should work. It has a huge corner where the builder's construction trailer was parked."

"You are a lifesaver," said Brighton.

***

As it turned out, Gina had a chance to meet Rhonda even before dinner that night. She was more nauseated than usual that day and had stayed in bed most of the morning. By noon she was getting cabin fever and decided to go for a walk. As she passed the long, newly-paved driveway of the Tucker mansion, Rhonda Tucker herself walked down the driveway to pick up the morning newspaper.

Within five minutes, the two were chatting excitedly and walking up Rhonda's driveway together. By the time they had shared a pitcher of Crabapple juice and a little gossip, they had become like old friends. Lunch for the following day was planned, and Gina had picked a place where they could have privacy and where a few of the other neighbors could drop by for introductions. The women's chance get-together was of course unknown to Brighton or Roy until the meeting at the restaurant.

That evening at Cisco's, the men were dumbfounded when the women met again and embraced.

"Can you believe our good luck?" Brighton said to Roy when the pair went off later to powder their noses. "How can she refuse to let us store the ore now? Turning down a request from Gina is like channeling a tsunami."

The term "dirt" had taken on a whole new meaning now that it was soon to be back in their possession. The dinner had gone well, and Rhonda consented to let Roy store the ore in her backyard. Gina and Brighton appeared oblivious to that portion of the dinner conversation. Rhonda did mention that she had received a bid for landscaping, and the company said they could start in two weeks. Time was now of the essence.

***

The second Hidden Canyon HOA meeting was called to order at eight o'clock sharp. There was no open bar or snacks. An agenda had been carefully planned and printed and would be adhered to. The meeting started on time, the first order of business being the officer election committee announcing the results of the election: a Dr. Mark Cooperman was to be the new president of the Hidden Canyon HOA. Mundane problems and finance issues were discussed. The conversation stopped abruptly when Dr. Patel walked into the back of the room.

"I want you to stop the person throwing dead things into my swimming pool." His high staccato voice made everyone turn toward him. With his arm extended straight outward, he held a dripping wet rabbit by its hind feet. It was quite dead—badly mangled and giving off the sickening odor of death.

"This is not the first time someone has harassed my family," Dr. Patel continued. "I am sick of it to death, and I will not tolerate it any longer."

He then walked to the podium, laying the rabbit on the edge so that everyone could see its sightless eyes and wet, drooping ears. Turning to face the entire group and pointing his finger at them, he said, "Shame on you, for shame on all of you. You would not like it if you were in my native country and treated thus. Why do you do this to my children and my wife?"

Charley was on his feet, and in a single, smooth move he picked up and brought the round metal wastebasket under the rabbit's head. Using an extra page of the meeting's agenda paper as a napkin, he picked up the rabbit by its foot and dropped the body into the basket. Charley then stood beside Dr. Patel until the frustrated man had stopped talking, and then with an arm around the good doctor's shoulder, gently escorted him to an empty seat on the front row.

Dr. Cooperman returned to the agenda briefly and resolved the remaining issues. At the conclusion, he thanked Dr. Patel for bringing his problem to the attention of the HOA and promised to look into it. He asked for a motion to assign the newly-promoted Clyde to the job of investigating. Charley breathed a sigh of relief when the meeting ended and no one had mentioned the desert lady nor reported any more of her actions. He was sure the dead rabbit was a prank by one of the teenagers in the neighborhood. The broken window the Dunns had reported was another problem altogether.

10

REFINED

The next day a large UPS envelope was waiting by the door when Roy came home from work. Inside were twelve computer-generated pages of mineral analysis along with a business letter printed on the letterhead of Pikes Peak Metals and Minerals, an assay and refining company in Colorado Springs, Colorado. The technical pages were difficult for Roy to understand, but the typed letter was clear: The residents of Hidden Canyon were sitting on a gold mine. Even better, they were sitting on a gold and rhodium and platinum mine. Again, Roy had written proof that the concentrations of mineral per ton were exceptional, and that the gold, platinum, and especially the rhodium were extremely high. The letter did ask where the sample had been obtained, but there was no mention of the federal government's need to know nor were any laws mentioned. It was more a question of curiosity.

Roy made three copies of the letter of the analysis pages. He hid all but one in a file cabinet with papers marked "Old Insurance." He looked up Brighton's fax number from his telephone book. He had his machine loaded and was ready to hit the "send" button when it dawned on him how really stupid that would be. Only three people knew about the value of the dirt in the Dunns' backyard. He decided he had better keep it that way for now.

Brighton had skipped the HOA meeting to avoid a confrontation with the Germans. Instead, he had spent hours searching cyberspace for a refinery that would handle small amounts of ore. Making phone calls between patients, he had found a company in Colorado that would refine ore but only of twenty tons or more. The dump truck driver who had just hauled Brighton's pool dirt back to Rhonda's guessed the total load to be eighteen tons. In order to use the Colorado refinery, they needed more ore.

Roy almost ran into Brighton's car as he pulled into the dentist's driveway. Brighton was pulling out at the same time.

"I've got good news!" Roy exclaimed, hopping out of his truck.

"So do I," Brighton explained.

That the two men had unknowingly contacted the same assayer/refiner in Colorado nearly gave them goose bumps.

Roy climbed into the Dunn's car, and they talked with the motor running and the air-conditioning on full blast, as the temperature outside was 108 degrees. After a short discussion they decided they needed to let Rhonda in on the secret. Since they had used her yard to store the Dunns' pool dirt, they hoped they could possibly scrape up an additional two tons of dirt and rock from Rhonda's yard. Roy doubted she would care and was sure that the adventure of it all would entice her more than the lure of riches. After all, she was already filthy rich.

Roy didn't share his evolving romantic inclinations toward the woman, but Brighton wasn't blind. Roy agreed to visit with Rhonda. They parted with a much clearer plan for the future of their clandestine mining operation.

***

When Rhonda answered the front door, she looked even more terrific than usual. She was wearing white jeans and a bright blue, pearl-button Western shirt. She was, however, acting ambivalent to Roy as they walked to the truck and headed out for a light supper. She wanted to go someplace out of the way where a fuss wouldn't be made over her and where they could talk. It didn't sound good to Roy.

He drove up the Apache Trail past Canyon Lake to Tequila Flat. The tiny bar and restaurant catered to anyone with a smile and a story. It had been a stagecoach stop until the late 1800s but had been burned down and rebuilt too many times to count. Now it was thriving from boaters, bikers, hikers, and anyone who wanted a drink and a bean burrito or cheeseburger. The clapboard walls were covered with memorabilia and keepsakes. Dry rattlesnake skins were the prevailing décor.

Roy had suggested the place with the hope that no one would recognize her and gawk or point fingers or make stupid comments. He had even suggested some sort of subtle disguise, but she told him that if she looked and dressed like the rest of the women her age, no one would give a second glance. The problem was that she didn't even come close to looking like the women her age, no matter how she dressed.

During the half-hour drive, her mood lightened, and she finally began talking. She shared a little of her unpublished life, finally starting to laugh at herself. Roy contributed an embarrassing story or two about himself. She finally confessed that she had been in a depressed mood, wondering if she was making a mistake dropping out of the music scene. She had wandered around her new mansion bored, lonely, and anxious. She admitted that taking two years off could cost her tens of millions of dollars and millions of fans. She didn't solicit his advice, but he was getting the idea that she would listen to it if offered.

Tequila Flat proved to be just what Roy wanted. There were just enough people for the pair to be anonymous. The music was upbeat and the service subtle. Later, after buffalo burgers and a bowl of prickly pear ice cream, Roy worked up the courage to ask her about the dirt. He tried to make it sound like nothing important, but she was curious. As soon as they were in the truck, she plucked the keys out of the ignition and held them away from him.

"Tell me the whole dirty story," she said, dangling the keys out of his reach.

"What do you mean, dirty story?"

He had already buckled his shoulder belt and couldn't escape when she reached across and started tickling him. His hand went for the keys, but she was too fast and dropped them into her shirt pocket.

He conceded the skirmish, settling back into the seat. He began at the beginning, explaining the story of seeing the glittering rock then getting it assayed. He went on explaining that he now needed twenty tons of it to process the ore and find out if the assay was for real or just a fluke. Rhonda was all ears, and acted more excited than he had ever seen her.

"What if it is for real, and all the rock under our yards is worth millions?" Rhonda speculated, laughing. "Imagine digging tunnels under our houses and hauling away the dirt at night in baskets like they did in that Steve McQueen movie. What was it, *The Great Escape*?"

"We won't hold our breath, okay?" Roy said.

She pulled the keys out of her pocket and dangled them just out of his reach. "You are going to include me in the fun, aren't you?" she teased. "Matter of fact, why don't you dig out the area where I want to put my pool and take that dirt too? It's probably cheaper to process forty tons than twenty."

He smiled. She was in. She clapped her hands like an excited eight-year-old and leaned across the truck's console giving him a subtle, yet affectionate kiss.

As they drove home to Hidden Canyon, they were both in a jovial mood. Roy was getting used to the idea of the ore adventure, and he was even getting used to being on dates with a celebrity. Thinking about getting rich from the ore was still too far beyond his imagination. He had never dreamed of being wealthy.

"Why don't you have your pool people start digging as soon as possible?" Roy asked her. "Have them pile the dirt and rock with the rest of the dirt from Dunns' pool. I'll contact a trucking company and tell them to pick up the dirt and rock next week."

As he spoke, the thought came to him that he and Brighton hadn't discussed the way they were going to pay for any of the expense of hauling and refining the ore. Roy was a paycheck-type guy, and didn't even have a home equity credit line. He had money in savings but had no idea what it would cost to move and process the ore.

As though she were reading his mind, she said, "Since you and the dentist are making me a partner in this adventure, y'all better count on me carrying my share of the cost. I just got a check from my perfume company's accountant. Having your own brand of perfume … isn't that the craziest thing you ever heard of? Anyway, it's burning a hole in my pocket. I'll be better off spending it before my ex hears about it."

Rhonda told him not to get out of the truck but to wait a second. She got out and came around to the driver's side and opened the door. She threw her arm around his neck and gave him a long, sensual kiss on the lips. Before he could respond, she had stepped away and shut the door. She just stood there smiling at him through the window, giving a little wave. He hesitated for a couple of moments, not quite knowing what to do next. With his heart and mind racing, he made his decision. He put his truck in gear and slowly drove down the circle drive into the night, tasting her lipstick and feeling the heat of her body pressed against his shoulder.

***

When Kara called Gina to ask if she wanted to go together over to the new neighbor's house to deliver some zucchini bread, she was surprised that Gina had already met Rhonda Tucker. Gina was vague about how they had met, and told Kara she couldn't go to Rhonda's anyway, because she had a doctor's appointment. Kara was just a little bit hurt and a great deal curious.

She wrapped the freshly baked bread in cellophane and put a bow around it. She changed into a new outfit and walked the short block to Ms. Tucker's house. Looking up at the magnificent home, she nearly turned away but took a deep breath, pressing forward.

As she walked up the driveway to the gigantic iron and glass door, she suddenly saw Brighton Dunn and the handsome single guy, the air traffic controller, walking down the side driveway leading from Ms. Tucker's garages and backyard.

"Hi, Brighton. How you doing?" she said, diverting her path toward them.

"Hey, Kara, how are you?"

He introduced Kara to Roy, and they made small talk for a couple of minutes. She asked, "What are you guys up to?"

"Rhonda asked me to keep an eye on the landscape people for her," Roy lied. "She is having a pool dug and doesn't know anything about the company."

Kara nodded toward the gaily wrapped bread she was holding. "I thought I'd bring a small welcoming gift. Do you know if she's at home?"

"We didn't see her, but she is usually around the house," Brighton volunteered, immediately questioning his own lame statement. How would he know anything about her daily activity or habits? "You should ring the bell. It's a huge house, so I'd give her some time to get to the door."

***

"You can't tell her anything about it, Gina," Brighton instructed emphatically. "Are you serious?"

He hadn't been home from work ten seconds when Gina was at his side, pleading with him to let Kara in on the gold ore secret.

"She called me a little while ago saying she saw you and Roy over at Rhonda's house. I didn't know you even came home for lunch."

"I had to meet Roy to look at the pile of ore in Rhonda's back-yard. Neither of us had any idea how many truckloads of it there were. We need to tell the trucking company how big of a truck to bring. We asked the guy running the backhoe, but he didn't even speak comprehendible English."

Brighton was tired and irritable. His leg was hurting worse than normal, and he had wasted another half hour on the phone arguing with an insurance adjuster about their broken window.

"Kara thinks something fishy is going on. I know she feels like I'm keeping secrets from her. She didn't say that, but I'm sure she feels hurt."

"The two of you have enough little secrets of your own for the time being," Brighton said in an uncharacteristically sarcastic tone. "Charley Banks is the lawyer for the HOA. If you tell Kara, then in essence you have told Charley. The last thing we need is to have the HOA lawyer snooping around. The whole plan could be shut down before we even have an idea what we have."

Gina looked away from him. "I need a friend, and I want Kara to be my friend. If I hurt her by not trusting her now, it will be all over for us," Gina said in a sorrowful tone.

Brighton put his arms around his wife and pulled her close to him. "Please don't say anything to her for now. Her husband is a big believer in spouses sharing everything. You know she'll tell him, and that puts him in an awkward position with us and the HOA. Keep quiet about it for their benefit too. Please! Just give us a few days to get the ore out of the neighborhood, and then everything will settle down. I promise you that you can talk to her about it, but first, let us learn a little bit more about what we really have." He leaned over and kissed her on the neck then went on. "Probably, it will turn out to be nothing and the big secret will be a big bust, but we need to have some options. Besides, it's not just up to me now. We have two other partners to consider. Roy talked to Rhonda last night. She's in and wants to finance the upfront costs."

***

Kara wasn't the only one who picked up mysterious happenings on Cactus Wren Circle. There were too many dump trucks coming and going from Ms. Tucker's backyard. The novelty of having a celebrity in the neighborhood made everyone more aware of anything that happened at or near her house, and there was a lot happening. Dean Shutter had noticed it, too. First, trucks had brought loads of dirt into her yard, and now bigger trucks were hauling dirt away. It didn't make sense.

Dean Shutter had started construction on his own house and now made a point of driving to his lot the long way around the block. He hadn't admitted to himself that the reason for the circuitous route to his construction site was Rhonda Tucker, until one day when his wife was with him and he took the long way out of habit. Sharron raised the question as to where they were going. "I just wanted you to see the changes in the development," he said.

"And what exactly would those be?" she asked in her usual sarcastic tone, picking up on his rubbernecking as they passed the recording star's house. They had already had an argument that day about the size of the porch in the front of their new house.

"No one sits on their front porches anymore. This isn't Mayberry R.F.D.," she told him. "Use the footage to make me a bigger master bath and closet."

The Shutter house footprint was already huge. Sharron was thrilled to finally be getting a house again and was making sure it would have everything she wanted. Four years ago, they had moved out of a large, luxurious home in Scottsdale when Dean sold it to finance the startup of Hidden Canyon. She and her daughter had been sharing the larger bath at their two-bedroom apartment after casting Dean into having the tiny second bath.

Dean hadn't even discussed the sale of the Scottsdale house with her. She had been defensive and frightened about their security ever since. Dean wasn't oblivious to the situation, and tried to reassure her that things would be better and that he would build her a new home. Now that it was started, she saw how wonderful it was going to be to live in the beautiful development, but she was panicked that someone would drive by the new house and like it enough to make Dean an offer he couldn't refuse. Knowing Dean, she knew that everything was for sale.

The two had lasted twenty years together, although it had been like a twenty-round boxing match. Sometimes she thought the only reason they kept fighting was to see who could outlast the other. The other reason they stuck it out was because of their daughter. However, she would be going away to school soon, and Sharron didn't want the insecurity of just the two of them without a real home in a real neighborhood, where she could make some lasting friendships. Living in a rental gave her no security whatsoever. Everything made her nervous about her life with Dean, especially single women like the new neighbor with lots of money and the good looks to go with it.

***

The Steiner brothers were getting bored with life. Otto wanted to learn more about his new neighbors and insisted that his wife make apple strudel for each of them, especially for the sexy redhead across the street. He was too chicken to take it himself, so he told one of his kids to leave it on the doorstep and ring the bell.

The prowling coyotes had enjoyed the strudel the previous night and had licked the pan clean. They had chewed on the welcome note from the Steiners as well. When she found the tattered note, Otto was watching her, focused on her front door with his binoculars. He was so disappointed that he told Helga to make another batch of the strudel and this time he would take it himself. Maybe then he could take a look at her backyard. "She must be putting in an Olympic-size swimming pool," he thought. "There have sure been a lot of truckloads of dirt leaving her backyard." He also wanted to see if she sunbathed nude like all the movie stars he had read about in the grocery store checkout line.

✳✳✳

There was activity everywhere in Hidden Canyon with the continuing buildup of the neighborhood. The construction of Rhonda's pool proceeded at a brisk pace, as did the framing of the Shutters' house. For several weeks there were no more dead animals, dog shootings or any other signs of mischief or sabotage. Occasionally there were sightings late in the evening of a woman with long, gray hair carrying a long walking stick. Most who saw her didn't know her name or from where she came. Slowly, however, her story was beginning to surface.

✳✳✳

Charley's secretary strutted into his office one Monday morning with a two-page list of all the neighborhood residents who lived outside the Hidden Canyon proper. Emily had an aerial map of the area. Within a few minutes, she and Charley had identified Alma Ziegler's property. A three-minute computer search of county records produced her name and address. A newspaper archive search of her name dug up the story of her parents' airplane accident. The desert lady now had a name and a history, though a sad one at that. Sitting back in his big office chair, Charley read through the findings. He couldn't imagine losing his entire family. As he read further, he discovered more information that gave Charley an understanding of her financial situation as well.

"Alma Ziegler is rich—very, very rich," Charley said quietly.

The original newspaper article said she had inherited her father's mining company, which was worth a fortune, but it didn't mention the problems with probate and how the attorneys had nibbled away at it until most was gone. The county records did state that she held title to hundreds of acres of virgin desert that butted against the Hidden Canyon fence line.

The sad story about her family made Charley begin to understand why she was a modern-day hermit. She apparently had no one except her animal friends and her desert shack. He concluded that he and the girls and everyone else in Hidden Canyon needed to leave Alma alone. Her behavior to date hinted at serious mental problems. He didn't want to create more. His instinct told him that he and his neighbors could very well be living near a time bomb.

***

A large certified envelope arrived at Brighton's office eight days after the first load of ore was scooped out of Rhonda's backyard and trucked to Colorado Springs. He was nearing the end of his day in the office when it arrived. The envelope contained three pages. First was a computer printout stating metal names and rows of numbers that were gibberish to Brighton. The next page was an agreement letter to sell the ore to Pikes Peak Metals and Minerals, a Colorado company. He was to sign and return it. The brief note on the third page stated that by cashing the attached check the ore became the sole property of the refinery company. The attached check was made out to Mr. Brighton Dunn. At the bottom left-hand corner of the check was printed the astounding sentence:

> *"Proceeds: 20.7 tons ore: gold, platinum, rhodium, and trace minerals, minus processing fee of 10 percent."*

On the amount line was written, "$191,055.36."

Brighton sank into the closest chair and stared at the check, then the letter, and then the check. He wondered if it was for multiple truckloads of the swimming pool dirt, but on close inspection realized it was for just the first large truckload. Who would have ever imagined? Elation and anxiety hit him simultaneously. What would he do with the thing? He wasn't alone in the ore deal. He had partners, even though there was no formal agreement. What should he do with the money? It was his name on the check and his name that would be reported to the IRS. He worried about the taxes and then about paying back Rhonda. She had already advanced six thousand dollars. Finally, he thought,

"How do we get more of this stuff and from whose yard?" He needed a meeting with the partners, and he needed it now. And the partners needed an attorney. A very smart and very sympathetic attorney.

He finished treating the last patients in his office and then called Roy. Roy agreed to call Rhonda, and they would all meet at Roy's at ten-thirty after Roy's shift. Gina was sick again, and staying up late was tough, but she agreed to do it anyway.

The meeting was calm and calculated after the first ten minutes—which were spent dancing around the room, waving the check in the air like a high school championship banner. When things settled down, they agreed to a forty/forty/twenty split, with Rhonda getting the twenty percent.

They decided that a formal business agreement was needed, and Rhonda suggested they set up an LLC—a limited liability corporation. The problem was that no one trusted attorneys for this job and no one could come up with the name of one other than their neighbor, Charley Banks. The more they talked, the better he sounded as a counsel and probably as a partner. This made Gina feel good knowing that Kara would, after all, be involved in the big secret.

They were pretty certain that there would be problems with the HOA rules if they weren't really careful in removing more of the natural ore. Another consideration was the Patel family. The shiniest specimen Roy had found was from samples right next to the Patel side of the of Brighton and Gina's lot. Could they get access to that ore?

"And what about taxes?" Gina asked.

None of them wanted to go to jail for failure to report income to the IRS, and the first check was made out just to Brighton. The IRS would consider him the person with the gain. They needed someone to keep them out of trouble.

The brainstorming session went on for another hour, and finally they each accepted an assignment: Rhonda had a Los Angeles accountant who owed her a favor. Roy would look into the HOA rules and state mining laws. Brighton and Gina agreed to open a bank account and keep records of the expenses and get to know the Patels better.

Gina mentioned the latest information Charley had obtained about the desert lady. She now had a name and a story. He had told his wife that the woman was still a threat. "He thinks she is a 'time bomb,' to use his words. We all need to be on the look-out for any weird stuff in the neighborhood."

"You mean like mining trucks rumbling through the streets?" Roy said in a rare attempt at humor.

Roy's statement produced a bit of stress-relieving laughter. The chiming, antique grandfather clock notified them that the meeting had gone on for over two hours. They were all tired and wondering if they hadn't caught a tiger by the tail.

11

FIRE! FIRE! FIRE!

A bomb of sorts went off that week. Who lit the fuse, no one knew.

Mike Salmon and his girlfriend, Tina, were the first to see the flames. Mike, a local high school senior, had followed a home-owner's car through the entrance gate into Hidden Canyon. Mike had turned the lights of his restored mauve 1958 Impala convertible off so that the car in front wouldn't even notice him. He found an awesome isolated spot on the highest road in the project, put down the convertible top, and shut off the engine. Soon he and Tina were talking a little, looking at the lights of the city a little, and kissing a lot.

The flash of light caught Tina's peripheral vision, something Mike probably wouldn't have ever noticed at that moment. Tina jerked her head toward the flash and gasped. They could clearly see the outline of a huge, partially framed house. Flames were crawling over the structure like giant red spiders. Within a few minutes the entire structure was ablaze. They heard the crackle of the fire and then, from a distance, came a single siren.

A chill of fear shot through Mike. They were trespassing in a private neighborhood, and a house was on fire. They needed to get out of there fast. His car, with the lights still off, crept down the hill and pulled in front of the automatic gate just as a security truck with its flashing lights drove into the development. It seemed like it took forever for the gates to open and Mike and Tina could drive away. Mike felt like everything was going to be okay until he remembered that his custom license plate frame would have still been illuminated. ROCKING 58 was not a plate number one had to write down.

***

Roy heard Chad whining and scratching at the glass door of his family room, and through it, Roy could plainly see the illumination of the entire mountainside behind his house. His first thought was of a desert brush fire. He threw on clothes and boots and grabbed his truck keys as he went out the door. To Chad's dismay, he was left behind. Roy only had to jog a few hundred yards before he could tell it was Dean and Sharron Shutter's newly framed house going up in flames.

Dean's house was on a deep cul-de-sac lot and sat up and away from any of the neighbors. The flames from the tinder-dry pine studs, timbers, and plywood shot into the sky like a rocket's tail flames. Luckily, the home's location reduced the danger of the fire spreading, and it was, at least, one of the unoccupied homes and wouldn't be destroying personal property or endangering lives. The structure, however, was obviously going to be a total loss. Seeing the fire trucks starting to roll into the development gave Roy a small sense of relief as well. He soon joined a group of the neighbors congregating across the street from the Shutters.

Charley's twin girls ran into their parents' bedroom screaming that their house was on fire. By the time he and Kara had awakened enough to collect their senses and get dressed, the guest parking lot across the street from their house was packed with people watching the inferno.

Brighton and Gina had still been awake when the commotion started. They dressed and joined the pack of useless observers. Unlike in the days of old when neighbors would have formed bucket brigades to try to save the house, people just assumed the presence of a good insurance policy and found comfortable places to stand or sit to watch. In the illumination of the fire, Brighton and Gina found Charley, Kara, and their girls. The four exchanged looks, and then Gina mumbled loud enough for the others to hear, "She did it; I know she did it. She has been waiting for a big revenge; and who bigger than Dean Shutter, the king of evil development? She is probably sitting up on a rock, sucking on coyote jerky and grinning from ear to ear."

"Come on, Gina, let's drive over there and see if her lights are on," Kara said.

"Hold your horses," Charley said, grabbing both women by their forearms in a grip much firmer than Gina thought necessary.

She jerked her arm away and said to her husband, "Brighton, drive me over there right now. I want to catch that witch sneaking back into her shack and beat the crap out of her."

"Settle down!" Brighton commanded in a hushed tone. He was embarrassed at her total reversal of personality, especially in front of the Banks girls. "No one is going to go anywhere except back to bed. You need to lay off those prenatal vitamins. They are making you way too energetic." He gave Charley a sideways glance and rolled his eyes.

In spite of his satirical statements and looks, Brighton was clearly sick inside. There were just too many coincidental and crazy things going on in Hidden Canyon.

When Dean Shutter rounded the corner in his Hummer, barely two of his four tires were touching the pavement. The fire chief was identified to Dean, and he rushed up to the man. Panic and anger were evident on his face as he approached the chief.

"What happened? Why aren't you pouring on water?"

Chief Rogers assumed by the intensity of the man's voice and the look on his face that he was the owner. He had ordered his men to back off from the main blaze and concentrate on containing the fire to the single building and lot, thus saving the surrounding desert plants and nearby houses. Stacks of building materials to the side of the house were being cooled with the spray from the fire truck's hoses. Rogers had been in enough situations post-incineration to know that the victims of fires had a need to know what and how and by whom the fires had been started.

With a firm grasp on Dean's arm, Rogers led him toward a red Suburban with its flashing lights. Once inside, he asked a few questions and clarified a few things to Dean, especially the reason for backing off the fire.

Dean finally cooled down enough to ask intelligent questions. Was anyone seen around the house prior to the blast? Did anyone hear anything? Was there an explosion? Was the lock on the construction gate broken, or had the firemen cut the lock?

When Dean was finished with the fire chief, he got out of the suburban and walked toward the glowing embers. The ninety thousand dollars' worth of two-by-sixes, plywood, engineered trusses, and the custom, hand-hewn beams had all been reduced to a smoking, crackling pile of charcoal. The entire mess would have to be scooped up, loaded into trucks, and hauled away. The concrete slab would be cracked, and the stem copper and PVC plumbing under the slab would be melted. It would cost a hundred thousand dollars minimum to dig up the foundation, haul it off, and redo the plumbing and concrete. Dean was doing the math in his head when he was interrupted.

"Sure hope you've got good insurance." The voice came from the shadowed side of the glow where Dean could barely make out the face of Roy Richards.

"Hey Roy, your pilot buddies in the friendly skies are probably reporting this fire from altitude." Dean's voice was subdued yet friendly.

Roy had been one of the first buyers in Hidden Canyon, and the two men had enjoyed many conversations the last couple of years.

"Did the fireman have any clue about the origin?" Roy inquired.

"Nothing obvious. They will have a forensics team out here when the thing cools down. He says they are pretty good at finding the place it started and how it started. That's one of the reasons they backed off with the water hoses once it was obvious that they couldn't stop it. I hope to hell that they don't do a reach and call it a terrorist attack; since 9/11 some insurance companies have used that dodge to not pay claims," Dean sighed. "Incidentally, the new sheriff, Tim Brice, called the fire chief while I was in his truck. Seems there have been too many problems in Hidden Canyon, and he wants some help with the solutions, whatever that means."

"Anything I can do to help, just let me know. I'm sure the rest of the neighbors feel the same," Roy said, nodding toward the group of ten or twelve people standing in a circle across the road. "When do you need to move out of your apartment? I had heard that you needed the house done in a hurry."

"We can stay as long as necessary. My wife is going crazy though, living in the tiny space. She wants to know why I didn't build the first house here. Let's just say that she's a great wife but hasn't figured out that you have to earn the money before you can spend it."

***

Brighton and Gina awoke early. The summer sun was streaming through their bedroom window like a laser. Since their backyard faced the mountain, there was no one to peek in the window, thus they hadn't been motivated to spend the money for shades or shutters. Gina got out of bed and threw the covers off of Brighton in a playful manner. He got up and fixed her a cup of her favorite hot chocolate and then walked down the driveway to get the paper.

Up the road, a single fire truck remained in front of Shutters' smoldering skeleton. Only the three stone fireplaces and a few plumbing pipes stood above the level of the cement pad. A couple of firemen were sifting through the smoking rubble using long probes that looked like giant knitting needles.

Brighton was studying the men and the house when his eyes noticed something different. An arroyo running behind the Shutters' lot had been obscured by desert trees prior to the fire. Now that the small trees had burned, the natural drainage area was exposed. It appeared to be the same arroyo that circled around a vacant area behind the Patels' place, which began in the back corner of Brighton's non-disturbed area. A long morning shadow from a distant peak was receding up the hill. As the direct sunlight finally struck the arroyo behind the Shutters' house, a glittering streak appeared, which in the changing light, ran like a giant snake up and around Brighton's house.

"Why are you running?" Gina yelled from the front porch. She was sitting on the lounge reading the paper.

"I've got to see something," he answered, disappearing around the corner.

He climbed a small hillock and positioned himself on an angle where he could see the arroyo from its first cut of erosion to a deep ravine eight hundred yards away. It bordered at least five of the lots, including his. As the angle of the sun changed and the shadows receded, it caused the glittering to decrease. Still, he could see some of the same type of reflection for the full length of the geological rift.

"What the heck are you doing?" Gina asked. She had walked across the backyard with her mug of chocolate.

"You won't believe what I saw as the sun lit up this little canyon. That same shining stone that is in our yard extends across the hill for half a mile. I hadn't ever noticed it because of the big Palo Verde trees by Shutter's place, but the fire wiped them out and the land looks different. Come see."

***

The next morning, Roy stood beside Brighton in the early morning dawn. Both held steaming cups and binoculars. A small topographic map, unfolded to show the exact contours and altitudes of the surface, lay on the nearby rock outcropping.

As the first rays of sunlight appeared on the distant hills in the west, the men put down their cups and, with binoculars ready, waited for the sun to hit the Dunns' backyard. Just as Brighton described, a long, fat snake of sparkling rock appeared and tracked its way directly through the Patels' backyard, part of the vacant area, and the far back end of the Shutters' blackened yard. In the other direction it headed east behind the Dunns' and Patels' houses straight into the desert.

"I can't believe it," whispered Roy in awe. "This vein is bigger than we could have ever imagined. Too bad we didn't find it before the houses were built and the yards were finished."

"There has to be a way we can access more of the ore and still keep the HOA and the tree huggers clueless. And what about our neighbor across the fence?" Brighton said, pointing to the east. As he looked into the distance, he saw a dull reflection from the roof of the desert lady's shack.

"Think about it, Brighton. If we could pull out twenty or thirty more truckloads of the high-grade ore, we could bank six or eight million bucks. That would make drilling teeth and babysitting airplanes a hobby instead of a necessity."

"Before you sail off into the sunset on your yacht," Brighton cautioned, "We need to get the group together and make plans. Maybe we should consider expanding the circle. Dean Shutter's torched building site could be ripe to do some serious deep digging while everything is torn up from the fire, and like you said, the Patels' backyard is possibly the richest area there is. If we could dig some of that area behind their pool, it would be awesome. There must be a full acre of relatively flat land there. I could probably use some more landscaping too, especially along the Patels' fence line," Brighton concluded.

Roy turned to Brighton and smiled.

✳✳✳

Gina stood at her bedroom window, watching the two men. She had the feeling that the secret of the precious shiny ore was getting very complicated. She had seen that look of determination on Brighton's face before. He had been obsessive on occasion: now she feared that the entire mining thing could trigger that behavior again. He still needed to make a living for them at his dental practice.

She also wanted to share the secret of the gold, rhodium, and platinum with Kara. She worried that if she didn't share the secret, she would lose her new, very dear friend. She realized at that moment that she cared more about Kara's feelings than she did about the possible money from the ore. The questions that kept cycling in her mind were: *Could the group trust Charley to keep it from the HOA President and board? Could Roy and Brighton and the rest with so little knowledge and no experience pull it all off?*

Shortly after the men came into the house, the phone rang with a call from the HOA secretary, informing the Dunns of an emergency meeting the following night.

12

MEETING OF GREAT MINDS

The emergency meeting of the Hidden Canyon HOA was getting out of hand again. The clubhouse was packed to the walls, and everyone was vocal and irritable. There were neither snacks, nor calming drinks. The stench of burned, wet building materials still hung like a fog over the development.

For three days, official police and fire vehicles as well as antenna-clad broadcast vans from each of the news teams had prowled the streets looking for story leads. Clyde had given up trying to monitor who did and didn't get through the gate; he finally opened the gate and left it that way. That allowed all the gawkers from town to cruise through the Canyon. Now empty soda cans and McDonald's wrappers were appearing on the sides of the streets.

Between Dean and Charley they recognized most of the meeting's attendees. Two of the homeowners on Prospector Lane, on the far end of the project, had gone in together and hired their own attorney. They were bending people's ears about how the HOA must build its own fire station and have a full-time fire-fighting team as well as a much more sophisticated security force.

Dr. Cooperman was about to call the chaotic group to order when silence fell over the crowd. All heads turned toward the entry door, staring at Rhonda Tucker, who had just walked into the room.

Her fire-red hair was braided and fell down her back. A row of small bows on each of her braids matched her frilly lace blouse, which gaped open, plunging nearly to her large silver-and-gold belt buckle. Her sequined, neon-blue bellbottom jeans looked painted on and had just enough length to drape over the tops of silver-tipped, black-ostrich-skin cowboy boots.

A pathway opened in front of her as she strolled forward toward the podium. She walked through the crowd, smiling at everyone who would make eye contact and mouthing hellos to those she had previously met. When she reached the podium, she nodded to Dean, Charley, and the HOA president, then turned to face the crowd. Roy, who escorted her into the room, leaned against the wall.

Cooperman rapped his gavel on the cherry wood podium. To everyone's astonishment, he motioned Rhonda even closer to the podium.

"Since the Fourth of July is just around the corner," he said, "I've asked one of our newest neighbors to start off our meeting with a touch of patriotism by singing the National Anthem. Allow me to introduce the newest resident of Hidden Canyon, Ms. Rhonda Tucker."

She didn't use a microphone. She didn't need one. When she stood ready at the podium, the room fell silent again.

"Thank you, Dr. Cooperman, for inviting me to sing for you all. I love living in Hidden Canyon and having neighbors like all you fine people here, and I love living in America. It's a great country we live in. Don't you agree?"

A restrained round of applause followed until she raised her hands, palms together, in a subtle sign of supplication and began to sing. Her voice pierced the four corners of the room with notes so pure and strong that hair stood up on the back of people's necks. As she finished the last few bars of the song, many were dabbing at the corners of their eyes. There were tears in Rhonda's eyes as well. She had found a real home and a wonderful new life.

Brighton and Gina worked their way around the room and stood next to Roy. They looked at each other with questioning eyes. America was a great country for sure, but American prisons didn't have the same reputation.

✳✳✳

The small "ore group" met at the Dunns' home. They had invited Charley and Kara Banks over to share a pizza, and Roy and Rhonda also were there. Dean Shutter had been invited, but was out of town for a funeral. The conversation had been light and fun until Gina had looked Kara in the eyes and explained that they had been keeping a secret. She went on to explain that she had insisted the secret be shared with Charley and Kara. Roy then handed Charley a hundred dollar bill, requesting a hand-shake commitment to represent the group as their attorney, thus assuring attorney client confidentiality.

Brighton and Roy explained some basic facts about the ore project. They were very careful not to name exact sites or even the exact dollar profits they were anticipating. They wanted Charley and Kara to agree in principle with the potential of the plan. They needed an attorney, plus they wanted their close friends involved. Yes, it was diluting the pot. Yes, it was increasing the mathematical probability that word would get out of the circle. However, with Charley there to build a legal foundation for them, they would be less likely to be stopped.

Kara rose from her chair and walked across the room to Gina. She bent down and kissed her on the cheek and said softly, "I knew there was something you wanted to share."

As Kara returned to her seat, Charley began to speak. "Let me get this straight. You plan to remove hundreds of tons of rock and dirt from Hidden Canyon to refine it and sell it? Then you plan to replace this dirt or ore with substitute dirt, all the time doing it without any of the neighbors outside our little group here knowing about it? Then you plan to do what with the money, buy your own country?"

A chuckle of released anxiety sounded through the room.

Charley paced back and forth a few times. Finally, he continued, "If we do this wrong we could all be sued for everything we own. We could also spend the next ten years in separate prison cells, away from each other and our children." Charley looked at each of them, then went on, "If on the other hand, we do it right we might have a pretty cool story to tell our filthy rich grandchildren."

Sighs of relief filled the room. Charley raised his hand, halting conversation. "I was told never to agree to a complicated case until I had had time to think."

Ten seconds later, he announced that he had thought long enough.

"We're in."

***

Dean Shutter's only paternal uncle couldn't have picked a worse time to die. Missing his uncle's funeral had not been an option. Going to the Dunns' for a late dessert and for something the dentist had described as "very important" was impossible.

Two days later, after Dean had endured lots of waiting at airports, the dentist called again. This time the meeting would be at Rhonda's house. He tried to persuade Sharron to come with him, but she decided to spend the evening with her sister. His wife kept such a low profile that he doubted whether most of his Hidden Canyon neighbors even knew if he was married.

Dean spent extra time dressing for the visit to the star's house. He had been around his share of rich people, but never someone whose face and voice were recognized by two hundred million people.

He was the first to arrive. He couldn't believe the pictures on the walls of Rhonda standing onstage with entertainment legends: Johnny Cash, Ray Charles, Bob Hope, John Wayne, and several U.S. Presidents, each with an arm around her. On one of the walls a shallow glass display case held platinum records, and in the middle stood a shiny gold Oscar for Best Original Song.

Roy was the next to arrive. After a handshake and a few pleasantries, Roy invited Dean to sit and talk. Rhonda wandered off into another part of the house.

"I need to ask you some difficult questions, and I need straightforward answers," Roy began. "How good is your word of honor?"

Dean looked at Roy, stunned. He could have asked him when he lost his virginity, and he wouldn't have been any more surprised.

"I'm a man who honors my word and the word of others. Why do you ask?"

"I'm going to tell you a story that you will have trouble believing, and then I'm going to offer you a part in the story, Roy began. "If you agree to join, then I, as well as several others, will be very pleased. If you reject the offer, I will understand, and you can leave knowing we are still friends. If, however, you share this story with anyone else for any reason, the rest of us will be severely disappointed. Disappointed in ways you might never imagine. Now is your chance to leave, like I said, as friends, or to stay and hear me out."

Roy gave Dean a minute or two and then asked, "Do I have your word to keep this conversation confidential?"

"You have my word," Dean said extending his hand to shake on the agreement.

No sooner had the men shaken hands than a door from the back porch opened and Rhonda came into the room accompanied by Brighton Dunn, Charley Banks, and their wives. Rhonda gestured for them all to be seated at the huge, round, country-style table.

Brighton opened a manila folder and displayed its contents. During the explanation, he presented various pieces of evidence, including a copy of the mega-dollar check. It still had not been cashed.

Charley gave a thumb-sketch version of where they stood on a legal basis. He had already prepared a mining claim for all the underground mineral rights beneath Hidden Canyon and the adjacent property owned by a Ms. Alma Ziegler, and for the surface rights for each of the lots owned by those present, including Dean and Sharron Shutter.

Dean listened carefully, too stunned to interrupt.

Roy added a few comments relating the firsthand conversations with the assay people. Then they all sat in silence. Rhonda produced glasses and a pitcher of ice water.

"This is for real, isn't it?" Dean finally said. "You guys plan to mine the ore under Hidden Canyon. Unbelievable! Why couldn't I have just discovered these minerals three years ago? It would have been a hell of a lot easier."

Everyone smiled but held their comments.

After a brief pause, Dean said, "You can count me in. What do you want me to do?"

"How is your wife going to feel about the situation? Her name is Sharron right?" Gina asked. "We all look forward to meeting her."

"To be frank, she and I have had our problems the last couple of years. Things were getting better with the closing of the project and starting the new house. Now with the fire, I'm not sure what's going on. She flew to L.A. yesterday to visit a sister. She seldom knows or cares what goes on with my business. I probably won't tell her much for right now."

The questions went on for a while longer, until Charley produced a paper for Dean to sign, agreeing to allow a substantial amount of rock and dirt to be excavated from the Shutters' lot while the cleanup of the burned house was under way.

"This is an all-for-one-and-one-for-all agreement," Brighton reiterated. "If it works, it is going to be a sweet deal for everyone."

Kara, being one of the new partners, didn't ask any questions or make any comments. She was a people watcher and sat fascinated at the faces and personalities in front of her. It was a strange, eclectic group, all of whom were successful at what they did. They definitely had a lust for adventure, excitement, and belonging.

Rhonda was having the most fun she had had in years. Instead of being onstage under hot lights and covered with makeup—she hated makeup—she was in the middle of a real adventure. No acting here. The drama and intrigue was genuine, with real people, not actors, putting their time, energy, and future on the line.

Roy was a person who had seldom been distracted from any goal or responsibility, but he was finding it harder to concentrate on work, or anything else for that matter. Sitting around Rhonda Tucker's table, remembering that he was the one who had started this entire pursuit of the valuable metals, his mind wandered. What would he do if they really struck it rich? Would he keep on working? Had he made a big mistake sharing the find with the rest of these people? Could he have, perhaps, had it all to himself?

At the moment, he faced the biggest distraction of them all. He was inches away from one of the most beautiful, desirable women in the world, and she was smiling directly at him. He knew he was letting her invade his organized life, and he could see many potential conflicts ahead, but still, he couldn't get enough of just being around her, watching her move and listening to her talk in her cute faux Southern drawl.

"Do you have anything to add, Roy?" Brighton asked, bringing the air traffic controller back to the conversation.

Roy just smiled and said, "Thanks for putting your trust in me."

13

ASSAULT

Brighton was in the middle of drilling out a nasty cavity when he had a revelation. As the tiny drill produced its maddening sound and ground away the dead dentine of the woman's tooth, a vivid picture came to his mind. *What if one were to drill out small cavities in the various backyards of Hidden Canyon then replace the precious ore with ordinary fill dirt?* "Auug!" mumbled the woman, bringing him back from dreamland. His assistant was staring at him, somewhat irritated. He had continued drilling past the cavity into the nerve.

Later, he did some calculations and figured he could remove about three or four thousand pounds of ore at a time. The hole wouldn't look much different from the large tree well needed to plant a huge boxed tree. He would have to find fill dirt and use a small truck to swap out the ore with the fill dirt. How to do it, he wasn't sure, but figured Dean would have an idea.

Brighton finished up with his last few patients and said good night to his weary staff. When his last staff member had finally gone home, Brighton picked up the phone to call Roy. He couldn't wait to tell him about the idea he had just hatched.

Brighton was startled when he heard the door open abruptly. He walked out of his consultation room and saw the self-closer on the door slowly easing shut. He looked around the room but saw nothing out of the ordinary. He shrugged off the incident thinking someone must have opened the door by accident and then left. He turned to walk back down the hall, and suddenly felt a crushing pain in the back of his head. Brighton's next recollection was hearing the telephone ring over and over. His head was pounding, and something was wet on the floor beside his nose. He tried to open his eyes, but everything was dark. The phone kept ringing.

Gina finally gave up calling Brighton's office. She had wanted him to pick up some fettuccine at the grocery store on his way home. She had thawed out a piece of salmon and planned to tell Brighton to hurry, because she was starving. Pregnancy was a nine-month roller coaster ride. She was finally getting over her nausea, and now was hungry from morning till midnight. Her hourglass figure was filling with sand.

When the office phone didn't answer and Brighton's cell phone kept going to voicemail, she became worried. She called his office manager at her home, and was told that they had finished up in the office more than an hour ago. She then called Kara to borrow some pasta—any kind would do—and inquire if Brighton had by chance stopped by there to brainstorm with Charley. Kara was an action type of woman. When she heard that Brighton was missing, she immediately called the police.

***

An ambulance crew lifted Brighton off the tile floor and gently placed him on a gurney. A long, dark, red string of clotted blood trailed from the white floor tile up to the laceration in the back of his head. Eventually, it pulled loose and fell back to the floor with a splat. The paramedics hadn't stopped to clean the wound but were concentrating instead on keeping his neck and spine stable.

The reflection of the rotating red police lights bounced off of the office building's windows and gave a surreal feeling to the otherwise sedate office complex. Inside the ambulance, Brighton could see the strobe lights and could hear the paramedics talking to him, but he couldn't make out any specific words coming from their mouths. He recognized a familiar voice or two but couldn't remember the names that went with them. He didn't remember the office door opening and closing but did remember the pain. Weirdest of all, as it would later seem to him, was that he remembered the idea of drilling he had conjured up to harvest the rhodium, platinum, and gold. As the ambulance drove toward the hospital, he remembered something else. He remembered seeing boots by his face—hiking or work boots, or were they cowboy boots? He couldn't be sure, but somewhere in his subconscious he knew that he had seen boots standing beside his bloodied head.

✻✻✻

"What the heck were they looking for? He didn't keep any drugs of interest in the office," Charley told the police sergeant. He was getting his information via cell phone from Gina, who was sitting in the Scottsdale Mayo Clinic emergency room. Charley had remained at Brighton's office with the police and had directed Kara to take Gina to the hospital.

When he first arrived at the office, Charley found that the front door was closed but unlocked, and the lights were still on. Nothing seemed amiss in the waiting room. He had never been in this office so felt a little shy about snooping. He had called out Brighton's name but received no answer. When he entered the consultation room, he found Brighton lying on the floor, blood oozing out of his head. He was still wearing his white lab coat, which was slowly turning red. The police arrived promptly with sirens shrieking and lights ablaze, followed shortly thereafter by the paramedics. After initially thinking Charley was the perpetrator, the police settled down, and evaluated the victim.

After Brighton was carted off to the hospital, Charley made his phone calls sitting on the tufted leather chair behind Brighton's desk, and refusing the police's request for him to leave. Charley stated that he was Dr. Dunn's attorney and he had the right and responsibility to remain there and assure that his client's property wasn't disturbed or damaged. In their search, the only suspicious thing the police found was Brighton's leather briefcase, which had been dropped or dumped on the floor near the back entrance hall. Papers were scattered all over the floor.

"Is the dentist some sort of amateur mineralogist?" asked the policeman. "The papers on the floor are some sort of mineral reports."

"I have no idea. I don't know him that well," said Charley, who suddenly felt a cramping feeling in his gut. The seriousness of the adventure he and Kara had jumped into with the Dunns, Roy Richards, and the Western music diva hit him like a bad chimichanga. His mind raced through possible assailants. *Who else knew what was going on in Dr. Dunn's life? What were they searching for?*

By the time Charley had finished up with the police, locked up the office, and met up with his wife and Gina at the hospital, Brighton was awake and sitting up in the bed. He had a new haircut and a dozen stitches across the back of his head. What could have been a time for a few Frankenstein jokes was suppressed by the sneaking fear that each of them was in danger. Charley didn't mention the policeman's questions, waiting instead for a chance to talk to Roy.

The doctors insisted that, because he had sustained a concussion, Brighton stay overnight for observation. They strongly suggested that everyone go home and let the nurses and doctors take care of the patient. Charley followed the women's car as they drove home. While en route, he phoned Roy. It was time to circle the wagons and start digging for gold.

The county fire chief called Dean Shutter a few days after the fire and requested a meeting at the chief's office. He wanted to discuss the house fire in Hidden Canyon and, in particular, wanted to learn why it was the original owner-developer who had his house torched instead of someone else.

When Dean walked into the appointed room, he saw serious faces. There were two men dressed in plain, gray, off-the-rack suits, the fire chief dressed in his pompous uniform with medals and ribbons like some African dictator, plus a wide-bodied woman with short-cropped, gray hair and bifocals. She was dressed in a plain black suit with a too-snug fit. The presence of Don Brice, the County Sheriff, was a huge surprise to Dean. Certainly, the sheriff had better things to do than attend meetings of little relevance to his elected position. It suddenly made Dean feel defensive. All were watching him with looks that his imagination immediately converted to suspicious stares. The fire chief introduced Dean to the group using formal terms. An inquiry board was the pretense; however, an inquisition was more the feeling.

"All of the forensic studies are complete, Mr. Shutter, and it is the determination of the laboratory team that your house fire was started by common accelerants. Actually, there were two probable starting points found. A small can of Sterno gel, like the ones used in chafing dishes, was near the epicenter."

"Epicenter … that means where the fire started," interrupted Ms. Grange, the gray-headed woman who had been introduced as representing Dean's insurance carrier. Her voice was like chalk on a blackboard. "The second probable site was from a small propane torch, similar to the ones the plumbers use to solder copper fittings. Both igniters are common to construction sites, as you know." She looked up from her papers.

"There also have been reports of other atypical activities in the development including shootings and beatings and even possible ghost sightings," added Ms. Grange's underling, Irving Malquist, a cadaver-skinny man with little more than a tuft of hair.

Dean didn't know whether to nod in agreement or break out laughing at the absurd presentation the woman and her co-worker were making. The female insurance investigator chimed in with absurd comments including she had heard rumors that Dean's wife said she didn't like the floor plan of her new house and wished they could start all over with the design. The woman's bold-faced inference was clear. Owner-planned arson was being considered by the two insurance investigators, if not by the authorities.

"So do you have any real evidence?" the sheriff asked.

"My best guess is that it was started innocently by one of the workmen either heating plumbing joints or heating lunch," the fire chief said. "It could have smoldered unnoticed all evening until the desert winds picked up enough to fan it into activity. Once it got started, it burned out of control. Another possibility is that some teenagers might have lit it on purpose or lit a warming fire, which then got out of control. The security guard saw a nonresident vehicle leaving the gated neighborhood as he was driving toward the fire."

The chief looked at the sheriff as if asking for further help but received none. Questions from the rest of the group were solicited. None were asked.

Dean had his I-Phone in his lap and made a few notes. Luckily he held his tongue and only looked at the fire chief with a questioning expression. "Is there more, or may I go? I have a new house to build."

The sheriff shrugged his shoulders and gave a nod of approval.

Dean turned to the woman he thought would make a good Nazi and said, "I'll be expecting the settlement money by the end of the week so I can order a new lumber package. Also, the cement contractor wants half up front. If you are not going to make the payment on time, I will need a letter for my attorney expressing the reasons. I encouraged over 70 percent of the homeowners in Hidden Canyon to use your company for their insurance. I'm certain that they will all want to know if you are willing to fulfill your obligation. There are lots of other companies out there wanting their business."

No sooner had Dean reached the parking lot when he received a call from his secretary telling him that the HOA office had called wanting to know when they could expect the debris from his lot to be cleared away. The HOA ecology committee would allow him just ten days from the time of the fire to have his lot cleared of fire debris.

Dean was furious. It was because of his hard work and effort that Hidden Canyon even existed, and now the damn HOA was placing restraints and requirements on him. He had some very serious doubts about the whacky mining plan, but he was becoming determined to do everything possible to make it a reality. The HOA could go to hell.

***

Otto Steiner had never seen a piece of landscaping equipment quite like the one sitting in front of his house on a giant flatbed trailer. The semi-truck transported the bright yellow machine into Hidden Canyon. Unlike a bulldozer or a front-end loader, it didn't have a blade. It was as tall as the largest Caterpillar but looked very strange. It was at least twenty-five feet long, with the driver's enclosed cab low and to the side. What it had in its front end instead of a scoop or a blade was an eight-foot-wide mouth with six two-feet-wide rotating heads just inside the opening. The smaller heads were similar to the giant drill bits Otto had seen in pictures—the kind used to drill oil wells.

"Wow!" Otto said out loud. "I want one of these."

Otto walked around the yellow machine several times studying it, approving of its engineering. He finished his beer then quickly walked over to his brother's house to discuss the novelty.

"I'm telling you, Heinz, that I tain't seen nothing like it except in dem coal mines in the hills by Dortmund back home in Deutschland. The man on the truck claims that they be digging some holes for some big trees, but I never seen no post hole diggers that size."

By the time Heinz put on a shirt and walked down the driveway with Otto, the burrowing machine was unloaded and out of sight, leaving behind only scraping marks on the asphalt roadway from its steel tracks. The brothers strolled around the neighborhood looking for the machine, and in not finding it, eventually lost interest.

***

It had been two weeks since Brighton had called Roy from the hospital, talking crazily at first about his brainstorm of some kind of weird digging machine. The refining mill in Colorado had put Brighton in contact with a mining company in New Mexico that owned just the machine Brighton had envisioned. They liked to call it the "Mole." Roy couldn't figure out how a dentist with a concussion and a lacerated head could envision a machine that he had never seen nor heard about before.

It had taken only a few days and a twenty thousand dollar deposit to get the equipment leased and the delivery arranged. Roy drove to the little mining town of Blue Water to inspect the machine. The Mole was everything they had hoped it would be.

Roy followed the Mole's tracks around to the back of the lot where it sat in the afternoon sun. At first he didn't notice Dean standing in the shade of a large mesquite tree.

"They tell me this machine can burrow through solid rock if it can get its teeth into a small crack to get started," Dean said.

"What did you tell the driver?" Roy asked.

"I told him that we were going to dig up the foundation of the burned-out house to see if any of that copper pipe can be saved." Dean answered. "With the price of copper over three fifty a pound, how could he argue?"

"I hope he showed you how to run this thing. When I went to inspect it, the operator was gone for the day."

They both studied the control panel in the cab, and then the rest of the machine, noting how the rotating teeth would pulverize the rock and dirt then spit it out onto the conveyor belt that would carry the ore, dropping it to the ground in a continuing row as the machine progressed forward. The ore could then be scooped up and loaded into a truck.

"I own a tractor with a scoop. We can push the ore into a larger pile until we have enough for a transport truckload. We'll have to see how fast this thing really digs. I'll bet a lot depends on how hard the ground is," Dean said.

"I doubt it will go through solid granite, but most of this stuff will crumble just like it did at Brighton's," he continued. "My tractor should be able to keep up with the output, and even do the loading onto the bigger trucks. If we work on it this weekend, we can get several truckloads out of here. If we're lucky, we may get deep enough to go safely under the fence into the neighbor's yard," Dean joked.

Roy looked at Dean over the top edge of his sunglasses with a gaze of questioning. The whole plan seemed to be evolving at a pace that surprised and excited him.

"If we dig the tunnels too close together, won't we run the chance of a collapse?" Roy's eyes and hands were all over the Mole as the two men talked. He had a thousand questions, but the most pressing right now was: *Will this weird-looking thing work?*

"We have to fill the holes, and then soak the filled ones to let them compact as we go along. I found a building lot down the hill near the gate that has lots of extra fill. We've just got to be careful. I'm not sure if the building inspector will require me to have another compaction study before I can redo the plumbing. How much noise do you suppose this thing will make?" Dean seemed to be excited about the digging and was unknowingly working himself into the leader of the mining part of the project.

"The HOA watchdogs will be all over us if we wake them up at night," said Roy.

"Actually, I was thinking of running the Mole in broad daylight and just doing the loading and backfilling at night. We might be surprised at how fast this thing is. How do we arrange for the trucks?"

Dean hadn't been in on the original trucking plan, and though he was in the mining deal up to his neck now, he still had only a small vision of the scope of the project. Brighton and Roy had sketched the entire plan out in their minds, often leaving the others wondering what would come next.

Later that afternoon, Roy dug out his well-worn topographical map and studied it with a magnifying glass. Roy marked the strata's flow with a yellow highlighter and made color copies for his partners.

If the Mole worked as planned, Roy didn't see any reason why they couldn't begin at Rhonda's and follow the flow of the ore-rich vein all the way out into the desert. If the quality of the ore persisted anywhere close to what the original truckload had been, then he calculated they could take out forty to sixty million dollars' worth before they ran out of real estate. By then he wouldn't care what happened. If he could bank ten million, he would disappear into the Alaska or Idaho wilderness, and the IRS and any litigious neighbors could spend their lives trying to find him. If anything ever became of his relationship with Rhonda, which he doubted, then so much the better. Roy knew that he was daydreaming. The forty hours a week he spent at the air traffic control center was his only real touch with the reality he was used to. What was going on in Hidden Canyon was the stuff of fantasy.

14

INVESTIGATORS

Azi Ziegler hadn't been the same woman since the two desperate housewives had played their missionary trick on her. She had been having an especially crappy day. It was the anniversary of the plane crash that had killed her family. She usually recognized that fateful day by hiking into the desert with a bag of Tostitos and a bottle of wine. She would eat and sip until her brain couldn't think of the family anymore, and then she would sleep. She would lie on the sand or rocks and not move until the insect scouts had found her and returned with their buddies. One year, a baby javalina woke her up by sucking on one of her toes.

Azi Zigler paced the kitchen, avoiding the dining room and living room because she didn't want to see any of the memorabilia and photos on the tabletops and walls. Once, she thought she had heard the sound of a car engine, but finally decided it was just the noise of a passenger jet plane. She daydreamed about getting in her old car and driving to the airport and hopping on a plane. She wouldn't even look at the list of flights; she would just tell the ticket agent to give her a ticket on the next flight out of Phoenix. The tiniest smile creased her mouth as she imagined the look on the ticket lady's face when she told them that she didn't care where the plane was going or how much the flight would cost.

She pictured herself dashing down the airport corridor waving her ticket in her hand and yelling for them to hold the flight because a very important person still needed to board. She didn't realize the hassle of current airport screening since 9/11. As for her appearance, she would look more at home at a Greyhound bus station.

As it so happened, a car did come to visit her that night, slowly moving up her driveway, producing a hushed crackling sound in the warm desert air as the tires rolled over the crushed granite. When someone pounded on her front door, she was still daydreaming. When she finally heard the knocking, she was so startled she had to hold on to the edge of the sink to steady herself.

"Ms. Ziegler, are you in there? Please open the door. We need to talk to you."

Azi grabbed a gun from behind the door and yelled for the people to go away. They knocked again, not bothering to identify themselves.

"If you won't talk to us, the sheriff will have to come out here and make you open the door," sounded a woman's scratchy voice. "We are investigating the fire in Hidden Canyon and must talk to you right now. Open the door. We know you are in there; we can see the lights and hear you moving around."

The chubby, insurance woman reached out for the door handle and tried to turn the rusty knob. A window sash opened. Then the shooting started.

Azi's night vision was fine-tuned; it was easy for her to fire five accurate successive shots from her Winchester rifle. The tan Crown Victoria was facing the house with the lights still on. The first shot took out the right headlight. The second and third shots shattered the right and left rearview mirrors. The fourth shot blasted through the windshield, destroying the inside rearview mirror with its built-in compass and exterior thermometer, leaving the whole assemblage dangling from a single wire. Alma took an extra millisecond with the fifth shot, putting a hole through the windshield directly into the padded driver's-side headrest. She still had two shiny, copper-jacketed cartridges left in the rifle.

The insurance agents thought their heads had exploded from the muzzle blast of the gun. The smoking barrel extended out of the window less than six feet from the doorway where they stood. When they came to their senses, they were lying in a heap on the dusty wooden door stoop with their arms wrapped over their heads and their ears ringing. They staggered to their feet, staring at the Ford then turning back toward the house expecting to be shot. When nothing immediately happened, they ran toward their car. The woman fumbled to get the car keys out of her purse, dropping them into the gravel. When she bent over to get them, she kicked them under the car.

Her partner was screaming at her to hurry, but it didn't matter. She couldn't hear anything but the high-pitched ringing in her ears from the gunshots. When she finally found the keys and got the car started, the glare from the shattered windshield distorted her view so badly that she had to stick her head out the side window to drive. Backing out of the driveway, she ran into and then over the milk-can mailbox.

Azi watched the whole post-shooting fiasco through a corner window, and although her ears also were ringing from the blasts, she had a big smile on her face. It was probably the first time in years that she had really smiled from within. *What will happen next?* She really didn't care. The wolves had come to her door, and who they really were or what they really wanted, she didn't know. She hadn't heard clearly enough to understand what they were saying—something about the house fire. She knew enough about the law to know that they were trespassing, and then they were trying to open her door without permission. If they came back, she was going to shoot the people instead of their car. The wolves were gone for now, but she had plenty of ammo and was ready and very willing to fight if they returned.

✳✳✳

Ms. Grange and her partner, Irving Malquist, drove their bullet-ridden car into the lighted parking lot of a 7-Eleven and shut off the engine. The ringing in their ears was still intense. Neither had tried to talk after the first failed attempt at communicating. They got out of the car and circled the wasted vehicle, assessing the damage. Only two of the six windows were intact. The three mirrors were gone or dangling from electrical wires. The hole in the headrest was the most frightening because it demonstrated just how accurate the woman could shoot.

"Go in there and use the pay phone to call the police. Tell them a sniper shot at us from a passing car. Don't even think about saying anything about the woman or the house fire investigation. If we try to tell the truth, the company will fire both of us and subtract the cost of a new car out of our pension accounts. Can you hear me?" Ms. Grange shouted.

Irving nodded, but he couldn't agree less on what they should do. He didn't have a plan of his own though, so he shook his head and said, "I can't hear you clearly enough to understand everything. I've got a terrible headache. I need you to drive me to a doctor." He walked back to the passenger side of the car and got in.

Ms. Grange got back into the car and looked Irving in the face. "Listen to me, you idiot. We could go to jail for trying to get into that woman's house. Forget about your ears. I know you can hear me. I don't want to lose my job, so let's stick with the drive-by story."

Irving couldn't stand her yelling at him anymore. He got out of the bullet-riddled car again and came around to the driver's side. He yanked the door open and grabbed Ms. Grange by the suit collar and pulled her out of the car. She let out a yelp of surprise but didn't resist. He jumped in behind the wheel, slammed the door, and stomped on the gas. He made it about thirty-feet before he ran headlong into a bread delivery truck. By the time the police arrived, the two insurance investigators were both claiming traumatic amnesia.

15

NITPICKING

Charley sat at his giant new ebony desk and rubbed its smooth surface over and over. His promotion had come with a handsome decorating allowance. He had seen a picture of a similar desk in *Forbes* magazine with Bunker Hunt, the silver baron, sitting behind it. He let Kara and his secretary, Emily, pick out the rest of the décor, but insisted on the desk. As his hand went over the glossy surface, his mind took a tangential direction to the treasures lying under his house.

He had gone to the Shutter lot at lunch to watch the Mole start its first dig. It worked like a charm, grinding an eight-foot-diameter hole into the nearly solid rock and spitting the pulverized ore out the end of its long conveyor. The only major problems were that it made some noise and required a lot of fuel. It would have to be used with caution for short periods of time. The machine had dug over twelve tons of ore in less than four hours. Charley did some quick calculations in his head. The money the machine could earn was beyond his imagination. He couldn't believe it. He could be a multi-millionaire in a matter of a few months—maybe even weeks! Although he had no idea if the mineral content of his own lot was as rich as Brighton and Gina's, he knew Kara was already counting unrealized riches and was scanning the Internet for expensive cruises.

Emily's voice came over the intercom, announcing a request from Mr. Fuller that Charley report to his office in ten minutes.

Charley stood in front of Fuller's marble-top desk, not anywhere as nice as Charley's new one. "I have a letter from one of your neighbors, a Doctor Patel, complaining that the HOA is not doing its job. Apparently, several people are not completing their landscaping within the time limit of the CC&Rs. He sounds pretty irate. It really didn't say anything specific, just complained that there were still too many construction trucks in the neighborhood hauling rock and dirt in and out of the neighbors' yards."

"I wasn't aware that there was a problem," Charley said.

"This HOA trash is your bag, Banks. You need to handle it. I don't ever want to see or hear anything about it again. And make darn sure that you aren't giving that HOA any break on the billable hours. All your rich, desert-rat neighbors can afford to pay us a fair price for our time," he concluded, waving Charley away with the back of his hand.

Charley took the letter and wandered back to his office, telling himself that his subservient situation was temporary. In just a couple of years the old man would either croak or retire to his mountain home or his beach house. In the meantime, Hidden Canyon's precious metals might just bring Charley's ship in a little sooner. It wasn't that he despised Fuller or any of the rest of the attorneys lined up ahead of him in the firm's pecking order; it was just that now that he was feeling secure and a little flush, the world looked different. He folded the letter from Patel and slipped it in Emily's shredder as he walked by.

Dr. Patel didn't answer when Charley knocked on the door. Going to the house and talking to the Indian expatriate seemed like a better way to discuss the problem. He rang the doorbell but heard nothing. He was about to turn for his car when the door opened, and Patel's son stood in the doorway. There was a smell coming from the house that made Charley take a couple involuntary steps backward. It was a mixture of garlic, curry, and big dog odor, but something deeper assaulted his olfactory nerves. He could barely concentrate on what the kid was saying. Suddenly, it hit him. The smell was burning incense. Maybe the kid was tooting marijuana. Charley almost started to laugh when he thought about Dr. Patel whining about the noise in the neighborhood when his kids were home smoking pot.

"Tell your dad that I came by to chat. I'll try again another day. By the way, how is your dog doing since he was shot?" Charley inquired, getting another disgusting whiff from the house's interior.

He took a business card out of his pocket and handed it to the young man. "Please tell your father that the attorney from the homeowners' association came by to discuss a few problems with him. I would like to hear from him between nine and ten o'clock in the morning. Tell him it is very important and not to miss the appointment."

The boy took the card and closed the door without any response. Charley looked around the lot. At the side of the house he could see over the fence into the backyard. He made a mental list of a few of the obvious features of the house and yard that were not in strict compliance with the CC&Rs of Hidden Canyon. The one other thing he noticed was the backyard was very deep, and there was a lot of empty space between the pool and the fence separating it from Brighton Dunn's yard. That could evolve into a very good thing.

***

Brighton was finished with the last patient of the day and getting excited about going home and eating dinner with Gina. He took the lid off of a bottle of Advil and swallowed four of the brown pills with his last gulp of watered-down, lukewarm Diet Pepsi. He had made it through his first full day back at work since the assault. His head pounded with a dull thud, but his mind was clear. Although the laceration on his head was itching, it seemed to be healing well. He had been wearing a Phoenix Suns baseball cap to the office the entire week, and had taken some kidding from patients and staff, but it was better than having to explain the railroad track line of sutures across the back of his skull.

The police had completed an extensive search of the office and the parking lot with nothing to show for it. There was some pressure from the newspaper that had picked up on the story, and had looked into the weird events in Hidden Canyon that affected the Dunns. The sheriff's office had no report on the original assault on Brighton or the thrown rock and broken window. They had sketchy information about a dog being shot and the house fire, but tying the events together was proving impossible.

Brighton had taken on the financial management of the ore project. He had met often with Roy and Charley and had set up an LLC corporation, in which Brighton would be the president and Roy the secretary. They opened a bank account in the name of the LLC and deposited the first check from the sale of the ore. Rhonda had given them a bridge loan to pay for the Mole lease until the LLC could be recorded by the state corporation commission. It was decided that the LLC would issue shares of stock based on the amount of time and work each member had put into it. Brighton and Roy would each receive an extra 10 percent for starting the ball rolling. It had been a very productive week for the group.

Now that Brighton was back to work, he was enjoying the challenges of dentistry, but he was having headaches and occasional dizziness and, even worse, a very hard time concentrating. When he finally walked into the kitchen that night looking for his pregnant wife, what he found was a note telling him that dinner was in the oven and that she was at the Banks' house. He ate the pork chops and rice while watching the last half of a lame crime investigator TV show. When Gina still hadn't returned, he got his mountain bike out of the garage, ready to ride over to his neighbor's and find his wife. The golden sky to the west made him pause to enjoy the view. The giant saguaro cactus in his front yard looked green and fat. He had been tempted to water it but realized that it had survived over a hundred years without his help.

He and Gina had been in the house now for several weeks, and had yet to sit on the front porch together and watch the sun go down over the horizon. Between decorating the house, finishing the landscaping of the yard, organizing the mining enterprise, and getting bludgeoned, he had little time to enjoy the very thing that had been so important to them from the start.

His legs were stiff and his sense of balance was a tiny bit off, but he managed to make it down the driveway and around the street to the Banks' home. The steep incline of their driveway had been the biggest challenge. He parked his bike against a travertine pillar and rang the bell. He was let inside by one of Kara's daughters, who pointed him toward the living room.

Gina and Kara looked up at Brighton from a letter they were both holding. Both had red eyes, and Kara's makeup was smudged. Charley wasn't anywhere to be seen. Gina got up slowly and walked over to him, rubbing her tubby stomach, hoping the move would distract Brighton.

"Did you get the dinner I left for you, sweetheart?" Gina asked in a subdued voice.

"Yes, it was delicious. She fixed my favorite, pork chops and rice," Brighton said to Kara. "That was the first meal she ever cooked for me the night after we returned from our three-day honeymoon. I still love it. So what's up? Are you having contractions?" he asked with a look of concern.

The women looked at each other with questioning expressions. Then Kara nodded, and Gina handed the letter to Brighton. It was handwritten on a piece of expensive stationery with the calligraphic letters "A Z" at the top. The handwriting was neat and precise. Brighton sat down and read the note knowing he wasn't going to like what he was about to read.

Alma Ziegler's letter told how she had tracked the license plate number of the car the two missionaries had driven on a recent visit to her house. She stated that she now doubted that they were really missionaries, but they had seemed so nice that she had prayed that they would return to visit her as promised. She said she was lonely and afraid because two other people had come to her house at night and tried to break in. She said she had seen Gina's car at the grocery store and had followed it to the Hidden Canyon Gate. She told how she used to be happy until the tractors and backhoes had invaded her land and scared away most of her animal friends. Now she longed for a human friend and wanted to know if by any chance the two women would come to see her again. She finished her plea with a flowing signature and a neatly printed verse from the Bible, which Brighton recognized as the Golden Rule.

When he looked up from the page, Gina and Kara were looking at him, eager to see and hear his response. He was somewhat touched by the sincerity of the letter but still could vividly remember the pain in his leg when this woman had struck him with her walking stick. Also, she was still at the top of the list in his mind as his attacker in his office; if she could track a license plate, she could look up his office address. He had no idea what the whole missionary acting thing was all about, but decided not to give them the first degree here and now. He handed the letter back to Gina and shrugged his shoulders.

"I've got a bad headache. I'll be home waiting for you. Watch out for snakes," he said to Gina and then turned and left the room and the house. As he rode the bike home, he asked himself, "What next?"

16

DIGGING DEEPER

Dean Shutter walked backward up the sloping grade of his driveway. He kept close eye contact with the driver of the enormous dump truck, guiding him up the hill as they approached the pile of burned rubble. The driver was surprised when Dean encouraged him to maneuver around the pile and continue to a second pile, this one of clean rock and gravel. The driver wasn't told what he would be hauling; just that it had to go to Colorado Springs.

Dean signaled him to stop the truck about ten feet from the pile. A John Deere tractor with a front-end scoop sat idling twenty feet from the pile of pulverized rock. The truck driver's first glance gave him doubts that the tractor's scoop could reach high enough to load the rock into his big rig. He was used to dealing with large equipment. He released the air brakes, and a loud gush of air spewed out, kicking up a small cloud of dust.

Dean crawled up on the John Deere and began loading the rock into the truck. With each scoop-load, a new cloud of dust appeared and settled toward the truck's cab. The driver was content to sit tight with his windows closed and the air-conditioning running while he waited. It was after three-fourths of the rock pile was gone and the breeze changed the direction of the dust cloud that he spotted a strange-looking, yellow machine sitting behind the pile. He wasn't sure he had ever seen anything quite like it. He was about to climb down from the cab to have a closer look when the passenger door opened and a tall, muscular man in a T-shirt and Levis pulled himself into the cab.

"Good morning. I'm Roy. I've got the paperwork you need to get you into the plant in Colorado." He handed the driver a large manila envelope. Attached to it with a paperclip was a blue, typed check for the hauling charge. The printed name on the check was "Hidden Gravel LLC."

The driver took the envelope and shook Roy's hand. He turned again to get out of the truck, but Dean was standing on the running board of the driver's side, blocking his exit. The driver rolled down the window and was told that the truck was full.

"I need to pull a nylon screen over the load so it doesn't blow out. That's the federal regulation," the driver told Dean.

"Why don't you pull down onto the paved street where it is more level to put on your screen?" Roy suggested in what sounded more like an order than a request. "Make sure you call me, using the phone number on the envelope, when you drop off the load. We'll see you back here in two days, right?"

Dean and Roy stood behind the truck, watching as the driver negotiated his way back down to the street.

"I think he was getting too curious about the Mole," Roy said. "We have got to hide that thing better from now on, or the word will be out that we are doing something besides landscaping."

Dean laughed as he watched the driver climbing over the top of the loaded ore, spreading a green nylon mesh as he crawled. "These guys aren't entirely stupid. I'll bet he knows something unusual is up. After all, who disposes of their extra landfill six hundred miles away? So, how much do you think we just loaded onto the truck?"

"It was a little more than the first load. That's a bigger truck. I'll guess there are twenty-five tons there. The question is, are we really just trucking landfill, or is there good mineral content there? We knew what we sent last time because I had it assayed. This time it's a shot in the dark. Keep your fingers crossed and say 'rhodium' over and over," said Roy.

"Maybe we ought to consider having a backup. What if the guys we're sending the ore to find out what rookies we are and don't give us an accurate assay? Didn't you get an assay from a company here in Phoenix on the Dunns' property?" Dean asked.

"I got an assay and paid four hundred bucks for it, and the guy who did it was the sleazebag of all time. The assay they did, however, was dead-on with the Colorado results."

The men shook hands then went their separate ways. Roy was off to his job, and Dean had a meeting with the two idiots from the insurance company.

***

Again the two Hidden Canyon wives were in the car on the gravel road, driving toward Alma Ziegler's clapboard house. They had decided to get dressed for a casual lunch and then drop by the desert lady's home to ask if she would join them. They had told no one where they were going.

The clapboard house looked even older and more in need of paint and repair than the last time they were there. A thick layer of dust covered the windshield of the old Mustang in the rutted driveway. One of its tires appeared to be nearly flat. The milk-can mailbox was no longer sitting on the railroad tie but lay along the road in the bar pit.

Kara was driving her minivan since Gina had been so sick that morning she was afraid to drive. She also just had her new car washed, and didn't want Brighton asking how it had gotten so dusty.

"What do you think, should we just pull in the driveway or park out here?" Kara asked, stopping at the entrance to the property.

"We made it this far; we might as well go all the way."

Both women were staring ahead, trying to catch any movement or hint that it wasn't safe to proceed. Slowly Kara pulled the car forward, its tires crunching loudly on the gravel. The sun was glaring on the windshield, making their close scrutiny difficult. Just as Kara slid the gearshift lever into park, there was a loud tapping on the passenger window next to Gina's face.

"Kara!" Gina screamed, practically jumping out of her seat belt.

"Crap!" Kara yelled, startled as much by Gina's screaming as the sudden appearance of a face distorted against the window.

Alma had a big grin on her face as she stepped back from the door and waved for the women to get out of the car.

Gina tried to re-contort her facial muscles into a smile. She pressed the button and lowered the window.

"Hello," she said through the open window, feeling the blast of hot air as it rushed into the air-conditioned car.

"You are the women from the church, aren't you?" Alma asked in an almost childlike voice. "Won't you come in and we can have some tea?"

Gina and Kara, recovered from their state of shock, looked at each other. They nodded in vague agreement and without speaking, got out of the car. Alma led the way toward the house.

"Why do you have all these broken bottles around your house?" Gina asked. There were hundreds of broken glass soda and wine bottles scattered around the perimeter of the house in a wide sweeping circle ten to fifteen feet in width. They had obviously been placed there recently.

"I had a couple of people try to break into my house last week, so I put this glass here to warn me and to scare any possible thieves or vandals away. It's also keeping the old javalina boar from rooting around the side of the house. He's been working on a hole that is getting big enough to bury a fridge."

She opened the frame door and ushered the women into the familiar room. It felt much more hospitable now that they weren't lying to her and were not so uncertain about what they were doing.

Once they were inside and the door was closed, Alma's voice became less friendly as she asked them, "Did you get my letter? Of course you did or you wouldn't be here. You really aren't from any church, are you?"

"No, we're not from any church. We came to apologize to you about the last time we visited," Gina began. "I'm Gina Dunn, and this is Kara Banks. The last time we came, we were being nosey and unkind, and now we would beg you to forgive us and let us take you to lunch like you said in your letter."

"We feel terrible about how we acted last time," Kara added. "Please forgive us and let us take you to lunch. It would be fun, and we could get to know each other. We don't even know your name," she said, letting the little white lie sneak out.

Alma studied the faces of the two women as she let her emotions flow over her. She felt hurt and anger at the confirmation of her suspicions about the two, but she also felt a tiny sense of joy that these women were here and asking for redemption for their previous transgressions, whatever their previous motivation was. She held out her hand.

"I'm Alma Ziegler. Some of my old friends used to call me Azi. I've lived here by myself for the last fifteen years. Where do you come from?"

They stood in the living room and chatted for several minutes before the subject of lunch was raised again. While they were talking, Gina couldn't help but notice a rifle leaning against the wall by the small window. In the far corner of the dining room she saw the other gun—the shotgun she had seen the first time they were there.

"I don't know why I mentioned lunch," Azi said. "I don't have any clothes to wear that you would want to be seen with me in. Thank you for the invitation, but you go ahead to your luncheon, and I'll be just fine here."

It was impossible to read Alma's mind. The women couldn't tell if she was mad or sad or wanted to be coaxed a little. When they tried the latter, Alma started to get a bit surly and so they backed off and started to leave—just then Gina was prompted to inquire about Alma's land. "Do you ever have any livestock on the place here—you know, cows or sheep or pigs or chickens?"

"What you think this is? Old McDonald's farm?" Alma asked in a defensive tone.

"No, not at all; it just seems like a nice place to raise some animals."

"I had a goat once. It wandered down the road one day and into the yard. I felt sorry for it, so I got it a pan of water and pulled some wild grass and gave it some cabbage. We became pretty friendly, and I started putting a rope around its neck at night so it wouldn't run off. One morning I went out to feed it, and nothing was left but its head. The mountain lion couldn't pull the horns through the rope, so it chewed through the neck and dragged the whole body off into the desert. I found some of the bones a few weeks later out in the hills. I haven't had any animals for pets since."

Kara and Gina were too stunned to reply. They made their way to the door and said their goodbyes without any mention of future plans.

"Well, that was a stupid idea. No wonder she lives by herself in the desert. She is insane!" Gina exclaimed as they walked back toward the minivan. "I don't know why I didn't listen to Brighton. Not only did we admit to being liars, but we let her know exactly who we are and where we live. We'll be lucky if she doesn't burn both of our houses to the ground with us in them."

"Do you really believe she was the one who burned Dean's house down?" Kara asked in a doubting tone. "She doesn't seem that malicious. She just seems lonely and a little frightened by all the changes occurring."

Kara pulled her car out onto the gravel road then turned away from the shack, heading toward the highway.

"She is a certifiable nut case, Kara. That's what I think. I would not be at all surprised if she single-handedly did all the weird things that have occurred in the neighborhood these last few months, including both assaults on Brighton. We really should report her to the sheriff. Geez, Kara! The weirdo put a ring of broken glass around her whole house. That's got to be a first in Psychoville."

17

THE JET SET

Rhonda called Roy from the phone in her Citation IV private jet as it passed over crop circles twenty-five thousand feet below. The half-mile sprinkler lines watering the fields in western Oklahoma made pretty green pinwheels on the ground when seen from that altitude. Rhonda hated her forced travel as such, but did like to look out of the window of her private jet on those clear days crossing the country at five hundred miles an hour. She had just been in Nashville to work on her new Christmas album and was flying home to Hidden Canyon for a long weekend.

"Hi buddy," she said to Roy. "I left a message at your house, but Chad was the only one home to hear it. How are you doing?"

"I'm fine. You caught me at a good time. I'm on my mandatory thirty-minute break from the radar screen. How are you? Where are you, by the way? Your phone is hissing."

"It's the jet engines," Rhonda answered, raising the volume in her voice to compensate for the background noise. "We're somewhere over the Great Plains, heading for home. I should be landing at Falcon Field in about two hours. When do you get off work? I'd love to see you and have dinner together."

Roy was a little confused by the phone call and especially at her request for a date. For the last five days they had been missing each other's calls. Her housekeeper wouldn't give him any information. *And why was she landing at a noncommercial airport?*

"I will be off at six o'clock. I have two steaks thawed out. Why don't you come over to my place about seven, and then we won't have to deal with waiters and gawkers? Besides, Chad wants to see you," Roy said.

"That sounds great to me. I'm getting tired of restaurant food, and I'd love to give my favorite dog a big hug."

She had been under duress the last few weeks trying to get her ex-husband out of her life. She couldn't remember the last time they had had a conversation without it ending in a fight. Finally, she agreed to do a Christmas album and do it fast enough to release it by November. She would give him full ownership of the album, and in return he would sign the final release of all her other assets. He already had stashed away millions of her money. This would be icing on his cake.

For Rhonda it would be an answer to her prayers. The recording studio had been great and had made it easy for her to zip through a long list of non-copyrighted songs. Though she had always been a perfectionist when it came to her recording, she had accepted some mediocre selections on this album just to get it over with. She wanted to get back to Arizona and her new friends in Hidden Canyon. She also was burning with curiosity about their current backyard mining adventure and the state of Hidden Gravel LLC.

The grill was smoking on the back porch, and the steaks were soaking in Roy's secret rattlesnake sauce, a home-concocted barbeque sauce he made by the gallon and used on every kind of meat one could cook. The sauce had nothing to do with rattlesnakes, but he enjoyed making people wonder about it. And wonder they did, since he absolutely refused to give away the recipe and always had a few sets of real rattles lying on his bookshelves.

He was setting the plates on the table when the doorbell rang. His heart jumped in his chest, and little beads of anxious sweat emerged under the collar of his new golf shirt. He had finally convinced himself that tonight was going to be special. Either he solidified their romantic relationship now, tonight, or he worried that she would probably walk out of his life forever.

When Roy opened the door, what appeared to be an angel dressed in white stood before him. He had to blink to clear the brightness from his eyes. When his pupils had constricted enough to focus, he realized that not only was it Rhonda, but she was stepping through the doorway with both arms extended. She took Roy into her arms and held him like he had never been held before. Her head was pressed against his chest, and he had to use extra energy to breathe. His arms were around her as well, and gently he increased the pressure. One of his hands went to her neck and then to her cheek and then under her chin. Softly he lifted her head, and their eyes met. They stared at one another for several moments before they kissed. At first it was a mere brushing of their lips then a slight parting allowing the tips of their tongues to touch, followed by the real thing. Slowly they worked their way toward the couch where they collapsed, tangled together.

The rattlesnake sauce tasted wonderful to Rhonda, but it did sting her now tenderized lips. She and Roy ate their steaks and salads in relative silence. The sun had long since set, and the vague shadow of a new moon was stretching out across the desert.

"Why haven't you ever been married?" Rhonda asked. "You have all the qualities that every sane woman wants. How could you have escaped for so long?"

At first he didn't answer her, and then he reached across the table and took her hand. "I've never met anyone I believed was right for me."

Their conversation was interrupted by Chad's barking. The dog had been sleeping contentedly on his oversize denim pad but now faced the door with his lips retracted and the hair on his back sticking straight up. Even with all the various desert animals that frequented the areas around Roy's house, Chad very seldom acted this upset. The motions sensor on the back porch had turned the floodlights on, lighting most of the yard. Roy released Rhonda's hand and walked to the bay window to have a look.

"Chad never gets this excited about something in the yard unless he thinks he is going to get to eat it," Roy said. "We had a big bobcat walk along the top of the pool fence a few weeks ago, and all Chad did was watch it." He saw shadows moving across the yard and into the cover of the cluster of Palo Verde trees at the far corner of the property.

"Do you see anything out there?" Rhonda asked, slipping her arm around his narrow waist.

Roy rummaged through a utility closet and came out with the biggest handheld spotlight Rhonda had ever seen. "My guess is that there is a person out there, not an animal." He held the light in his left hand. His right hand was hanging to his side, out of her clear view. In it she saw what she imagined was a handgun.

Rhonda wasn't a wilting flower, but the reality that she could soon be in the middle of a gunfight sent a chill down her spine.

Roy asked Rhonda to stand behind a wall, out of view from the backyard. He walked directly to the back door, opening it less than a foot. Roy scanned the backyard with the bright beam and in seconds detected motion again near a cluster of Palo Verde trees. Suddenly, a human figure jerked up from the hiding place and dashed for the distant fence line. The baseball cap on the person's head flew off as the concrete and wrought iron fence was cleared. Even after entering the desert behind Roy's yard, the figure could still be seen clamoring over the rocks, ducking in and out around desert plants then scampering over the darkened horizon. At first Roy yelled at the disappearing figure, but then concentrated on keeping the light on it, trying to see anything identifiable.

Rhonda seemed very calm about the intrusion, but by the time he had locked the door and laid the giant light on the countertop, she was shaking and her eyes were full of tears.

"Were you going to use that if that man stopped running or came toward the house?" Rhonda asked with a quiver to her voice. She was staring at his right hand.

"You mean the wasp spray?" he asked, raising his hand to display a silver aerosol can with a cone-shaped nozzle. He set the Kirkland Wasp Control can on the countertop next to the light. "It will only reach out about twenty feet but will turn a coyote or lynx right around if they get a whiff. I grabbed the first thing I thought would chase something big away. "

Rhonda was staring at the spray can, wondering how she had let her mind convince her that Roy had a gun in his hand.

"Are you going to call the police?" Her voice hinted to Roy that she wasn't happy about talking to the police about what she was doing at his house. Rhonda had had far too much publicity over the years and didn't want to deal with another round of hanging her private life, heart, and soul out for the public to shred.

"I don't see any point in it unless you want me to," he answered, feeling good about their ability to communicate nonverbally. "Tomorrow I'll take Chad out there with me, and we'll see what we can find. For now I'd better get you safely home. You've had a long day."

***

The Hidden Gravel LLC partners were generally too busy with their own lives to spend much time on the mining project. Because the Mole was presently on Dean's property, he was the only one who had taken the time to fire it up. The results and subsequent yield from the second big truckload were still unknown. He had removed the base of earth under his entire original building pad, which went down eleven feet deep. The hole was refilled with fill dirt from a nearby orange grove development, then was compacted and leveled, ready for the new concrete floor to be poured. There were two additional very tall piles of native gravel awaiting the return of the previous assay, and then transport to Colorado if that second load proved to be valuable.

It was just before sunset when Dean started the powerful engine and manipulated its spinning jaws into the area where he wanted to dig his swimming pool. This area wouldn't have to be backfilled. The engine sound echoed off the rock walls of the nearby canyons. It was a Friday night, and most of the neighbors would be off to dinner for the evening at their summer homes in the mountains or at beach getaways in Southern California. Summers in Arizona were only for the desert dwellers that had to be there.

Dean ran the Mole for about fifteen minutes until he noticed a major change in the color of the water running off to the side of the machine. It started out chocolate brown, but as the Mole reached eighteen inches below the surface, the water took on a more grayish hue. Dean disengaged the drill teeth and pulled the throttle into idle and climbed down to examine the ore. It was in a pile about two feet high with small rivulets of water seeping out to the base. It was different from any of the ore they had dug out from under his house. The sunset's light was failing, so he scooped some of the ore into an old gallon paint can to study later. He climbed back on the seat and reengaged the drill clutch. Out came more of the gray material, and then, strangely, the chocolate water started to flow again. At this point, the depth gauge on the drill head read twenty-six inches.

Over the next three hours, he took the hole down to six feet, until he noticed the gas gauge showing near empty. Dean brought the engine speed back down to idle then shut it off. He retracted the jaws of the Mole and put them back down at ground level. Still curious about the gray water, he shined a flashlight into the hole. From about fifteen inches down to thirty-six inches, the color of the ground differed drastically.

Sticking out from the wall of the soil was what Dean almost certainly thought to be a long, white bone. He could make out the articulating joint, probably a knee joint, at the end of a femur. Dislodged from the side wall, it reflected the flashlight's glare. Around it the ground looked ghostly gray. He reached down to extract the bone, but it was just out of his reach, and he didn't want to jump down into the muddy hole. Dean stepped away from the dig and, picking up the paint can with the sample of the gray soil, he hurried toward his truck. He couldn't wait to have Brighton and Roy take a look at his find.

***

Brighton and Gina were at the new mega-movie theater watching a new Julia Roberts' flick. Brighton was getting irritated at the negative intonations about marriage and families. It seemed that Hollywood wanted America to be portrayed as one big happy singles' party. He was relieved when his office pager vibrated. In reality, if there was a dental emergency, patients could go to the nearest emergency room or wait until the next time the office was open. Nevertheless, Brighton liked to be available. "If you want to have a successful practice, keep your shoes shined, go to church on Sundays, and always be available," is what his old family dentist had told him when he was first starting his practice.

"Hello, this is Dr. Dunn," he said as he stood in the corridor.

"Brighton? It's Dean Shutter. I apologize for interrupting your evening, but I need to see you tonight. I called your house and just got your voicemail. Listen, I dug something up with the Mole and need you to take a look at it. I think it's a human bone. I tried to call Roy, but he must be at work. When will you be home?"

"I'm at a movie with Gina. Could we meet at your building site at ten thirty?" Brighton asked, knowing they would have to skip the ice cream on the way home. Gina's pregnancy cravings were requiring a large dish of rocky road every night.

"I'll see you then."

Gina insisted on knowing what the call was about and then insisted on staying with Brighton. When they arrived, Dean was down in the Mole hole, standing on the edge of a ladder covered with mud. He had set up a portable light. When he heard the footsteps and muffled conversation approaching the pit, he climbed the ladder and out of the hole.

"Hi Gina, Brighton, I'm glad I got a hold of you. Thanks for cutting your date short."

"No problem. What have you got?" Brighton asked, leaning over the edge of the pit and looking down into the lighted hole. There was mud everywhere, and he could feel his new loafers sinking into the goop.

"Climb down here and tell me what you think we've got."

Gina stood back a few feet to give them room and avoid the mud, but when Brighton gave out a loud whistle, she crowded toward the edge. Gently, Brighton extracted the bone from its loosened grave. The bone wasn't dry as he had expected but still had tiny fragments of slimy skin or tattered muscle attached to it. Brighton reached up to the ground level and laid the bone at the edge. Not commenting, he took a few steps down further into the hole and poked around the gray edges of the side wall with his finger. He had seen something shiny that had disappeared when he moved the bone. He couldn't tell if it had fallen or just been covered by the loose dirt.

"I think this gray color is ash from a fire. My guess is that whatever or whomever the bone came from was burned and then covered with dirt. Were the top few feet of ground hard dig?" Brighton asked Dean.

"Not hard or soft. There were some big rocks in the middle. Maybe the gravesite was covered with rocks to keep the varmints out. How old would you guess the bone is?"

"From his vast experience in forensic pathology, from watching *CSI* on TV that is, he should be able to pin it down to within centuries," Gina said, unable to resist the chance to lighten the mood.

The men had taken the bait. They looked at each other and then had a good laugh at themselves. One thing certain in the minds of all three as they stared at the bone and the wall was that this new finding, if made public, could destroy any chance they had of keeping their precious metal find a secret. The history of major archeological finds disrupting and halting construction sites throughout the world was legend.

"I don't consider myself a heartless SOB, but until we prove that this is a real gravesite, my inclination would be to keep digging," Brighton said. "Just to be safe, why don't we move the Mole east twenty feet and work this direction. That should give us another truckload of ore and, in the meantime, we can probe around here when the light is good and see what else we can find."

The men agreed to meet early Saturday morning. Brighton said he would get a hold of Charley and Roy to bring them up to date on the new discovery. Gina gave Dean a peck on the cheek as the three parted.

✳✳✳

The big surprise early Saturday morning wasn't that the team all showed up, but that they were so organized. Rhonda had made a run to Starbucks and had something for everyone to eat and drink. Dean had topped off the fuel tank and greased all the bearings of the Mole. Roy had his folder with the latest information from the refinery, and Charley had a binder with his research on the mining laws and how he thought the newly founded LLC would have to deal with the Hidden Canyon HOA. Brighton and Gina had spent two hours in the middle of the night searching the Internet for any history of Indian habitats in the area of Hidden Canyon and hadn't found anything of importance.

Once assembled, the group members found a place to sit in the shade of some mesquite trees. Dean explained what he had found. Each of them had already looked down into the hole and had their own opinion of what the apparent gravesite meant. They were across the spectrum with their ideas, from a recent murder to an ancient burial ground for the Anastazi Indians with leprosy. Rhonda surprised them all by saying it could have been the grave of a murdered prospector after he found the Lost Dutchman's gold mine.

During the last weeks, with all the events regarding finding the rhodium and platinum-rich ore, no one had ventured that it had anything to do with the Superstition Mountain legend of a gold treasure left there by the Indians, Mexicans, or the German prospector who died in Phoenix in the early 1900s. The words of his dying breath, given to his girlfriend and caregiver, was purported to be the secret location of a rich gold strike in the desert hills east of Phoenix, and that he had left a fortune of gold hidden somewhere among those hills. Most people who lived in the Phoenix area knew bits and pieces of the tale, but in spite of a great deal of searching and writing, no facts had ever surfaced.

Dean started to explain the story to Brighton and Gina, who hadn't heard of it, when Charley insisted they get back to the problems at hand. He needed to get his office. Even on a Saturday he had hours to bill.

Brighton caught the group up to date on the digging thus far, and then Roy broke the bad news. The assay report on the last load of ore, the one from the area of Dean's garage pad, had shown less than 60 percent of the amount of platinum group metals and 30 percent of the gold and silver had been found in the first load, the load that had come from Brighton's swimming pool. It was still worth a lot of money, certainly enough to dig and ship it to Colorado, but they were disappointed.

"Show me where the ore came out of the ground," Charley insisted.

They walked out of the shade and over to the edge of what would someday be the Shutters' swimming pool. Charley pointed out to the group how the fault line of the canyon shifted from behind the Dunns' house to across the Patels' backyard and into the middle of Rhonda's yard then took an abrupt turn through the Steiners' two yards, crossing the street and going straight toward the mountain. It didn't even come close to Dean's yard but went instead through the vacant lot across the street.

Charley mentioned for the first time that his minor in college was geology and that he had spent a summer working and studying at a mine in Montana. He made some suggestions about where to dig. It was concluded that they finish digging Dean's pool and ship the ore; it was still worth thousands of dollars even though its content of precious metals was less than the other sites. Next, they would move the machine back to Rhonda's and dig up her backyard, claiming a leaky waterline of some sort.

"We'll make up some sort of excuse if anyone gets too nosey," Rhonda suggested.

"Let's just move the Mole," Brighton said, not waiting for discussion or arguments. He didn't like the idea of them digging on the gravesite. "Let your swimming pool people finish here, and we'll ship what they dig out. Dean, would you refill this hole and let the pool excavation guys dig up the gravesite? If they say anything, then you can call the authorities and let them deal with it."

18

HOT AND HOTTER

The next two weeks went by with the kind of routine only a summer desert dweller could imagine. Construction workers throughout Hidden Canyon started their saws and tractors at early dawn trying to get a jump on the heat. Dean showed up each morning and started the Mole's engine as soon as the first noise from the house construction sites began. The rock around Brighton and Gina's yard was harder the deeper he dug, and the incline of the gullies and small hills at the back of the lot required skill to position the Mole. By nine o'clock, Dean would stop the digging and start backfilling each of the eight-foot-wide holes. Ten truckloads of ore were produced in those two weeks, and the word back from the mill was "higher content than the very first load received."

Charley had taken his wife and girls to Newport, California, to a rented beach house. Roy was working extra hours so he could get time off to fly to Nashville with Rhonda for the finishing touches of her Christmas album. She had caught a summer cold and insisted on staying home alone until she recovered her voice. Brighton and Gina had been gone for eight days to a family reunion in Park City, Utah, but had left the lights on in the backyard just in case Dean wanted to dig at night.

"How in the heck did I get stuck here in the summer doing the dirty work?" Dean asked himself out loud. Carlos, his Mexican helper, looked up from his shoveling as if worried that he had done something wrong. Dean sat on the green John Deere tractor drinking a warm Gatorade. He unclipped his cell phone from his wide leather belt and selected Sharron's number to call. It was temporarily quiet in the neighborhood, and he could hear the phone ringing on the other end. He hadn't seen his wife for days. She had been back and forth between her mom's and her sister's all summer, trying to avoid the heat as well as the rental house they were living in until the Hidden Canyon mansion could be completed.

Sharron's phone went to voicemail again. Dean had no sooner clipped his phone back onto his belt than it began to ring. "We've got trouble in River City," Charley's voice said. "My office just emailed me a copy of a complaint filed in the Maricopa County Court against Brighton Dunn for environmental damage and destruction of native habitat. The HOA got a copy and sent it on to my office. Are you still digging in his yard?"

"As we speak, I'm boiling my butt on a tractor loading your money into a truck. What do you want me to do?"

"It's probably best if you get the Mole out of their yard and hide it someplace. Have you refilled the dig holes?"

"I've got a couple to fill as soon as I can get the ore onto the truck. Do you have any idea who filed the complaint?"

"No idea at all, but we have lots of possibilities, starting with the Steiner brothers or the Patels," Charley said. "Try to get out of there today. It will take a day or two before the sheriff will send someone out there to check on it. See if you can get the landscape people to re-vegetate the yard before someone comes snooping around. It will be a lot better if the law doesn't find anything wrong when it gets there."

Crap, is this guy ever going to hang up? Dean thought. *I'm roasting in the sun, and he's yapping away thinking he's billing by the hour.*

"Listen, Charley, thanks for the heads-up. I'll do my best to take care of the problem. Right now I've got to get this truck loaded. Give me a call when you get back in town." Dean pressed the "Off" button and looked at Carlos.

"I'll bet your lawyers in Mexico talk only half as much as these American attorneys. I'll bet if there were twenty-five hours in a day, they could talk for twenty-six."

Carlos looked up from his work to listen to his employer. He didn't understand one word of what was said, but was certain he was in trouble for something. He put his head down and continued shoveling.

❊❊❊

Brighton and Gina were having the best vacation of their lives. Just escaping the Arizona heat had been good, and the resort atmosphere of the Park City area had been awesome. Gina's family had planned lots of activities, including river rafting, horseback riding, golf tournaments, and mountain biking.

"This place is amazing," Gina said. "Let's look into buying a condo."

"That would be great if we could afford one," Brighton said.

"What about the rhodium money?" Gina had asked as the two lie in bed watching the early morning sunrise. They could see a doe and her fawn feeding on the edge of an aspen grove. The hotel had the softest bed linens and the most comfortable mattress either of them had ever experienced. They were snuggled in together with a window open, letting a breeze into the room. It was just cool enough that neither of them wanted to stir out from under the down duvet.

"We can't factor that money into our lives yet. We don't know how much we're going to get out of it in the long run nor can we calculate the expenses that have been hidden so far."

Gina rolled into an upright position, kneeling and leaning over Brighton, her hair catching a glint of the reflected sunlight. Her pink satin nightgown fell away from her neck enough that Brighton became distracted from his train of thought.

"Let your imagination go, Brighton. We're going to be rich, rich, rich, and just think of all the fun we'll have." Gina giggled as she spoke. Her exuberance was contagious and arousing. Brighton gently pulled her down close enough to kiss her lips. When they separated, he reminded himself that half the fun of having anything was the anticipation of the thing.

"We can go looking today. Who knows, maybe putting a deposit down on something here would be a good hedge, just in case the Mole hole does pay big time. We might need a place to invest it in, rather than just blowing it all on curtains and shoes," he joked.

He had never seen her happier. Her pregnancy gave a new fullness to her face and body. There was a radiance he loved. He couldn't believe how lucky he was to have her to share his life.

✳✳✳

Kara was watching the same sunrise from the top of a hiking trail six hundred miles south of Park City and six hundred yards from

her house. She was in severe pain. The family had arrived home
from the beach the previous afternoon, hot and tired from sitting
in the car. She and the girls had unpacked the Suburban while
Charley made a quick trip to the office to check his inbox. When
he didn't come home for five hours, she had called him, and they
had had an argument that was irrelevant, but had ruined the
evening just the same. She had been unable to sleep, and had gotten dressed at the first hint of dawn and headed out for a walk.
Ruminating over her life with Charley and the girls and the ob-
session he had for his legal work made her adrenaline flow. She
climbed the rocky desert mountain trail faster and higher than
she was used to doing. The visible trail had disappeared, but she
kept climbing anyway.

She wasn't a hiker as a rule and didn't even have standard hiking boots. Suddenly her Keds deck shoes slipped on a crumbling
stone, and she fell backwards. Trying to stop her downhill skid,
she put both hands behind her, instantly scraping skin off her
palms. Using her feet to try to stop her descent, her left ankle
snagged on a rock outcropping, twisting it hard enough that it
tore the shoe off of her foot. The shoe tumbled twenty feet down
the hill and wedged itself between a rock and a cholla cactus. She
realized there was no way she could reach it. Her right foot
smashed into the trunk of a small tree, finally stopping her slide.

She cried out in surprise and pain, astonished at how quickly
gravity had yanked her to the ground. The cotton cargo shorts
had saved the skin on her bottom, but her thin halter top had
snagged on a brittle brush plant, pulling up the top and allowing
the rough rocky mountain to gouge a long, deep abrasion into
her back. She looked at the palms of her hands. They were both
oozing blood where skin had been torn away and tiny rocks had
become imbedded. She tried to brush away the dirt, rocks, pieces
of dried twigs, and cactus spines. The pain was unbearable.
Childbirth had been nothing compared to the pain she felt right
now. *How could it have happened so quickly?*

She looked around, trying to orient herself. She had been so
intent on climbing that she was much higher than she imagined.
In the glare of the rising sun, she could make out the tiny shack
where Alma Ziegler lived, but didn't see anyone on the dirt road
leading to Alma's. In the other direction, the rock outcroppings

blocked her view of Hidden Canyon and the city in the distance. Looking up, she saw the rocky ledge she had fallen from, which was surprisingly far above her current position. She tried to pull herself up enough to put weight on her right foot, not wanting her bare left foot to step on the rocks. Another volley of pain exploded in her brain as she realized she had sprained her right ankle. She sat back down and began to cry.

By the time she gained control of her rational thought, some of the bleeding had stopped, and the pains had decreased slightly. She reached into the Velcro-fastened pocket on the leg of her shorts for her cell phone, only to remember that her phone was still connected to the charger in the Suburban. She took the shoe off of her sprained right foot and loosened the laces. She slipped it onto her left foot. The shoe hurt her toes but was big enough to allow her to tighten the laces and drag herself to a standing position. Holding onto the jagged rocks and hopping on one foot, she maneuvered herself over a small ridge to a point where she could finally see the rooftops in part of Hidden Canyon. She tried yelling for help, but couldn't see a soul.

She pulled a broken branch away from a dead tree and hit it against a rock, breaking off the excess limbs and branches to make a crutch. She inched her way down the slope. Once she could see the rooftop of her own house, she gained a little confidence. Her throat was burning from yelling in the dry desert air, but it was her back and hands that hurt the most. Another wave of pain from the injured ankle hit her. She sat down on a rock, convinced she could go no further.

Looking out over the Hidden Canyon development, she could now see the rooftops of twenty or thirty houses. She could see the club home with the now active HOA office and the light poles of the community tennis courts. A shimmer of light came from the Olympic-size pool. "That water would feel great right now," she thought.

Then she saw the intruder.

Someone was crawling over the stone and wrought iron fence into Gina Dunn's backyard. Kara knew that Brighton and Gina were still in Park City; she had talked to Gina just yesterday. She watched a person of medium height wearing a baseball cap and black tennis shoes move behind a stone pillar. A second later,

Kara heard the delayed bark of a dog. Standing on his hind legs with his black-and-white face looking over the fence toward the Dunn house stood Harley, the Patels' enormous Great Dane.

The intruder froze in his tracks for a few seconds, then moved slowly toward the electric and phone line box at the edge of the house. The mystery person then pulled something from a hip pocket and began cutting wires; then smashed a rock through the utility door and disappeared.

Kara was watching and she wanted to kill. She had forgotten her pain and difficult circumstance for the moment. She had no way of notifying anyone of the intruder's presence and wasn't about to scream again. *The best thing I can do is to try to identify the person and hope they don't steal anything too valuable.* And then it struck her. *The mining information!* Brighton was in charge of keeping all the paperwork on the gold, platinum, and those other metals. *Was the intruder trying to steal the documents about the HOA gold?*

Kara wiped her bloody hands on her cargo shorts to get a better grip on the mesquite tree limb. Rivulets of sweat and blood trickled down her back into her waistband. The laceration on her back burned hot and deep. She tried to walk normally, but her ankle wouldn't bear any weight without sending pains up her leg. The sun was beating down on her now, and she started to feel dizzy. She found a flatter rock and sat down again. It was hopeless. The trail down was too steep, and if she fell again, she might end up wedged between rocks where no one would ever see her. She would just have to wait for help.

Kara had lost sight of the person in the Dunns' yard. Harley was still standing and looking in the direction of the house. Suddenly, there was the figure again. The back door to the patio was sliding open, and out walked the intruder with an armful of manila folders.

"Stupid, stupid, stupid!" she muttered out loud to herself. "No phone, no water, no binoculars, and terrible hiking shoes. No one knows where I am or when I should be home. I'm just plain stupid."

Finally, she couldn't take it anymore. With a tear from the pain and fear in her eyes, she forced herself to a stand and screamed at the top of her lungs, "I see you down there, you thief! I saw you break into the house! You're going to jail! Thief! Thief! Thief!" she screamed, surprising herself at the volume of her voice.

The intruder, almost reaching the back fence, turned toward the mountain to see the source of the verbal assault. Kara tried to clear the mist from her eyes to focus on the culprit below but still couldn't recognize the intruder, even with the sun shining directly on the person's face. What she could make out was the body language of intense anger. The figure turned and ran toward the gate at the far side of the Dunns' yard. Kara could now see the yard better and noticed the Mole sitting off in the corner. The two most recent drill holes hadn't been completely backfilled. The running figure glanced in her direction and disappeared.

Kara couldn't believe her eyes. One second, the figure was running toward the gate. The next second, there was nothing but a cloud of papers flying into the air. She watched, astonished, as a light breeze scattered them around the yard, and a small cloud of dust erupted from the shallow abyss. A muted yelp echoed up through the canyon toward Kara.

After a few moments, there was a motion in the hole. First came one hand and then another as the thief tried to get enough of a grip on the surrounding edge to pull out of the round trap. Luckily for the intruder, a small manzanita bush had been crushed by the Mole, and the edge of it hung down far enough for one to get a firm grasp. It took time, but the culprit finally squirmed out of the hole and headed back toward the side gate, stooped over and clutching at one leg. The idiot made no effort to retrieve the scattered papers, instead quickly fled around the corner of the house.

Kara again tried to walk on her swollen ankle and, in spite of the intense pain, slowly started her way down the mountain.

***

Dean had slept in late. After a Grand Slam cholesterol fix at the local Denny's, he headed out to Hidden Canyon. Sharron had shown up at the rented apartment the previous evening and they had gone out for sushi, which Dean could barely gag down but was assured how healthy it was. Sharron was gone when Dean awoke, leaving a note that her Mom had text messaged her, and needed her help immediately.

Dean parked his Humvee at his home's construction site. He did a quick walk-around to inspect the plumbing installation, and then climbed onto the tractor. When the little diesel engine made a loud clattering sound, he hoped all the neighbors were already awake. He drove the green machine to the Dunns' and pulled up the driveway, stopping automatically to open the double gate. "That's weird," he thought. He could have sworn he had closed the gates, yet they swung open on their hinges. He drove up into the yard and guided the front-end blade into the larger pile of fill dirt. Several loose papers were floating around the yard with the gusts of breeze. When they caught his eye, he shut off the engine to investigate. That's when he heard the desperate cries from the adjacent hill. Staring into the rising sun, he could make out the figure of a lone woman.

Kara's ankle was the size of a ripe cantaloupe and throbbed with each heartbeat. She had given up the idea of walking any further down the steep trail with its loose footing when she heard and saw the little tractor pull into the yard. Dean had heard her yells for help right away, and when he got close enough to recognize Kara, he pulled out his phone and called Charley.

***

"What the heck are you doing up here?" Charley demanded when he arrived a few minutes after Dean's call, quickly ascending the trail to meet Dean and Kara. Dean was lifting up the back of her shirt, rinsing the wound on her back with what was left of the bottle of water he had given her to drink.

"I'll explain everything when we get down," Kara answered, trying to suppress her sobs of relief as the two men made a cradle with their arms and started slipping and sliding their way down the steep trail.

"We've got to get to Gina's yard and gather up those papers!" Kara told the pair.

"Sweetheart, stop worrying about the Dunns' problems; right now we need to get you to a doctor."

"But they are the rhodium and gold records. You've got to gather them up and not let anyone see them," Kara insisted between moans. The pressure of the men's arms around her back had reopened the long laceration, leaving an occasional splatter of blood on the dusty trail.

Once the men made her comfortable in the backseat of the Banks' BMW, Charley made a call to a doctor friend, asking him to meet them at the hospital. Kara would not let them leave the neighborhood until every last one of the scattered papers was picked up and the Dunns' sliding back door had been secured and locked.

After hearing bits and pieces of Kara's story, Dean couldn't resist taking a look into the hole where the intruder had supposedly fallen. He could see where the walls of the hole had been disturbed by the person trying to climb out. At the bottom of the hole, under a thin layer of dirt and rock, he saw the corner of a piece of material. He found a long-handled swimming pool brush and fished a silver-and-blue baseball cap out of the hole. The hat was quite new, though dusty and soaked with sweat. The logo on the brim spelled out in large cursive writing: *RHONDA*. Smaller printed words across the back declared: "COUNTRY IS A STATE OF MIND." Dean dusted it off and threw it on the dash of his truck.

19

WHO DUNNIT?

Roy was ready to commit murder. By the time he heard Kara's story from Dean and had driven to the hospital emergency room to see just how bad off Kara really was, he had started to feel guilty for finding the ore. As Kara filled in the details of the morning's events, his guilt was slowly being replaced with anger. Whatever was wrong in the neighborhood had to be fixed.

Kara was admitted to the hospital for observation. She had refused any pain medication at first, but when the technician started scrubbing the cuts and laceration with a plastic bristle brush soaked in disinfectant soap, she had quickly changed her mind.

"Are you sure you couldn't tell if it was a man or not?" Roy asked in a calm, controlled voice, though he felt anything but calm. Patience was Roy's strong suit, but he was losing patience with Kara.

Charley had pulled Roy aside when he arrived at the hospital room and given him the rumpled handful of papers that were gathered up hastily from the Dunns' backyard. A quick glance had confirmed the worst of Roy's fears. They were the assay reports and other financial documents of the Hidden Gravel LLC's project, including the transportation and sale receipts.

Although Kara had injured herself sliding down the mountain, she was way better off than if she had been attacked. Roy's frustration was that she had seen the intruder and couldn't make any kind of identification. *How hard is it to tell a man from a woman?* Roy asked himself but hesitated to say any more, remembering his own backyard intruder whose sex still was unknown.

"I'll call Brighton and find out when he'll be home. If it's not today, I'll ask for permission to go back into his house to see what we can find. I don't think he will want the police snooping around his house. At least we can pick things up and make sure it's locked up securely," Charley said.

While Dean agreed with their plan of leaving, Roy felt more like staying and shaking Kara back into a state of alertness and making her recall more of the details. He was experiencing a flow of emotions totally foreign to him. Roy felt the need to comfort her some way but before the men could leave the room, Kara had rolled over on her side and was sound asleep.

***

"Show me the hat," Rhonda Tucker requested. "We design a different one for each concert. At least we can figure out when and where the culprit got the hat."

"You shouldn't worry about the hat. It has nothing to do with the break-in or the mining operation." Roy stood in the kitchen beside Rhonda's chair. He messaged the back of her neck gently, trying to soothe her nerves. Rhonda had been in the middle of her workout with her personal trainer when Roy knocked on her door.

The worried expression on his face was transplanted to Rhonda as he recalled the story of the climb, fall, and sustained injuries and then Kara's witnessing the break-in. His anger had dissipated only slightly on the drive back to Hidden Canyon. Now his main concern was to get over to the Dunns' house and check out the damage. Charley had spoken to Brighton from the hospital parking lot and had received permission for Roy to enter the Dunn's house. He felt uncomfortable, going through their personal things by himself and had thought of Rhonda. Perhaps he could get her to go with him to the house.

Rhonda excused herself to make a quick change of clothes. She asked Roy to advise the trainer that the session was over, so Roy found his way to the back of the house and into the mirror-lined workout room. The female personal trainer was in the middle of a long set of sit-ups on an inclined table; rather than disturb her, Roy watched and looked around the room. It was an incredible assemblage of apparatus and chrome weights. Three of the walls were floor-to-ceiling mirrors, while the fourth was a solid pane of glass looking out over the pool site and onto the desert and the rocky hills beyond. Roy tried to not stare at the trainer, but the mirrors made it nearly impossible to not see her no matter which direction he looked.

He walked over and stood flush against the window, staring out but not really looking for anything—just staring into space—when he suddenly sensed a motion in the backyard. Right there in front of him, less than two hundred feet away, was Otto Steiner. He was standing in a clump of small trees, leaning on the stone and wrought iron fence looking into Rhonda's backyard with a small pair of binoculars. The glasses were focused on the area where the master bathtub sat in a stained-glass rotunda. Roy couldn't believe his eyes. The idiot was window peeping in broad daylight.

Old Otto was still ogling the stained-glass window when Rhonda joined them, now dressed in jeans and a low-cut cotton top.

"Do either of you have a camera handy?" Roy asked, still staring at the peeper.

"Here," the trainer said, digging a small Nikon digital out of a backpack that hung on one of the large chrome hooks. Roy took the camera and zoomed in the lens on Otto, and clicked off five frames of the wishful voyeur. Roy then slipped out of a side door and circled around toward the back of the fence. He selected three apricot-sized round stones and, stepping away from the driveway wall, threw the stones in quick succession toward Otto. He couldn't see where they had landed, but he heard each of them hit something, followed by a loud cursing in German.

The two women in the house watched the whole thing develop, including seeing one of the rocks landing directly on the base of the binoculars and glancing over Otto's forehead. He jumped around a couple of times and then took off running as fast as his chunky legs and the terrain would let him.

"If we had been at my house, I probably would have gotten my pistol out and shot the old fool," Roy said when he returned.

"I'm glad you didn't ask for mine," Rhonda said, rising and walking through the huge kitchen to a nook where a desk and computer center had been built in. "You could have tried this." She opened a drawer and withdrew a pistol with an extended barrel. When Roy opened the cylinder, he noted that the gun was loaded.

"It was a gift from Clint Eastwood. Supposedly, it was one of the guns from one of his old spaghetti Westerns, *The Good, the Bad and the Ugly*. I don't even know if the thing works. Is it loaded?"

The woman never failed to amaze Roy.

Soon Roy and Rhonda were out the door on their way to the Dunns' house, where after a thorough search of Brighton's office and the rest of the rooms, they found everything in place except the open plastic file box that Brighton had obviously been using for the LLC records' storage. It sat empty with the lids flipped open. In less than ten minutes, they locked up the house and left.

✳✳✳

Brighton and Gina had just returned from a long hike down the mountain from the top of the Deer Valley ski lift to the shuttle stop at the base. They had ridden the free shuttle back to their hotel and had both collapsed on the bed, when Gina noticed the message light blinking on the phone.

After listening to an irritatingly long menu, Brighton finally heard the voice of an operator who explained how he could access his hotel voice mailbox.

"Phone me on my cell, and do it now!" said the recorded message from Charley Banks.

It took Brighton and Gina less than an hour to pack up and check out of the Hotel Park City. The anxiety of the moment made Gina start cramping, which prompted her to call her OB doctor in Phoenix. The triage nurse told her to drink a large glass of water and go to bed for twenty-four hours ... fat chance of that.

"That was a waste of time," Brighton said. "By the time we could check back into the hotel so you could lie down for an hour, we could be home and you could be lying in our own bed." By the time he and Gina had cleared security and boarded the Boeing 737, they were both having cramps. He thought about taking something to calm his shattered nerves, but he didn't even have a drink of water to wash down a pill. He took some deep breaths and imagined himself doing a difficult root canal. Soon he calmed down, his anxiety controlled.

***

Alma Ziegler was getting smarter every day. Yesterday, she had gone to the office of her old real estate attorney. She found his son there instead, anticipating another big sales contract to negotiate, after looking up her file. In the file was a faded Polaroid snapshot of his father and an attractive young blonde woman. The son remembered how surprised his father had been when the woman had paid for her land purchase with stacks of hundred dollar bills. The man had freed up extra time to spend with her.

Alma had left early that morning, having first gone to the bank to pick up a credit card for her savings account. Prior to that day, she had never owned any plastic banking cards. It had been years since she had opened the statements from the bank, electing to write the occasional check as needed for utilities and taxes and getting what little cash she needed by writing for extra when she bought groceries. When she picked up her card, she studied the paperwork and had to have the bank assistant explain the new statement's format to her. The lady explained to her that her credit limit was sixty thousand only because she was getting a card for the first time and that actually she was free to use the full amount of her balance as a debit card. The pen Alma was holding slid from her hand when the attendant circled her current balance of over four million dollars.

From the bank she had driven to a store in a new shopping mall. She hadn't even heard the name of the store before those women, supposedly from the church, came and offered to take her to lunch and shopping. The clerk at the Nordstrom's store couldn't have been nicer. Within an hour they had picked out several new outfits including a dress, skirts, blouses, shoes, and several casual pair of pants. They also found a new purse to go with all the ensembles, as her old macramé bag was falling apart. Next, the nice sales lady took her downstairs to the makeup department where a skinny woman who smelled like a combination of every perfume in the store taught Alma how to put on the newest trends in makeup. The beauty salon fit her in for a quick wash and trim. When Alma finally left the store, she wore a new slacks outfit, leaving the clothes she had worn to the shopping mall in the dressing room garbage can. Her hair and makeup were a definite improvement; however, her skin was still tanned leather, and her hair was still pretty long. Her hair color remained a scattering of course blonde strands slowly being nudged out by gray.

Mitchell Johnstone had met Alma in the lobby and walked her back to his mahogany-paneled office. His secretary brought in a tray with chilled bottles of water and crystal glasses. There was a small sterling ice bucket and a tiny crystal dish with quarter-size wedges of fresh lime. Mitchell helped her put the ice cubes in her glass, adding a piece of lime, and then poured the water from the condensation-beaded blue bottles. Water had never tasted so good to her. Her busy morning hadn't included stops for anything to drink, and it had been hot in her non-air-conditioned car.

"It's certainly a pleasure to finally meet you, Miss Ziegler. I remember my father speaking highly of the times he worked with you … buying a piece of desert property, wasn't it?"

She knew he was full of crap and had never heard of her until he saw her old file. She answered with a smile anyway.

"That's correct. It was nearly fifteen years ago. I bought a little piece of desert land far out in the east end of the valley. My parents were killed in an airplane crash, and I was quite helpless at the time. Your father was extremely kind and took care of all the details for me."

Her sophisticated, educated voice was far from what Mitchell had expected upon his first look at her. In spite of the clothes, her rough hands and broken fingernails confirmed his feeling that she was newly but not completely groomed. She did, however, have a hint of natural deep beauty under the wrinkled, copper-colored skin.

"That must have been a horrible time in your life," he said. "I still remember reading about that incident and thinking of how that must have been to have to pick up the pieces of your life afterward."

That's enough of this bull crap, she thought and just sat there looking at him. She was starting to have second thoughts about having chosen this jerk to carry out her game plan, but then realized that the polished two faces of this man would be just what she needed.

"Exactly how can those of us here at Johnstone and Son be of help?" he asked, spreading his hands as if offering the whole company to her.

"It's very simple, actually. I want to sue my neighbors for everything they have. I want their cars and their houses, and I especially want their land."

20

HOMEOWNERS' ASSOCIATION

Mark Cooperman had been the perfect choice for president of the Hidden Canyon HOA. He was a retired doctor who had spent his entire adult life working like a dog to provide for his family and patients. For years he had practiced his specialty and asked for only a reasonable reward for his ninety-hour work-weeks.

He had closed his office doors at the age of sixty, getting pennies on the dollar for his thirty-year-old practice. He and his wife, Janet, had sold their eight-thousand-square-foot home on the country club's sixteenth fairway and had bought the cheapest lot in Hidden Canyon. Dr. Cooperman, with the help of his sons and sons-in-law, had designed and built his home at a fraction of the costs of most of the homes in the Canyon and had moved in to live out the rest of his life in modest comfort and peacefulness.

It had taken only two months after the last touches were finished on the home before Mark had started to get antsy. The first sign his wife noticed was when he came back from a walk around the development, carrying a trash bag overflowing with debris. Next, he traded in his Audi V10 and bought a midsize pickup truck so he would have "room to haul things." She had no idea what the heck he needed to haul. He became buddies with Clyde, the security guard, and would even cover for him on his occasional days off.

During the second HOA meeting, Dr. Mark, as the neighbors had started calling him, saw that there really wasn't anyone who wanted the job all that badly, a job that Charley Banks was desperate to unload onto someone—anyone for that matter. The doctor agreed to be nominated.

He loved the need to get up in the morning. He loved checking on the swimming pool and ensuring that the lights of the tennis courts were turned off. He could hardly wait for the executive steering committee to meet each week to report and counsel on the affairs of the development. He really started to bond with the HOA job when weird events began to occur. Now, the stories were rolling in on a nearly daily basis: snakes and scorpions in the swimming pools, dead animals at the HOA meetings, paint taggers at the tennis courts, and garbage cans left on the street overnight. Dr. Mark was having so much fun dealing with all the challenges of his new job, that he had forgotten how much he missed the practice of medicine. Most of all, he was beginning to love the power of the bylaws of the Hidden Canyon Homeowners' Association. The bylaws made him feel like a king.

He got along wonderfully with Dean Shutter and even better with Charley Banks, even though he was an attorney and a bit on the arrogant side, but then Cooperman had his own ego to deal with too. He had to be careful talking to Charley though, because each time he did so, the HOA would receive another bill. Mark's wife loved the job he had taken on. For the first time in twenty years, her husband was working without complaining every day about how the insurance companies were stealing from the doctors and how little he was getting paid. At Hidden Canyon HOA, the president was being paid nothing.

When he picked up the crisp, heavy envelope with the gold-embossed logo and return address of Johnstone and Son Esq., Mark broke out in a fine, total-body sweat. He had always dreaded mail with an attorney's letterhead. He sat down at his desk in the HOA office and read through the two-page notice carefully.

Basically, the letter informed the members of the HOA that they were in violation of the original land-use laws of the Old West. They were obstructing the view of nature. They were destroying the habitat of the wildlife of the area. Some people had even killed animals indigenous to the desert—snakes, rabbits, and coyotes; the list of animals read like the index of a National Geographic magazine. Mark didn't realize that even half of the animals listed lived in the U.S. It stated that illegal digging was occurring, raising the dust level in the air, thus blocking out the ambient moon and starlight. Sound pollution exceeded any natural or prudent level. It stated that representatives of the Hidden Canyon had harassed the adjacent neighbors with upsetting visits and late-night intrusions, requiring violent force to keep them away. It mentioned possible destruction of ancient burial grounds. Its most startling revelation claimed the entire Hidden Canyon project was sitting on a valid subsurface mining claim that gave rightful ownership to the plaintiff.

Demands in the letter required that all construction come to an immediate halt and that any further extraction of rock or soil of any kind would be reported as theft, and criminal charges would be filed. It demanded finally that all the homes, driveways, pools, patios, unnatural landscaping, and enhancements be removed from the property. The letter also requested that the natural desert be restored to its original natural state at the landowner's expense. The plaintiff would hold the Hidden Canyon HOA responsible for the enactment of the requests, since the HOA had the legal right to fine homeowners for infringements of any codes, covenants, or restrictions. Should the collective homeowners decide to resist the requests, a formal lawsuit would follow. The only option to full compliance acceptable would be a single payment to the plaintiff in the amount of twenty million dollars. The letter asked for a response within thirty days.

Mark Cooperman rose from his small desk and walked to the window. He took a deep breath and said, "Maybe there is a life after retirement. This was going to be fun." He unsnapped the cell phone on his belt and speed-dialed the office of Fuller and Fuller.

***

"This is the stupidest thing I've ever read in my entire life," Charley said to his colleagues as they sat around the conference table nibbling at their breakfast. The casual daily get-together was a good sounding board for problems and ideas.

"The first question is, does the plaintiff really own the mineral rights to the land? If she ever filed a claim, is it still in force? Since the county granted building permits on the land to the Hidden Canyon developer, I would seriously doubt it. The title company records will make the truth evident," commented the junior member of the firm, Mr. Jack Fuller. He was two years out of law school and thought he knew it all, but he usually had to have his briefs revised by his secretary.

The other men and woman in the room all rolled their eyes and looked at Fuller with careful distain. He was a jerk, and in spite of their patience and subtle advice over the last two years, he hadn't changed a bit.

"I'm sure you have some special knowledge on the desert and mining laws, having grown up here in the desert," Charley said. "Maybe you would be interested in helping me out on this one?" No sooner had he uttered the words than he immediately regretted the invitation. The last time the young Fuller had helped him, they had lost in court on a technicality due to Fuller submitting a document that turned out to be a bogus reprint from the National Enquirer.

The more Charley thought about it, the more he favored a different approach. He needed to round up his troops and circle the wagons.

***

Rhonda Tucker's house was ablaze with lights. Cars lined the long, steep driveway, and the living room was filling with excited people. Charley had called the emergency meeting of the Hidden Gravel LLC. Rhonda had offered to host the get-together.

Brighton and Gina Dunn were the first to arrive. Gina helped Rhonda set up a table of snacks and fill a sterling silver punchbowl with lemon ginger ale. As they prepared for the guests, Rhonda filled Gina in on the last week's events and more of the details of her celebrity life.

"I have to do a couple of Christmas concerts to promote my new album and help the Salvation Army with its holiday drive. I also accepted an invitation to be part of the Rockets' annual Christmas extravaganza at Radio City Music Hall in New York. Maybe you'all could come to the concert. It'll be my Christmas treat to my new friends."

Brighton answered the door, showing the guests into the cavernous great room. The huge fireplace was unlit since it was still one hundred and four degrees outside, but a row of ocean-blue candles on holders of varying heights filled the firebox, giving a cozy atmosphere. The walls were covered with original art, including corral scenes by Howard Post and two large watercolor horses by Carl S. Dahl.

Roy arrived with a cardboard box full of papers. He spread out the disorganized documents on an oval glass-top table with a slab base of petrified giant redwood.

"Brighton, you'd better spend a few minutes and straighten out this mess."

Everyone went to the foyer when Kara and Charley made their entrance. Kara was on crutches, sporting a hot pink fiberglass cast on her fractured ankle. Her normally smooth, tan skin was covered with scrapes and bruises. Her smile, however, was radiant. She was sincerely touched by the group's outpouring of concern. Sharron Shutter had even shown up with her husband and was expressing concern over Kara's recent accident.

"Let me start with a short report on the finances of our LLC," Brighton began after everyone had served themselves and found a place to sit. Rhonda pulled a chair up alongside Roy and had taken his hand, making him feel uncomfortable in front of the others.

"Thus far, we have sent eight truckloads of ore to the processing mill in Colorado. There hasn't been any new digging now for almost a week, but the Mole is in position here at the back of Rhonda's lot, ready to start up again in the morning. We are digging a larger than normal swimming pool. Matter of fact, they might want to hold the next Olympics here." A round of laughter followed Brighton's joke. "The checks from the ore total about nine hundred and fifty thousand and change. We paid back the loan from Rhonda, and she has refused any interest on the loan." There was a subdued applause of gratitude from the seven members of the group.

"I hope we can keep on digging where the ore is the richest. The terrain extending from my yard into the Patels' backyard seems to be the best. Another option is to dig out further; Roy and I both agree that the vein with high concentrations of rhodium is probably just over my property line extending into the desert. There is another rich vein right in the middle of the Steiners' backyards." This produced a moan from Rhonda. "There are several clumps of Palo Verde trees there to obstruct the view of the area from the road. We could probably get a few good loads out of there in less than a day if all of us pitch in."

"What if somebody turns us into the county?" Rhonda asked.

"There really isn't any law against digging if we have the permission of the landowner," Roy replied.

"Who owns that desert land? I thought it was state of Arizona land. That's what you always told me since we started this project, Dean," Sharron said. There was more than a little frustration in her voice.

"I'm not sure who the real owner is, but if we file a claim on the mineral rights, we might be able to mine the subsurface ore and then replant the surface." It was Gina who spoke, adding a bit of guesswork.

Kara finally spoke up and volunteered that her husband speak on the subject. "Charley, tell them about the lawsuit."

Charley was trapped in an ethics dilemma he didn't know how to handle. Scriptures say that no man can serve two masters; Charley was beginning to wonder how he could even serve one.

He stood to speak. "There was a letter sent to the president of the HOA, Dr. Cooperman, which he in turn forwarded to my firm. The letter claims that the entire Hidden Canyon project is built on land that sits on top of an existing mining claim. The letter states that every house, driveway, and swimming pool must be removed so that the mining claim can be worked."

Dead silence fell on the group.

"Who owns the mining claim?" Roy asked Charley.

"Listen, I really shouldn't be even telling you any of this until it can be investigated and then presented to the entire HOA." Charley knew he was being dragged from the frying pan into the fire. "But let me go on."

"Do we know who sent the letter, and if so, does he really have the right to the minerals?" Brighton was on the edge of his chair and getting very red in the face.

"The answer is yes and no. My investigator is going to check into all that. In the meantime, we need to put level heads together and create a working plan."

"Let me venture a guess at who it is and how that party can be satisfied." Brighton spoke in a pseudo-British accent, more David Niven than Sherlock Holmes.

"My guess is a certain middle-aged woman who speaks softly and carries a big, fat walking stick. I would venture to guess that she doesn't want to take our homes away. She just wants to be a thorn in our sides and make us as miserable as she is. Maybe she wants some money too. Am I close, Charley? How much does she want?"

"As I already told you, we don't know all the details. As for the money, whoever it is would settle the alleged claim for a cool twenty million dollars."

"I'm no lawyer, but I'll bet it would take months if not years to reach an agreement that will affect us," Roy stated. "Matter of fact, I took an Introduction to Law class my senior year, and that claim sounds a lot like extortion."

"Let's just keep digging and banking the money," Rhonda suggested with lots of positive emotion. "I know that what we will earn will be more than you could ever earn on your regular jobs. It's a chance of a lifetime. What is the realistic worst that can happen anyway, a court order to stop digging? I vote we make hay while the sun shines."

Dean had been quiet thus far. He finally stood and began pacing around the room as he talked. "I agree with Ms. Tucker," Dean began. "I've sat out on the Mole for lots of hours now and find that, though it is doing a good job, it's pretty slow. I also have learned that the deeper we dig, the richer the ore appears. The material removed from my place was the least concentrated, but we took it all from a scraping of six or eight feet.

"What we need is a real mine shaft. We need a tunnel, and if we have a tunnel we don't have to cross property lines on the surface but can dig under them. Take the Patels' yard, for example. Starting in Brighton's yard, we could tunnel under the ground and follow the vein of rich ore for fifty or a hundred feet. It would require a different approach, and we would need to hire day laborers to do the work. I hire Mexican laborers all the time. They work hard, and if they get paid each day, they will be loyal to their employer. I also have all the equipment we need. I've got plenty of shovels and picks and wheelbarrows."

"How do we conceal the digging?" Gina asked.

"Maybe we need to hire a special security guard or rent some guard dogs," Kara suggested sincerely.

"No way am I going to have some strange attack dog wandering in my backyard, nor am I comfortable with a bunch of guards hanging out, expecting me to feed them and use my bathroom," Gina said with tears forming in her eyes.

Finally overcome by the silence, Roy said, "Gina, how about if the little group here gives you a birthday gift of a new pool house sitting on top of an underground racquetball court? We could have Dean here design and build it, and the Mole could dig the initial basement for the underground court. I knew a guy in Phoenix twenty years ago who built an underground court complete with men's and women's lockers and a snack bar. I'll bet he hauled out forty truckloads of rock and sand to build that underground court."

"I like that idea," Brighton said, surprising everyone. "We could build it right up to the property lines of the Patels' and to the desert boundary in the rear."

"The county will probably issue me a building permit, and the best thing is we won't have to backfill the hole. Property setbacks apply only to the surface," Dean added.

The idea started to sink in. Roy tore off a piece of Charley's yellow legal pad and sketched out a rough drawing and passed it around.

"Hey, how about if I wanted an underground basketball court?" said Rhonda with a smile. "I read about one at that basketball player Carl Malone's house that could host an entire NBA game. You know what I mean, a big deep hole in the ground where we all could exercise and become healthy ... healthy rich."

For the first time that evening, everyone laughed. And a couple of them rose from their seats and started nibbling again on the snacks Rhonda had spread out on a teak buffet table. They threw around more ideas and laughed some more.

Brighton pulled out his flip phone and punched in the calculator mode. He entered some numbers and then reported to the now chatty group, "If, and I mean if, the quality of the ore stays anywhere near what we've received and the price continues to hold, I estimate that one truckload out of the, let's say, forty truckloads of ore would more than pay for Rhonda's basketball court or my racquetball court with a couple of paddles and balls thrown in. The other thirty-nine loads will earn over ten million dollars. If we get going on the project, there won't be time for anyone's legal maneuverings to interfere. We just need to keep a tight lip and start immediately."

The hour was getting late, and all the men had work the following morning to attend to, but their spirits were too high for anyone to leave. Rhonda thawed out a couple of gourmet pizzas. The drinks were refreshed while deeper, more detailed plans were made. The party moved to the patio and pool area where they could look out on the desert landscaping and envision a deep, dark hole in the ground and forty trucks headed for Colorado.

✳✳✳

Roy thought he recognized the car as it made the turn in front of his house. The red Mustang with a white stripe down the hood was exactly like the one he had seen the blonde mineralogist woman driving. Lori, he remembered her name. He watched it pull into the next cul-de-sac and stop. The driver and a passenger got out. The two of them walked onto the empty lot next to Shutter's and looked around, pointing in different directions.

Roy quickly went into his house and grabbed his binoculars and took the side door out of the house. Standing at the corner of the house in the shade, he focused in on the couple. Clear as clear could be, there stood the Lori Pederson of Geological Associates. Roy turned the Nikon glasses toward the man and there, bigger and uglier than life, was Big Bill, big disgusting Bill, with his gut hanging over his belt buckle. Roy didn't have to ponder long to realize why the two of them were here in Hidden Canyon. Somehow, they had figured out the location where he had found the precious ore. After a few minutes, the pair got back into the car and slowly circled the project. Finally, they headed for the exit, and he could hear the guttural roar of the big V-8 as it accelerated away from the front gate.

Roy became conscious of his own hyperventilation. Just as Lori Pederson was physically stimulating, so was Big Bill physically intimidating because he was such a creep. Roy often thought of himself as a tough guy. The reality, however, was that in spite of his rugged Marlboro Man looks and his finely tuned body, Roy had never been in a real knock-'em-down fist-fight. He was more likely to talk them down—just like in the tower. The first question that popped into his mind was whether or not to tell the rest of the group about the suspicious visit. Would it make a difference in what they were planning? Probably not, he surmised. Best let it go un-discussed for now. He didn't want to add more paranoia to the already anxious group.

21

EXCAVATION

The backhoe that rolled into Rhonda's backyard was enormous. The articulated arm was at least as high as the top of her roofline, and the tracks it rolled on stood taller that the hood of her new truck. The driver had unloaded it off a huge flatbed trailer down on the street and drove it up the driveway, the metal tracks clattering as it climbed the gentle grade. He stopped it just short of the back gate before coming to the side door for further directions. Rhonda was in her full cowgirl get-up when she came to the door. She had a smile on her face as she greeted the tall, scruffy man.

"You look just like Dale Evans—you know, Roy Rogers' wife?" the driver said.

"I'm on my way to a photo shoot," Rhonda explained after introducing herself. "It's for the cover of a charity Christmas album."

"I was just joking about the Dale Evans thing. The guy who hired me gave me a heads-up about who you are and told me not to bother you, but I really do need to know where to dig this hole and where to pile the dirt. By the way, my wife is a fan of yours. I was hoping to get an autograph." The man spoke in soft, pleasant tones, suggesting a much higher education level than his present job indicated.

Rhonda blushed, looking into the hefty older man's green eyes. She stepped back away from the door, at first intending to let him into the house, but something about his eagerness stopped her. She held up her hand.

"Would you mind walking around to the back, and I'll meet you there? If I get these boots dusty, my photographer will kill me."

"Strange," she thought, her own word, "kill," relayed a tiny chill down her spine. Something about this guy was putting her into a defensive mood. She closed and locked the door behind him and went straight to the phone. Roy didn't answer. Next she tried Dean Shutter, but his phone went straight to his voicemail. She speed-dialed the Dunns and got Gina on the first ring.

"This is Rhonda Tucker. Honey, I hate to be a pest, but the big tractor is here to dig our racquetball court. You know what I'm talking about, right? Well, anyway, this guy says he needs me to show him where to dig, and after the other night I think I'm too nervous to go out there by myself. Is Brighton home, or could you come over and give me some moral support?" Rhonda asked. "I answered the door without thinking and probably ticked this guy off. He's big and creepy and has eyes that look like a guy who played a murderer in one of my movies."

Finally able to get in a word in over the obviously rattled Rhonda, Gina said, "Don't go out until I get there. I'll just grab my pepper spray and be right there. I'll knock four times so you will know it's me." Gina surprised herself at how clearly she was thinking.

When Gina pulled into the circular drive near Rhonda's front door, her hands were starting to shake. By the time she got to the door, she was feeling her heart pound so hard she needed to gasp occasionally to catch her breath. She knocked four times as planned, and the door opened immediately.

Rhonda closed the door behind Gina, locking it. The women embraced, holding each other momentarily. There, for the first time, Rhonda felt a bond that had been missing for most of her adult life. An unspoken sense that they and their friends and family were into something dangerous was beguiling. The lure of riches and the mystery of the unknown were unifying.

"Thank you so much for coming. I am not a paranoid woman, and heaven only knows how many times I have put myself in real danger. This is probably some cute kid's grandpa, but something about him set me off. I think he drove the digger around to the corner. I can't see either of them from the kitchen. Wow, honey, you're shivering! Are you okay?" Rhonda guided Gina to a chair and crouched down, holding her shaking hand.

"I was just about to eat a late breakfast, and by the time I got here my hands started shaking," Gina explained, taking deep breaths and trying in vain to get control.

There was a loud pounding at the back kitchen door that made both women jump.

"You stay here, and I'll tell him to wait or go away or something."

"Here, take this with you." Gina said, handing Rhonda a small silver aerosol canister. "It's pepper spray."

Rhonda took the canister and looked at it, shaking her head as she went around the corner to her study. "To hell with this toy; I'll get my gun," she said.

The man was pounding on the door again by the time she had taken her .32 caliber automatic out of the center drawer of her massive hickory desk. Walking toward the door, she tucked it into the waistband of her jeans, at the small of her back. She had packed the same gun in a couple of scenes in one of her movies, but it had real bullets in it now. Unlike the Buntline Special she had shown Roy, she had practiced firing this gun. The tractor man was pacing restlessly on the patio, looking at his watch when Rhonda opener the door.

"I'm so sorry to have kept you waiting. A friend came to the door, and she is pregnant and not feeling well. I've got to get back in there and help her. Those are the perimeter stakes, and the ground is painted as well. It needs to be fourteen feet deep. You can pile the dirt up against the wall on the driveway side, and someone will be here later to load it onto a truck."

"Why aren't we loading it straight into a truck as we dig it?" the man said in a tone that was vastly different from the one he had used at the front door.

"I think that there wasn't room for all the equipment at the same time," Rhonda said through a crack in the doorway. "Just do the best you can. I've got to go help my friend."

The man stared at the now-closed door. He walked toward the excavator and climbed up the yellow metal ladder and positioned himself inside the cab. A black poof of smoke shot out of the stovepipe-size exhaust stack, followed by a window-rattling roar from the engine. The excavator's metal tracks rotated, and the giant machine inched forward toward the orange stakes. Dust billowed out from the inverted jaw as it dug deep into the ground, and then, tilting upward, the shovel removed a huge bite from the ground, leaving a cavity big enough to hide a Volkswagen Beetle.

Rhonda peeled Gina an orange and toasted a cinnamon raisin bagel. They sat at the table visiting and wondering if the yard would fill up with ore before Dean arrived with his little green tractor and the transport trucks.

Later, having become used to the tractor noise in the back and the presence of the man outside, Gina had a surge of energy and bravery, so she fixed a big glass of ice water for the tractor driver.

He powered down the machine and opened the glass-frame door. "That looks great! Thanks for thinking of me. I sure would like to take an autograph of Rhonda home to my little daughter," he said after taking a big gulp of the cold water. "I must have said something to make her mad when I first got here. Would you mind asking her?"

"She is very nice, and I'm sure she will fix you up with a glossy picture or something. What is your daughter's name?" Gina asked, feeling more at ease, and beginning to think that Rhonda had been imagining a risk.

"Better yet, if she will do it for me, have her make it out to Bill and Lori."

Dean arrived soon afterward, leading a convoy of five trucks all lined up behind his front-loading John Deere. He had been surprised when Brighton was able to arrange for so many trucks at a time. Dean went right to work and, within a couple of hours, had loaded all five trucks and was starting on the second wave.

Later in the day, Dean took a break from the loading and came to the kitchen door. Gina had gone home and Rhonda was sitting at her grand piano's keyboard in the great room, trying to re-arrange a few lines of a song she had started writing. Dean's knock at the door nearly jolted her off her piano bench. Standing behind him was Big Bill, the excavator driver.

"This gentleman is done digging and mentioned that you might give him an autograph."

✳✳✳

It was nearly dark when Brighton and Roy showed up at Rhonda's house. Driving through the gate of Hidden Canyon within seconds of one another, they parked out on the street in front of Rhonda's then walked up the driveway together. The noise from the side and backyard was daunting. Two diesel tractor engines and three idling diesel truck engines broke the normal early evening silence. A big blue dump truck pulled down the drive and out onto the street, spilling a few fist-size rocks and a couple of shovels-full of loose dirt and rock as it turned the corner. Rhonda's sculptured paved driveway with its borders of newly planted flowers and low-stemmed ground lights had been run over in spots and was covered with a thick layer of dust.

Dean and the excavator driver were standing beside the huge yellow backhoe talking and exchanging handshakes when the new arrivals cleared the top of the hill. Before they could get very close, the driver of the backhoe had crawled into the cab and closed the door. The machine let out a grinding sound as he put it in gear and headed down the drive toward its trailer, parked up the street.

Dean was covered in dust and had a brown outline around his mouth where the dust and moisture from his mouth coalesced. He looked tired but had a smile on his face.

"We got the hole completely dug and sixteen truckloads of ore headed up the road toward Colorado. We have about three or four loads left to put on the trucks. I can't believe how lucky we were that you lined up all the equipment on such short notice," Dean said.

Roy was standing on the edge of the cavernous hole in the ground. "You didn't hit any hard dig?" he asked, studying the layers of strata and sediment in the dimming light.

"Like I said, we have had one lucky day. The excavator showed up at eight sharp, and by the time I arrived he already had a mountain of ore ready for me to load. He only had to stop for fuel. The ladies fed us sandwiches and drinks as we worked."

The men turned to see Rhonda and Gina walk up the driveway from the front. "Rhonda just took an autographed picture down to Bill," Gina said. "She was so nice to give it to him, especially after the way he frightened her this morning." Roy quizzed her about the incident, and was losing interest in the story until Rhonda made the comment.

"It was weird then, and it still feels a little weird that he wanted my signature to read 'To Lori and Bill, all my best on your new fortune.' When he first asked, he said it was for his wife or mother. He didn't want to tell me what his new fortune was, then he changed his mind and asked that it be made out to him and someone named Lori."

Roy turned to face the group with his mouth agape. "Did you say Bill and Lori? What did this guy look like?"

Gina answered, feeling that she needed to diffuse the apparent jealous anger Roy was verbalizing. "He was 6'2" or 6'3" with a big belly and a hard look to him."

"He tried to con his way into the house when he first arrived, but I made him wait outside until Gina could get here. Then he went straight to work and didn't cause any problems. He worked like a dog and wouldn't even stop long enough to eat lunch; he just wolfed down the sandwiches while he worked. He did a lot of talking on his cell phone. He was kind of weird when I gave him my picture. He said thanks for the 'windfall' instead of 'picture.' I didn't have a clue what he was talking about."

Roy sat down at on a patio chair and stared at the enormous hole in the singer's backyard.

"Did you recognize any of the truck drivers from the previous loads?" he quizzed the girls.

"I don't remember seeing any of the drivers before, and I didn't recognize any of these guys," said Gina. Rhonda nodded in agreement.

"Maybe we'd better call the trucking company and see where the trucks are right now," Brighton added. "How many truckloads of ore did you say they picked up?" he asked Dean, who was slumped in a patio chair almost asleep with fatigue.

"Sixteen trucks gone and two more to go. The sign-off sheets are in a stack over there by the air-conditioning compressor, under that bucket," Dean answered.

Brighton was calling the trucking company on his cell phone as he and Roy picked up the crumpled stack of yellow receipts. They were covered in dust, and some were wrinkled where sweaty hands had held them. Roy took them back to the patio table and counted them out one by one, smoothing and straightening them as he stacked them.

Brighton lifted the phone away from his ear. "The dispatcher says the trucks have all reported in and are strung out for six hundred miles along their way to the mill in Colorado Springs."

"Ask him how many trucks reported," Roy insisted.

Brighton gave Roy and the others an annoyed look but went ahead and asked the person on the other end of the phone.

"Are you sure about the number?" Brighton asked the man. "Thanks," he said and hung up.

"Let me guess," said Roy as he smoothed out the last of the yellow receipts. "He said that there were eighteen trucks total from his company. Am I right?"

Dean jumped out of the soft padded patio chair to join the circle of people gathered around the table. "How many did you get?"

"We are short two receipts, unless these guys still waiting to load have already added their paperwork. That's assuming you counted correctly," Roy answered, looking at Dean.

"I graduated in accounting, not construction. A long time ago I learned that if I wanted to make a profit building, I had to keep good records." His tone of voice was defensive but mostly exhausted. He pulled a pocket-sized spiral notebook out of his shirt pocket and leafed through the pages, finding what he wanted and laying it out on the table for the others to see. "I always keep a backup record."

Listed in the notebook were the names of drivers and the license plate numbers of the twenty separate truckloads. Gina looked over the shoulder of her husband and was the first to pick up on the problem. Two of the plate numbers started with a different prefix than the other twenty. When she pointed it out, Roy lost his composure and stomped away from the table.

"We've been had!" Roy yelled, walking out into the now pitch-dark yard.

"What is he talking about?" asked Rhonda.

"Someone has stolen two truckloads of our ore," Gina explained, exhibiting less than her unusual amount of patience with the singer. She had ignored her own needs all day long to spend most of the day with Rhonda and was tired and nauseated.

Roy rejoined the group and told of his experience with the people at Geological Associates and of having recently seen them in Hidden Canyon. He explained how they had nearly demanded the location of the original ore samples and how he had felt threatened. The final stab was when he told these people were named Lori and Bill.

"Oh my gosh! I signed the photo for him like he asked and then added, 'Thanks for all your hard work.' What an idiot I am," Rhonda said.

"No one did anything wrong," Roy said. "Dean kept good records, and I should have taken off work and been here so you ladies didn't have to meet the driver and trucks. We do, however, have a huge problem. If these two find out just how good the ore samples are, they are going to want more."

Brighton picked up the yellow papers from the table and addressed the group. "Well, there is nothing we can do about it tonight, and we all look beat. I vote that we all get some sleep. Tomorrow I'll check into the license plates on the trucks and try to trace their locations. Maybe we're overreacting. I'll call Charley and bring him up to date. The good news is that we sent out twenty truckloads of ore to the mill. That should be over three million dollars' worth."

There were subdued gasps from the rest of them and then some comforting hugs among the group. No one hugged Dean. He was already crawling onto the bright yellow seat of his green tractor. He still had to load the two idling trucks with the last of the excavation's ore.

22

COMPLICATIONS

Alma Ziegler was running out of patience. Getting back into the current system of modern society was only reinforcing the wisdom of her previous decision to drop out. She had been talked into buying a cell phone by the saleswoman at Nordstrom's. Alma thought her new phone was quite unique, until she was on the way to her car and saw a group of pre-teenage girls all carrying the same phone.

Once at home, the phone kept ringing an irritating tone, and she couldn't figure out how to change it. None of the calls were for her personally—who would even be interested in her? First it was a woman trying to sell her time-share condominiums, then a call to solicit a donation to Greenpeace. The call she really had wanted was the one from her attorney. She was naively expecting that her threat to the Hidden Canyon HOA would yield immediate results.

"Why haven't you called me?" Alma scolded her attorney after running out of patience and finally calling him herself. "Have you received any kind of a settlement offer? I remember that Dad sued a miner in Colorado once, and the guy showed up at the house with a bagful of hundred-dollar bills."

The attorney assured her that he had received a call from a Mr. Banks, verifying that the letter had been received. He didn't tell her that Charley had had a good laugh over the letter and had passed on the opinion of several of the HOA members that the whole idea of the thing was pure bull. He also didn't tell Alma that Mr. Banks had recommended that a psychiatric consult was indicated before wasting any more of either law firm's time.

"What am I supposed to do in the meantime?" Alma asked him. "I know they are digging big holes over there and hauling away my valuable minerals. I remember hearing about a thing called a restraining order. Can't you get one of those to at least stop them from digging until a judge makes them all move off my land?"

"I've been giving it considerable thought," said Mr. Johnstone. "I think it would be a good idea if you stay far away from the Hidden Canyon area for a couple of weeks. My wife recently was showing me a vacation cruise flyer that has a terrific late-booking bargain price. Have you ever been to the Caribbean, or how about the Mediterranean? My secretary could get you a suite on the ship and make all the flight reservations for you."

"What the heck are you trying to do? Get rid of me? Maybe someone could just push me overboard while I'm there, and you and your friends could split up my land and have it all to your-selves."

"No, no, no. I just think that if you were away from the area that the people there would have time to make a decision on the complaint. By the way, do you know a Dr. Brighton Dunn?" The question for Alma was followed by a long silence. "He claims you attacked him several months ago while he was standing on his property and that you may have come to his office, broken in, and attacked him, causing him severe injuries." The hair on the back of Alma's neck stood on end, and her pulse quickened on hearing the information. "I'm sure it wasn't you, but staying clear of the development is a wise idea," Johnstone continued.

"That is more pure javalina crap," she answered, not denying the charges.

"Why don't you seriously think about the cruise? By the time you get back I'll have some word for you about the land, and we can get the whole thing settled."

"I'll tell you what I will think about, Mr. Johnstone. That will be how I can bring charges at the Arizona Bar Association against you and your firm for incompetence and insult. If I haven't heard back from you within ten days, I will go to another attorney and to the State Bar. You seem to think that just because I don't be-long to your country club I'm stupid. I haven't lived on my own for all these years because I'm a wilting blossom." Alma hung up on him.

✳✳✳

Charley answered his door early on Sunday morning to the faces of three people he vaguely remembered, but to whom he couldn't place a name. He had been up late the night before with a sick daughter.

Standing on his doorstep was the unlikely team of Heinz Steiner, Otto Steiner, and Kashmir Patel.

"Good morning," Charley said, wiping sleep out of his eyes and having a moment of concern as to whether he had zipped up the fly of his cargo shorts in his rush to get dressed.

In his usual mixed-up context of idioms, Dr. Patel said, "We are being so sorry to bother you at an early time, Mr. Banks, but the three of us are concerning quite badly that a crazy something is placing itself in our neighborhood."

"We've been thinking that many trucks and diggers and wrecks and crazy things are going on here, and we want you to explain why we aren't been given no clues to all these crazy things," Otto Steiner added.

Heinz spoke much better English than Otto, but ever since the HOA meeting, he had carried a grudge against every neighbor except Rhonda, whom he was certain had secret lust for him.

"I'm not sure what exactly you men are talking about, but if you would like some time on the HOA agenda for next week, you should call Mark Cooperman and let him know. Or if you would like, I could drop him an email and let him know that you have some concerns."

By now Charley was reading their minds and needed to turn on his charm, in spite of trying to deal with a rising tide of stomach acid.

Dr. Patel said, "We have belief to reason that our friends here on our house circle are taking away something in trucks that is not in accordance with the law. We want to know if it is something dangerous like a nuclear poison, and if so we want to get rid of it also."

"My wife says its radar gas," interjected Otto.

"It is nothing like that, nothing you need to worry about, but why don't we get together tonight here at my place, and we can talk about it with all the neighbors here on Cactus Wren Circle?

I'll invite the other homeowners here, and we can discuss what we know. Would that be all right with the three of you?"

The three ex-patriots seemed unsure what to think about such a friendly offer but couldn't come up with any alternatives. Otto acted put off. He started to argue for an answer, but Heinz gave him an elbow in the belly to make him be quiet. The three then looked at each other and nodded their heads in agreement.

23

ONE BIG HAPPY FAMILY

That evening, decked out in their nicest evening dinner outfits, the Steiner brothers walked down their driveway and past the Tucker mansion toward the Dunns' house. They looked up ahead to see a new Mercedes Benz sedan slowly ease its way down the drive of the Patels' home and then take an immediate turn into the driveway of the Dunns. When Bavana Patel exited the car and approached the front door, her gold-thread-lined sari and her gemstone-covered fingers, neck, and ears sparkled like a Murano crystal chandelier. Kashmir was in an Armani pinstripe suit complete with a diamond tie tack and ruby-and-diamond pinky ring. The Steiners looked at each other's newly purchased Sears slacks and shirts then shrugged their shoulders.

Rhonda and Roy walked up the driveway together, holding hands and laughing. They had spent most of the day together hiking in the Superstition Mountains.

Having changed the meeting location after both daughters became ill that afternoon, Charley felt like a nursing student after caring all night and day for sick kids and a crippled wife. Now he was feeling like an ambulance driver. He brought Kara in their car. She was still on crutches and could never have made it up or down the steep driveway. He also had picked up the Shutters, trying to befriend the antisocial Sharron.

Roy had discussed their new plan with Dean, and though he had some doubts about it, he guessed that the only thing they had to lose was fifty million dollars.

Gina seemed excited about showing off her house and the new living room furniture; every light in the house was on when the guests arrived. Gina had trays of snacks placed on the granite counter in the kitchen and on the coffee table in the great room. Since the Dunns didn't drink alcohol, none was served. Most everyone chatted and became acquainted, especially with the three new families in the circle. Least conversant of the group was Sharron Shutter.

Eventually, the room started to quiet down, and the group began taking their places in the chairs and couches that were carefully arranged. Couples sat by one another, and Brighton stood at the head of the group and began speaking.

***

Alma Ziegler sat on a rock up the hill from the Dunns' back property line. She had spent the last several days and nights sneaking around the hills and observing the strange activities of the residents of Hidden Canyon.

She had watched gatherings of various groups of Hidden Canyon neighbors before, but this appeared different. "Maybe they are together to collect the money to pay me off? Or perhaps they were plotting to have me murdered," she thought.

Alma had pondered the impulsive action she had taken in hiring an attorney. She was still wavering over whether she should drop the suit or keep it going. She had already received an attorney's bill for twenty-five hundred dollars. "Would it be worth it to harass these people I have to live near? What will I really get out of it in the long run?" she wondered. She knew that the attorney would keep encouraging her to pursue the matter, just because that is what they do. She, however, had to live the rest of her life with the decision.

Alma got off of her rocky perch and worked her way carefully down the trail, taking the cutoff that led behind Rhonda Tucker's house. She crawled over the rock fence and started to cut through Rhonda's backyard. She was looking at the sparkling water in the newly finished pool and thinking about the lawsuit when she stepped off into space and fell into a deep hole she hadn't noticed. She screamed as she fell, but before her echo stopped reverberating off the canyon walls, she was out cold.

***

The Hidden Gravel LLC meeting officially started with Brighton inviting everyone to have a seat. Charley Banks handed a clipboard to Kashmir Patel. On it was a disclaimer.

> *The undersigned agrees to maintain absolute confidentiality of all things discussed at the meeting. The signee also agrees to hold harmless any activities and actions taken prior to this meeting by any of the residents of Cactus Wren Circle.*

"If you sign this you will shut up and listen closely. Then you will continue to shut up." Those of the original LLC had already signed alongside their names.

Kashmir scanned the page quickly and signed the page with a John Hancock flair, then handed the clipboard and pen to his wife and nodded toward the document, giving her a slight smile of consent. She signed the document after a momentary scanning and handed it back to Charley.

Next, the clipboard was handed to the Steiner brothers who sat hip to hip and read the two paragraphs over and over. They both looked around the room suspiciously, but finally Otto asked Kashmir if they could borrow his gold pen. They each signed the paper and passed the clipboard back to Charley. Heinz tried to pocket the pen, but it was too long to fit in his shirt pocket and fell on the travertine floor with a guilty thud.

"There is a line to sign for each of your wives as well," Charley said to the two brothers. "Since they are not here, and Arizona is a common property state, I am going to ask that you sign this for your wives; otherwise, we will need to meet again another night."

The others in the room knew immediately that what Charley asked wouldn't hold up in court, but they kept their silence. It would be in everyone's interest to abide by the agreement.

The Germans shrugged their shoulders in unison, reaching again for the all-important clipboard. Each signed the release paper for his respective wife.

Sharron Shutter had been asked to sign the paper earlier in a private meeting in Brighton's study. She had done so without argument or hesitation.

With the preliminaries out of the way, Brighton again stood in front of the group. "What I am going to tell you will be both surprising and exciting. Again, I remind you of the obligation you have to keep everything we talk about here secret."

He proceeded to tell the newcomers the story of Roy finding the sample of ore and having it evaluated by two independent companies and of having some of the ore sent to the mill and refined. He omitted the dollar amounts and the specific areas where the ore was harvested. He went on to tell the group that there was every reason to believe that there was a great deal more of the precious metals still to be found and removed, especially rhodium, platinum, and gold. The first two metals didn't raise much in the way of facial expressions, but the word "gold" had the same impact it had had on man for millenniums. The five neophytes to the group were sitting upright in their seats with mouths slightly agape.

"As you all know, we are all members of the Hidden Canyon HOA, and as such have many restrictions placed on us regarding our individual properties. There also are restrictions placed on us by the county and federal governments. We do, however, have some rights not mentioned in any of the deed restrictions or HOA rules and regulations. One is the right to make our own subordinate HOA in our own cul-de-sac of houses right here on Cactus Wren Circle. With such an organization, we could make some of our own rules. Roy has already filed a petition that will grant us mineral rights under the entire twenty acres of home lots and common area that is impacted by our little circle."

Roy stood and spoke. "By having access to the entire acreage through some of our individual lots, we think we can extract about twenty thousand tons of ore from the richest veins. This vein of metal runs through most of our lots and the common areas between them. All of the extracted ore would have to be replaced with fill dirt of similar appearance and the surfaces would need to be compacted and completely re-landscaped." Roy paused, looking at each of the group. "We think it will take about a year to complete the job."

Kashmir raised his hand like a grade-school child asking to get a drink, and when acknowledged, asked, "How many dollars will it cost each of us, and how do I know I am not about breaking up the law?"

"That is a very good question," Roy answered. "The upfront cost to each of us will be nothing since we will finance it with some of the funds from the original extraction. As we earn money from the ore, we will pay back those funds and the legal expenses to the original lenders."

"How much money we gunna get?" interrupted Otto Steiner, having lost patience with the legal mumbo jumbo he barely understood.

"A very conservative estimate is around ten million dollars," Brighton said, cutting his real estimate by half.

"I count seven individual owners of the houses in our circle. If I am correct, there are eight building sites," interjected Bavana Patel. They were the first words she had spoken since the meeting began. "I am not familiar with the other lot owners, but assuming eight owners, you are estimating approximately $1.25 million apiece?"

"Actually," Brighton said, "the estimate is for approximately ten million dollars per lot, give or take a few million."

There was a blanket of silence in the room that rolled over the group like fog. The ticking of the grandfather clock standing in the entry way sounded like the tolling of Big Ben.

Rhonda was the first to break the silence. "Who owns the eighth lot?" she asked.

Every head turned toward Dean. He stood up before he began speaking. He was eager to get some movement in his aching legs and stiff neck. His shoulder hurt the worst. He had done too much heavy work the last couple of weeks.

"The lot was originally sold to the Andersons, a retired couple from Bismarck, North Dakota," he said. "The man owned a big trucking company and was in the process of turning it over to his son. They were going to build a winter home here. Then the poor guy was diagnosed with pancreatic cancer. He died two months ago. I spoke with Mrs. Anderson today, and she is willing to sell the lot. She smells money and wants fifty thousand more than she paid for it. I told her there would be an offer coming in the morning. I suggest we buy it in the name of the LLC."

"Do you think we can afford it?" Heinz Steiner asked in a serious tone.

Everyone in the room looked at him as he broke into an ear-to-ear smile. His attempt at humor had succeeded. The room burst into laughter.

"Where I went to school, ten divided by seven would be an extra $1.25 million dollars, give or take a few hundred thousand," Kara added, sparking another round of laughter.

Details of the overall plan were discussed. The LLC would use the empty lot as a storage spot for the ore and fill dirt as it accumulated and was replaced. The empty lot would be the final digging sight.

Roy turned to the Steiner brothers. "Your backyards probably have the richest vein of ore the whole neighborhood. What we would like to do is start the excavation in your yard until we can close the transaction on the Anderson lot. Once Dean teaches me how to run the Mole, I can get started. I plan to take a two-week vacation to dig for gold."

"I'm going to be right there with you, sweetheart," Rhonda said, drawing a quick look from most of the room. "What? You guys think I can't swing a pick or throw a load of dirt with a shovel?"

The meeting broke up with everyone in agreement that the best plan was to dig and dig fast before anyone could stop them. It held to the old premise that, "It is much easier to obtain forgiveness than permission."

✳✳✳

Alma awoke in a fog of panic. She dragged herself into a sitting position and took inventory of her body parts. She could hear the voices of some of the party group at the Dunns' as they were apparently leaving, but she had no idea how long she had been in the hole and couldn't understand how it had been dug with her not knowing it. Her major joints seemed fine, but her head was throbbing, and her hands were scraped with small rocks imbedded under the skin. Putting both hands against the dirt wall, she staggered to a stance and tested her legs for walking. The tractor's path leading out of the hole was a steep incline with crumbled rock at its base. She stumbled and fell on her injured hands several times before she made it to the top of the hole and into Rhonda's remaining backyard. Eventually, she could see the outline of the abyss she had just walked out of. She figured she had fallen about fourteen feet. The only reason she wasn't more severely injured was that she had landed on plastic sheathing.

She could hear voices echoing through the otherwise still neighborhood. Alma could see the shimmer of starlight coming off the surface of the swimming pool. She was dirty, bloody, and now sweaty from the exertion of crawling to level ground. She walked to the pool's edge, pulled her shirt up and over her head, unbuttoned her jeans, and unlaced her new hiking boots. Kicking off the boots, she stood and dropped her jeans onto the pool deck.

Carefully she waded down the steps. She let her whole body sink into the cool water and sensed for the first time in what seemed like hours that she was going to be fine. The water felt so wonderful. She tried to remember the last time she had been swimming. She moved her arms and legs slowly back and forth through the water, rubbing her hands gently over her body and picking cactus spines from her knees and tiny rocks from their embedded sites in her palms and elbows.

She dove under the water then, breaking the surface, shook her head and ran her fingers through her hair and over her entire body. Popping up to the surface over and over, she felt clean and comfortable for the first time in days. The memories of swimming in her family's pool returned in vivid color. She could almost see the tall leafy trees and rolling green grass that stretched out between the family house and the pool.

Finally, cleansed and exhausted, she lay still in the water, leaning forward on the pool steps, and slowly kicked her legs.

The house lights came on without warning, the pool area suddenly brightly lit from the uncovered windows.

Alma swam to the edge nearest her shoes and clothes. She pulled them together in a wad and, holding them above the water level, swam to the deep end of the pool where, just a few feet away from the edge, a large double lounger with a canopy blocked any direct view from the house. She put the shoes and clothes on the deck and took one last plunge under the water, coming up by a love seat that was cut into the wall of the swimming pool. Like a snake slithering out of a hole, she emerged from the water and slinked over to the lounger, leaving a trail of water on the stone decking. She crawled up onto deep, soft cushion and pulled her clothes up off the deck. Holding her breath, she waited to find out what would come next.

Minutes passed, and one by one the lights in the house went out. By then she was feeling a blanket of fatigue envelop her body and then her brain. She leaned her weary head back against the soft fabric and fell fast asleep.

***

Hidden Canyon's new security people were doing a mediocre job of keeping the neighborhood safe and secure. The new HOA president held meetings to train the amateurish group of part-time guards, but getting them to understand that they had a serious responsibility was like pouring syrup into a small-mouth bottle.

Clyde, now the day-shift guy, had noted an increase in truck traffic in and out of the far end of the project. When Clyde asked Dean Shutter about it, Dean had assured him that things were as they should be.

"After all, Mr. Shutter is the original owner and developer and knows what is what," Clyde told Cooperman and the new security employees.

Dr. Cooperman had kept a log on the attacks and break-ins in the neighborhood and had noticed that a lot more problems occurred at the far end of the Canyon. He was already getting tired of the job of HOA Nazi, noting that some of his close friends were starting to avoid him. The latest call to security that had been immediately passed on to Cooperman gave him chill of fear. It was from a house on Cactus Wren Circle.

A workman, preparing to pour the concrete walls of Ms. Tucker's racquetball court, called on his cell phone reporting to Clyde of seeing something very weird. He claimed that just after dawn, as he had pulled his pickup truck into the side driveway of Ms. Tucker's mansion, his headlights shined into the backyard and startled a naked woman asleep on a chair by the pool. The workman was so shaken, thinking it was the movie star herself, that he had started to turn his head away but then couldn't resist looking.

He noted that when he woke up the woman, she jumped to her feet, mumbling and rubbing her eyes. She gathered up her clothes, stopping to pull on her boots, and then ran across to the far end of the yard, where she climbed over the metal fence and disappeared into the desert.

"You mean she had nothing on?" Clyde asked.

"Just hiking boots," the man said. "I swear she was like a ghost, a gray-headed ghost. One minute she was there, and the next minute she was over the fence and gone."

Dr. Cooperman waited for a couple of hours before going to Rhonda's backyard to investigate. He was too embarrassed to bother her, so he walked to the backyard with the pretense of talking to the construction guys. He nosed around a little and finally edged his way alongside the pool, keeping a lookout for Ms. Tucker. There on the lounge chair, plain as day, were streaks of dark red with a fly or two buzzing the area. He was certain it was blood. The pool edge also had diluted droplets of wine-colored liquid that had long since dried in the morning sun. He promised himself that he would tell Mr. Richards about it. Mark had picked up on the fact that Roy and Rhonda had become an item, and he was afraid to bother the diva herself.

✳✳✳

"Have you got two minutes?" Brighton asked Charley. He had wasted several of his own minutes waiting for Charley's secretary to put his call through.

"Shoot, but make it quick; I've got an appointment with my dentist. Just kidding," Charley answered with a laugh.

He had had a good morning: breakfast by the pool with Kara and the girls, a fast drive to the office in his Beemer, and four short appointments with clients who needed advice on a regular basis and paid their bills on their way out the door. To top it off, he had just scored two lower-section, mid-court season tickets for the upcoming Phoenix Suns season.

"What have you got?"

"Did you hear that Rhonda had some naked woman sleeping in her backyard last night?"

"It's just a rumor," Charley said, upset that he was being bothered again with the story. "Cooperman called me first thing and told me about it."

"I'll bet big bucks that the story is true and that it was our old friend, the desert witch," Brighton insisted.

Charley was still a bit aggravated when they said goodbye. He had been having such a great day before the call.

As the phone disconnected Brighton and Charley's lines, there was a third click at the desk outside Charley's office. Emily Ashworth was getting an earful of information that bit by bit and piece by piece she was beginning to fit together into a very interesting puzzle. She was a very smart girl and thought she was certainly wasting her time playing girl Friday to insecure men like Mr. Banks.

24

DIG IN

A large flatbed truck loaded with chain-link fencing arrived in front of the Patels' home on Monday morning. Two hours later the entire back perimeter of the property was surrounded with the fence. Dean drove the Mole out of Rhonda's yard and into the Patels' backyard. The slope of their yard was perfect for digging, and with the angle of the Mole just right, the hole deepened as the machine moved forward. Roy ran the Mole and Dean drove his tractor, moving the ore as it came out and loading it into the caravan of trucks.

Dr. Patel had gone to work, but Mrs. Patel and her sons were home and were soon running water, soft drinks, and sandwiches out to the two men. Harley came out of the house periodically to bark at everyone and to make puddles in the newly dug earth.

Roy noticed that there was a significant difference in the color of the ore as they dug deeper, especially as they neared the geographical fall line between the ridges of stone. It was taking about an hour to dig enough ore to fill one of the trucks. When the Mole had worked its way up to the back property line bordering on Alma Ziegler's property, Roy stopped and had a short conference with Dean.

"What do you think? Should we push our luck and dig under the fence for a few feet and then refill this part of it first?" Dean asked Roy while wiping the sweat and dirt off his face with a red bandana.

What he was proposing struck Roy as the same as driving a wheat thrasher into the next-door neighbor's field and taking a couple of swaths. Roy hadn't seen this side of Dean before, and it surprised him.

"I'd be more comfortable staying on this side of the fence. Who knows, maybe the ceiling of the tunnel could collapse and the fence could cave in. The desert lady over there hates us enough as it is. If she thought for even a second that we were on her property, she might just shoot all of us. You know, thinking about it, she would probably be within her rights to do so."

Dean took a long pull on his Pepsi, shrugged his shoulders, and restarted his engine. Roy studied the man, wondering what made the guy tick. He was wealthy in his own right but clearly wanted more. He had an attractive wife but couldn't keep her happy and at home. He had a house that had mysteriously burned to the ground, and yet in all the conversations Roy had had with Dean, the cause of the house fire had never been mentioned. "Oh, well, to each his own," he thought.

***

Kara and Gina sat out on the Banks' patio and listened to the whining and grinding and dumping going on just up the street.

"Thank goodness the breeze is blowing the dust out toward the desert," Gina commented. "I'll bet that even with the wind, my patio and the interior of my house is layered with dirt and dust."

"Layered with gold and platinum dust, you mean," Kara answered. "You could probably have the most valuable mop and dust rags in the country."

They both laughed and smiled at each other. They listened again in silence to the many motors and wondered where and how it might all end.

Perhaps it was more the adventure of the project that fueled the fire more than the hint of riches.

***

Alma Ziegler was listening to the same motors. She had just been visited by a strange man who not only had the nerve to cross her driveway full of broken glass and knock on the door just inches from where her rifle was leaning, but he had had the nerve to offer her cash money to buy her land.

The man had come to her house in a silver Cadillac, which most seasoned travelers would recognize immediately as an airport rental with its Florida license plate and a coded decal in its window. To Alma, the crested hood ornament meant wealth. Pulling up in front of the house, the man had been smart enough to honk the horn before getting out of the car. It was a good thing, since Alma had heard the gravel crunching under the tires and had retrieved her rifle, checking it to be sure she still had bullets in the chamber.

She thought to herself that she had developed her own shooting gallery and that the targets even came to her to get shot at. She laughed at her own joke. The emotion made her thirsty for a Dr. Pepper. She had been laughing a lot lately for no reason that she could figure. Since her fall into the pit and the narrow escape from detection a few nights ago, she had adopted an attitude of ambivalence and near foolhardiness. Still, she had her rifle handy and wouldn't hesitate to use it should this man threaten her.

"Are you Alma Ziegler?" he called, leaning out his window.

"What do you want?" she called out through the space between the glass and the window frame.

"I'm Albert Hicks, a friend of your attorney, Mr. Mitchell Johnstone. I need to talk to you about your land. It's very important. Could you spare a few minutes to talk to me?"

Alma stowed the rifle behind the kitchen door and opened the door for the stranger. Albert was an impressive-looking guy with neatly trimmed salt-and-pepper hair. He wore a blue-and-white flowered tropical shirt. His slacks were tailored, and his belt and shoes were of tanned alligator hide and he carried a leather briefcase.

"Thank you for taking the time to see me," he said, entering Alma's house. "I represent a group of men and women who are very concerned about the environment and want to save what little is still left for the future generations." The words made Alma smile.

"You can sit on that chair if you want to. I don't drink liquor, but I can offer you a Dr. Pepper," Alma said, feeling a bit uncomfortable at being in her house alone with a man, but quite interested in what he had to say. She felt an attraction to him that she tried to ignore; it was making her even more nervous than usual. She hadn't been alone in a house with a man since her college days. She went to the small kitchen and pulled a dusty bottle of soda from an open shelf. At the last moment, she noticed that there were mouse droppings beside it on the shelf, so she took it to the sink and rinsed it off. She dried it with a wadded paper towel that was already lying on the tiny counter and then took the drink to Mr. Hicks.

"How long have you lived here?" he asked.

"That's a story you don't need to hear. Why do you want to talk to me about my land?" she asked, surprising herself at the abruptness in her voice. "It isn't for sale, and it is already protected from the developers."

She went on for several minutes about the intrusion of others into her natural desert and how the dust and noise were getting worse each day. She just wanted to be left alone with her desert animal friends and the trees and cactus. When she finally took a breath and gave Hicks a chance to talk, he just stared at her, shaking his head from side to side.

"Why are you shaking your head?" she asked, surprised by this action. "You don't have to agree with me. You just have to understand that I'm not selling my land to anyone. Not to you or that developer in Hidden Canyon or to the federal government. Not to anyone. If you want my land, then come around in fifty years when I'm dead."

Hicks was listening and still shaking his head like a disagreeable teenager being told to clean his room. This made Alma even more nervous.

Hicks stood and walked to the dirt-streaked window. He pointed out at the broken glass surrounding her house and the piles of broken and discarded trash strewn around the side and back of the house.

"I didn't mention wanting to buy your property. I said that I represent people who want to protect the natural lands," he said, waving at the desert in front of him. "You obviously don't care anything about the desert or your property or the value of your neighbors' land. You live here like a desert pig. I can see clearly what a trash heap you have created outside. There's junk everywhere. My people want it changed. We are going to have your shack here condemned and scraped away along with all filth out there that you have accumulated in the burn barrel and the rusted tools and all that scrap lumber." He turned to face her and stabbing a finger toward her chest said, "If you don't sell, we are going to force you to pay to restore the desert to its original habitat and vegetation. And we will see that the courts fine you thousands of dollars and use it to clean up the surrounding area."

"You get out of my house, mister, and don't ever come back. If you don't get out, I'm going to shoot you," Alma said, rushing to retrieve her rifle.

Hicks took two steps toward her and slammed the door closed, nearly smashing her hand in the door jam. He gripped her by the arm, forcing her against the wall and shoving her face to within inches of his.

"Now Ms. Ziegler, you listen to me, and you listen well. Next Monday at 2:00 p.m. your attorney will have some papers for you to sign. If you don't do anything stupid like attack your neighbors again or shoot at their dogs or attempt to burn down their houses, and if you take a bath, comb your hair, and show up at the attorney's office on time, there will be a check waiting for you for one million dollars. The federal and state taxes will be calculated and will be prepaid for you. You will take the money and start looking for a new place to live—maybe best in another state. In fifteen days, this dump you call a house will be scraped into a pile of rubble and hauled away."

"You are hurting my arm, you bastard. I'm going to sue you and have you thrown in jail," Alma whimpered, trying to twist away from his grip, which he tightened even more.

"Let me add, Alma, that if you don't do exactly as I say, you can expect to awaken some night soon to the roaring sound of flames, and you can watch from your bed while this disgusting shanty burns to the ground with you in it."

"I thought you said you didn't want to buy my place. Now you have changed your story," she said trying to hold back tears.

"We're giving you a going-away present. You, in turn are giving your property back to someone who appreciates it for what it really is." Hicks released her arm, pushing her away from the door. He opened the bottle of soda and set in down. He took the rifle and with the barrel of the gun, intentionally tipped the bottle of Dr. Pepper over onto the floor where it shattered, spewing the fizzing brown liquid across the concrete. He then opened the front door and turning to the stunned Alma said, "Monday afternoon. Don't be late, and don't think for a second of mentioning our little interlude to anyone, not that anyone would even care."

Alma staggered to a chair and sat in a daze, listening to the crunch of the tires as the horrible man drove away. Her emotions were a spinning combination of fear, hate, and lust for revenge against the man and for her attorney who apparently sent the demonic man. *Why would Mr. Johnstone expose her to such a vile person?* Then, she turned her confused mind toward the neighbors in Hidden Canyon.

She needed a friend, not just an attorney with ulterior motives. Though she was still hurt by the deceptive and sacrilegious actions of the two Hidden Canyon women who had visited her a few weeks ago, she asked herself if there was anyone else who could or would possibly help her. Her mixed emotions of fear and anger, and a desire to retaliate against this Hicks, this carpetbagger of an evil man, forced her to make an unexpected decision.

✳✳✳

Charley couldn't believe his ears when Emily, walked into his office and announced that a tall, slender woman dressed in jeans and a "Rhonda for President" sweatshirt was in the foyer asking for an immediate conference. When Charley began to protest that he didn't accept walk-in clients anymore, Emily held up a hand, insisting that he stop talking.

"The woman has someone with her you know."

Charley walked toward the door only to be met face-to-face by his wife. Kara was in full motion on her crutches and didn't even look up as she, Rhonda Tucker, and Gina Dunn blew by, followed by a woman he had never seen before, but was sure he could identify by name.

Kara sat on a chair at the head of the conference table. The other women took her lead and seated themselves without invitation. Charley stood near the mahogany door and stared, unsure how to react. He slowly took a chair on the opposite end of the table from Kara.

"Hello Kara, Gina, Rhonda." He then turned his attention toward the fourth woman and smiled, feeling that he knew and disliked her already but still maintained the polite manners his mother had instilled in him. "Who might you be?" He extended his hand to shake hands, but the woman didn't react. She just looked at him with eyes like a caged panther watching the zoo patrons walk by.

"Charley, I would like you to meet Alma Ziegler," Kara began. "She lives alone in the desert about a mile from us. Actually, Alma owns the property that backs up to most of our houses. She is a fine lady and came to us this morning asking if we might be able to lend a hand with a neighborhood problem of sorts."

Charley again extended his hand, and this time Alma responded with a limp, clammy handshake and a subtle nod of her head. Her eyes didn't blink but continued to watch him. Beneath the unkempt hair, broken nails, and leather skin, he suspected there was a woman who had once been beautiful.

Kara explained how she and Gina were in their car on their way to Kara's physical therapy when they received an urgent call from Rhonda. They had turned around and gone back to see what was needed. Once at Ms. Tucker's house, they recognized Alma from their encounter at her house a few weeks prior.

This confirmed Charley's impression of the identity of the woman. This was the desert lady: the gray-haired witch, Brighton's assailant, the perpetrator of several of Hidden Canyon's crimes, assaults, and possibly arson attacks. What the heck was going on?

Rhonda rose and walked around to the back of Alma's chair and placed her hands on the woman's shoulders to help calm and reassure her. Rhonda began speaking in a slow and clear voice devoid of her usual Southern accent. "Alma, or Azi as she prefers to be called, has a very interesting and disturbing story to relate to you. She has, as well, a confession to make. She asked us to be here with her ... for moral support."

He had spoken to Roy and Brighton about it, and they concurred. Gina was to drive to Alma's house and pick up some overnight essentials. They were then to take Alma to the nearest Courtyard hotel and check her in under Kara's name. Emily, Charley's secretary, would come by later to check on her and take her food. Charley was in the process of setting up a meeting for the following morning with all the attorneys and the county sheriff. He would help Alma file a complaint against Hicks for assault and trespassing along with a lawsuit against Mr. Johnstone for breach of attorney-client confidentiality.

Charley and the other partners agreed to meet after dinner at Roy's for a brainstorming session. There was a great deal on the agenda. They needed to come up with a feasible plan that would get rid of the problem of Alma's newly filed lawsuit against the Hidden Canyon HOA. A big question on everyone's mind was: Who was the person harassing Azi about selling her land?

The priority became keeping the desert lady happy and convincing her to let them have access to the mineral rights she was claiming. Urgently needed was a plan. Getting access to the land that Alma rightfully owned would be a major windfall. It would be worth millions if they could get her permission to mine the barren land. Of course they would expect to restore it afterward to its perfect, previously natural state: coyotes, snakes, broken-down shack and all.

25

PLAN B

The Cactus Wren LLC's executive committee members were greeted at Roy's front door by the sparkling smile of Rhonda Tucker. She was wearing a simple pink cotton dress with a full skirt and a scooped neckline. After hugs, she led them into the family room where refreshments were waiting.

"Isn't it amazing that whenever a woman is present, a room seems to take on a healthier air, and food and drink appear out of nowhere like magic?" Dean said with a smile and a peck on the cheek of the superstar.

It took a while for the group to get their fill of snacks, visiting, and catching up. Then Roy handed Brighton the receipts from the digging that had been accomplished since the Patels and Steiners had thrown their hats in the ring.

"I counted twenty-five truckloads. We are making a copy of the driver's license of each of the trucks' drivers, and only the one company is sending trucks. We shouldn't lose any more loads," Roy said in disgust.

Brighton had been swamped for days at his office, trying to catch up from his injury and planned vacation. He hadn't been by the Patels' for three days. "How close are you to being done?" he asked.

"I would guess that we're about two-thirds done with the backyard. There may be some more on the side of the house that is retrievable. Their lot is by far the largest in the development. The ore we're pulling out of the arroyo is soft and digs fast, plus, it looks just like the high-grade stuff we got out of your yard. You know? The stuff that looks and smells like money," Roy said to Brighton with a grin.

Absent and uninvited from the meeting were the Patels and the Steiners. Kara, Gina, and Sharron all had begged off claiming other obligations. Charley was the last to arrive; having made sure that Alma was secure and well-hidden.

Charley took the lead and brought everyone up to speed. He felt that fighting the desert lady was a losing battle and that letting her in on the deal would save the group millions of dollars in lost time and legal fees. What kind of a real threat presented by the man who had assaulted Alma was anyone's guess.

"So what do you all want to do to settle this with psycho-woman?" Brighton asked, rubbing his aching knee.

"You know her best. What do you think of her personality and attitude?" Dean asked, directing his question to Rhonda. "Charley said you have spent some time with her."

"I really don't know her at all. I don't think anybody does. Kara said that Charley did some research on her a few weeks ago and found she has had a tragic background. Her family was all killed in a plane crash when she was here at ASU, and then the family fortune went up in smoke and legal fees. Apparently, she had enough to buy some land and to continue to pay the taxes on it, but other than that there isn't much she has done other than live out here like a recluse." Rhonda looked at Charley to confirm that her thirdhand review was accurate.

"Obviously I'm not a doctor, but having met the woman, I think she is depressed and lonely and maybe even a bit schizophrenic," Charley said. "We know that she can be violent, but I think she has a mature intelligence that can be reasoned with. Rhonda met her for the first time today and won her over with her good ol' girl routine."

A laugh sprang up from the group at Rhonda's expense, but she laughed along with them.

"If y'all are implying that it takes a crazy woman to know a crazy woman, then I'll have to agree with Charley: she is as nutty as a jar of Skippy. I also think she is scared to death of somebody killing her. Yeah, she beat up Brighton here, because to her he represented the devil. And yeah, she shot up some idiot insurance adjuster's car with them in it. Maybe you guys didn't hear about it; my friend at the Chevy dealership told me about that one. I think the insurance people were trying to blame Alma for burning down your house, Dean."

"Do I think she can be convinced that we can help her by becoming her partner? I doubt it, but I think it's worth a try,"

Charley chimed back in. "Hey, did y'all know that she has a Bachelor of Science degree in geology?" he asked, taking a long pull on his glass of Diet Mountain Dew.

"Don't expect me to say anything good about the freak," Brighton said. "Just think about it. Who shot the dog? Who killed the rabbit and threw it in the Patels' pool? Who threw the rock through my window? Who really did set your house on fire, Dean? The most important thing for me to know is: who beat the hell out of me in my office, leaving me to die? She puts up a good front, but if you ask me, I think she is a whole lot smarter and a hundred times crazier than we think. She needs to be locked up and have the key thrown away," Brighton paused. "But not until we have an agreement signed to mine her land."

His well-timed punch line brought the house down.

"You are so hormonal," joked Rhonda, getting up and passing a plate of vegetables with dip around the circle.

"And who spent the night in Rhonda's backyard, bleeding all over the patio furniture?" asked Roy. He was staring at Charley. Even Roy was getting emotional, and that was unheard of in this circle of friends.

"We have no proof, no witnesses, and not even a thread of circumstantial evidence," Charley began, using a courtroom voice with an edge of aggravation. "We might as well try to blame all of this crap on Santa Claus. The only thing we know for sure is that someone else out there knows what we have found, and they are willing to go to extremes to get it. Trust me on this one. She is scared to death. Sure she may be schizophrenic, but even they have enemies. This man who came to her house today is real, and he frightened a woman who has lived with rattlesnakes and mountain lions for twenty years. He is our enemy. I think Rhonda, Kara, and I can get her to sign on to our deal and dump the lawsuit. We need to find out who else knows about our rhodium."

"What about the people at the assay office, Roy? They had to have been the source of the leak about the original find. Is there any way we can follow up on them?" Dean asked.

"I can't just walk in there again and ask them what they are up to, but I suppose that we could invent a sting to find out how much they are involved."

"Don't even think about getting involved with them again," Charley insisted. He was standing again, pacing back and forth. "Maybe it's time to spend some of our hard-earned money on a professional investigator. There is a guy who works for my law firm who might be able to find out who the mystery man is."

The meeting melted down early. Charley made some minor assignments but left any additional decisions for a future date. Even Rhonda didn't linger at Roy's but left with the others.

***

Roy awoke early and decided to take Chad for a hike up the mountain. The air was clear with the sun just breaking over the horizon. Chad was in an unusually playful mood. He would run ahead of Roy then hide behind a rock and lie in wait before rushing out at the last second to bark and growl as Roy walked by. The game went on for several cycles until Chad was exhausted and came to lie by Roy's feet. Roy was pouring Chad a drink in a wide-mouthed cup when he scanned the horizon and spotted the curl of smoke. At first it was a small, white wisp twisting into the morning sky, much like a dust devil, but too white. Soon, a much blacker cloud blossomed high into the sky, thicker than any ordinary brush or trash fire.

"Chad, stay close to me and leave the poor rabbits alone!" Roy yelled as he stood and began jogging up a small knoll to get a better look at the source of the distant smoke. When he reached a spot where he could see the base of the smoke, he yanked his phone from his hip pocket and dialed 911.

"I'm hiking near Hidden Canyon and have spotted a large fire. I can't be sure whether it's a house or a downed airplane."

As Roy gave directions, there was a bright flash. A huge fireball at the base of the smoke plume was followed in less than two seconds by a bone-shaking explosion, which he felt as well as heard. He stopped in mid-conversation, letting the hand with his cell phone fall to his side. In all his years of living, he had never witnessed firsthand anything quite as spectacular or potentially dangerous. Chad lay at his feet, shaking and whimpering.

It took him a couple of minutes to hike to a better vantage point. From his new location, he could finally confirm what he had feared from the start. He could make out the denuded stripe of the county road and follow it where it snaked by the source of the smoke and what had been the old frame house belonging to the desert lady, Alma "Azi" Ziegler.

By noon the news helicopter had left, but the reporters' broadcast trucks were still cruising the area. Although Roy had called in the report of the fire to the 911 operator, it was the rural postman who called the sheriff's office in the mid-afternoon stating that Ms. Ziegler was in her house when it burned and blew up. "I have been telling that stubborn woman for years that her propane gas tank was too big and too close to her house. She told me to mind my own business."

The postman retold the details of the fire to anyone who would listen. Each time, his story changed just a bit. The deputy and the rural fire chief had both heard him tell a version of the story, insisting that the woman was in the house. Unfortunately, they heard it enough times that they believed it. It was late afternoon before the fire burned itself down enough that the investigators could get into the house. Once the incendiary experts had the opportunity to look for the woman, it became obvious. She wasn't there.

When the word got out that there wasn't a body in the house, someone asked the postman about her car. "It's always there behind the house. The thing hardly runs, so she doesn't go anywhere except to the grocery store."

When the deputies bothered looking for the car, they found that it wasn't burned up at all; it wasn't even on the property but abandoned a quarter mile farther down the dead end of the road with the keys still in the ignition. The mobile news teams, not having a cremated corpse to show off to their dinner-hour news addicts, had lowered their satellite dishes, packed up their cameras and were making dust clouds rolling away on the gravel road.

✳✳✳

Alma Ziegler was sitting straight up in a chair at the Courtyard hotel, watching the news flash that interrupted the rerun of *Green Acres*. She had tried to understand the reporter's story of an explosion in the desert but pressed the mute button on the remote control by mistake, and couldn't find the button to get the sound to come back on.

The TV news photos taken from the helicopter showed a blackened area of desert. Alma hoped they would get back to the comedy show before another commercial came on. The medication Ms. Tucker gave Alma the night before had really made her sleep well. She still felt really good—almost as good as she used to feel after those sorority parties at ASU.

The doorbell of the motel room rang, and when Alma answered, there stood Mr. and Mrs. Banks. The poor lady still had to use crutches to walk. Standing back in the hallway behind them was that pretty secretary, carrying several folders and a shopping bag full of clothes and toiletries.

"I didn't expect you until six o'clock," she said, standing in the doorway in a cotton nightgown that Kara had loaned her for the night. It didn't fit very well, drooping in front for lack of any body fat. She wore no make-up, of course, and hadn't even bothered to comb her waist-length gray hair, which was in snarls.

Charley started to turn away when Kara gripped his arm and nudged her way into the room dragging him with her. Emily followed carrying a stack of legal papers with her as well as her notary public stamp.

"Are you all right, Alma?" Kara asked.

"I'm fine, but I need to finish the show I'm watching. It's *Green Acres*. I used to watch it with Mom and Dad when I was in high school. Do you like it?"

"Alma, maybe you can watch the TV show later. Charley has some important business he needs to talk to you about. It's about your house. And we brought you some clothes."

Kara pulled a chair up beside Alma and put her arm around the woman. Alma almost jumped as though she had just realized that there were other people in the room. Charley stood in front of the TV for a moment, blocking her view, and then reached down and turned it off.

"Alma, listen to me. There was an explosion at your house this morning."

Alma stared at the blank TV for a minute then said, "I told you that that creepy little man was going to burn my house down."

Alma didn't look up. "He did it, didn't he?" Strangely, instead of expressing grief she acted somewhat smug as though her predicting the fire had made her important in their eyes.

"We don't know who or what caused the fire, but he is a good possibility," Charley went on. "There was a huge fire and an explosion. The firemen tried to put out the fire. It was really bad. For a while the police thought you were inside."

"I saw it on television," Alma said in a flat voice. "I thought it might be mine. Everything burned up, didn't it? Everything is gone, isn't it?"

It was Emily this time, with big tears cascading down her cheeks and her nose running as she knelt down in front of Alma and took both of her hands. "We are going to help you and take care of you. You can come and live with me in my guest bedroom until we find you a new house."

"He can't take my land away from me. I am going to shoot that man for burning down my house," Alma said in a flat voice as though it was on her to do list along with feeding the coyotes or putting the washed clothes on the line to dry.

"Come sit at the table. Charley needs to explain a way for us to help you," Kara said in a firm but kind voice.

Alma complied, listening closely to Mr. Banks and what he suggested be done. She asked some surprisingly astute questions and seemed satisfied with the answers. Somewhat out of the standard of usual practice, Charley had called Mitchell Johnstone, Alma's attorney, and brought him up to speed on the house explosion and the threat Alma had received from a Mr. Hicks. Once Johnstone admitted he had given Hicks Alma's address, Charley had no problem convincing Alma's old attorney to approve a change in counsel and fax a paper to that effect.

In addition to the other legal documents, Charley had drawn up the paperwork dismissing Alma's lawsuit against Hidden Canyon HOA and created an addendum to the limited partnership, including Alma in the group. She would own 30 percent of the subterranean mineral rights and would be a 5 percent partner in the LLC. With little more than a sigh, she took Charley's slender gold pen and signed away most of her land, apparently understanding that it was useless to her without the help of her new friends. Emily notarized the signatures. When Charley asked her if she needed some cash, she showed them her backpack and wallet containing two platinum credit cards and a wad of large bills.

"That man said he would burn up my house, so I had my backpack ready in the trunk of my car. The trunk has some garden tools too. Did he burn my car?" she asked with vague attitude of detachment. "I just want to stay here for a while and watch television. When you find that man, please tell me where he is so I can shoot him."

***

The three of them left the motel room and walked to the car in silence, each thinking about the strange hour they had spent in the presence of a woman who none of them could figure out.

"Wow! I think she is going to kill that Hicks guy," Emily said. "I'll bet you anything that the gun you saw at her house is in her backpack and that she is going to find the guy and shoot him. I probably would too. I can't believe that he burned down her house and maybe even believed that she was in it when he set it on fire. What do you think, Mrs. Banks? Is she going to kill him if she finds him?"

"She won't come up with a plan, and even if she does, she won't be able to carry it out," Kara said in a quiet voice.

"By the way, I thought you said you lived in a small apartment. What's all this about inviting her to come and live with you and taking care of her?" Charley asked Emily in a teasing voice.

"I've been looking for a bigger place to live, and think I've found one. Don't forget that I was the one who did the research on her assets. I know she can afford to pay for a place to live and for someone to help her try to get her life back in order."

"I'm starting to agree with Roy and Gina," Kara interjected. "I think she is flat-out nuts. She doesn't need a roommate; she needs a room in a psychiatric hospital."

26

PARANOIA

The Mole was louder than normal, working its way through an unusually dense vein of granite. The smoke and dust that the diamond bits were kicking up were as thick as an Arizona dust storm. Even with the car windows closed and the air-conditioning on high, Brighton could hear the grinding. He had arrived home early from work and changed into jeans and hiking boots; then walked next door to the Patels' yard to lend a hand with the excavation. Roy and Dean were covered from head to toe with a thick layer of dust. Both were wearing respirator masks to protect their lungs. When they shut down the Mole's engine and removed the masks, their pink noses and mouths appeared surrounded by a circle of gray. As the throbbing sound of the motor came to a stop, a layer of stillness settled over the neighborhood, and the clouds of dust slowly drifted away in the evening breeze.

"How is it going?" Brighton asked.

"We've had a great day. This machine is the sweetest thing I've ever worked with," Roy answered. "All it needs is gasoline and a solid surface to grind on, and it's happy. We were so lucky that you found this baby."

"In spite of our getting a late start, we've sent sixteen trucks full of good-looking ore up the highway to Colorado. I think we've about dug as much as we can here. Maybe we can get another one or two truckloads, and then we'll have to move the Mole to a new spot. What is the story with the desert lady?" Dean asked Brighton.

"Charley and Kara worked magic on her. As of four o'clock she is our partner on about 140 acres of that land," Brighton said, pointing over the Patels' back wall toward the desert. High fives were shared by the three men.

"She also has dropped the lawsuit against us and hired Charley as her new attorney. He and Kara have found a place to hide her for a couple of weeks."

"That's a huge relief. Has anyone heard anything about the fire from the sheriff's office or the rural fire people?" Dean asked.

"The way you described the fire, Roy, it had to have been set by someone. Maybe the mystery man did it, or maybe she set it herself, and it just smoldered for twenty-four hours before it blew. She's certainly nutty enough," Brighton said. There was no way she would ever win his trust in anything she did or didn't do.

"So far, there is no news from the sheriff or fire forensics people that I've heard. Charley is positive that she didn't do it herself," Roy said. "One thing is for sure, we have got to have our antenna up for anything unusual around here."

"I spoke to Clyde and warned him to raise his level of suspicion with everyone who drives through the gate," Dean said.

The men heard the solid sound of an expensive car door slam shut and looked up to see Kashmir Patel walking toward them. His highly-polished shoes were getting duller with each step he took toward the men. Roy took one look and shook his head in friendly disbelief. Patel was a dandy. He liked to wear his wealth on his sleeve, just the opposite of the way Roy had been raised. The diamond-studded Rolex, the mother-of-pearl cufflinks, and the ruby-and-diamond-encrusted tie tack, not to mention the pinky ring, would collectively appraise higher than Roy's net worth.

"Good evening," Dr. Patel said as he nodded to each of the three individually and offered a gentle handshake. "I must explain to you three gentleman that there is a situation that is not good. My wife, Mrs. Patel, is going insane because of the constant digging, digging, digging. It was her day off from her work today, thus she was here, as you know. Is it to be soon when you will have extracted all the valuable earth and can take this giant ground squirrel to another place?"

This brought smiles and a collective laugh from all four men.

"Bavana—that is my wife's name—rang me up seven times today insisting I make you stop the digging. Also, Doctor Dunn, she has received telephone calls from her friends saying that a house residing close to our area was started on fire by an arsonist. They told her it was on the television. That would make two houses burning into the ground in our very neighborhood.

Bavana is very frightened that our house too will be set on fire by some pyromaniac. Can you help me?"

Brighton explained to Patel that the work on his lot was almost done and that the fire had nothing to do with the Hidden Canyon neighborhood. Patel stood patiently listening and nodding his head in agreement, but all three of the men doubted that he understood completely or that he believed them—"and why should he?" Roy thought. "It was a damn lie."

Roy, more than any of the other men, knew that what he had witnessed that morning could happen to any of their homes at any time. Until the Mr. Hicks, if that was his real name, was found and dealt with permanently, no one could count on being safe. Even then there was the risk that the sweet smell of money under the ground would draw other unwanted flies.

"Why don't you take your wife and boys out to a nice dinner tonight? The digging will be done when you return home. Make it a long dinner," Brighton told Dr. Patel, giving his most reassuring smile. "Save the bill, and the LLC will reimburse you."

***

Later that night, after a long soak in his hot tub followed by a cold plunge in the pool, Roy had dressed and straightened his great room. Rhonda had let herself in, juggling two plastic bags and a two-liter bottle of sparkling cider. She had come by the Patels' yard in the early afternoon to drop off a supply of cold water and sodas and to tell the men about the surprise visit from the desert lady. She had hinted to Roy not to fix any supper that evening, but to wait for her instead.

The spread of tossed salads, coconut shrimp, and hot, juicy steaks from Outback Steakhouse immediately filled the room with savory aromas. Roy helped her with the plates and silverware and then pulled out her chair. As she took her seat, Roy leaned down and gave her a kiss on her neck. Her hair smelled so good that it was all he could do to refocus his attention on the meal.

"Thanks so much for bringing everything. I probably would have settled for a bowl of Frosted Flakes and an apple. This looks great, and so do you," Roy said with a cheery voice and a big smile.

They caught up on the busy day's events. Rhonda hadn't re-turned to town until late the night before, having been in Los Angeles to meet with her tax attorney and to do a photo shoot for a new Corvette commercial. In spite of her saying that she was taking a leave of absence from the entertainment world, she still had a hard time saying no to offers that were fun and lucrative and kept her name out there in front of the public.

She had been paid big bucks for the half-day commercial shoot, plus as a bonus the regional manager of G.M. had offered her the use of a new truck or car for a year as part of the deal. She was excited about it, mainly because she had decided to give the truck to Roy as a surprise. His truck had seen better days.

After the meal was finished and the dishes cleared, they settled down together on the deep leather couch. Rhonda brought out an envelope with a thank you card and a picture of a red Chevy 4x4 truck.

"What's this all about?" Roy asked, somewhat embarrassed.

"I just want you to know how much I appreciate your being my friend. I moved here to be able to get my feet back on the ground and refocus on the real people of the world and write a few songs. Since the first day I met you, you have been sincere and helpful without asking for anything in return, and I truly ad-mire and appreciate you for it," she said, looking into his eyes then down at the ground. "As for the truck, heck, I couldn't re-fuse the guy when he offered it to me, and I sure don't need two of them. My Bentley is sitting in the garage gathering dust as it is. I just want you to use the truck for the year." She looked back up at him and continued, "A year from now, who knows where we'll be or what paths our lives will have taken." She leaned over and took his cheeks between her hands and kissed him.

✳✳✳

Brighton and Gina went to bed late. Gina had experienced more nausea than usual after the ordeal of the fire and the trip to the attorney's with Kara and Rhonda. Though she couldn't stand the Ziegler woman, and was certain she was mentally unstable, she still couldn't help but feel sorry for her awful loss. Gina lay on Brighton's arm, curled against his side until she relaxed enough to finally fall asleep. Gently, Brighton slid his arm from under her head and tried to get comfortable himself, but sleep wouldn't come.

Here he was in his dream house, lying next to a dreamingly beautiful pregnant woman, having spent the day working at a job he loved and had dreamed about for the last ten years, yet his life contained a nightmare. The yellow Mole that was sitting just over the neighbor's the fence was supposedly earning him thousands of dollars a day, but he knew that the entire operation was on the thin edge of being illegal. Now on top of it all, there was a new psycho out there threatening helpless women, burning down houses, and apparently trying to kill Alma Ziegler. *What next?*

He got out of bed and went into the dark kitchen and turned on the dim hood light over the stove. He poured himself a glass of milk and took a couple of frosted oatmeal cookies he kept stashed in a drawer. He sat down at the counter and saw his reflection in the octagonal windows of the kitchen nook. *Do I really look that old to the others?* It wasn't the crow's-feet by his eyes or the slight paunch above the string tie of his pajama bottoms; it was the lack of a smile and the slight droop of his shoulders.

Brighton moved to the couch and tried lying down and forcing himself back to sleep, but his guilty thoughts of not wanting to do something to help Alma were too annoying to ignore. He got up and walked out onto the rear patio where he sat in a patio rocking chair.

Who was this Mr. X who Charley had told him about? How did he find out about the precious ore? Were the assay office people involved? How did any of them know what was taking place with the mining? Would the whole neighborhood be going to jail for breaking some obscure law or worse still, was this lunatic arsonist going to murder everyone? Brighton's brain wouldn't stop churning.

He hated this late-night mental process that wouldn't give up. Brighton finally got some peace of mind when he resolved to find out who, when, where, and why. To do anything less was asking for even more risks to life and limb and more sleepless nights.

Gina startled him. She was standing in the doorway into the kitchen, leaning against the door jam and watching him.

"What are you doing awake? You have patients in the morning," Gina murmured as she walked back inside to the sink and poured herself a glass of water. She came out into the warm night air in her flimsy nightgown and sat down next to Brighton and began stroking his arm and hand. "Come to bed and get some sleep. You have a busy day tomorrow." He turned and put his arms around her waist and rested his head on her protruding belly. He thought about how his life was changing and the new pressures that were mounting. He leaned back and looked into her eyes and said a little prayer of thanks for the beautiful person in his arms and the new life in her belly. He had to be a better protector. He had to find and get rid of those who were a threat to his family. He stood and led her back into the coolness of the house and the comfort of their bed.

✳✳✳

The following day, Brighton was at Roy's doorstep at seven sharp. He wasn't due in the office until nine and knew that Roy and Dean wouldn't start up the Mole until the neighborhood was awake. A light knock on the door was all it took to ignite a round of concerned barking from Chad. Roy answered the door fully dressed in work clothes.

"Good morning, Brighton," Roy said with a smile. "You look like a man with a mission. Don't you have some dangerous teeth to attack today?"

"I thought you and Dean were going to finish up the Patels' place today. You look like you are on your way to the airport."

"We finished up at the Patels' last night after dark and moved the Mole over to the Steiners' properties. I just got called in on standby status. There is another terrorist threat. This time, a group of luggage handlers working together spotted suspicious activity. The information is highly classified. Promise me you won't say anything or else I'll have to kill you … just joking," Roy said, with a big grin on his face.

"I'm glad you are in a good mood. I slept like crap last night. I can't get the house fires out of my head. I came by to get the information about the assay office people from you. You know, the

one you went to first. I want to stop in there and ask some questions and check them out with the better business people. What
do you think?"

"I think you should stick to fixing teeth before you end up
needing a dentist yourself. If you go down there and they are involved in the fire they might get even more violent. We've got
plenty of operating money. I'll call Clyde. He knows a lot of the
city cops. For a couple hundred bucks, we can find out a lot more
than you will by sticking your nose in a hornets' nest."

Brighton feigned agreement. In principle, he knew that Roy
was right. He still had his mind made up to make the next two
hours count. Without asking directly, he managed to get Roy to
mention the name of the assay company. He had already heard
Big Bill's name mentioned by Gina.

Brighton said goodbye and headed toward town. On a last-
minute hunch he drove back by his house and, without opening
the garage, snuck in the patio door. He went to his bedroom and
opened the bottom drawer of the nightstand. In a shoebox
wrapped in an oily rag, he found his revolver, a .38-caliber Smith
and Wesson his dad had given him when he moved to the Bay
Area. He had never fired it nor had he even cleaned it. He slid
the cylinder open and saw that it was still loaded. His dad had
been adamant that an empty gun was very safe; safe for the intruder or the mugger or the rapist, that is.

He slid the gun into his waistband as he had seen in so many
movies, only to find that it hurt like heck, poking his hip bone
and then, after shifting it to the back, poking his butt. He loosened his belt after he was outside and moved the gun to the front
of his pants, which he found much better until he slid into his car.
"Ouch!" he yelled, pulling the gun out and rubbing his thigh and
groin and tossing the gun onto the passenger seat. He started
driving toward the gate and passed Clyde in the security truck.

Brighton immediately felt conscious of the danger the mere
presence of the gun placed him in. He reached over and slid the
revolver into the glove box, but then the box wouldn't close. Finally, he stopped the car and popped the trunk lid; looking
around to be sure no one was looking as he got out of the car.
Holding it close to his body, he secreted the gun to the trunk and
hid it in his gym bag.

He found the industrial area near the airport and drove up and down the side streets until he saw the sign. He hadn't thought about what he was going to say but figured he could come up with something if he had to.

He heard the top-of-the-hour beep on the radio just as the national news network started their 8:00 a.m. broadcast. He looked up from his newly found parking place and saw a strikingly beautiful woman walk up to the inside of the glass door. She flipped over the white-and-red closed sign that dangled from a suction cup on the glass so that it now read "Open." He got out of his car and walked to the door. A low-volume bell sounded as he entered the tiny waiting room. The woman looked up from behind the counter smiling. "Oh crap," he thought. "I left the gun in the car."

"What can I do for you?" Lori Pederson asked in a sweet Boston accent. She had the makeup, dress, and body of a Madison Avenue ad executive. He could not imagine her stomping around in the desert in combat boots.

"Good morning, I'm looking for some information on good areas to do desert rock collecting. I just moved here and want a new hobby." Brighton looked around the room as he talked, trying to pick out anything that would in any way give him clues. Clues to what, he wasn't quite sure.

"Well," she said, drawing out her speech and studying him in return. "We aren't exactly a tourist information center. Maybe you should try one of the rock shops. We are strictly in the assay business. When you find some pretty rocks, you are welcome to bring them in, and we can tell you what they are made up of and their scientific names."

"But I see the rocks on the shelves over there, and gosh, that's just the kind of things I want to find. I'm decorating my office and want to add some local novelty. Are any of those for sale?"

The woman shook her head, and though acting patient, her body language hinted at the need to get rid of him, the pest.

Brighton was learning nothing new or helpful and didn't want to dig himself into a verbal hole. He made an obvious sweep of the room again and said, "You have a nice place here. Thanks for your help."

He headed for the door, and as he opened it he noticed the reflection of a man in the glass door. He looked back, and there standing beside the woman was huge, hairy man with a no-nonsense face. The description Roy had given of him matched this Neanderthal to a tee. Brighton's adrenalin had long since kicked into high gear. He turned back toward the counter and looked at Bill.

"Good morning, sir. Maybe you could help me. I'm looking for a good place to find some desert rocks, sort of like you have right here." Brighton motioned toward the shelves.

"The lady already told you that you have the wrong place, so maybe you should get your skinny butt out of here before I come around the counter and throw you out."

Brighton expected some polite assistance from the woman, but she just stared at him with a conspiratorial look on her face. Then it came to him, plain as the light of day. This woman standing in front of him had an unmistakable resemblance to one of his neighbors. Without another word he turned, left the building, and got into his car.

27

THE MILL

By the time Roy arrived at work, the terrorist emergency had been cancelled, and he was told he could go home. He called Dean on his way to the parking lot. He could hear the throbbing of an engine in the background.

"I'm on my way back home. They took care of the problem, so I'll be there to help you in half an hour."

"Why don't you take the day off?" Dean said. "One of the best workers I've ever had showed up on my doorstep this morning needing work. He just snuck back across the border at Nogales and hitched a ride to Phoenix. His name is Jorge, but the men always called him Eveready, because he never stops working."

"Sounds good to me," Roy said. "I could use a day to get caught up on things."

Roy's next call was to Rhonda. She was an early morning riser and was hopefully still home. She also answered on the first ring. This was turning into his lucky day.

"How about lunch and taking in a movie?" Roy asked her, smiling into the phone at the sound of her voice.

"How about lunch and a plane ride?" Rhonda came back. "I've got to fly to Denver for a one o'clock meeting. It won't take but an hour, and then we could stop in Colorado Springs and visit the refinery mill that you keep saying you need to see."

"Do you think we'll have time?" Roy asked.

"My meeting is at the airport with a promoter who is working on a concert for me for next year. My agent arranged the meeting. This particular man is the best in the business. The guy can't leave Denver this week because he is setting up for the Stones on Friday. Sixty thousand people in the Bronco's stadium. The flight to Colorado Springs from Denver should only take thirty minutes. What do you think?"

"Sounds like fun to me. I've never ridden on a private jet with a movie star."

Rhonda laughed and they agreed Roy would pick up lunch on

his way to meet her at the plane. He knew a place near the airport that made terrific shrimp tacos.

✳✳✳

He could see her pickup truck in the general aviation parking lot. When he pulled into the empty space alongside her truck, he saw she was sitting inside, talking on the phone. She gave him a sign to wait for one minute and then turned away to finish her conversation. Sixty seconds later, she hopped out of the truck with a big smile on her face and promptly planted a kiss on his lips. He had a feeling something negative had happened, but she acted sincerely happy to be with him, and she looked fantastic. She had on a non-country outfit for a change: a tailored red dress with a short hemline and jewelry of which he could only guess the value.

The flight was smooth, and the food was tasty. The inside of the small jet was a bit more cramped than Roy had imagined and made moving around difficult. However, Rhonda wore just enough of a light custom fragrance to make being close to her constantly intriguing. When the food was gone, they cleared wrappers and folded away the table between them. Rhonda moved to the seat beside him and buckled in. She looked tired as she took his hand in hers and laid her head on his shoulder. She was asleep within seconds and, to his surprise, made a soft snoring sound that nearly made him laugh.

True to her word, the meeting at the Denver terminal was short. Before he could even stretch his legs for a walk, the pilot was looking for him, telling him they were set to get the multimillion-dollar bird in the air again. They were landing at Colorado Springs general aviation terminal by two-thirty. Hertz had a shiny black Range Rover waiting for them, and with a few directions from the GPS, they were at the locked gate of the Pikes Peak Metal and Minerals by three. The phone at the gate was answered after a few rings by the owner himself.

✳✳✳

Jerry Sorenson had been a big help to the Hidden Canyon partnership. He looked just like he sounded on the phone: big, strong, and very bright. His large body filled the doorframe of the office as he greeted them. He wore Levis and a starched plaid shirt under a chocolate lambskin jacket. His alligator boots were scuffed with everyday wear.

He offered them a drink and a tour of the plant. It was smaller than Roy had imagined, but the equipment was new and being put to constant use. The crews all wore matching coveralls and white hard hats with a clever gold logo. The traffic flow of trucks coming and going was timed like a Swiss railroad station. Each truck backed in and dumped its load of ore onto a huge grate, where it fell onto a conveyor belt. The ore then headed toward a crushing machine on its way to the furnaces. After they had inspected the various phases of the process, they worked their way back to his office where Jerry handed Roy the latest assay report and production figures.

Roy was astonished at the numbers. He thought the ore coming out of the ravine at the Patels' looked good, but the report showed it to be nearly 20 percent richer than anything they had mined to date. Rhonda was charming Jerry with stories of the rich and famous while Roy studied the numbers.

"By the way," Jerry said, "I received a call last Friday from an old classmate of mine at Texas A&M. He told me about a pile of ore someone had dumped alongside the gate of the small company he works for in Clovis, New Mexico. He said no one even saw the trucks dump the stuff, but they had received a call telling them that if they would process the pile of rock they could keep half of the proceeds. My friend said his boss is a real piece of work and told the caller to get lost. The ore is still sitting there." He got up from his desk and retrieved bottles of water from a small fridge.

"My friend did send one of the cleanup men out to the pile with a wheelbarrow. They assayed a couple hundred pounds of the stuff and were blown away with the figures. It's off the charts for rhodium, lots of platinum, and plenty of the yellow stuff. He couldn't believe the figures, so he wanted me to cross-check. I just ran the sample this morning. It matches the first several loads of ore you sent to me to within one percentile. It's got to be your missing two truckloads."

"Any good ideas how we could trace the origin of the phone

call they made to your friend's boss?" Rhonda asked. She had been trying to stay in the background of the conversations, acting on the dumb side of normal.

"I'm not into high tech stuff, but I'd bet that there is someone around Phoenix who could track down the telephone information you want. The question is, do you really want to get your nose into something like that, or is it better letting the police handle it?" Jerry asked.

She looked at him and quieted down again. Roy nodded in agreement and suggested they get the phone number of Jerry's friend and let someone official look into the situation.

Jerry walked Rhonda and Roy to their car and extended an invitation to come back anytime.

"What a nice fellow," Rhonda commented as they drove away. "We ought to be sure he is getting paid enough for his work."

"Don't worry. So far we have sent him over fifty truckloads of ore, and he has charged us more than ten thousand dollars per load. Unless I've done the math wrong, he has cleared well over a half million dollars."

28

ESCAPE

Alma stared at the walls of the motel room that had seemed so far apart when she first arrived. They were getting closer together, and the room was getting smaller by the hour. The mattress on the metal bed frame squeaked each time she got in or out of the bed. Though it was quite a bit larger than her worn-out mattress at home, this one was as hard as granite. Her own mattress had developed a cozy sag in the middle that surrounded her like a soft nest of down feathers, keeping her warm on long winter nights and cool during the scorching days of summer. These sheets were scratchy, and the pillows were so hard she had long since relegated them to the floor behind the dinky little table where she had eaten the last four meals.

She stood naked in front of a window that looked directly into the back side of a chipped and rusted green dumpster. Every so often she could hear footsteps outside the window, followed by a screeching noise as the lid of the metal box was raised then a loud metallic clank as the lid was allowed to fall closed. She couldn't see the person hauling the trash, as the space between her window and the green box barely let in any light.

"This must be the worst room in the motel," she thought; just like they used to try to give her dad. Once he got smarter and richer, he told the desk clerk to start him off with the best room in the hotel, not the worst, and then he would decide whether to stay there or to go down the street to the competition. But perhaps, Mr. Banks was just trying to hide her from the other guests and that evil Mr. Hicks.

The television had begun to lose its fascination. The same commercials were repeated over and over, and the volume of the ads was twice that of the *Leave It to Beaver* or *Bonanza* reruns she had enjoyed so much that first night. She kept replaying in her mind the television image of her house in the desert, smoking and burning, and then the later helicopter view of her yard and surrounding land, revealing nothing but a big black smudge in the middle of the desert plants.

Who would fill the rubber water trough she had recessed in the ground so her desert friends could get a drink? Who would scatter seed and bread for the chipmunks and quail? She needed to get back there.

She filled the shallow fiberglass bathtub with hot water and even put some of the body wash in it to make bubbles. It reminded her of the weekend her family moved from the rental house into the mansion in the foothills west of Denver. She had her own bedroom and bathroom with a huge tub with jets that sprayed water all over the room if the water level in the tub wasn't high enough. Her desert house didn't have a tub, just a shower that dripped water day and night.

She was lying in the motel tub when the idea came to her. She would find Mr. Hicks and put him in a bathtub and let him get pruned just like her fingers.

Mr. Banks had been very specific about her not leaving her room. He had told her that if she needed anything, she should just call the front desk. She had already called them for hot tea three different times and asked them to show her how to turn on the TV and how to use the controller, so she thought it would be okay if she called to have a taxicab ordered for her. Mr. Banks had left her a twenty-dollar bill since her smallest bill was a hundred. He told her to charge anything else she might need to the room.

She got dressed in the clothes the women had loaned her and wrote a note to the secretary, Emily, and left it on the tiny table. She walked out the door and down the long, smelly hallway to the front of the motel. She thanked the man at the desk for calling the taxi and asked him to change the twenty-dollar bill into fives and ones.

The taxi took nearly half an hour to show up. By then Alma was starting to lose her resolve to find Mr. Hicks. The honking horn of the cab broke her wandering thoughts. She got into the car and settled back into the hot, sticky, and very smelly plastic seat. Even her old Mustang was nicer than the inside of this disgusting clunker.

"Where to, lady?" the driver asked in a Brooklyn-accented slur and without as much as a hello.

"Eh, I'm not quite sure. I'm trying to find a man."

"Really? Well, I'm trying finding me a woman, but don't ya think you're a little too old for me? Just kidding, lady," the bearded driver joked, checking her out in the rearview mirror. "So where's it going to be?"

"Where is what going to be?" she responded.

"Where … do … you … want … me … to … take … you?" He spoke to her with a raised voice as though she were child or hard of hearing.

She suddenly felt confused. Tears started flowing as she tried to answer. The fresh air had helped her feel more alert, but she still couldn't think clearly. She had made a plan when she was in the hotel room. She would find that awful Mr. Hicks and punish him. But she couldn't remember how she was going to find him.

The cab sat with its engine idling and air-conditioning re-circulating the car's fetid air. The driver was trying to be patient. He was used to hauling the oddballs of society around. Cabs in Arizona weren't like Manhattan where he had picked up hot-looking women or captains of industry or even an occasional sports figure. In the desert, most everyone had their own cars, thus it was the type sitting in his backseat right now who needed his service. "I'm sorry I made you cry, lady. Maybe you should go back into the hotel and get a map so you know for sure where you want to go."

He got out of the car and came around to her door to open it for her so she could get out, but she just sat there.

Then it came to her. "Do you know where Hidden Canyon is?" she asked.

"Sure, is that where you want to go?"

"Yes, please," she answered, sniffing and dabbing at her eyes and nose with a tattered tissue.

He was about to ask her if she was going to be able to pay him, when she pressed a hundred dollar bill into his hand. He closed the door and, shaking his head, got back in and headed the cab toward the foothills.

❋❋❋

Clyde saw the yellow Crown Victoria coming toward the gate and stopped eating his sandwich long enough to squint and try to see who was in the backseat. He was parked about four hundred yards from the electric entrance gate. Charley and the HOA president both had told him to be alert to any strangers rather than sit in the office and wait for complaints as usual. The driver of the cab stopped at the gate's code-and-call box, but apparently didn't have a code or even a name to call from the box. After the car had blocked the entrance for three or four minutes, he saw the back door open and someone get out. The cab pulled away, making a U-turn to leave. Then he saw her. "Oh my gosh!" he exclaimed out loud. "It's the desert lady."

By the time Clyde drove onto the paved part of the road and negotiated driving over a concrete median to shorten the route, he had lost sight of Alma. She was not on the roadway or any of the nearby driveways. There were three separate arroyos into which she could have disappeared, and he wasn't walking into any of them. Just that morning, he had seen a diamondback rattler slither across the road. He got out of the truck and yelled for Alma to come onto the road, but she was gone.

Charley got the call just as he was pulling into the Courtyard's parking lot. At first he doubted Clyde, but the manager of the hotel confirmed that the woman in Room 1178 had left in a cab an hour ago. *What was she thinking?* He had some additional paperwork in his car that needed her signature to finalize the partnership and to drop the suit against Hidden Canyon.

Charley thanked the hotel manager and told him to hold her room for another twenty-four hours just in case she wandered back into the hotel.

✳✳✳

Alma knew the arroyos of the Hidden Canyon like fat people know the way to the refrigerator. In a matter of minutes, she was out of the gated area and heading to the far end of the development. She had heard Clyde's bellowing voice calling her, but since he didn't follow her, even in his truck, she supposed he had gone back to whatever he had been doing. As she got closer to the top of the canyon, she could hear the grinding sound of that weird digging machine. It was good to be back on familiar ground.

✲✲✲

Dean caught sight of her out of his peripheral vision and shut down the Mole's engine. He climbed down and stood in the shadows of the machine until Alma was close enough to grab.

"Can I help you?" Dean asked, stepping into her path.

Alma gave a little yelp and then turned to run, but Dean latched onto her arm and held firm. "Aren't you supposed to be hiding at the motel?" he asked, keeping a firm but gentle grip on her arm. As far as he was concerned, she was no different from a spooked horse. One had to establish who was in charge, and then cooperation would follow.

"I couldn't stand it there in that smelly motel. Besides, I need to get to my house to feed and water the animals. And I need to get my gun before that man comes back."

They were standing near the back gate of the Steiner's yard. He figured that with another three feet of digging, he would have finished the first truckload from the new dig. Another empty truck was just pulling up, and he needed to man the loading tractor. Roy hadn't been helping today. Dean and Eveready were doing double duty.

"If you will sit there in the shade and have one of those sodas," he said, pointing to the small white cooler by the corner of the house, "I will load this truck with the tractor and then drive you in my truck to what's left of your house."

Alma drank two cans of Dr. Pepper and sat patiently in the shade, drawing patterns in the dirt with a long mesquite branch. When Dean finished loading the truck, he shut off the tractor and accepted the paperwork from the truck driver. He had kept his eye on the woman the entire time, ready to run after her if she took off, but she was being obedient. Once the truckload of ore was gone, Dean grabbed a can of soda for himself and motioned her to follow. He closed the Steiner's gate and headed for his new red Hummer. He opened the passenger door for Alma and helped her climb onto the high, tan leather seat.

"This is a real neat truck you have. My daddy used to have a red truck, but it didn't have a backseat, just a big bed to put stuff in. Don't you think it's funny that they called it a bed?" She smiled at him. "Us kids would ride in the back of that truck and sing songs and throw water balloons at the stop signs. One time, my brother—he's dead now—threw a water balloon at a car, and the lady called the police. Daddy had to pay a big fine."

Dean gave her a sideways glance before he started the engine, not wanting to interrupt her dialogue. The air-conditioning blew hot at first, and then within seconds cool, fresh air invaded the cab. When the air combined with the new car smell, the eighty thousand dollar price tag seemed reasonable. He headed toward the entrance gate and didn't even slow down when he passed Clyde's security truck.

Dean and Alma were half a mile down the main road, headed toward the county road intersection, when Dean spotted Roy's pickup coming toward him. He flashed his lights and slowed down, rolling down his window and waving at Roy to stop.

Roy checked his rearview mirror for cars and, seeing no traffic behind him, stopped in the middle of the road. His eyes nearly popped out of his head when he saw who was in Dean's new Hummer.

"Park your truck at the Circle K and come ride with us," Dean told Roy, not giving him a chance to question or disagree.

Once Roy was in the Hummer's backseat, Dean explained the situation and said they were going to drive over the hill and down the dirt road so that Ms. Ziegler could see what if anything was left of her house and find some of her property. He didn't mention that she wanted to find her gun.

Driving around the bend in the road, Alma was finally able to witness firsthand what had happened to her beloved little house. Tears filled the corners of her eyes, and her nose ran as she muffled her sobs of grief. Dean pulled a small box of Kleenex from his console and placed several tissues in her hand.

"We are so sorry," Roy offered, speaking for both men.

The scene in front of them was dismal. A couple tiny whiffs of smoke snuck up out of the blackened debris. The blackened frames of her refrigerator and stove were all that stood above ground level. A thin streamer of crime scene tape wound around bushes and cactus, creating a yellow ring around her blackened homesite.

Alma got out of the truck and stood looking over the charred ruins, and then she ducked under the tape and walked out toward the back of her yard. She stopped at an old rusty wood-burning oven, junked when she got electricity in the house. She stooped down, opened a hinged door, and pulled out an army-green backpack. Brushing dust and soot off of the bag, she walked straight back to the truck, not giving the smoldering remains of her home another glance. She climbed into the Hummer and pulled the door closed.

"Thank you for waiting for me. If you could just let me off at the Circle K, I can call a taxi. Do you know the name of the hotel where Mr. Banks left me to stay? I can't remember."

"I think he said the Marriott Courtyard. Does that sound familiar?"

"Yes, that's it. I remember now," she said in a flat tone.

Dean pulled up alongside a row of trucks in the parking lot of the convenience market. "Why don't you come over to dinner at our house? Sharron can get you some clean clothes and fix us a nice meal, and then we will take you back to the hotel. I'll bet Charley would like to talk to you too."

"It's okay. I want to pay you for taking me to my house." Alma's hands were shaking as she unzipped the backpack and reached in. She pulled out a woman's wallet and opened it, revealing a driver's license and a new MasterCard. Inside the encircling rubber band was a stack of crisp new bills. She peeled off two hundreds and offered them to Dean, thanking him again for the ride. He refused them flat out, leaving no room for discussion. As she turned to get out of the truck, her backpack slipped off her lap, landing on the floor of the truck. Out slid a chrome-plated Smith & Wesson .44 caliber revolver. She bent down to pick it up, but Roy had come around the truck to open the door for her and gently lifted the gun out of her hand.

"Are you sure you know what to do with this thing?"

"You could never count the number of sick and injured critters that I have put out of their misery over the years. I just have one more to take care of," she said. She took the gun back from him without his resisting and placed it in her satchel, climbed down out of the Hummer, and walked into the Circle K.

Dean and Roy watched her go. Alma entered the store then came back out to the pay phone on the entrance wall. She pulled the receiver from its hook, dropped in a quarter, and dialed a number. She glanced up at him and smiled.

***

The Steiner brothers and their wives had been on another gambling vacation. This time it was to the casinos at Lake Havasu, Arizona. They were already well into having spent the next year's installment of their lottery annuity. They had lost thousands of dollars at the crap tables and had consumed tens of thousands of calories in rich and greasy buffet food. The amount of alcohol they put away was quickly forgotten. Otto had passed out twice in four days, and one time the paramedics had been called to extract a catfish bone from the throat of Heinz's wife after she had tried to eat dinner on a full tank of margaritas.

When Otto opened the entrance into his house from the garage, an overwhelming sense of fear struck him. There on the kitchen counter was a stack of dirty dishes and numerous containers of unfinished Boston Market fast food cartons. The dialogue that followed was reminiscent of a parent telling the story of Goldilocks and the Three Bears. His wife screamed German obscenities as she wandered through the house, saying over and over, "Someone has been eating in my kitchen; someone has been sitting on my couch; someone has been sleeping in my bed." But no one was there, and no clues pointed to who it could have been. She didn't notice that there had been somebody digging in her backyard.

***

When Rhonda came home from grocery shopping after she had left the airport, she saw the deputy sheriff's cruiser parked across the cul-de-sac with its lights flashing, raising her curiosity. *What was going on at the home of the newest partners in the neighborhood mining group?*

When Otto answered the door, he was so excited that his new best friend, the singing movie star, had shown up on his doorstep that he completely forgot about the break-in. He insisted on introducing her to the two uniformed cops and made her a cup of coffee. She politely refused the beverage, and little by little, she gleaned the whole story of some stranger having slept and eaten in their house for the last two days.

Since it had occurred less than two hundred yards from her front door, she considered the possibility that it could be a paparazzo or even a stalker, but then she found something. Lying near a telephone book on the coffee table was a single piece of yellow legal-size paper. She picked it up and read the beginning of what was apparently a contract to purchase, for the sum of one million dollars, the acreage of Alma Ziegler. There was no name of the buyer, nor were there any more pages nearby. She got down on all fours to see if there were more papers to be found.

"What are you looking for?" one of the deputies asked, as he admired Rhonda.

"I might have dropped my contact," she improvised, sliding the paper out of the angle of view of the policeman. "Did y'all look on the back porch for the squatter? I had a stranger spend the night sleeping on my patio furniture just a few nights ago."

When he turned to look toward the back patio, she folded the paper and slipped it into her loose-fitting top, flattening in out against her belly and turning away toward the door. Before Otto could make any more fuss over her, she excused herself and walked out the door.

29

EXECUTIVE DECISION

"So what do you think, Roy?" Rhonda asked. "The guy who was camping at the Steiner's has to be the same guy who threatened Alma and broke into Brighton and Gina's house last week. It's got to be someone who knows the neighborhood and has an idea who is here and who is out of town. Where is he getting his information?"

He had fallen asleep in the hot tub and was still a bit dizzy having hurriedly jumped out of the water to answer the door. Luckily he had worn a swimsuit this time, but in Rhonda's state of agitation, she might not have even noticed the difference.

"You're probably right about it being someone who has an insider helping him. The problem is trying to investigate this thing and not raise the sheriff's curiosity. The last thing we need is some nosey cop trying to figure out why we are digging up the neighborhood."

Roy was still dripping water on the entry floor. "Have you eaten?" He walked toward his bedroom. "Help yourself to the food on the counter."

She assessed the dinner prospects, but found only a jar of peanut butter, an open packet of Ritz crackers, and a plastic knife smeared with Skippy. The only other choices were a brown banana and a half-eaten hotdog. She opened the fridge, searching for anything healthy to eat and settled for a Fuji apple.

"How does this guy stay so fit looking?" she asked Chad, staring up at her, probably hoping for a handout. "He really needs a wife."

Fifteen minutes later, they were walking across the street to Rhonda's house and saw the red Hummer pulling up with Dean and Sharron inside.

"I was just headed over toward the Patels' to have a look at the excavation," Dean said when the vehicle rolled to a stop.

Rhonda repeated her story to the Shutters, giving them a shortened version.

"I moved the Mole to the Steiner's this morning. Maybe that scared off the visitor," Dean explained. They exchanged an abbreviated version of the day's events including the trip to Colorado then returned to Rhonda's story about the squatter. Except for a couple of nods and soft exclamations, Sharron remained quiet. Rhonda couldn't see into the tall truck very well but got the idea that Sharron was dressed in just a robe.

As they parted directions and the couple resumed their walk toward Rhonda's, it was Roy who mentioned Sharron and how she seemed almost like a zombie.

"Think about it. In all the time this mining thing has been going on and all the meetings and all the weird stuff, not once has Sharron given us little or no help. Do you think she is a stoner?" Rhonda asked.

Roy laughed and said, "You would be the expert on stoners in this neighborhood. I thought all of you entertainers were required to remain stoned for as long as you were under contract."

Rhonda turned and slugged Roy in the shoulder.

"Ouch! Where did you learn to hit like that?" he said, rubbing the welt on his deltoid.

"I thought you told me that you had seen every one of my movies. Don't you remember when I was in that pirate movie with Johnny and had to hit the guy with the patch on his eye? They made me practice hitting a punching bag for weeks just so I had the swing correct; you know like in golf, it's all in the swing. They also trained me for occasions when smart-mouth guys make snide comments so I can defend the honor of the motion picture industry."

They both laughed and went on to more lighthearted subjects like who was fixing dinner for whom. They walked up the driveway to the Tucker mansion.

Getting back to the subject of Alma and the Hidden Canyon gold mining, Roy reminded her that she had agreed to call around and set up a meeting with the partners to bring everyone up to date. It was a moot point. When they walked inside, her message light was flashing, and the voicemail was from Brighton. "Nine o'clock tomorrow at the Banks' house."

"I swear," said Rhonda, "that boy has been sniffing too much of that dental anesthesia lately. He used to have a sense of humor. Now it's all business and numbers and dig, dig, dig."

"More likely is the fact that he had a near-lethal blow to his head and has a wife who's pregnant. You would be grouchy too if you had to look at rotten teeth all day and put ice packs on your throbbing head at night. I'm amazed he gets so much done every day."

"Why honey, all of you men are just amazing. All those difficult things you do each day. I mean sleep, eat, and ride around in your trucks and everything." She looked at him teasingly and then dodged the fake punch he threw her direction. She laughed and ran around to the other side of the island countertop. He tried to catch her, but she was too quick and kept the counter between them. Finally, he gave up and sat on a bar stool. She came around behind him and wrapped her arms around his neck. She put her soft lips on the top of his head and left them there for several moments. Finally, he stirred, and she released him. She walked over to the refrigerator to look for something for them to eat. At least her fridge was full.

✳✳✳

The meeting started late. Charley was the host, and though Kara was still limping and expressing an occasional grimace when she moved, her house was still perfect, with a lovely spread of finger foods and beverages. Rhonda had dropped by earlier with ten pounds of fresh prawns and homemade cocktail sauce on a bed of shredded butter lettuce.

The Patels showed up with their sons and the Great Dane. Dr. Patel held a leash in his hand, but it wasn't attached to the dog. Kara opened the front door, and the dog walked right into the living room as though he were the guest of honor. When he let out a bark to announce he was hungry and could smell the shrimp, the Banks girls ran out of their room to investigate. The Steiners showed up with their wives and three of their four kids. Dean and Sharron came with a teenage daughter, of whom no one had ever even heard about prior to that evening.

By the time the rest of the group arrived, the room was hot

and bursting at the seams. Harley was behaving nicely until Heinz Steiner's ten-year-old fed him a handful of shrimp tails and four radishes. The dog staggered into the middle of the kitchen, gagging and gasping for air. Bavana Patel screamed something no one could understand. It finally was repeated in English by one of her boys that the dog was allergic to shellfish. Harley barfed in the middle of the travertine floor. The crowd scattered, and the patio doors flew open to let in fresh air.

"I thought this was a business meeting," Kara whispered into Brighton's ear as he walked by looking for more paper towels. She was sitting on a high-back stool, resting her foot and observing the raucous scene and the demolition of her house.

"Fat chance of that ever happening with the Heidelberg Hillbillies and canine clinic open for business," Brighton answered back.

The teenage kids, eight of them at best count, had led the dog into the backyard and had found a boom box by the pool. Bob Marley and the Wailers were soon jamming into the cool desert air. The snacks and sodas were long gone, and the guests were reduced to getting drinks of water from the kitchen sink.

With no booze present, the Steiner brothers had managed to act quite civil, and their wives were pleasant and well-mannered. Everyone wondered where the wives had been hiding. The Steiner kids, however, were acorns off the proverbial tree. When the younger of the Banks girls asked them why they talked funny, the oldest one grabbed her by her skinny arms and threw her into the swimming pool. The Patel boys came to her rescue, both jumping into the water and dragging her to the steps. Her sister had run into the house crying and screaming for help. With all the yelling and shouting, Harley had gone postal, barking and growling and finally jumping into the pool himself.

At this first sign of trouble, Sharron grabbed Dean and her daughter and headed for the front door.

"Please don't leave yet; we need to have our meeting," someone had shouted to the Shutters, but Sharron hadn't glanced back. They were gone, and so was the evening's chance to make any democratic decisions regarding a new separate HOA, the LLC's plans, and a possible Wren Circle gold mine.

Roy and Rhonda stayed in the kitchen, helping Charley clean

up the mess. Gina started having contractions in the middle of the melee and had gone in to lie down in the guest bedroom. Kara had taken her girls back into the shelter of their rooms to warm and quiet them. Brighton was on the front porch accepting apologies from the Steiner wives. Howls could be heard from the direction of the Steiner homes, and probably not from coyotes. The Patels felt like the whole confusion was their fault and offered to pay for the food. It required a nearly rude rejection of a handful of greenbacks.

Brighton walked back in and related the story. They looked at each other, and started to laugh.

"Could you believe it when they all walked in with their kids?" Brighton asked.

"And how about the dog?" Roy added. "I can tell you now that I'm going to be in big trouble when I get home and Chad finds out that we had a party without him."

Rhonda laughed, putting her arms around both of the men, pulling them into her sides in a collegial hug.

"I swear you two have provided me with more laughs and gotten me into more trouble than all the boys at Cotton Creek High School combined."

They separated, and Rhonda finished wiping off the countertop while the men carried out the garbage sacks. When she looked up, Gina was standing in the hall, leaning against the wall with a nasty frown on her face.

"Gina honey, are you feeling all right?"

"I'm feeling okay, Rhonda. How does my husband feel?" she said sarcastically.

"Whoa there little lady, don't let your imagination run away with your good senses," Rhonda replied.

"Isn't one man at a time good enough for you?"

"Gina, Gina, what you saw were friends sharing a laugh and nothing else." She took Gina by both hands and looked into her eyes. "You don't need to worry about me, honey, or any other woman coming between you and Brighton. He is a lucky man to have you, and he knows it. I apologize for making you uncomfortable. I'll be more sensitive from now on. And to answer your question—yes, one man is more than enough for me."

She took Gina in her arms and held her close. After a moment, Rhonda pushed her gently away and said, "Holy catfish! You are getting a big tummy!"

By the time all three men were back, the women were laughing, and Kara had joined them. They settled onto the couches and talked about the bizarre evening. They decided that Brighton and Roy would call all the shots with the legal help of Charley and that the democratic way of running the partnership would have to go by the wayside. They would pay Dean extra to oversee the actual mining. The rest of the partners could just take what they got.

Walking back to their homes, Brighton and Roy had reminisced about the beginning of the whole mining project. They ruminated on some things they could have done differently from the first, but soon the biggest questions of all: Who had attacked Brighton, and who had set the torch to Alma's house? Were they the same person?

30

PARTING WAYS

Mark Cooperman was mad. Not only was he intentionally not privy to the events in the upper canyon, especially on Cactus Wren Circle, but he was the one having to deal with the complaints from his other neighbors. In frustration, he filed a written complaint on behalf of the entire Hidden Canyon HOA. He presented it personally to Mr. Fuller, of Fuller and Fuller, by driving a golf cart out to the seventh green at the country club and standing in the middle of Fuller's putting line until he had gained the full attention of the attorney. The letter demanded the replacement of Charley Banks as the legal representative for the firm, maintaining that he was incompetent and conflicted with the good of the development. It also demanded that the firm file a lawsuit against the eight homeowners on Cactus Wren Circle to stop them from whatever they seemed to be doing up there with their trucks and the digging machine.

Fuller let his putter drop to the ground when he read the letter. He hated all HOAs. In his mind they were the devil's very own workshops. He couldn't care less what went on in them, but now it seemed that Charley had crossed the line. In thirty years of law practice he had never had a client interrupt him on the golf course; why, the man might just as well have come into Fuller's bedroom with the letter of complaint. In his most tolerant voice, ignoring the doctor's title and mispronouncing his name intentionally, he assured "Mr. Copperman" that it would be taken care of.

Charley received a summons to Fuller's throne room the next morning.

"I have decided to relieve you of the Hidden Canyon HOA account," Fuller stated. "I'm also relieving you of your position in the law firm. You are to clean out your desk and be out of the building by noon. As per your original employment agreement, you will not, and I emphasize, *not*, contact any of the firm's clients, nor will you discuss this conversation with any other employees of the firm. You have created an intolerable situation by not controlling the clients to whom you are assigned. This is not a discussion. You have disappointed me and the firm, and I wish you a permanent goodbye."

Charley knew that arguing with the idiot would be useless. Had this happened six months ago, he would have been devastated, but now things were different. With his partnership in a secret venture already worth millions he couldn't care less about this arrogant law firm and its senior partner. He turned on his heels and left the room without a word.

So Cooperman didn't like the activities of the neighbors up the hill. "Well," Charley thought, "Maybe we'll just have to dissociate ourselves from them. Maybe we'll have to restructure the project." He walked into his office and took a legal-size file box off the corner of his desk. Charley dumped the box upside-down in the middle of the floor and placed his pictures of Kara and the girls in the box. He took the paperwork of the purchase of Alma's property from a neat stack of briefs and placed it on top of the pictures, removed his diplomas from the wall, and walked out the door. The firm owed him money, but he would concern himself with that later. He was going to recreate the Hidden Canyon HOA into the Cactus Wren HOA, and it would take an order from the United States Supreme Court to stop him.

***

Brighton woke up early and put on hiking boots and a light jacket to ward off the morning chill. He wandered over to the site of the reconstruction of the Shutter house and circled the property, keeping his eyes to the ground for clues and trying not to let his mind wander. There had to be clues in the fire's rubble, and there had to be a connection between all the maddening events. He circled the property twice and found nothing.

As much as he disliked Alma Ziegler, he just couldn't picture her as an arsonist, nor could he imagine her finding her way to his office and timing an attack on him so perfectly that even the police couldn't come up with any ideas to pursue. He climbed on an outcropping of rocks overlooking the Shutter's building site and found a smooth rock to sit on. There was a nagging cobweb in his mind about the attack in his office. It was a smell or, more correctly, a fragrance. It kept returning to his sense of awareness. It was vastly different from the earthy scent he had been aware of when he had first encountered Alma.

He checked his watch and decided he still had time to walk out to the burned remains of Alma's house. It was a brilliant and clear morning. There was still a hint of dew on the cactus, and the desert birds were flittering around the plants, picking up an insect here and there. He saw the usual ground squirrel and rabbit, but it wasn't until he went over a small rise just yards from the edge of Alma's yard that he saw the pack of coyotes. Five or six had found something edible in the charred rubble.

They didn't take the intrusion of Brighton lightly. The alpha male in the pack turned on Brighton, giving a guttural growl that raised the hair on Brighton's neck. He froze at first, avoiding eye contact with the coyote. He glanced around until his eyes spotted a shovel with a partially burned handle. He moved closer to the shovel and, with a quick move, picked it off the ground and began yelling at the coyotes while swinging the shovel from side to side. The charred handle promptly broke in half, sailing the blade into the desert, leaving nothing but a short piece of wood in his hands. The younger and smaller animals took flight, but the large female and the alpha male slowly increased the distance between each other while keeping their heads near the ground and their beady eyes focused on Brighton. He was astounded that they weren't running away from him. Whatever they had found to eat must have been something special. The strings of drool from their jaws raised a fear in Brighton that they might all be rabid.

Taking steps backward, he moved behind a bundle of burned tin roofing and finally saw some items that could act as real weapons. Grasping a broken ax handle, he was surprised at how heavy the thing was. He doubted whether he could throw it more than a few feet, let alone hit the coyote with it. He didn't have long to find out. From behind him came a growl and the thud of heavy paws. Turning, he saw a third adult coyote rushing him with jaws open and eyes ablaze. In a purely reflexive move, he swung the ax, letting it fly toward the closest animal. Whether the blade would have stuck in a logger's target he would never know, but it did knock the beast off its feet and drew blood. A single yelp and then a whimper was all that was left of the three-sided attack. They all ran off toward a dusty trail, which disappeared through the cholla and brittle brush. Brighton had won.

Other than swinging the ax and dodging the wild canines, Brighton hadn't exerted much physical energy, but mentally he was spent. His entire body was shaking, and his shirt and pants were soaked with sweat and coated with sooty dust.

Searching the rubble, he found a blackened refrigerator lying on its side with the door partly open to the freezer compartment. This is where the coyotes had been feeding. He nudged the fridge into a better angle with his foot and jerked the charred door completely open. There, amid the defrosted food and rapidly spoiling meat, was a sealed plastic food container. Inside it, he could make out a folded, brown, business-size envelope apparently hidden and forgotten.

He knew that he was about to invade Alma's privacy and that he was trespassing. He looked around to be sure he was alone and then opened the partially melted plastic container and withdrew the envelope. There, clear as a harvest moon, was the return address of Geological Associates. The Phoenix assay company was showing its colors in interesting places. Brighton slid the content out of the envelope and found a single-page letter telling Ms. Ziegler that her property might be the site of significant mineral deposits. It went on to say that the assay company would like to help her study some samples of the rock at no expense to her. There was just the single sheet of paper that had at the bottom the neatly written signature of Lori Patterson, President and CEO.

Brighton had all he needed. He took the paper and dropped the envelope and container near the spilled food and thawed-out vegetables, stomping them into the mix with the trampled mess. Dragging his feet across the charred rubble to cover any distinct shoe prints, he made his way across the driveway to the road. He tucked the letter into his shirt and began jogging back to Hidden Canyon.

31

COLLAPSE

It took several hours for Dean and his workman to move the Mole and accumulated equipment to the new site behind the Steiner brothers' two houses. The Patels' had been surprisingly cooperative. Replacement dirt and vegetation had been placed and drip lines to all the separate plants installed. The yard looked terrific. The Patel boys had already started to wash off the thick layer of dust from the pool and patio areas. Dean had lost track of the number of loads of ore they had taken from the Patels, but he knew that the proceeds would yield a king's ransom.

The arroyo connecting the Steiner brothers' homes was proving to be easier to dig. The access to the backyard, up a steep incline, had required moving a couple of large cactus, but otherwise the situation was going to work out well. Dean had already dug a small trench the evening before and knew the type of earth he would find.

Otto had greeted him that morning with the good news that both families were going to go back East to visit friends and attend Oktoberfest in Minnesota. Dean laughed out loud at the thought of being able to tear up the Steiners' properties without so much as a yodel from them.

He fired up the engine of the Mole, positioning the huge machine just beyond a fractured rock outcropping that he would leave intact. He started the actual digging just beyond it. Pulverized rock and dirt began pouring out of the conveyor end of the Mole, and a dust cloud erupted from the front end, completely obscuring his vision of where the diamond-studded teeth were chewing away. His helper, Eveready, had dragged an extra garden hose from Otto's patio and was spraying the area to settle the dust that the yellow beast was spewing. Dean stopped the dig to attach the hose to the front to help settle the dust.

He had been working for about two hours into the deepest hole he had dug thus far. Mountains of ore lay in a neat row behind him. Dean first heard the problem before he felt anything. A change in the pitch of the engine was followed by the distinct new ripping sound of metal on metal. Before he could shut the engine down, he felt another sensation. The Mole was sinking. The angle of the seat shifted drastically forward, nearly throwing him against the control panel. The engine sputtered to a stop, and the sinking motion slowed. When it finally stopped, he found himself sitting at a forty-five degree angle, ten feet below ground level, looking into a dusty, dark tunnel. When the dust cloud began to settle, he wiped his eyes and saw a double row of metal rails disappearing into a hole in the side of the mountain.

"Madre de Dio!" exclaimed Eveready, leaning down over the edge of the collapsed tunnel.

Dean brushed the dirt and debris from his shirt and Levis, removed the respirator and goggles, and crawled over the front end of the Mole to get a closer look. He was staring into the mouth of an ancient mine shaft. The narrow metal mine cart rails had been twisted and mangled by the jaws of the Mole. They had in turn fouled the six grinding bits and jammed the conveyer, causing the engine to stall.

Looking deep into the shaft, he saw no sign of a mine car or any other tools. Thick cobwebs were hanging from the ceiling. Beyond was darkness. He motioned for his man to stay back and not walk near the roof of the tunnel. As he spoke, a cascade of new rocks fell from the overhanging ceiling. He slipped his cell phone out of its holster and hit a speed dial button. "You need to come up to the Steiners' casa. You are never in a million years going to believe what I'm looking at."

***

Roy walked briskly up the steep approach to the Steiners' homes, eager to find Dean and the Mole. Dean's truck and tractor were sitting off to the side, but the Mole was not in view. A long, deep pile of ore that looked freshly dug lay at the far end of the property near an outcropping of distinct red boulders. As Roy walked closer, he could see Dean and Eveready sitting on the edge of the boulders, looking downward into a gaping sinkhole. The yellow roll cage of the Mole was barely visible above the level area of the yard.

"I knew there were old mine shafts scattered around these hills, but I had no idea we were building homes right on top of one," Dean said, still staring into the hole.

Roy walked up to the edge of the hole and gave a long whistle. He walked the full circumference and stomped at the loose edges, creating an occasional new landslide. Then he took a seat on one of the boulders beside Dean.

"Have you checked it out inside yet?" Roy asked.

"I know you think I look stupid, but do you really think I am that stupid?" Dean said. "There are still rocks falling from the roof of the tunnel. I tried to look up into it for as far as I could see by standing on the hood of the Mole, but every few seconds another rock falls and kicks up a new cloud of dust. It looks like there is some equipment at the far end of the tunnel. I'm pretty sure it takes a turn deeper into the mountain."

"Where do you suppose the entrance is?" Roy asked, deferring to the man who had been developing this whole area, yet had overlooked a mine shaft less than fifteen feet below the surface.

"My best guess is that it is over on the other side of the hill, a few hundred yards from here, probably on our newest best friend's property. My guess is that the Mole collapsed an air vent, and we are at the far end of the tunnel. The steel tracks are probably spares that were stacked upright in the shaft. I'll bet the main entrance has long since been covered up, and vegetation has grown over it."

"Did you get a hold of Brighton and Charley?"

"Brighton was tied up with patients. He started late today and now says he has to work late, but he has his own story to tell if he can get here at lunchtime. Charley's secretary said to try his cell later and not to call him at his office … something about him not working there anymore. I think she was crying."

***

It took several hours for Dean to a have a D9 Caterpillar tractor brought up to the Steiners' properties. It had been clearing one of the remaining few lots near the entrance gate. It was a giant yellow machine that shook the ground as it clanked and clattered its way up the hill to the back of the lot. It didn't take long for it to dig out an inclined, ramp-like ditch leading down to the back of the sunken Mole.

Brighton had arrived at noon as promised and, like Roy and the others, couldn't believe his eyes. As yet they still hadn't seen or heard from Charley.

The CAT operator attached a huge chain with links the size of footballs to the back of the Mole. Using the blade end of the CAT to lift one end of the sunken Mole as the CAT pulled backward, it was able to free the Mole from the collapsed sides of the tunnel and, inch by inch, back it out of its earthen trap. Dean knew the driver from previous excavation work, and not wanting to anger the man, allowed him to walk down the ramp and take a look at the entrance to the shaft. "Don't ask and don't tell," Brighton said to the driver of the Cat, handing the man five one hundred dollar bills as agreed upon.

"Just another old useless but dangerous, abandoned mining operation," Brighton said loudly to the men standing around the hole. "It's a good thing it didn't collapse out from under a group of kids."

The CAT driver departed with his giant Caterpillar, clattering down the driveway to the empty lot across the street. The rest of the men stood at the top of the edge, looking into the hole.

"Time to take a look, don't you think?" Roy said to his two friends. "I'd better get rid of Eveready before we do too much in the way of further exploration."

He gave the man forty dollars and asked him to go to the closest Taco Bell for late lunch and to buy them all large Cokes. Dean retrieved two long, black flashlights from the back of his Humvee and waved for the other two men to follow him into the abyss.

The loose dirt and rock made an unstable surface to walk on. Brighton's loafers quickly filled with tiny stones. Boulders the size of footstools had to be circumnavigated, and without warning, watermelon-sized rocks fell from their millennial fixations in the roof of the newly disrupted cavern. The three men proceeded slowly to the boundary of safety, holding their breath quickly as they headed into the deep tunnel.

Shining the flashlights into the newly created entrance, they began inspecting the tunnel. The bent mine cart tracks were the only obvious sign of man's previous presence. A few yards deeper, they found an old oil lantern hanging from an eight-by-eight-inch timber wedged in the corner of the tunnel. From there the walls seemed to curve out of sight. At best, they could see less than thirty feet into the cave before it made a descending turn into the mountain.

"Have any hard hats in your truck?" Brighton asked, turning toward Dean. "We really need to check this thing out, but I've already had my allotment of concussions for the year."

"Forget the hats; just get by that new ledge and you'll be fine!" Roy called out from thirty feet inside the tunnel. He had dealt with danger his whole career and didn't think twice before entering the tunnel. His light flashing on the walls past the turn was soon joined by the second flashlight's beam. Past the hanging lantern there were more relics. Old rodent-eaten ropes, wooden buckets, rusted picks, and shovels with splintered handles lay in orderly stacks against one of the walls. The narrow mine car tracks, like those that had fouled the jaws of the Mole, stretched out before them into a tunnel that disappeared into darkness beyond the illuminating power of their flashlights.

"Look at the ceilings," Roy said. "It looks like this is partially a natural cave, not just a man-dug tunnel. I would guess they dug a new exit or air vent back there where the Mole fell in. There is most likely another natural exit or two at the other end of this thing."

Once past the falling rocks at the entrance, none of the men showed any hesitation at going deeper into the cave. They let Roy lead the way.

"Look here," Roy said, shining his light into a side area off the main tunnel. There had been obvious digging into the cave's wall going back fifteen or twenty feet. "They could have taken twenty tons of ore out of that area alone. And look up here." He shined his flashlight toward the far end near the ceiling where a metal spike had been hammered into the rock wall. Glistening around the spike like twinkling lights on a Christmas tree was a wide vein of rich metals: gold, silver, probably some platinum, and the most precious of them all—rhodium.

"We've found the mother lode and in a natural cave. It's unbe-lievable!" Brighton said in a nearly reverent voice. "Let's find out what else is in this place."

Roy led the way carefully and slowly. Since there was no apparent branching of the tunnel, they weren't afraid of diffi-culties in finding their way back. Dean had relinquished his two flashlights to the other men and was getting a tad dizzy following the darting lights as they flickered to and fro from floor to ceiling. The three men followed the cave back an-other eighty feet before they found an anteroom, where the digging had created a twenty-by-thirty-foot area. There again they could see a vein of glistening ore streaking across the wall. Indentations from picks and stone axes pockmarked the three walls, and the floor also had been dug down two or three feet. In the far corner lay the mummified carcass of a small coyote that had probably wandered into the cave and become lost. Brighton felt a chill run up his spine.

All along the cave the men could see where the floor had been chiseled and hammered to make it level and smooth for the narrow-gauge rails to be placed.

By now the men were a good hundred feet into the tunnel, and the ceiling was getting lower. There an abrupt shift in the strata appeared. An opening angled upward at sixty degrees, and a blast of fresh hot air could be felt pouring down into the cave. With a flutter of wings, a dozen or so bats took flight, screeching as they were interrupted from their slumber. They scattered up and out through an opening about fifty feet above that appeared to be no larger than a man's fist.

Off to the right, the tunnel opened into another cave. This one had much higher ceilings and still had a few stalactites point-ing down at the men. It was a dry cave and most likely only had moisture during the summer monsoon season, when the moun-tain soil became saturated enough to allow a few drops of water to seep through.

At the furthermost end of that cave, one hundred feet from the vent, they found a stack of rails and a small hand-made, wooden ore car. Only the wheels were metal. One of the axles had col-lapsed with several hundred pounds of ore still in the box.

"This must have been the coup de grâce for the operation. It looks like they cleaned up the tunnel, stored their equipment, and left for a while," said Dean.

"Or, maybe they locked it up so they could go to town and spend some of their money," said Brighton.

"They left it for a long, long while," said Roy. "I doubt anyone was using wooden mine cars after the 1880s. This place probably hasn't been touched for a hundred and thirty years. We'll have to look at the history of the area and see if there were any claims filed. Back then this place was at least twenty-five miles from the nearest commerce center. That's almost a day's ride by mule or wagon."

"You don't think this could be that Lost German's mine, do you?" asked Brighton.

"You mean the Lost Dutchman's mine?" Roy asked.

"No way in hell. That thing, if it ever existed, had to have been up in the Superstition Mountains. They're another ten miles from here," Dean answered.

"No one has ever proven where it was, but its having existed is hard to refute," Roy added with the confidence of one who had read more than a thumbnail sketch of the legend. Once, he had even rented a pathetic little donkey to go back into the Superstition Mountains. He wanted to see for himself what all the legends were about. What he had found were many beaten-down trails and scattered trash. He had come away from that mountain range vowing not to waste his time there again.

Both of the flashlights were getting dimmer, and the men decided to head back to the entrance at the Steiners'. They had seen all they needed for now. Eventually they would want to find the location of the air vents and the main entrance. The location where the Mole had collapsed the tunnel was a possibility for the entrance, but there had to have been a major earthquake or deluge from a cloudburst to have buried it that well. The men were nearly one hundred and fifty feet from the sinkhole where the Mole had rested earlier that morning when the snake struck.

All three men heard the snake's warning buzz. It was mixed in with the sounds of their six shoes crunching on gravel as they walked in the dim light. Before anyone could react to the sound of the high-pitched rattle, the snake struck Brighton's right ankle, easily penetrating his thin sock. Both fangs sank through his sock, deep into the soft flesh of his lower ankle.

"Ouch!" Brighton yelped, his brain not registering at first what had caused the pain. Then he knew. "I've been bitten!" he screamed out in more panic than pain.

Roy grabbed Brighton's shoulder, jerking him away from the area where they had heard the sound of the rattles. Dean shook his flashlight to try to get more light out of it but to no avail. He couldn't see the snake and wasn't sure where it was safe to step. Roy steadied Brighton, who was hopping on one leg, but not reaching for his ankle in fear that the snake would strike him in the face or arm. Roy shined his dim light on Brighton's ankle and saw a tiny trickle of blood oozing through the gray sock. He pulled down the sock, exposing two oozing puncture holes. The snake had stopped rattling.

"Where did the damn thing go?" Brighton asked.

"Forget the snake. We need to get you out of here and to the hospital," Roy said in a calm yet commanding voice. "Grab his other arm, Dean. Brighton, try not to put any weight on your foot. Your ankle is bleeding; that's good. It will allow some of the venom to be washed out with the blood. It's fall instead of spring; that's good too. The snake's venom is much less concentrated this time of year."

The two partners' strong arms and legs soon had Brighton at the entrance to the tunnel. The newly loosened dirt and crumbled rock slipped under their feet as they climbed the last ten yards up the incline.

Looking around the yard with the bright sunlight making him squint, Brighton felt like he had just had a nightmare and was suddenly waking up. Then he felt a searing hot pain shoot up his leg into his crotch. He looked down at his bloody sock and shoe, and then, with the desert, the mountains, and the Steiners' houses spinning around in his head, he fainted.

"Why don't you drive your Hummer around here to the back, and we can load him in the backseat and go straight to the hospital? It's one way for us but a round trip for the ambulance."

"My truck isn't here. Remember, we sent Eveready to the store. He must not be back." Dean was half squatted on the ground, holding Brighton head. He could feel his own pulse pounding in his temples and chest.

"You stay with him. I'll get Rhonda's truck. She is in L.A. today and had a limo take her to the airport. I can get into her house for her keys to her truck faster than I can run home." Roy ran from the yard before Dean could respond.

Dean stretched Brighton out on the patio, shielding him from the blazing sun, and gently set his head down. Dean then cut a piece of nylon cord from a staked tree trunk and put a loose tourniquet around Brighton's leg just below the knee. He felt for Brighton's pulse and was reassured by a strong throbbing in his neck. Before he could do much else, he looked up to see the tailgate of a black pickup truck backing up the dusty drive toward him. The cavalry had arrived.

***

Alma was stretched out on the hotel bed in a trance, staring at the stained ceiling, when she heard the knock on the door. She had her hand on the doorknob when she remembered that she should look through the little peephole first to be sure it was safe. Standing in the hall, glancing up and down the hall each way in a nervous manner, was a young blonde. Alma observed the woman as best as she could through the tiny fish eye.

"Ms. Ziegler? I have some important information for you. I'm not going to hurt you. I'm from a company that wants to help you rebuild your house and replace your lost belongings."

This woman didn't look anything like those weird people from the insurance company. She had never seen this woman before. It was strange to stand two inches from the door and have someone six inches on the other side, yelling at her as though she were deaf. It was all she could do to not answer or even open the door, but she remembered Mr. Banks' warning. "Don't talk to anyone but the hotel employees, and do not open the door for strangers."

The woman pounded on the door a few more times and finally left.

Alma thought about calling Mr. Banks but was sure he would have heard about her leaving from Mr. Dean and would be mad at her. She paced in front of the TV, not able to concentrate on any of the shows. When the phone rang, she was glad for the feeling that someone cared about her.

"Hello?"

"Is this Alma?" the voice on the telephone said.

"Yes, who is calling?" Alma thought the voice sounded familiar but wasn't sure which of the men it was. She had talked to so many new friends the last three days.

"I was sorry to hear about the little accident at your house. That's a real shame—all your furniture and clothes and everything burning up. I'll bet you are getting tired of wearing your neighbors' clothes and living in a motel room."

A cold chill followed by a wave of nausea struck Alma as she realized who it really was on the other end of the phone. Hanging up would have been a smart thing to do, but she was too stunned to move.

"Who are you?" Alma asked.

"You know who I am. I'm the guy who wanted to give you a million dollars for your dried-up desert land and that shack you called home. Now, there isn't a house on the property, and it will cost lots of money to clean up the mess you made by burning it down. The offer to buy still stands, but the price has gone down. You have until noon tomorrow to sign the papers, or the price will go down more, a lot more."

"I can't go to the attorneys. I don't have a car to …"

"You don't have to go anywhere. My secretary will come by with the papers. We'll even take the money to the bank for you, but you have to sign the papers."

The phone went dead in her hand. She was drained of emotion and couldn't think straight. Maybe if she had a short nap, she would think more clearly. She would call Mr. Banks when she woke up, and he would know what to do. She was so sleepy that maybe she hadn't really needed the Nytol she had taken just before the phone rang.

***

The waiting room at the hospital was beginning to seem like home. Roy and Charley had been sitting on the cheap plastic chairs for hours. Gina had insisted that Kara, Rhonda, and Dean go home when it became apparent that it would be a long vigil before they got an update from the doctors.

Gina had already been calling around the neighborhood trying to track Brighton. He was late for his afternoon office appointments. Her first, though fleeting, thought was that he was with Rhonda—hormones again. Then realizing how stupid that thought was, she suspected that another bad-luck event had occurred. The confirming phone call came moments later.

Turning again to Kara for help, Gina had explained what little she knew and asked for a ride to the hospital. By the time Kara dropped the girls off at the piano teacher's and they fought the mid-afternoon traffic, Brighton was out of the operating room and in an ICU bed. The trauma team leader met her in the hallway with news that Brighton's vital signs were beginning to stabilize. The doctors had cleaned the bite area and started him on anti-venom. As to the condition of his leg, it was too early to know if circulation would ever return to the poisoned area.

Rhonda heard the news from Roy and had her driver take her straight from the airport to the hospital. She was tired and bedraggled when she joined the others in the waiting room. Charley also arrived, looking like he too had been dragged through a wringer. It was a tearful and daunting reunion as the neighbors waited together and prayed that Brighton would pull through.

The women couldn't believe the story that Roy told them as they sat in the waiting room: the collapse into the tunnel, the abandoned mine shaft, the ancient mining tools, and then the rattlesnake bite. It made it all seem like an episode of Twilight Zone.

✻✻✻

Several hours later, reassuring word came from the team of doctors. The anti-venom was working, though slowly. Brighton's dusky-colored leg was starting to turn pink as the circulation of healthy blood returned. Roy felt a huge weight lift from his shoulders with the news. Earlier, he had overheard one of the nurses mention amputation if circulation couldn't be restored.

Brighton was sedated and resting when they finally let Gina into the room to see him. He was too snowed to respond to her kiss on his forehead or her rubbing his arm and shoulder. She stayed for just a few minutes before she broke down sobbing. Doctor Patel had come by the room and, after consulting with Roy, offered to take the exhausted Gina home. She agreed, to everyone's surprise.

It was late in the evening before Roy and Charley finally had time to discuss the events of the day. The ICU waiting room had cleared out, and the men were finishing the last of a cold pizza.

"You are not going to believe this cave," Roy said, trying to contain his exuberance. "I could see the veins of gold as clearly as if they had been some tagger's spray paint. Whoever mined that tunnel probably just got to the surface of the good stuff when something bad happened, and it was abandoned."

"On whose property is the main tunnel?" Charley asked.

"That depends on whether or not you got the papers signed. It starts somewhere out in the desert east of the Steiners' and winds its way around to their yard. You won't believe the hole in their yard. It will take ten or twelve truckloads of dirt just to fill in the hole where the tunnel collapsed."

"What about access to the other end?"

Roy shook his head. "I haven't figured it out. Our flashlights were going out when the snake hit Brighton. We had only two to start with. We need to go back with good equipment and plenty of lights."

"I'm not going in there! I don't deal with snakes of the nonhuman variety," Charley said. "Speaking of snakes, let me tell you about my delightful day at the office."

***

Alma Ziegler ran away again. After the call from the man she thought had burned down her house, she made the decision to run. She took the time to shower and fix her hair. She even put on some of the lipstick her new friends had bought for her. She put on the best of the clothes lying around and packed the rest in a plastic laundry bag.

She called Mr. Banks but only got his voicemail. She left him a voice message telling about the visitor and the threatening phone call. She then stuffed pillows and extra blankets and towels under the sheets, making it look as though she were asleep in the bed. She cracked the window shade enough for someone to see into the room and even left the TV on. As she slipped out the door, she hung the "PRIVACY" sign on the doorknob and left through an exit at the end of the hall.

She was a lot smarter with this escape than the previous attempt. She walked down the street to the next brightly lit hotel and went into the lobby. There she asked an attractive black woman sitting at a fancy desk where she could get some money. All she still had in her purse were hundreds. The lady led her to a box about the size of a gas range and said, "Here is our ATM."

Alma gave the woman such a perplexed look that the girl read her mind and offered to help.

"How much money can I get out of it? I have never used one of these machines," Alma said with a childlike curiosity.

"May I have your card? We can find out."

The woman slowly slid the card through the slot, explaining the steps to Alma as she went along.

"Could you please type in your PIN number?"

Alma carefully typed in the number and then pressed the enter button. The machine asked for instructions, and with coaching, Alma pressed the balance button. A small grinding noise rumbled inside the machine as if it had come to life, and a narrow piece of paper extruded from an open slot in the box. Alma, again with coaching, tore off the paper and tried to read it. She handed it to the woman who then pointed to the number.

"Twenty-five thousand dollars!" the concierge said out loud. "Honey, don't you be losing that credit card. Do you want to get some money now?"

"Yes, please. How much can I get?"

"Want to try for a lot or a little?"

"As much as I can get," Alma answered.

The woman slid the card through again and had Alma type her PIN in again.

She typed in $200 then changed it to $600 and pressed the enter button. The machine came to life, spitting out twenty-dollar bills. The stack got higher and higher. When it finally stopped, Alma picked up a stack of bills as thick as a sandwich.

"Amazing!" the two women said at the same time, staring at the wad of bills.

The woman helped Alma close out the transaction and started to leave to return to her desk. "Wait, this is for your trouble." She handed the woman two of the stiff, new bills and asked for a taxi.

32

MISSING

Charley had been as busy as a one-armed juggler. With the loss of his job, the finding of the mine tunnel, and Brighton in the hospital with a serious snake bite, his phone wouldn't stop ringing. Now Alma was missing.

Charley had stayed up half the night rewriting the paperwork for Alma to sign. It was clear that the mine shaft and its untold riches were primarily on or under Alma's property. They would make her a partner in the Hidden Gravel LLC, and would give her an additional percentage of any income that came directly from mining on her land. The mineral rights to both the surface and the subterranean area would belong to the LLC, but when all mining was completed, the land would revert to Alma. It was a sweet deal for everyone. Charley had done some quick calculations and figured the deal could be worth over twenty million dollars to each of the partners and twice that much to Alma.

He also had spent significant time on the addendum to the Hidden Canyon HOA bylaws. He had written up a deal that the other twenty-eight members would find hard to turn down. The new Cactus Wren NOA (Neighborhood Owners' Association) would function as a sub-association, agreeing to all the basic rules of the Hidden Canyon HOA but would install its own security gate and have a different set of rules within its boundaries. The other owners would not have access to the Cactus Wren NOA property nor the pool and recessed tennis court it planned to build on the recently acquired empty lot. For agreeing to the conditions, the Hidden Canyon HOA would receive one hundred thousand dollars, which would cover the HOA dues for each of the Hidden Canyon residents for the next two years.

Charley was confident that they would sign off on it, even though there were some real jerks involved. It would take only a majority vote. Now all he had to do was get a hold of the officers of the HOA and find Alma Ziegler.

He had tried the hotel's staff and the bank where she had her account and even her old attorney's office. Desperate to find Alma, he had called Roy at the airport.

Roy was off in an hour and planned to go to the hospital. He promised that he would find the missing woman and said he would even check out the assay company and talk to Lori Pederson, if necessary.

"What about the airlines or the bus stations? What about the other hotels?" Charley suggested.

✳✳✳

Roy decided to check out the hotels near the Courtyard before he went to the hostile territory of the assay office.

He struck pay dirt on his third try. The Hampton Inn didn't have a large staff, and when he asked the front desk clerk if he had seen a middle-aged woman with long, gray hair, the clerk laughed and pointed to the black woman at the other end of the counter.

"You need to talk to that lady. Did she get away with your credit card?" joked the clerk.

Ms. Suggs was polite to Roy. She recounted the experience of helping Alma with her credit card withdrawal and even mentioned the huge tip that Alma had given her.

"Did she mention what she needed the money for?"

"She just had me call her a cab. But I did follow her out, and I heard her ask the cabdriver where she could find a restaurant that had tacos. You know how you can get hungry for Mexican food sometimes?"

"You didn't happen to know which cab company?"

"I sure do."

Roy called the cab company, and with a little sweet talk and a plea for compassion to help him find his mentally handicapped cousin, he was put through to the cabdriver. The man was helpful and said he had worried about the woman after he dropped her off at the airport.

"She wanted the old terminal, where Hughes Air West flew out of. I've never heard of such an airline," the man said in an intelligent voice with a strong Middle Eastern accent. "I left her at Terminal #2 at about four o'clock."

Roy was making a U-turn as they spoke.

Finding her at the airport was easy. She was sitting on a bench in front of the entrance to the departure doors, talking to a policewoman who was writing something in on a notepad. Roy was hesitant at first, but Alma saw him looking at her, and a smile of recognition warmed her face. Roy parked the truck with his flasher lights on and approached the two women.

"Do you know this woman?" the policewoman asked.

"Yes, officer. She is a neighbor of mine, and I have been looking for her."

"She created a scene here trying to buy a ticket with cash and no I.D."

"Are you okay, Ms. Ziegler?" Roy asked, trying to win the woman's confidence. "I'm Roy, remember me? Rhonda's boyfriend? Remember Rhonda Tucker and Kara, who took you to their house and gave you those clothes to wear?"

At the mention of Rhonda Tucker, the officer became more alert and gave Roy a closer look. Alma acted as though she had lost interest in the whole conversation. She was looking around, watching the cars come and go and the people unload their luggage, giving hugs and kisses to one another. Then out of the blue she stood up, picked up her bag and jacket and started to walk away. The alert officer gently took her by the arm.

"This nice gentleman is going to give you a ride to your neighborhood. You should go home and get some rest."

He took Alma's unfastened bag of clothes, noting a stack of greenbacks held together by a rubber band sitting on the clothes. He clutched the outside of the bag and was sure he felt a gun inside. She was lucky they didn't sell her a ticket and then find the gun at the security counter. He led her to the passenger side of the truck and opened the door. She got in without protest and sat, staring out the window.

He got in, started the truck and drove slowly away from the terminal, asking himself how in the heck he had gotten himself into this mess. All it would take was Alma to start screaming or acting nutty again, and Roy could end up in jail for assault or kidnapping. Probably, stupidity would be a more reasonable charge. He barely knew the woman, and now he was suddenly her self-proclaimed protector.

***

Charley was sitting at Brighton's bedside in the hospital, working on his laptop, when he received the call from Roy. He went into the hallway listening intently as he walked. He wrinkled his brow and then began laughing at Roy who was pleading with Charley to give him some advice about what to do with the woman.

Roy had stopped at a gas station to let Alma use the restroom. She promised she would return and not try to run away again, but he kept her travel bag anyway, as insurance. Luckily for Roy, she returned without him having to go in after her.

Charley and Roy agreed that Roy would take Alma to Charley's and then maybe see if Rhonda would allow Alma to stay at her house for a few days. Going back to the motel didn't seem like a good option.

The whole conversation was nearly one-sided after Alma returned. She was sitting next to Roy in the truck, listening to every word.

When they disconnected and Charley told Brighton about Roy's version of the incident, they both laughed—the first laugh for Brighton in days. Not only did his swollen leg still constantly throb, but as he thought about it, he probably could use some advice about women. His normally happy wife was changing personalities by the hour.

***

Gina had never been materialistic and had always been more than happy with whatever meager income she and Brighton had earned. When Brighton started providing a better income, she seemed grateful and had found prudent ways to use the extra money. Now, with all the craziness of the last few weeks, her mind was working in a different way. She was pregnant, and for the first time in her life, she felt fat. She wanted the attention of her husband, but he had been spending more hours every week managing the details of the Hidden Gravel LLC or recuperating from bodily injuries. He had now been in the hospital more days in the last three months than in both their entire lives combined.

She and Brighton hadn't been out to dinner or to a movie since she first got pregnant. Lately their moods and libidos had been on a different schedule. She now blamed all of her problems on the neighbors and their lust for riches. In Gina's mind there were two big reasons their life wasn't perfect: rhodium and Alma Ziegler.

She was sitting on her bed, trying to decide whether to fix herself something to eat at home or to drive all the way down to the hospital for the second time today and eat hospital food with her husband. Her feet were swollen, and her earlier nausea left her drained. She was ambivalent about eating and driving in traffic to the hospital. *Brighton was probably coming home tomorrow anyway.* She would have much rather gone out for pizza and a Coke with girlfriends like she used to do when they were in dental school and Brighton had a study session with classmates.

The ringing phone brought her back to the present. She looked at it and let it ring four times before she finally picked up.

"Hi honey," Brighton said in the most upbeat voice she had heard in days. "Did you get some rest this afternoon?"

"I laid down for a while, but the baby is moving a lot today and I couldn't sleep."

"I've got good news. The doctors said I can go home tomorrow, and maybe if the swelling is down in a few days, I can try going back to work."

His voice was mellow from the drugs, but still had his sincere tone. He was excited to share the news, but she had difficulty even mustering an answer.

"Gina, are you there? Honey?"

"I'm here; the phone must have cut out," she lied. "That's great about you coming home. Listen, Brighton, I have a really bad headache," she lied again. "Would you mind terribly if I don't come to see you tonight? I think I'm just going to heat up some soup and go to bed."

"Sure. I'm sorry you don't feel good. I guess I won't bother you with the other thing I called about."

"Don't be silly, Brighton. What's up?" she asked.

"Well, remember I told you that Alma was missing from the hotel?"

Gina didn't answer.

"Anyway, Roy found her at the airport. Charley and Roy decided to keep an eye on her for a few days. She still needs to sign a couple more documents to finalize the deal, and the title company is still preparing them. Kara is having friends of the girls sleep over, and Rhonda isn't due back in town until really late tonight. Charley even called Dean to see if Alma could stay there, but you know they only have an apartment. Sharron was close to agreeing but in the end said they didn't have an extra bedroom."

"Brighton, get to the point," Gina said in an impatient tone. Her mind was trying to process this incredulous request. Brighton was calling this horrid woman by her first name like an old friend. She was a total nutcase. She had attacked him at least once, fired a gun at her and now he wanted his pregnant wife to play hostess to the witch?

"Well, Charley was wondering if Roy could bring her by and let her spend the night at our house … you know, in the guest bedroom?"

Another dead silence followed. When she said nothing, he went on. "It's a bad idea. I'll call and tell him to forget it." Brighton had read her mind over the phone and didn't like the reading. "Maybe she can stay at Roy's, or maybe Dean and Sharron have a couch she can sleep on. It will just be for one night anyway. Gina, are you still there?"

"She can stay here if you think that's the best thing," Gina relented.

"Are you sure?"

"No, I'm not sure," she thought, but then had a wave of empathy for the woman who had just lost her home, and had no one in the world but strangers to turn to. Plus, how could she turn her husband down when he was lying on scratchy sheets in a hospital bed, and she was sitting on a six-thousand-dollar leather couch watching high definition TV on a seventy-two-inch plasma screen, and sipping a Cherry Coke?

"Tell Roy to bring her here to the house, but please tell him to be sure she has had supper first. I'm really not up to cooking for anybody." She paused for a minute, and with a sigh of surrender said, "I guess I could leave some snacks on the kitchen counter. Tell him the front door will be open and to have her come in and go to bed in the blue room. I'll leave the lights on for her. But Brighton, she has to go somewhere else tomorrow."

Gina hung up the phone without saying goodbye and walked to the kitchen. She fixed herself a salad and ate it in bed watching an old replay of *Murder She Wrote*. When she heard a car door slam, she turned the TV on mute and turned off her bed-side light. She didn't want to see or talk to that desert witch.

✳✳✳

Roy walked Alma to the Dunns' front door and found it unlocked as promised. It was nearly dark, but the yard and porch lights were on, giving a welcoming aura. He opened the door, ushering Alma into the house. He was familiar with the layout just enough to show Alma the family room, kitchen, and guest bedroom where there were clean towels on the bed. Gina had left half a pizza and a plate of cookies on the kitchen island.

He thought about trying to talk to Gina, but there were no lights on down the hall toward the master bedroom, nor were there any sounds in the house. Alma's bag lay half open on the kitchen counter with the stack of bills still in plain view, almost as though she were intentionally displaying it to Roy. "How strange was that?" Roy thought. Alma looked around the family room, orienting herself, and then, without a word, disappeared into the guest powder room, closing the door behind her.

"I've got to get out of this place," he told himself and tiptoed to the bathroom door.

"Ms. Ziegler?" he said, talking through the door, "I'm fixing you some supper, then I'm going to leave. Please don't leave the house until Mr. Banks comes to pick you up in the morning."

There was no response from the bathroom. Roy walked down the hall to the family room and cut a couple pieces of pizza and heated them. He had been told to feed her but didn't want to be seen with her in a restaurant. She had rejected driving through McDonald's because she had heard years ago that they added red night crawlers to their hamburger meat.

He walked back down the hall and met her coming his way. Once she sat down at the counter, he got her a drink of water, showed her the refrigerator, and then excused himself. He was out of the front door in a flash and in his truck. Moments later, as he pulled into his driveway, he questioned whether he had locked the Dunns' front door behind him.

"Forget it," he said out loud. His hot tub beckoned. This had been one of the strangest, most uncomfortable evenings of his life.

33

INTRUSION

Brighton's throbbing right leg awoke him shortly before eleven o'clock. The Percocet he had taken at eight o'clock was not lasting nearly long enough. He had been worrying about Gina before he went to sleep, and now his conscience kicked into high gear. Why had he agreed to let Roy drop the desert lady at his house? Gina had said yes, but in his heart he knew that she had a problem with it.

He also was ruminating about the legal problems from mining without a permit. The old HOA would fry them in court if they found out what really had been going on. Eventually, his mind went back to Gina and the desert lady. *Would she hurt Gina? What about the baby?* He had to get some sleep. He pressed his bedside call light, but the TV came on instead. He kept pushing buttons until finally someone answered on the intercom. It was twenty minutes before a nurse showed up to see what he wanted.

"My leg is killing me worse than ever. I need more pain pills and a sleeper, please," Brighton pleaded.

The nurse was a short, round-faced girl who didn't seem old enough to be out of high school, but still had a smart mouth. She told him it wasn't time for his pain pills and that she wouldn't be passing out regular medicines like sleeping pills until midnight. She was gone before he could get over the shock of the denial. He rummaged around in his shaving kit and found some old Percocet. He swallowed two of them with a big swig of water just as the door opened.

It was Sara, an older nurse who remembered him from his last stay. She apologized for the young nurse's rudeness, saying she had been standing just outside the door when she heard the conversation. She had a tray in her hand and said she didn't like any of her patients to hurt. She plunked two Lortab and a ten-milligram Ambien sleeping pill from a tiny paper cup into his hand and refilled his water glass.

He began to protest and for a split second, pictured himself in front of the Board of Dentistry, trying to explain his self-administration of a narcotic. Sara smiled as he took the pills. He knew he would be stoned if he swallowed them, so using his tongue; he let them settle in the corner of his mouth. Then she handed him water.

"Drink the whole glassful. Since they took out your IV, your urine output has gone down."

Trying as hard as he could not to swallow the additional pills right on top of the Percocet, he pushed them further into the corner of his mouth, but they still washed away from his cheek and down his throat. By the time Sara left the room, the pain in his leg was pretty much gone, and the room was beginning to spin.

Brighton dragged himself out of bed into the closet-size bathroom. Leaning over the sink, he stuck his finger down his throat, trying to vomit up some of the medication. In spite of repeated tries, all he got for his effort was a sore throat and a near fall on his way back to bed. He drank another cup of water before realizing that he might be too sleepy to get out of bed again. By then his thoughts were jumbling into nonsense.

***

Albert Hicks didn't have as hard a time finding Alma the second occasion; all he had to do was wait for a phone call from his boss. His job had changed considerably in the last few days. He was no longer commissioned to buy the property from the weirdo Ziegler woman but instead, to see that she would not sell it to anyone else no matter how he had to accomplish it. He and his superior would work on the details of getting possession later.

He arrived at the Dunns' home just before Roy pulled into the driveway with Alma. He had parked up the street from the Dunns' house and waited, observing it from a distance. Once the woman arrived, he left the car and worked his way closer to the house. With his binoculars, he watched a man and the Ziegler woman enter the house. He thought it strange that the man with Alma had opened the door and walked into the house without knocking. What was even stranger was that when the man left a few minutes later, he didn't seem to have locked the door. Hicks watched the truck leave and could hear it pull into another driveway close by. He couldn't help but think this was going to be a quick ending to his assignment.

Albert wasn't just any run-of-the-mill hoodlum. He had a graduate degree in business that he obtained online while serving time making license plates at a minimum security prison in California. It was there that he also learned about precious metals. His stepsister had sent him a letter just before his release, which mentioned finding precious metals in the area where she lived. Moments after the prison gate opened, he had caught the first bus to Phoenix.

With his sister's help, it had been just a matter of time until he had learned a great deal about the people of Hidden Canyon. One might even say that he had become a part of their daily lives without them even knowing it. He had observed goings and comings and was informed about the value of the land and its precious content. He had made contacts and pseudo-friends, especially with some of the older retired women in the development and had formed his own sort of info-network. His car was a common sight for the security boys.

Due to temporary lack of operating capital, he wasn't the designated boss. He had demonstrated an exceptional proficiency in the practical parts of his assignment. Unfortunately, Alma Ziegler had been a tougher nut to crack. One thing he felt for certain was that she was now frightened, and would most likely agree to turn over her property. He just needed to get her alone for a long persuasive conversation. Taking her out of the unlocked house shouldn't be a problem.

✳✳✳

Alma found the Dunn's guest bedroom to be wonderful. In contrast to her old house, and even compared to the hotel room, this place was like heaven. It made her remember the room her mom had decorated for her when her parents moved into their new house. Everything smelled so new.

She felt dirty in such a clean, beautiful room, so she filled the tub with steaming hot water and added some eucalyptus bath oil from a robin-egg-blue bottle. She stripped off her wrinkled clothes and slid into the heavenly hot water. *What was she thinking of, going to the airport by herself?* She couldn't even remember where she wanted to go. The bubbles snuggled around her neck, and the hot water drained the tension and anxiety from her soul. She was so relaxed that she found herself humming a song she had learned at Brownie camp when she was nine; something about popcorn popping on an apricot tree.

Her thoughts turned to her neighbors in Hidden Canyon. *Why had she hated them so much?* Every one of them was kind and forgiving, especially the dentist she had struck out at and his wife, who was so pretty and sweet. Now, in her helpless and dependent state, she was lying in their bathtub, enjoying the safety and luxury of their home. She thought about the Banks family and how Mr. Banks had helped her and dressed her and fed her, and how he was going to take care of her finances and make her a partner in a business that would make her even richer than her daddy used to be.

The hot water was making her thirsty. Beads of sweat ran into her eyes, making them burn. She added some cold water to the tub and splashed it on her face. She even cupped her hands to drink some of the cool, chlorinated water. Just as she shut off the faucet, she heard a noise. *Maybe it was Mrs. Dunn, but why would she be in the bedroom without knocking or calling out her name?*

✳✳✳

Gina had moved around her room like a mouse in the dark. She didn't want to talk to Alma and didn't even want to look at her. Washing her face with just a trickle of water, she then put on her nightgown in the dark closet and slipped into bed. It was much earlier than she and Brighton ever went to sleep. She lay on her back, feeling the baby do barrel rolls and listening to the stranger's noises from down her hallway. What a weird feeling, to be like a prisoner in her own bedroom. She wanted a cookie or a cup of hot chocolate, but didn't dare risk an encounter with the desert lady.

She had heard the bathwater run for a long time. Fifteen or twenty minutes later it ran again, and just as it shut off, Gina thought she heard the front door close. It was a quirky little sound that the hinges and latch made at the same time. It hadn't changed since they had moved in. She had asked Brighton to oil it or adjust it, but of course, there was always something else going on to distract him. Chills ran up her spine when she remembered that it couldn't be Brighton, and Alma was still in the tub. Roy had left nearly an hour ago, and he wouldn't just walk in the house again without calling or ringing the bell.

Gina's first thought was to pull the covers over her head and hope the noise would go away.

***

Alma's first thought was that she was lying naked in a stranger's house, and there was someone in her bedroom on the other side of the door. At her old house she always had kept a gun handy and knew how to use it. Her pistol was in the nylon backpack with her extra clothes and money, but they were lying on the kitchen counter. Slowly, she stood up and stepped out of the bathtub. A skinny plastic bottle of men's shampoo sitting on the counter caught her eye.

***

Gina did have a gun but had never held it or fired it since the first week Brighton bought it for her during dental school. They were living in a bad part of the city, and he often stayed late to team-study with classmates. He thought it would make her safe in his absence.

She slid open the nightstand drawer and felt the cold steel behind the box of Kleenex tissue and some old magazines. Quietly, she hefted the gun out of the drawer and tried to remember how it worked. He had told her something about taking off a safety.

***

Both women in their separate rooms moved silently. Gina slipped out of the bed and tiptoed to the door, listening intently for the slightest sound. Her breathing was getting faster as her anxiety level increased. She couldn't wait much longer. Probably her ears had tricked her. She needed to be reassured that the front door was locked, and maybe she could even raid the refrigerator while she was tiptoeing around.

Alma was beginning to doubt the reality of hearing the doors opening and closing when she heard the distinct sound of a man's cough.

***

Albert heard the sound of both doors opening at the same time. He was standing in the open doorway between the guest bedroom and the hallway. Through the doorway to the bathroom, a hand darted out and flicked off the light switch, throwing the guest bedroom into darkness. From far down the hallway, a new dim light appeared.

He took several quick steps across the darkened bedroom, grabbing toward the woman's hand only to feel his face splattered with a cool slime that filled his nostrils and mouth and sent intense bolts of pain from his eyes to his brain. Ear-piercing screams bombarded him from both doorways. Then the light in the room came back on. He grabbed the nearest piece of material his hands could find—a satin throw pillow from the bed—and wiped his eyes. Squinting and rubbing, trying to see anything, his vision finally cleared enough for him to see the skinny, gray-haired woman standing naked against the wall. Her body was ghostly white except for her neck, face, and muscular arms, which were the color of beef jerky and wrinkled. In one hand, she held a plastic bottle that was dripping green liquid. In the other, she held a bright blue towel with which she made no attempt to cover her nakedness.

As his vision cleared, he turned to face the hall doorway. Standing there in a lacy blue nightgown with a swooping neckline and the fullness of her pregnant abdomen was the woman he knew as the dentist's wife. Though the encounter thus far had happened in seconds, there now came a period of frozen time. The screams had stopped, and in their place was a deathly silence.

There, surprisingly, in the pregnant woman's right hand was a gun. At first, he thought it was a joke, but as his tearing eyes cleared his vision, he could discern the no-nonsense look on Gina's face.

"Now ladies, let's not get too excited. There is some kind of mistake. I don't want to hurt anyone. I'm in the wrong house. Please accept my apology, and I will leave quietly. Please put down the gun before you hurt someone."

Except for the small, blue chintz pillow he had been using to clear his eyes, his hands were empty and held out away from his body. Tears were streaming down his cheeks onto his flowered Hawaiian shirt. Neither of the women had made a sound since their synchronous screams. Each held her position. Water was still dripping from the naked Alma, and Gina's once-steady gun hand was wavering, getting tired holding the heavy steel pistol.

"If you won't drop the gun, at least step away from the door so I can leave."

"Don't let him leave," whispered Alma. "He is the mean bastard who burned down my house. Let me take the gun so I can shoot him like the rabid dog he is."

Unabashed by her nakedness, she walked slowly across the room toward Gina. As she passed in front of Hicks, she abruptly turned toward him and slapped him across the face. He reacted by grabbing her other wrist and pulling her in front of him like a shield, but the combination of his shampoo-covered hands and her still dripping wet body allowed her to jerk away. She nudged Gina into the hallway, slamming the door behind her, trapping Hicks in the bedroom.

"Give me the gun and go call the police!" Alma commanded in an out-of-character voice.

Gina would not give up the gun. Instead, she ran toward the master bedroom to call 911, leaving the enraged intruder in the guest room and Alma standing unarmed and unclothed in the hallway. Alma could hear the man's cursing behind the bedroom door, thus she backed down the hallway toward what she remembered to be the family room, where she had left her backpack. The hallway was pitch black with only the thin line of light showing under the master bedroom door.

The house became hauntingly silent except for the muffled sounds of Gina's voice talking to the emergency operator. Suddenly, the bedroom door burst open, and the intruder came rushing down the hallway, screaming at her. She turned and ran full speed ahead in the direction of the front door.

***

Roy was walking up the moonlit street, hand in hand with Rhonda. Dropping Alma off at the Dunns', he had gone straight to Rhonda's. He needed to unwind. He let himself into her house, as had been his custom of late, and started fixing a light supper. She had called from her plane, saying she hoped to be home by seven but didn't walk through the door until nearly eight. Rhonda was famished and delighted with the salad and quesadilla Roy had prepared. As they ate, they caught up on the day's crazy events. After dinner, she changed into some jeans and a frilly top and suggested an evening stroll to help Roy unwind. He was still bothered by not being sure if he had locked Gina's front door, so they turned toward the Dunns'. As they started up the steep walkway to the darkened house, they saw a flash of light through the living room window, followed by the unmistakable report of a gunshot.

Roy's worst fears streamed through his head as he pushed Rhonda behind a tall travertine pillar near the entry and ran to the front door. Just as he reached for the knob, the door jerked open from the inside. Roy ran face first into a fast-moving body. The momentum carried both their figures outward, onto the stone floor of the porch. Roy automatically grabbed the person to maintain his balance but only managed to drag both to the ground. His head hit the stone with a thud, followed instantly by a crunch to his nose as Alma's face crashed into his. Stunned by the fall, he struggled to make his scrambled brain understand what had happened, and to think of what he should do next.

"Let go of me! Let go now!" Alma screamed into his ear.

"Okay, get off of me!" Roy responded, realizing that the person on top of him was Ms. Ziegler, and that she was not only wet, but stark naked.

The lights came on first in the hallway, then in the entryway and on the porch. Standing in the doorway was the beautiful, pregnant Gina in a flimsy blue nightgown, holding a big silver pistol. She had it pointed at the wet and naked woman who was struggling to get off Roy.

"I shot him! I shot him!" Gina screamed as she lowered the gun. The screams brought a new wave of pain to Roy's ringing ears.

Rhonda reacted first by pulling Gina out of the entryway and behind the pillar. Next, she grabbed Alma's arm, helping her to her feet and pulling her close to Gina. Roy struggled to his feet and gently, but quickly, took the pistol from Gina. His head was now clearing rapidly.

"There was a man attacking us in the house. I shot him and heard him scream. Maybe he's dead! He ran into the backyard," explained Gina in a rush of words.

Slowly, with gun in hand, Roy entered the house. His head was throbbing from hitting the stone floor, and he was still in shock from the takedown by the naked desert lady. Listening and looking for a sound or sign of whomever Gina claimed she had shot, he walked around the entry's corner, turning on lights as he started down the hall. No one was to be found, but a smeared trail of blood caught Roy's eye. It led from the long hallway with its polished stone floor onto the deep-pile carpet of the family room. Turning on more lights as he went, Roy could plainly see that the blood trail led to the massive sliding glass back door then out onto the patio. The door was still standing wide open. He turned on the backyard floodlights but couldn't see any movement.

Thinking clearly now, his attention turned to the women and especially to the naked Alma. He grabbed a throw blanket off the couch as he dashed to the front porch.

He found the women where he had left them, Gina and Rhonda on each side of the now shivering Alma, forming a human shield and warmer. Rhonda was in the process of calling the sheriff on her cell phone only to be told by Gina that the sheriff was already on his way.

"The house is clear. Wherever you hit him, he's losing a lot of blood," Roy told Gina. "And he is long gone. Let's go back into the house." No sooner had he said it than they heard the rumble of a big V-8 engine come to life in the distance.

Feeling that the danger was gone, Roy helped the three traumatized women into the house. Rhonda led Alma down the
blood-spattered hallway back to the guest bedroom where she
helped the woman into a hot shower. The evaporating dryness of
the desert night air had chilled Alma's skin to a mass of goose
bumps, turning her white, naked body a blotchy blue. The room
was a mess with smears of green shampoo strewn on the dresser
and walls.

Assured that the sheriff was on his way, Roy took Gina's cell
phone and called Charley Banks. The presence of an attorney
was going to be essential to assist Gina, plus Roy needed the
presence of another man in the house. He was careful to keep
Gina away from the bloody trail, well aware that touching anything would aggravate the sheriff and impede the work of his
crime scene experts. However, he held onto the gun just in case
there was a reappearance of the assailant.

When Alma was warmed and dressed, Rhonda led her down
the hall into the living room where Roy and Gina sat, talking
softly. The two women joined them, and the four sat in stunned
silence awaiting the arrival of the police. Roy felt so guilty for
leaving the front door unlocked that he could hardly stand it. He
was certain that the three women were sitting there silently cursing him.

They could hear the sirens for several minutes before there
was a knock on the door and the first pair of deputies streamed
into the room. Don Brice, the county sheriff, arrived moments
later. Sheriff Brice was getting accustomed to making visits to
Hidden Canyon. Off the top of his head he counted six incidents
involving the residents of Cactus Wren Circle alone. This place
was right up there with East L.A. in his frequent idiot index.
Over the years he had become cynical, coming to the conclusion
that the majority of crimes and police-required investigations involved at least one stupid victim—often many stupid victims.

He introduced himself to the group of four, taking a few extra
seconds to study the familiar, gorgeous face of Rhonda Tucker.
He recognized the names of the others from previous reports.
The other three officers searched the house and grounds and
reported little or nothing in the way of obvious clues. The trail
of blood led across the patio, then disappeared into the desert

landscape. There was no sign of a bullet hole in any of the walls of the house; he thought the target must still be carrying the slug. Another group of men and a woman arrived to check for fingerprints and carry out the forensics on the blood found trailing along the floor. Maybe they would be lucky enough to get a DNA match.

The four were asked to stay in the living room until the investigation was complete. The sheriff had many questions, but Roy held firm on his pledge that no one would answer anything until their attorney showed up.

Charley arrived fifteen minutes later dressed in a coat, white shirt, and tie. He was ready to play lawyer. He went first to Gina, kneeling in front of her and speaking softly enough that the others couldn't discern the conversation. Next, he went to the chair where Alma sat in a catatonic-like state. Again, he knelt in front of her, taking her hands and exchanging muted phrases. Finished with Alma, he nodded at Roy and Rhonda then spoke to Chief Deputy Brice.

"Just for the record, Sheriff Brice, I am Charles Banks, and I represent both Ms. Ziegler and Mrs. Dunn. I want it made known that there has been an attempt on the life of both of my clients tonight, and I expect the sheriff's department and the county attorney to make every effort to find and punish the person who broke into this house and threatened the lives of these two ladies. Ms. Ziegler has reason to believe that the intruder is the same man who threatened her two days ago, and then torched her house, burning it to the ground. Ms. Ziegler has been in hiding but was tracked down twice by the intruder, threatened, and now physically attacked."

Brice wanted to roll his eyes in response to Charley's legalese but thought better of it. He knew Alma Ziegler from her own set of bizarre activities over the past ten years: trapping animals, burning trash on no-burn days, shooting up the insurance woman's car, probably bludgeoning the local dentist, and destroying federal property—a United States mailbox. The list of complaints went on and on. *How did she ever get mixed in with this affluent bunch?* Looking at Alma sitting next to Rhonda Tucker and the very attractive Mrs. Dunn, even in her obvious pregnant state, was like watching his kids' video of *Beauty and the Beast*. Ms.

Ziegler looked like she must have combed her hair with a garden rake.

After a round of questions, the lab team finished their work, and Brice told the group of four that they could go home. Rhonda realized that there was no way she could leave Gina and Alma to spend the night alone and insisted they come to her house. The ladies gathered up essential overnight items and followed Rhonda and Roy out of the front door.

Charley, now alone, wandered around the Dunns' empty house, picking up scattered towel and dishes, straightening as he went. He examined the bloodstained carpet and elected to leave that cleaning job to professionals. He checked and locked all the windows and doors before he walked down the hill to his car and put in a call for Brighton. This was going to take some explaining. He hoped his friend the dentist was awake and prepared for a shock.

34

TIME OUT

Not only was Brighton unable to take Charley's call; he was chemically comatose. Nurse Sara came in to take his vital signs forty minutes after his medications were administered. When she saw the patient slumped over the bed, she panicked. Brighton's respiratory rate was half normal, and his pulse nearly twice what was considered safe. His heart was trying to compensate for his slow, shallow breathing and a poor oxygen exchange. She tried to wake him, but he was so sound asleep that even grinding her knuckles into his sternum didn't get a response.

Luckily for Brighton, Nurse Sara stopped to think for a minute before she pushed the literal panic button. *Could I have given him too much pain medication all at once?* Maybe his liver was affected by the snakebite, making the drug relatively stronger and last longer. She decided to follow her basic medical training: "First, do no harm."

Sara could hear the phone ringing down the hall at the nursing station, but she didn't want to leave Dr. Dunn. The phone calls would just have to wait.

***

At the other end of the line, Charley was getting angry. *How could a hospital nursing station not answer its phone?* He finally gave up trying as he pulled into his driveway and shut off his car. He sat there listening to the sounds of the engine cooling and the distant howling of a lonesome coyote. This whole mining business was getting very complicated and more dangerous by the day. He thought he had covered all the legal angles, but no one taught him in law school how to handle a kidnapping or shootout.

What the heck were they going to do with Alma? She was an educated, well-to-do woman in the prime age of her life, yet she now seemed like a seven-year-old who was now 100 percent dependent on the members of the Hidden Gravel LLC. He could deal with the goofball Steiner families and even the naive Patel gang, but Alma was an enigma. For sure Gina, who didn't like the woman in the best of circumstances, and whose husband was a walking medical disaster, was not going to let Alma spend another minute in her house. Kara had to protect their girls and had told Charley that the desert woman staying at their home was not an option. Roy had the extra room, but Rhonda would probably throw a fit if they moved Alma to Roy's. She would put up with the houseguest for a night or two, but Charley was certain that the country hospitality and big smile would fade away quickly.

He had to find another solution. Again he asked himself, *How in the heck did I become her keeper, and what the heck am I going to do with her?*

***

Albert Hicks thought he was a dead man. The bullet felt like someone hit him in the leg with a golf club, and the pain was getting worse. He should have waited for the woman to go to sleep or tried another time. Now he was in big trouble. Not only had both of those women seen his face, but his leg was bleeding like an open faucet, and his eyes were still burning so badly that the tears obscured his vision. He could try to get to the woman some other way later, but right now he needed medical help.

He removed his belt and wrapped it around his thigh to stop the blood. The leg was already getting stiff from the bleeding into his knee joint. By the time he crossed the open lot and made it to the car, he was dizzy and could feel the blood squishing in his boot. He opened the door of the borrowed Mustang and found he had to use both hands to pull his left leg into the car. There was an intense pain shooting into his groin, but the feeling below his knee was now gone. He reached down find that his boot was entirely full of blood.

Albert was trying to be quiet on his the trek to the car, but realized it had been futile. The car's engine sprang to life with a throaty growl that he was certain echoed throughout the canyon.

He was sure it would be only a matter of minutes before the cops arrived. The gray-haired witch had recognized him, and now the dentist's wife could pick him out of a lineup.

If caught, he would rot in prison the rest of his life. He tried to focus on the drive out of the development, but nearly ran through the closed gate, locking up his brakes to stop just in time.

On the main road heading toward town and freeway, he passed a sheriff's car with flashing lights and a screaming siren heading toward Hidden Canyon. His first thought was to make it to the freeway and out of town, south to Tucson and then into Mexico. He made it onto the freeway without seeing another police car. As his muscle car quickly caught up with the traffic on the busy freeway, he began to feel as though the car were flying. He didn't hear the other cars honking as he swerved from lane to lane, increasing his speed without realizing it. Nor did he see the gradual banked turn of the main highway, but followed the straight exit lane instead.

The highway patrol officer later investigating the crash scene estimated that the Mustang was racing at ninety-five miles per hour when it hit the concrete wall beyond the stoplight.

***

At nine o'clock the next morning, Lori Pederson called in a stolen auto report to the Phoenix police and then to her insurance carrier. When questioned later by the officers, she told them that the last time she had seen her Mustang was around dinnertime the night before. That much was true.

***

Roy went by the hospital early to check on Brighton. His seven o'clock shift gave him just enough time for a ten-minute visit. He had already spoken with Charley and Dean on his way in. Dean was up to speed on the intrusion and shooting, having received a late-night call from Charley. He had nothing else to do after he checked on his house construction, so he was planning to spend most of the day on the Mole. Lot #29 still held many secrets and tons of precious metals.

It was decided that they would leave the cave-in site at the Steiners' for investigation when they could all inspect the tunnel and do so with the proper equipment. Having legal access to the Ziegler property also was essential, and Charley was going to get the final signatures from Alma notarized and the documents recorded.

When Roy arrived at the hospital, Brighton wasn't in his room. The clerk at the nursing station reluctantly told him that Dr. Dunn had been transferred to the ICU.

Roy asked for directions and then broke into a run, heading down the long corridor toward the ICU. Before he could get into the ICU area, he had to wait by the locked and coded door, talking through a stupid metal box as though he were ordering cheeseburgers. Finally, the double doors swung open, and he was met by a woman dressed in a starched white uniform.

"He's in the third room down, but he probably won't hear you. He's been in a coma all night," she said. "The night nurse gave him too much pain medication on top of a sleeping pill. He almost stopped breathing. He seems to be doing better now," she added.

Roy opened the door expecting the worst. He parted a white curtain that hid the bed from the hallway and found Brighton sitting up in bed, drinking a Pepsi out of the can and watching the morning news.

"Hey Roy, what's happening on the home front?"

Relieved to see Brighton alive, alert, and in good spirits, he was hesitant but asked, "Are you sure you really want to know?"

Roy told him about the break-in and the shooting. He saved the best part of the story for last, where Alma had landed on top of him "buck naked and slippery from dripping bathwater." Both men laughed until they had tears in their eyes. Brighton still on the pain medication high, was trying to feel panicked, but a bit of anxiety was all he felt. He was assured that Gina was fine and that the house had not been damaged. Roy shared other good news about the newest dig.

"The last thing you need to know is the guy won't be back to bother us. He was killed in an auto accident during the night. His body is lying on a slab at the county morgue."

Brighton's emotions had been close to the surface while hearing the story and, being reassured that Gina and the baby were fine, drew from a well of seldom shed tears.

"Now what do we do?" Brighton asked.

It was a straightforward question, but one that couldn't be easily answered. The men looked at each other.

Finally, Roy answered, "I'm going to the airport tower; you are going to get better and resume filling teeth, if you remember how. Charley is going pick you up this afternoon, if the doctors will release you, and take you home to your wife. Then he's going to straighten out all the legal crap. Dean is going to keep digging starting on the empty lot. I don't know about you, but I still want to become filthy stinking rich." They smiled in silent agreement, and Roy left for work.

***

After the previous night's chaos, Roy and Rhonda had gone back to Rhonda's to settle in the midnight houseguests. Rhonda was a strong woman, but once back in the safety of her own home, and after the other two women had been gently tucked in, she had broken down. Seeing the stark reality of the scene on the porch with its scrambled emotions had frightened her. *What if Gina had fired the gun at Roy or Alma before she realized who they were? What if the bad guy had had a gun and shot Roy when he went back into the house? What if the bad guy has friends or accomplices who return to finish what the first guy didn't accomplish?*

"Why don't we get out of here while we are still in one piece?" Rhonda propositioned. "We can just get in my bird and fly to Hawaii. I have a little house on Kauai that I probably never mentioned. We can hang out there for a while until the sheriff solves this whole mess and it's safe for us to return. Forget about the rhodium and the platinum and the old gold mine and the money."

Forgetting the money would be a no-brainier for Rhonda. She would usually clear ten or twelve million on a two-week concert tour and always made at least ten million when she showed up in a movie. Roy himself had seen her open her mail and glance nonchalantly at residual recording checks for fifty or a hundred thousand dollars. For Roy, the mining operation was a once-in-a-lifetime grasp at the Holy Grail. He earned civil service-grade pay that in his lifetime was unlikely to exceed one hundred thousand per year, and he worked hard for the money.

He hadn't answered Rhonda. They were both too tired to daydream about some Walter Mitty-like existence on a tropical island.

Now, standing in the ICU with his friend and business partner incapacitated, Brighton's "now what" question had put Rhonda's Hawaii proposal to rest, at least for the time being. As he walked out of the hospital into the pleasant fall air, he resolved to see the Hidden Gravel LLC mining operation through to the last possible grain of precious ore. Rhodium, platinum, silver, beryllium, or just plain gold—they all looked like greenbacks to him.

***

Dean heard the news of the events at the Dunns' house after Sharron was fast asleep. She slept like a rock and never heard the phone once she was in bed, so he passed the general story onto his wife the next morning. She listened with detached interest, engrossed in reading a pile of glossy catalogue ads for online shopping and looking up only when she heard the part about the auto accident. Home furnishing items were at the top of her list today.

"I need to order furniture for the new house, Dean. I found some fun teen girls' bedroom sets at Pottery Barn. Which credit card do you want me to max out?"

Sharron's sarcastic comment about the credit card was an ongoing fencing match between the couple. Regardless of how much he gave or made available, it was never enough.

Dean stood up from the small breakfast table in the apartment and walked to her side. He brushed her cheek with the back of his hand, and then leaned over and kissed her on the forehead. He loved his wife, but never in a million years would he be able to figure her out. She was from a huge Appalachian family who had ignored her as she grew up. For the first twenty years married to Dean, she had been clingy and always at his beck and call. Now that they had real financial security, she seemed to have backed off from their relationship in subtle ways.

The most apparent change in Dean's impression of Sharron was her frequent absence from the house—the apartment. The burning of the framed-up new house had seemed to push her even further away from the new neighbors. Dean had tried to arouse her interest in the mining project and to get her to do something sociable with the other neighborhood women, but she was non-committal, agreeing one minute and backing out the next. In spite of the probability of making a king's ransom from the mining, she seemed withdrawn from the whole ordeal.

"I'm going to go over to the empty lot and start some digging," Dean explained to the back of her head. "Charley and I both think we can get a lot of ore out of the center of Lot #29, and if we don't build an association pool or tennis court, we can use one of my preapproved plans to build that Alma lady a house. That way we can get it up and going faster and have the mineable ore long gone before any questions start flying around the lower neighborhood. What do you think?" He rubbed her smooth, muscular shoulder under the silk material of her dressing gown and hoped for a response.

Finally, she looked up at him and smiled, taking his hand. "That sounds like a good idea. Did you want to look at any of the furniture before I order it?" She stood and started down the narrow hall to the bedroom. "Okay with the Visa card?" she asked, not waiting for an answer.

Dean finished his breakfast frustrated. He left the cereal on the table for his daughter, who was on fall break, thus sleeping in this morning. He pulled on a jacket and hat, smeared some sunscreen on his nose, and headed for Hidden Canyon.

✳✳✳

It was a fabulous fall morning in the desert. The sun was hitting the hills and distant mountains at the perfect angle to highlight their colors and odd shapes. It seemed to Dean that every time he drove through the gate and into the various streets and cul-de-sacs of his development, he saw a new giant rock or a different multi-armed cactus he hadn't noticed before. He loved it here. It felt like home. He had never slept one night on the property, but this was where he wanted to spend the rest of his life.

He and Eveready had cleared and repaired the damage done to the Mole's cutting bits by the metal rails in the mine shaft. He sprayed some starter fluid into the carburetor and, settling into the seat, engaged the starter. A slow churning came from the engine block followed by a pop from the exhaust stack and a rumble as the cold diesel engine came to life. A black stream of exhaust smoke billowed up into the clear desert air. Dean let the diesel engine warm up for several minutes, studying the layout of the lot.

Lot #29 was one of the flattest lots in the project, so he expected it to be the easiest to dig and to build on. It also had one of the worst views, explaining why it had sold last and for the least amount. It galled Dean to think how much the LLC had paid the lady to buy back the lot, but what the heck? He could dig that much out of the ground in an hour. What he could dig out this afternoon would more than cover the cost of a fancy pool and tennis facility or a new house for Alma if the assays continued to be as good as they had been.

Dean couldn't believe how easy it was to dig on this lot compared to the hills and rock piles and arroyos he had been working on at the other four lots. It took less than an hour to dig out one long swath that extended the full length of the lot. After three full passes, he stopped to refresh and refuel and walked up the hill to his truck.

Normally, Roy or Brighton would have brought the tractor to the site, saving him time. Now he was faced with the choice of waiting for one of the truck drivers to give him a ride or walk the half mile down to the construction yard to get his tractor. He set off on foot and even cut through a few yards to shorten the distance.

It took half an hour to get the tractor started and fueled and back up the road to the dig site. On the way he pulled out his cell phone to call Sharron and ask her to bring him something for lunch. She didn't answer.

As he approached the lot, he saw someone standing beside the Mole—a tall, blonde, good-looking woman he didn't recognize.

She was giving the Mole a more than casual exam. He loved the way she had pulled her thick blonde ponytail out through the back opening of the baseball cap. It gave her neck and head a foxy appearance.

Dean pulled the tractor up to one of the ore piles, driving the blade deep into the loose rock. He throttled the engine down, put the transmission into neutral, and climbed down to the ground. The woman was still checking out the Mole when he walked up to her side. When she turned to face him, he couldn't believe his eyes.

"Lori? What are you doing here? I haven't laid eyes on you since we were at the family reunion in Aspen. What was that … five years ago? You look great!"

"Dean! I'm fine, thanks. And you?" She was talking, but making no eye contact. "This is a very interesting machine. What the heck does this thing do?" she asked, walking around. She stooped and looked in the cab at the controls.

"It's a type of excavator. We're using it to clear off this lot to get a level foundation," Dean lied, hoping to change the subject. "How is your family doing?"

"Doesn't Sharron keep you up to date? I talk to her all the time."

Dean didn't answer, acting as though he didn't hear the question. He was inwardly flabbergasted that his wife had kept in touch with her second cousin at all.

Lori was the black sheep of the family and had been for as long as Dean had been around them. She had caused some sort of scandal when she was a teenager, and though no one would ever clarify the details to Dean, it was clear that she was a persona non grata to the majority of the clan. When she had shown up at the reunion, where Dean met the woman, the relatives had parted like the Red Sea when she walked by.

Sharron had befriended her cousin, and she had joined them at the picnic table for the family's big potluck meal. They had laughed together at some of the peculiar dishes and the stranger relatives. Dean had even danced with her in the obligatory square dance. That, he remembered, had ticked off his wife. He hadn't seen Lori since then, and was certain that Sharron had never mentioned hearing from her.

Dean recalled that Lori ran an assay company. Where, he didn't know, but the pieces of the puzzle started to fit together one by one. Lori's company must have been the one that Roy had used at the beginning of his search into the mysterious shiny rocks, which had led the whole neighborhood down the crazy path to their King Solomon's mine. He remembered Roy telling him that the blonde owner of the company had been very nosey when the assays showed to be high quality platinum group metals.

"It's good to see you. Did you come out to visit someone?" Dean finally asked, breaking the uncomfortable silence.

"Sharron told me your new house was framed up, so I thought I'd stop by while I was on this end of town and take a look."

"Framed up for the second time," Dean commented in a disgusted tone. "Did she tell you that it caught on fire somehow and burned to the ground?"

"She did mention that. I sure hope you had good insurance," commented Lori, still having little or no real eye contact with Dean. He thought it strange that she didn't inquire further regarding the fire. She seemed much more fascinated with the Mole and with the freshly ground soil that she kept picking up and running through her fingers.

"I guess Sharron told you that we are still living in a two-bedroom apartment like college students."

Dean could tell that she was barely listening to him, but instead was sifting through the pile of ore, spreading layers out with her foot so the sun illuminated them at different angles. She reached down and scooped up another handful and let it drain through her fingers. She spit into a small remaining amount in her hand and stirred it with a finger. The whole time, Dean was studying her and trying to not let his imagination run wild about the possibility of her being the epicenter of all the problems that had struck Cactus Wren Circle and his partners.

"Something catch your eye?" he asked.

"Sorry, habit of the trade." She dropped the dirt and wiped her hands on the back of her jeans. "I was just thinking that this is an interesting-looking rock base. That's what I do for a living. You know, test the soil and mining samples. You probably don't remember. I own a small assay company here in town. Nothing big, but it pays the bills and is way more fun than working for Phelps Dodge or some of the other mining giants."

"I guess I didn't remember that," Dean replied at a loss for words. "Do you run it by yourself?"

"I had a partner until recently, but he got in some legal trouble, and I had to buy him out so he could pay the attorney. Now I heard he's left town. He's probably got some bail bond guy looking for him." By now she was looking Dean straight in the eye and making no secret that she knew exactly what he was thinking. "Today, I've got a new problem. I loaned my car to a friend last night, and he ran off with it."

"I'm so sorry to hear that. Won't he bring it back?"

"Who knows? He just got out of jail, and I was trying to give him some help getting a new start. You know, find a job, that stuff."

"What kind of car did he take?" Dean asked, unable to resist the question.

"It's a new Mustang GT."

Dean's head was spinning, trying to process the possibilities of her or her partner or both being involved in the happenings at Hidden Canyon. He wondered, "Was that the guy who broke in, threatened the desert lady, probably torched her house, and who Gina had shot? Alma sure didn't describe a big guy like Bill when she told the sheriff her side of the break-in story."

Dean commented in a sincere voice, "I'm sorry to hear you are having so much trouble. Let me shut off the tractor, and I'll walk over to the new house with you. It's only a short walk. Who knows? Sharron and her decorator may even be there."

They hadn't made it to the house when the blast of an air horn signaled the arrival of a convoy of four huge trucks. The first driver stopped Dean on the road to ask where he wanted the trucks while they waited to be loaded. When Dean finished speaking to the man and turned back toward Lori Pederson, she was gone.

35

HOTEL TUCKER

It had been a night from hell for the three women. Gina had insisted she was fine to stay at her own house, but in the end, had gathered up her necessities and had gone with Alma, Rhonda, and Roy.

She was exhausted and had refused anything to eat, but instead drank a large glass of water. She sat at Rhonda's table, watching Alma wolf down a big bowl of Ben and Jerry's chocolate ice cream, wishing the whole time she hadn't been so stubborn. Neither of the women wanted to talk anymore about the break-in. The five empty guest bedrooms allowed each her choice of a master suite-size room, each a different color with a theme décor based on Rhonda's past movies. After a warm shower, Gina turned out her lights and was soon fast asleep.

Roy had enjoyed a mug of hot chocolate with Rhonda cuddled on the couch, visiting like old married people. Rhonda's proposal to escape it all and go to Hawaii had taken Roy's breath away. He was still too shocked to give her an answer. It sounded seriously like a marriage proposal, and yet really wasn't. They had kissed goodnight, and Roy, checking all the doors before he left, walked up the road to his own house. Chad had greeted him at his door with a leather bone and an invitation to play. Roy was exhausted but still engaged in twenty minutes of hide-and-seek with his canine pal, whom he had been ignoring lately.

Rhonda ran a steaming hot bath in her enormous jetted tub, adding eucalyptus bath oil. When the tub was filled to nearly overflowing, she peeled off her clothes and slipped into the heavenly, liquid cocoon. After just ten minutes she was having trouble staying awake, so she pulled the drain plug, washed her face with cool water, and stepped out to dry off. The door to her bedroom was closed, and in spite of three closed, solid, wood doors and fifty-plus feet of hallway separating her from the source of the sound, the bloodcurdling scream pierced her ears.

She ran into the bedroom and, grabbing her bedside can of mace, opened the hall door. Standing down the hallway with hall lights ablaze was her houseguest, Alma Ziegler. Her hair was tousled and her hands were bunched into tight fists, yet her eyes were closed; she was sound asleep. Alma looked twenty years older than her real age. She had on a green robe that was two sizes too big through the shoulders and chest, allowing the neckline to droop nearly to her navel. She made no other sounds and didn't move.

Rhonda had a large, white towel wrapped around her and was dripping water on the stone floor. Gina had opened her door less than an inch and looked through the crack. Slowly, Gina opened her door fully and came into the hallway. To Rhonda's surprise, she was holding another gun. Before either of them could signal or speak, Alma let out another scream, this one shorter and directed at no one.

"She is sleepwalking. For heaven's sake, put that gun down. Haven't you shot enough people tonight?" Rhonda barked. This highly atypical refute in such a sarcastic tone shocked Gina, and immediately embarrassed Rhonda.

Gina laid the gun on the ledge of a hallway niche and approached Alma, who was starting to awaken from her nightmare and was babbling apologies to the other two. Rhonda slipped the mace spray canister next to the gun on the shelf and helped Gina lead Alma back into her bedroom.

Sleep came to all of them in bits and pieces for the rest of the night. At six o'clock the alarm went off and Rhonda, a morning person by nature, would normally have gotten up to get ready and meet with her personal trainer. Instead she rolled over, throwing a pillow on top of the clock and pulling another one over her ear. Instantly, she went back to sleep.

Gina awoke in a panic, momentarily not knowing where she was. Once she remembered the previous night and that her husband was still in the hospital with a rattlesnake bite, a new wave of panic overcame her. She had to see Brighton and be reassured that he was all right.

She picked up the portable telephone and dialed Brighton's cell phone number. There was no answer, and after six rings it went to voicemail. Next she called 411 for information and was eventually connected to the hospital operator. She asked for

Brighton's room by number, and again absent ringing was her reply. After what seemed like fifty rings, the operator picked up again. When she was told that Dr. Dunn was in a different room—an ICU room—she dropped a water glass, shattering it on the hard stone floor. Her scream was nearly as loud as the sleepwalking Alma's.

Before Rhonda could drag herself out of her bed, her door flew open.

"Rhonda, wake up! You have got to help me. Please, wake up!"

Gina exclaimed, giving details of the emergency in such babbling terms that Rhonda was sitting up in bed and wide awake before she understood what Gina was saying. When they called the hospital again, an ICU nurse had reassured the women that Dr. Dunn was awake and just fine and was in the ICU because of a medication reaction. Moments later, Brighton came on the line and spoke to them for several minutes, finally convincing Gina that he was okay. Roy had just left and had filled him in on the break-in.

"Go back to sleep, and then come and pick me up later in the afternoon," he told Gina.

Rhonda laid the phone on the bed stand, pulled back the covers, and nodded at the other side of the king-size bed. Without reply, Gina, with her pregnant belly protruding over the elastic waistband of her pajama bottoms, waddled around to the other side of the bed and crawled in. Rhonda turned to the panel of buttons on her inlaid Italian bedside table and pressed a large black button that lowered the blackout curtains, snuggling the room into a comfy but unusual darkness. Within minutes, the relaxed breathing of both women's sleep filled the room.

***

By mid-morning, the area of Cactus Wren Circle outside the Dunns' house was a beehive of activity. Cars were driving up and down the road, and neighbors from the other parts of Hidden Canyon were walking by, ostensibly for their morning hikes, but in reality they wanted to investigate the previous night's sirens and police cars.

Dean was working away on Lot #29, watching the parade of passersby as he dug, loaded, and sent off six truckloads of ore from the newly acquired lot. He had given up any sense of caring if people saw the Mole or suspected what he was doing. It was none of their business.

Kara arrived at Rhonda's around noon with fresh bagels and hand-squeezed OJ. Rhonda had put on her game face after the lengthy ordeal, and was back in the perfect hostess mode when the much-needed food arrived.

Gina, recovered and refreshed, picked up Brighton from the hospital, although his discharge process was unbelievably annoying. At Brighton's insistence, they had stopped by the dig site to talk to Dean on their way home.

Charley had stopped by to have Dean sign off on a house plan building permit for Alma's house. The men were still ambivalent about having her for a neighbor, but until something better came along, they were keeping the option open.

Sharron had surprised Dean with a sandwich and Gatorade from his favorite deli.

After brunch, Rhonda called Roy at the airport and left a message to call back when he had a minute. Seconds later, her phone rang.

"How are you holding up?" Roy asked. He had handled twenty-five landings in the last two hours and was taking a well-deserved Pepsi break.

"Things are better than I had expected. Alma got up and combed her hair and put on a little of my lipstick. My studio makeup people could reinvent her in four or five hours time." Rhonda was walking around the pool with her portable phone as she talked. "Roy, honey, could you do me a huge favor and call another meeting of the LLC? We need to make some decisions with Alma present. I want to help the cause, but this babysitting definitely is not my thing."

Roy agreed to set up a meeting and went straight back to his radar post to keep the air traffic flowing. Concentration was his strong suit, and he was back at his chair only seconds when he pushed the whole Hidden Canyon ordeal out of his mind. One thing that did creep into his thoughts every several minutes was the odd circumstance ever since the snakebite: no one had mentioned anything more about what to do with the discovered mine shaft. It was as though everyone was waiting for Brighton's recovery before even approaching the subject.

36

SPELUNKING

Lori Pederson was smarter than she had ever been given credit for by high school teachers or college professors. Scores on exams were relative to her interest level in the subject and the intensity of her partying the night before. In her Survey of American Opera class (Broadway and movie musicals), she had scored perfectly on every paper, report, and test. The same was true of chemistry, where there was nothing she didn't understand, but the higher mathematics courses left her with a cold feeling of wasting her time. "Let the computers do the math," she had told one professor after he gave her a low C and a warning that her scholarship was in jeopardy. Intuitive thinking was her forte.

When she met Roy that first time, she picked up clues about the discovery of rhodium that she hadn't let go. Not only was she enticed at the dollar value of the ore sample that he originally brought into her shop, but she was enthralled that the platinum group of ores could be that concentrated and so near the city. She spent hours doing online twiddles and searching through the stacks at the ASU library. Her findings confirmed her instinct: this was either the find of the century or major fraud. Rhodium was just not that rich and concentrated anywhere else in the world.

Her employee, Big Bill, put the greed spin on the subject when he got out his calculator and started in on a "what if" scenario that turned quickly from curiosity to lust. Their problem was that they had no clue where the ore sample had been found. A fifth grader could have discerned the false fabrication Roy had invented, but although the story was bogus, the ore sample wasn't. Bill insisted on spending time away from his responsibilities at the assay shop to solve the mystery. With a lot of tracking and some phone calls, he got lucky. He had called in the license plate number on Roy's truck to a highway patrolman friend and, for the promise of a pair of Suns tickets, got Roy's address. That he had shared with her. Then he went over the line and stole a couple of truckloads of ore. Now days had gone by with no word from the man.

It wasn't until Lori bumped into her distant cousin at the Biltmore Mall had she learned about the "silly waste of time" project that was distracting Sharron's husband from finishing their new house. Sharron even mentioned the theft of a couple of truckloads of "very valuable dirt" that if found, could pay for the new house blocks, locks, and, shingles. Lori had made a few observation runs of her own to Hidden Canyon, and it didn't take a Sherlock Holmes to figure out that large volumes of ore were being hauled out of the area and replaced with fill dirt from other construction sites.

Lori had met Albert Hicks years before in Tucson at a big national gem show. He was a classy guy compared to most of the rock geeks and their fluffy, tattooed girlfriends. They had had a few drinks and a meal or two together before they realized that they were related, but it had perked Lori's interest in minerals enough to eventually lead to her opening her own assay business.

When he called her a couple of months ago, she had been happy to hear his voice but not his story of having been parked in prison for the last five years. After his release, he showed up on her doorstep. They had a drink together, and Lori, always one to share a good secret, told him all about the rhodium. Albert became all ears. She agreed to pay him if he would help her buy a piece of land in the desert. He had promised to do some research and get back to her. He even borrowed her Mustang a couple of times to check out some of the leads.

Stories of the shoot-outs and the threat on Alma's life had come to Lori, not from Hicks, but from her cousin Sharron, whom she had latched onto like a pilot fish on a great white shark. After Sharron called Lori and told her about the dentist neighbor getting bitten by a rattlesnake in a cave that ran under one of the lots in Hidden Canyon, she closed her shop for the day. Lori packed up some old spelunking gear from her college days. She had to use the old company pickup since Hicks had borrowed her car again.

She couldn't believe how easy it was to sneak into Hidden Canyon and find the tunnel and explore its branches and the mine shafts. She, unlike the novices who had preceded her, had plenty of candlepower to flood the walls and floor with light. She packed her long-barrel twenty-two pistol that was loaded with snake shot and immediately found not one, but three rattlesnakes sleeping in a corner of the tunnel where a family of packrats had lived prior to providing Sunday dinner for the reptiles. She disposed of the three snakes with three single shots from eight feet away—just out of striking range.

The mine's old, original exit and the airshaft had been easy for Lori to spot. She used small smoke bombs to find the entrance. When they were lit, the smoke was picked up by the prevailing draft of air and was carried like a dandelion seed straight to the airshaft. Further down the tunnel, another smoke cloud easily found its way to the collapsed mine entrance.

Exiting the tunnel at the Steiner's lot, she hiked around the hill to the opposite side on Alma's property to find the pink smoke curling gently out of a pile of lichen-covered rocks and silver brittle brush. No one in a thousand years would have suspected that there was an entrance to a tunnel, a hundred-year-old cave-in beneath this mature desert overgrowth. There was even a ten-foot-tall saguaro cactus growing right in front of the main tunnel.

Before she left the mine tunnel, she found a vein of shiny metal running along the side of a lateral tunnel. She took out her titanium pickax and hacked off samples of the rich-looking rock. She recorded the stacks of antique equipment with her digital camera and even left some name tags on the ancient mine cars, claiming salvage rights to the physical property. She placed a tin can nailed to a timber at both the caved-in entrance and the collapsed shaft under the Steiners' yards, claiming the mine to be her property. This was the traditional method of staking a claim, and as far as she could remember, no one had bothered to change it.

Satisfied that she had seen and marked most everything of importance in the mine, she shot another twenty digital photos of the shafts and equipment and even took pictures of herself standing beside some of the more valuable items by setting the camera on time delay and resting it on the mine car. The photo of her smiling and holding a piece of paper with the date and the simple words, "Claimed by Lori Pederson" secured in her mind that she was going to be rich.

Hicks hadn't known about the tunnel with its collapsed entrance on the edge of the desert lady's property, and Lori had no intention of telling him yet. The surface minerals were his goal. He had called her twice the day before, first to say he couldn't bring her car back for a few hours and next to brag that he had a foolproof way to get the woman to sign over the land. Two days later, she was called by the police and told that her car had been involved in a fatal accident.

***

Charley Banks had a busy Sunday. He had spent the morning at his ex-office when no one was around to make him leave. He called his most valued clients, catching them at home or on the golf course, informing them that he was leaving Fuller and Fuller and inviting them to allow him to remain as their attorney. He then packed up the files of the potential clients. By noon, assured that he still might have some sort of law practice, he focused his attention on his dysfunctional and accident-prone neighborhood.

He called to be sure that Brighton was doing better and that the women at Rhonda's house were fine and then climbed into his BMW and drove to Hidden Canyon. He stopped at the clubhouse where he still maintained a small office. Now that he was no longer the attorney for the HOA, he took some time picking through the HOA files, stopping to make copies of a few more important ones. He was about to leave when Clyde walked up to the door.

"Hey, Mr. Banks. What are you doing here? Mr. Cooperman told me your law firm had fired you and that you weren't allowed to use this room anymore. I couldn't believe it. Say, did you hear that someone broke into the Dunns' house?"

Charley figured that the lonely guard would go on talking all day if he didn't stop him. He held up his hand.

"Excuse me for just one minute, will you, Clyde? Then I'll answer all your questions." Charley then picked up the box of files he felt would help him with the subjugation of the Cactus Wren Circle's own HOA. He handed the file box to Clyde and motioned toward the door.

"Just set those in the backseat of my car, would you please?"

Clyde, with a dumbfounded look on his face, took the box and walked out of the office toward the car. Charley took one last look around the room and then typed a delete command into the computer that held the HOA financial records. He knew that Cooperman had a backup disc somewhere, but a little passive-aggressive behavior seemed appropriate at the moment. Cooperman had been a good guy to work with, but his head had started to swell, and his self-imposed importance had blossomed.

Clyde was standing beside the car, waiting for Charley to give him an answer to his questions about the Dunns' break-in. Charley ignored him, got into the driver's seat, and started the car. Clyde's face was turning red when Charley lowered the window.

"I'm sorry, Clyde, I almost forgot." He stuck his hand out the window and handed Clyde a twenty-dollar bill. "That's for carrying the box." Up went the window, and off Charley drove with a tiny screech of gravel from under the tires.

37

SPY

The neighborhood of Hidden Canyon had seen an occasional helicopter buzz the area before, but this modern-looking MD chopper, with its strange rear rotor and whisper-quiet engine, seemed like it was going to stay in the sky forever. It arrived in the late afternoon and slowly worked its way back and forth across the project, like a wheat thrasher cutting swaths through a rolling Kansas wheat field. Occasionally, it would make a wide arch toward the Ziegler property and then return, concentrating on the upper canyons and cul-de-sacs of Hidden Canyon.

At first the kids and dogs were the only ones giving it more than a cursory glance; however, after thirty or forty minutes of circling, suspicion was aroused and people started to come out into the streets. Many of the neighbors presumed it was searching for a missing hiker or a child that had wandered off.

Dean was busy on the Mole, and though he had seen the helicopter earlier, he had dismissed it, concentrating on his excavation. When Roy pulled his pickup into the dig site and got out, he immediately pulled out a pair of binoculars and focused on the bird. He waved at Dean to shut down the Mole and take a look. It took a couple of minutes, but soon Dean was studying the graceful single-rotor machine as it swept methodically back and forth.

"Do you see the camera pod on the front? The guy is photographing every inch of the neighborhood—especially the upper circles," Roy said, passing the binoculars back to Dean. "Now look at the round thing hanging out of the door on the rope."

"What the heck is it?" Dean asked.

"I'm pretty sure it's some kind of seismographic sounder," Roy said.

"Can they do that? Fly low and slow over the houses like that? One would think it is illegal or dangerous."

"As long as it's not a congested area and he isn't disturbing the peace, he can hover there all day. The big questions are what is it really doing, and who is the guy working for?"

"We had an aerial photo study done of the area before we ever cut the roads and laid out the lots. A woman named Kristen did it for us. She flew an old Hughes chopper out of Falcon Air. She had lunch with me and the engineers several times. I could give her a call and find out whom that bird belongs to," Dean offered.

"Find out what you can. I'll bet anything that it's more of the same group that wants to butt in on our little project."

***

Alma looked out of Rhonda's kitchen window at the helicopter, remembering the first time a helicopter had buzzed her house. It had frightened away the animals that she always fed out behind the shed, some of which never saw again. It wasn't long afterward that the grinding and scraping sounds of the tractors with their black smoke and clouds of dust filled the air of the previously pristine desert.

Now as she watched this helicopter, she noticed it was working its way toward the hills on her property. She thought maybe it was looking for the opening to the old mine tunnel she had found years ago. All this digging and hauling away dirt and talk of partnership with the neighbors confused her. *Why couldn't she turn back the clock and be alone in her house listening to the coyotes and owls?* Rhonda had told her that the lot just down the street where that weird-looking machine was digging might be the site of her new house, if she wanted it. *Why couldn't they just rebuild her old house on her own property, and then go away and leave her alone?*

"Is the helicopter still there?" Rhonda asked.

Alma walked to the window and looked at it then answered Rhonda saying, "What helicopter?"

Rhonda had spent the day feeling like she did when she babysat for her younger cousins. She had fixed meals and picked up clothes and combed hair as though she were the maid instead of a member of *Time* magazine's "Fifty Most Interesting People," not to mention the owner of eighty million dollars in an offshore account that her investment bankers had safely hidden away for her. She knew she could have had her regular help come in and take over the duties of caring for her guests, but she felt a strange and growing empathy for Alma.

She had promised to keep an eye on the nutty woman, and that she had done. She expected Roy to arrive anytime and couldn't wait. He had called on his way from the airport and offered to take them out for dinner. She was in the mood for a good steak and a hot baked potato, although Alma's table manners at a four-star restaurant would be a sight to behold. That she had ever belonged to a national sorority was difficult to believe, especially when Rhonda observed her drinking her soup from the bowl and then mopping up the residual with a piece of white sandwich bread.

When Rhonda heard the door open and then softly close, she thought it must be Roy arriving. Turning toward where Alma had been standing, she blinked in surprise. "Oh crap!" she said. The woman had disappeared.

She couldn't see which way Alma had gone but got a clue when she heard Harley barking from the back of the Patels' yard. Roy returned her panic call just as she was headed up the Steiner's driveway. She had to stop to catch her breath and talk to Roy.

"She is a nutcase, Roy. A wild raccoon would be more predictable. She hasn't said three words all day, and then she started watching the helicopter that keeps circling the area—then all of a sudden, she just took off."

"I've been watching it too," said Roy, walking up behind Rhonda and placing one hand on her hip. He had been in his truck approaching her house when she ran out the door and up the street. "Which way did she go?"

"I guess she went into the Steiner's backyard. I heard the Patels' giant dog barking, and their gate looks like it's open."

They walked up the rest of the driveway together and went through the back gate. Roy was used to coming and going from the Steiners' yards and didn't think much about trespassing or invading their property. They walked toward the collapsed tunnel entrance and could see fresh footprints in the deep dirt, which led down the slope into the tunnel. Harley was barking wildly and lunging against his collar over the temporary fence. As far as Roy knew, no one had even been down into the tunnel entrance since Brighton's snakebite. The Steiners were gone most of the time, and the Patel boys had kept an eye on the site of the collapse, plus Harley had been outside watching just over the fence. The Steiner families were due back anytime, and already had been warned to stay out of their backyard and away from the cave-in.

Roy stood at the edge of the collapsed dig, looking into the tunnel. He yelled Alma's name. Rhonda took up the chorus and was ready to go for a good flashlight when the gray head of hair emerged from the dark entrance.

"Somebody has been in my tunnel!" Alma walked out of the dusty tunnel carrying a piece of paper.

Rhonda and Roy assisted Alma up the steep, dusty ramp. Alma relinquished the note to Rhonda, who held it out for them both to read. *I, Lori Pederson, hereby make legal claim to the subterranean mineral rights of this property, including but not limited to this tunnel and all the contents therein. I claim access and egress on any surface property as may be deemed necessary in order to remove the ore and the contents of this tunnel. NO TRESPASSING.* It was signed and dated.

"Do you believe this?" exclaimed Rhonda. "Who is this person?"

"Remember the woman I told you about who ran the first assay company I took the samples of ore to?" Roy asked.

The women both gave a shrug.

"She is the one. How in the heck she found out about this place, I could never guess, unless she had some inside information or her partner did. Obviously, she has been down there, and the writing of this note would indicate that she has some knowledge of the mining laws."

"Wasn't Charley going to file a claim on the mine and property?" Rhonda asked in a voice that was sounding more agitated.

"Remember, he had to get signatures from Alma and the rest of the LLC."

"Oh crap! Do you think she's filed the claim yet with the county, or whomever, yet?"

Alma just stood there with her head turning back and forth as Roy and Rhonda exchanged comments. "Her claim is worthless," Alma said. "When I first bought my ranch, the attorney had me

322 Steven I. Dahl, M.D.

sign a mining claim to all the land above and below the ground. That's when I got the idea to cover up the entrance to the tunnel on the other end."

"How the heck did you close off the end?" Roy asked in amazement. "I looked for the other end of the tunnel, and all I ever found were huge boulders covering where I thought it should be."

"That's easy," Alma said with a laugh. "Meximite."

"Meximite? What the heck is Meximite?" Rhonda asked.

"Meximite—that's a handful of Mexicans and two handfuls of dynamite."

Roy and Rhonda shook their heads and smiled as the trio headed back to Rhonda's house.

Rhonda scolded Alma as they walked down the road, admonishing her to be more careful. "There could still be someone out there who wants to harm you, especially if they find out you own the mining rights under your ranch. You can't just run out of the house any time you want like a puppy on an adventure."

"I needed some fresh air, and I wanted to see the tunnel all of you were talking about. You have been very nice to me, but you tend to talk about me like I'm a retarded child. I'm not stupid. I'm confused about some things is all. I appreciate what you are doing for me and want to make this whole thing work out, but how about including me in the conversation and, more importantly, in the decisions?"

Roy and Rhonda looked at each other in amazement. Did this woman just wake up from a twenty-year coma?

***

The next LLC meeting was at Brighton's house that evening. No chatter, no snacks, and no drinks were served. Brighton sat in a recliner with his leg elevated and wrapped in a cooling blanket attached with plastic tubing that led into a green-and-white Igloo ice chest. The quiet hum of a battery-operated motor circulating cold water to the blanket was the only sound in the room.

Gina was still resentful about the break-in and having had to tend to Alma, but she agreed to host the meeting in her home only because she didn't want Brighton to have to move his leg.

The pink color had returned to most of the foot, but gangrene in his toes was still a remote possibility.

The room was full of people, and most of them hadn't done anything to further the success of the mining operation. Yet they all were drooling about the possibility of getting rich over Brighton and Roy's discovery. When someone asked Gina for a drink of water, she told them there was a drinking fountain on the back porch.

Charley stood and called the meeting to order. He made a big deal about imposing on Gina and Brighton, apologizing profusely. Kara had read Gina's expression and had given him the word. He gave a ten-minute summary of the publicly known events of the past few days and then reminded them that the rest of the meeting was strictly confidential. He passed around a new letter of nondisclosure that he insisted everyone sign, giving their word that they would not discuss the affairs of Hidden Gravel LLC with anyone.

Dean then took the floor and summarized the progress of the mining operation and gave them a ballpark idea of the account balances provided by Brighton. He had visited with Alma earlier in the evening and had shown her a plan for a new house on the vacant lot. She now sat in the corner next to Rhonda, nodding approvingly.

"Why should she get a new house?" blurted Otto, looking around the room for someone who would agree with him.

"Shut up and listen!" Heinz said, elbowing his brother.

"That is a fair question," interrupted Brighton. "Everyone here has contributed time or effort or dirt to the project. Alma, however, has suffered the most and will ultimately contribute the most. She has agreed to allow the LLC to mine her entire ranch, including the old mine shaft and whatever it contains. She has decided she would like to live in a house in our neighborhood and to be a part of our little community. As compensation, she will have a house of similar value and quality to the rest of us and will receive a double portion of the total proceeds."

"That's not fair," said Otto's wife, in accented yet passable English. "All she has done is create problems. She should be paying us for saving her life."

Glances were exchanged, but no answer to her complaint was

voiced. Perhaps the fact that she had spoken at all surprised them as much as the articulation and obvious greed.

Charley asked for a motion to support the plan as Dean had explained it. Bavana Patel made the motion and was promptly seconded by her husband. The Steiners gave each other questioning glances, having understood little of what had just happened. Charley asked for a vote, which passed unanimously, except Alma, who prudently abstained.

Charley had waited until after the vote before he told them that there was a chink in the armor, a woman named Pederson. He had made a couple of after-hours calls to learn more about the mining claim laws. As far as he could tell, Alma was probably the rightful claimant to the minerals both above and below ground, but to be sure he had put in a call to a law school classmate who lived in Helena, Montana and was a mining and environmental expert. Thus far, he hadn't heard back from the man.

Otto let out a purposeful grumble, drawing the attention of the whole group. "What is wrong with your laws here? In Deutschland, we don't have no problems."

"Then why don't you move back there?" said Bavana Patel, glancing sideways at him.

"Don't any of you lose sleep over this," Brighton added, trying to diffuse the tension. "If we need to, we will go to court to get control. In the meantime, we are going to keep digging."

This brought a heightened awareness to each of the partners. The stage was set, the battle lines drawn, and the war coffers overflowing. What had started with a tiny sparkling rock was turning into an avalanche.

38

DECEPTION

It took all week for the aerial photos to be processed and the computers' seismic studies to run their programs before they were ready for evaluation. A group of two men and a woman surrounded the fake walnut table.

It had taken Big Bill Butler nearly two weeks of following ore trucks out of Hidden Canyon and finally tracking them to the refinery in Colorado before he devised a plan. Once he knew for sure where the ore was going, he had applied for a refinery job at Pikes Peak Metal. On the third day in town, Bill hit pay dirt. One of the grinder operators had crushed his foot in a hydraulic compactor trying to retrieve his Denver Bronco's cap.

Bill received a phone call at the Motel 6 and was dressed and at the plant's gate in thirty minutes. From there it was just a matter of planting the seed in the foreman's head and waiting for it to germinate. At first he was treated like another walk-on employee, but his knowledge of the minerals and the assaying process did not go unnoticed. Even the most innocuous of comments caught the attention of the bosses. Between his formidable size and unique knowledge, he was a natural to advance quickly.

In just one week, he was promoted to a mill assistant foreman's job. Soon he was introduced to Jerry Sorensen, the plant manager and owner. It was the break he had choreographed. He knew that the trucks loaded with ore from Arizona were from Hidden Canyon. If he hadn't been so stupid as to try to steal the two truckloads of ore at the first, he might still have a position in the Arizona company and wouldn't have to include Jerry Sorensen in his plan. But he got gold fever, and Lori Pederson wasn't interested in being involved at the time.

Now his plan was complete and very simple: Let Sorensen in on the magnitude of the Hidden Canyon find, and then work together to figure out a way take control of it. In the meantime, he was drawing twenty-five bucks an hour for standing around and telling minimum wage workers what to do.

Bill had tried to get in touch with Lori to give her a second chance to be involved in his project, but she wouldn't talk to him. He knew Lori would have hatched her own plan by now.

Bill had snuck a look at the computer data regarding the Hidden Canyon LLC account. The numbers were staggering. He updated his knowledge of rhodium and concluded that the Hidden Canyon find had to be close to, if not the richest, in the world. No other recorded finds had been anywhere near to the yield per ton of rhodium ore from Hidden Canyon. How Sorensen had remained so blasé about the job was astounding. This strike by rights should be written up in the mineral and mining journals.

Big Bill sauntered into Jerry Sorensen's office and laid down a proposal. Two days later, the helicopters were in the air, and the data was being downloaded to the new HP computer in Bill's motel room. The following Monday, Bill assembled the new team at the office of Jerry Sorensen. He had collated all the transmitted data from the seismologic studies, along with the aerial photos of the foothills behind Hidden Canyon. Now he laid it out in front of the others.

Lori had been the last to agree to his plan. She had vacillated between coming or not. For years, she had trusted Big Bill, and then he did that stupid truck theft thing. His phone call and proposal shocked her. She had been studying up on the mining claims laws, and her dream of an easy takeover of the Ziegler woman's mine was starting to become less likely. True, she had made a claim, but the days of hammering a stake into the ground and putting a tin can with one's name in it over the top of the stake were probably gone. She had listened to Bill's plan and finally agreed to drive up to Colorado.

For years, she had watched others make good money in the mining business. She had also seen a fair percentage lose their "grubstake," dreaming of lucky strikes and bonanzas that never materialized. Now she was taking huge risks to share in a part of the pay dirt. The memory of the dead Albert Hicks' smashed and lifeless face kept creeping into her thoughts as well.

Bill introduced her to Jerry Sorensen and then gave her a short tour of the refinery.

Lori heard a reiteration of Bill's plan and how he had brought the three of them together. When the meeting broke up, there were cautious smiles and nods of approval. The presence of the successful and quite handsome Mr. Sorensen had given Lori the feeling that the plan might just work.

✳✳✳

Alma had promised to behave herself and remain a part of the Hidden Gravel LLC. Charley had secured all the necessary signatures from her, and she had already made a few changes to the plans of the new house that was to be built. But she still needed someplace to live until the house was built.

It was Rhonda who had the perfect brainstorm. She called her travel agent friend in L.A. and asked him to scan the cruise ships' calendars. "I need a very long cruise for a close friend of mine. The sooner it sails from port, the better."

The friend had come up with a perfect Oceania cruise that started in Barcelona, spent two weeks in the Mediterranean, and then headed across the Atlantic to the Caribbean. There was one premium suite still available. The ship left in seventy-two hours—just enough time to fly to San Francisco to get an emergency passport.

Alma and Rhonda spent the whole morning at Nordstrom's and Macy's buying clothes, luggage, and makeup. They had Alma's hair colored brown with blonde highlights, trimmed, and styled. She had a pedicure and a manicure. She was nearly unrecognizable with all the superficial changes. Charley made a few calls and by noon had Alma's temporary passport work started.

At noon the following day, Rhonda's Citation jet was in the air on its way to San Francisco with two excited women on board. Rhonda agreed to go as far as San Francisco with Alma, where they would swing by the passport office and then put Alma on the overnight flight to Spain. By the time she got back, they would think of something else to keep her busy and safe. If all went as planned, there would soon be a new house for her. Also, by the

time she returned, they planned for heavy equipment to be working the east end of the hundred-year-old tunnel, using access
from the newly acquired land—Alma's land.

***

The newest reality check for the Hidden Gravel LLC came when
Charley Banks went to the Bureau of Mines. The Director of
Mines was an elected position that Charley had voted for at every
general election without ever knowing what the position was or
what the elected official really did. He was soon to find out.

"Take a number," the clerk said.

For a minute he thought he must be back at the hospital ER
or maybe 31 Flavors. After waiting twenty minutes with no one
in front of him, the woman pushed herself to her feet and waddled up to the counter.

"Yeah?"

"I need to speak to someone about verifying and then changing the name on a mining claim," Charley stated.

"You can file it online and then bring the final signatures in
when it's all done." The woman's voice was soft and quite con-
genial.

Charley opened his briefcase and retrieved a folder containing
all the papers he had filled out and the notarized papers signed
by Alma.

"I already did that and have them all ready for you." He
handed the stack to the woman who immediately withdrew to
her desk. Not another word was said, and the only sound was the
soft thumping of the computer keyboard as the woman's sausage-
like fingers flittered up, down, back, and forth across the keys.

After ten minutes, she heaved herself to her feet and approached the printer, which had come to life. She lifted six or
eight papers out of the collating rack and moved to the counter.

"Everything looks okay, but didn't someone in your group
start to file this claim last Wednesday?" the woman asked.

"Not that I know of," Charley answered, a bit confused.

"Well, someone started the paperwork online and then
stopped at the question of the social security number of the previous owner. That was an Alma Z-something, right?"

"Right," Charley answered with a question in his voice. "Does it say who the person was?"

"They didn't get that far, but they did give a Colorado mailing address."

"Would you mind giving me that so I can clear up any confusion?"

"And then you won't mind me giving them your address if they should ask, right?" the clerk answered with a cutting tone in her voice. "This isn't the hospital, but we still have our privacy rules."

Charley felt chastised to the bone. He looked at her eyes, which were sunken deep in puffy pockets and staring at him over the half-rimmed peach-colored glasses perched on the edge of her bulbous nose. He had all he really needed; his side had won. It was time to get out of there. He gathered up the papers from the countertop and started to leave.

"Don't forget to fill out and submit the EPA form. The last miner who skipped that part is sitting in Leavenworth. That's a federal prison, you know." She laughed in a deep, lusty rumble.

The parting words were like a stiletto jabbing into Charley's back. In all the hustle and hassle, he hadn't thought about the EPA and the environmental impact statement they would undoubtedly require. He walked out of the state building with his blood pressure rising with each footstep. Beads of sweat were cascading off his forehead and down his chest. The EPA! He had read volumes about their interference and the economic debris they left in their path. Why hadn't he thought about them? They would probably get automatic notification that a claim was active and would have their inspectors on the job.

"Crap!" he yelled out loud, causing a group of passing bureaucrats to spin their heads toward him. He unclipped his cell phone and punched in Brighton's number.

"Hey Charley, how are you doing?" Brighton said. "I hope you are calling to whet my appetite for some Chinese food, which I hope you are planning to bring to me."

Charley laughed and felt himself relax a little bit.

"Actually, I was calling to invite you and Gina to a line dancing lesson at the Bronze Bull. You know? It's the new catfish and rib place over on Main and Superstition."

They both laughed at the joke then paused in a silent calm before what Brighton suspected was going to be a storm.

"Now that's my style ... line dancing in cowboy boots. I'll tell you what. You line me up with Rhonda, and I'll try it—leg bandages and all."

"Brighton, I need your help. Can you think of anyone you have run into over the years, maybe at Stanford, who is connected to the EPA?"

"Do we have a problem?" Brighton asked, "Other than my getting my Chinese food and Rhonda agreeing to be my dance partner?"

Charley went through his experience at the Bureau of Mines and his concern about getting sanctioned by the EPA. They kicked the problem back and forth and brainstormed about the best- and worst-case scenarios. By the end of the discussion, Charley felt much better. The mental exercise had stimulated his brain to allow another storm to materialize.

✳✳✳

Roy had spent the day preventing head-on aircraft collisions over the Arizona skies, and Dean had ripped out another zillion particles of rhodium from Lot #29. The trucks bringing in the back fill were finally keeping up, thus the gaping cavity was looking more like a leveling and compaction effort than a strip mine.

"I got a call back from Brighton," Roy said. "And he gave me the name of an EPA guy he met while he and Gina were in Palo Alto. I talked to him; Allen Lee is his name. It turns out he's now a private consultant to the timber industry in Tacoma. He is the king of slash and reforest. He agreed to fly down and look at our problem. He didn't sound like he was bragging particularly, but he did say that he has never consulted on an EPA-muddled project where his clients lost. When I told him I might be able to arrange a private jet to pick him up, he agreed to clear his calendar for us."

"I still believe in the 'ask for forgiveness rather than permission' theory," said Dean. "My advice is to get the Mole and a couple of big Caterpillars on the job right here and work the gullies running off the east side of the hill toward Alma's house. If we can get Brighton's friend to stall the EPA for a couple of months, and if the ore is anywhere close to being as rich as on the other side of the hill, we could pull out enough wealth to satisfy everyone in the LLC and then convert the surface into a tree-hugging park and the mine tunnel into a tourist attraction."

Roy and Charley sat silently for a few moments digesting the idea and then nodded in agreement, not because they thought it a necessarily brilliant idea, but because they just didn't have a better one.

**

Big Bill and the Pikes Peak Metal group were in their own planning meeting. A fourth person had joined the group and kept silent through the first part of the proceedings. His name was Fred English, and he was an ex-procurement officer for the U.S. Air Force. When he took his retirement, he stayed in Colorado Springs, hoping for a teaching job at the Air Force Academy, but instead had shifted his way down the food chain to doing dirty tricks for companies trying to get contracts with the military. Jerry Sorensen had met him at a mining seminar in Leadville. His name had been the first to pop into Sorensen's head when Big Bill had crossed the line of ethics and legality.

"The way I see this thing evolving," English explained, trying to make his voice sound professorial, "is to scare the present group away like a covey of quail being blasted with twelve-gauge shotguns."

Jerry Sorensen interrupted the new arrival. "I've met some of these people, and they don't strike me as the kind who will be easily frightened away. I mentioned that Rhonda Tucker, the country movie and singing star, is one of them. She and her boyfriend came up here in her private jet and looked over the refinery. The guy is smart and has no intention of being displaced from this project. Your first idea won't work, and your plan of fighting for the mineral rights in court sounds like it's not going to work for anyone but a bunch of attorneys. As for me, I think that unless you have a legal and realistic plan, I'm going to leave you to your scheming and forget that I ever met any of you folks."

"Did we get all the data from the aerial survey yet?" Lori asked Sorensen.

"We're still short of some of the data, but we have more than enough to confirm your story of there being a tunnel with several laterals," Big Bill answered for Sorensen.

Lori Pederson stood up in front of the group and spoke for herself. "I've been in the mine, and I've run the assays, and I've met the woman who owns the land with access to the mine tunnel." The last part of the story was a lie. "The artifacts in the tunnel alone are worth hundreds of thousands as collectables. There is a good chance that this is one of the old Spaniard's mines, if not the famous Lost Dutchman's mine itself. If we can get control of the thing, there are millions to be made even without the rhodium and platinum and gold. I think we can have it all and do so without any court battles," Lori explained.

Mr. English interrupted, trying to save face. "I have looked into the laws regarding special metals that have military and national security implications, rhodium certainly one of them. I have a variety of the government forms, most of which are still in use. Among them is this one."

English held up an official-looking U.S. government form headed in bold type: CEASE AND DESIST.

"This is used for a variety of situations, but the one I used it for on occasion was to get construction or excavation and even mining projects stopped in areas that were sensitive. We ran off more than one prospector from strategically sensitive areas using just this form. It scares the heck out of them. Some think we're storing aliens in the area."

"So how does that help us? These people all live like a stone's throw from the area. Even if we could scare them off, the minute we started to remove anything, they would be all over us." It was Sorenson rebutting this time, and he was losing his nerve. "My guess is that since we can't get the mineral rights, and if they have control of the Ziegler woman, we are toast."

"But nobody has control of the weirdo woman," said Lori, trying to keep the plan together. "She is so nuts that she can be influenced and turn a one-eighty in a heartbeat."

"Go ahead and explain the plan. I've got other work to do today," Sorensen said in a disgusted voice, feeling that the whole thing was a big mistake and already firing Bill in his mind. How he had been talked into even listening made him question his own sanity. He didn't need the money, and he for sure didn't need legal problems, or worse still, criminal charges. Fake documents scared him. Since he had recommended English to the group, he could already be in deep trouble.

English took the floor again and laid out his plan: a simple government order to back off from any disturbing of the Ziegler property, followed by another fake court order requiring an EPA study, followed by a diversion while they raided the tunnel of its artifacts. Then with a little persuasion, they could coax the Ziegler woman into signing the mineral rights over to them.

"The whole strategy is simple," concluded English, "and the minimal yield will be several million dollars."

Lori had to bite her lip to not admit that she and shoestring relative Albert Hicks had already tried to buy out Alma Ziegler and failed fatally.

"The whole plan is idiotic," said Sorensen, getting to his feet to leave. "And I'm an idiot for having agreed to host this little conspiracy. We all need to go home and forget that this meeting ever took place. If anyone ever mentions my name with any of these harebrained plans, I will make you regret it." He stepped away from the small conference table and headed out the door. "Say, Bill, would you mind stopping by my office after you have straightened up the room here?"

✳✳✳

Bill was not smiling when he entered Sorensen's office an hour later. He had cleaned up the room and agreed to meet the others for lunch at Denny's. Sorensen had made him wait over half an hour before the secretary nodded for Bill to go into Sorensen's office. She had then asked permission to leave for lunch.

"We have a huge problem now," Jerry began, not offering a chair to Bill. "The so-called plan you first suggested has obviously fallen apart, and the temptation to get English to rescue it was my fault. I have been on the phone with my attorney, and he is of the opinion that unless we all want to go to jail, we need to follow my suggestion and scatter. I'm going to let you go, and I suggest that you leave town immediately and not return. I hope the rest of the group will do likewise. I'll take care of English since he was my suggestion. I had Margo cut a severance check for you with a little extra for your travel expenses. You were a good worker, but obviously it was a front to get close to me. I'll admit you made it sound too good to be true, and you were right."

Jerry stood up and then, remembering that the check in front of him was unsigned, he bent over the desk with his pen in hand. Just as he put the last swirl on Sorensen, he felt a blinding, sharp pain in his head, and then he felt nothing.

Bill laid down the heavy amethyst paperweight and slid the blue check out from under his former boss's hand. With Sorensen's gold Cross pen, he carefully added a zero to the numbered amount on the check and pocketed the pen. He would fix the written number amount later.

39

PLAN B

Roy was the first to hear about the attack on Jerry Sorensen. One of the truck drivers had pulled up to the Pikes Peak Metals and Minerals gate with a fresh load of ore only to be turned away by policemen guarding the entrance.

"That place had more yellow crime scene tape around it than O.J. Simpson's mansion. When they told me about the owner getting his head bashed in, I backed out of there like Richard Petty in reverse," the driver told Roy, calling him from a pay phone in town. "What do you want me to do with this load? I need to dump it and get back to Scottsdale for my two-year-old's birthday party. Should I just dump it at a landfill and head back?"

Roy couldn't believe what he had heard on the phone. Jerry Sorensen had been so easy to work with, and the refining was going so well. *What a disaster!* This was going to take some real brainpower to re-direct the ore and start over with a new refiner—if they could find one.

Roy told the driver to keep the load onboard the truck. If he couldn't find a safe place to park it, he should get out and fly back to Arizona. Roy would take care of his air fare and any extra costs. Heck, Roy would buy the truck if he had to. The last calculations had shown that the average truckload of the rhodium ore was worth over two hundred thousand dollars. They had to start searching for another refiner. And they needed to do it immediately.

He called Charley and Brighton and spread the bad news. They set up an executive meeting for that night, and Brighton agreed to get a hold of Dean. There was the refinery in New Mexico where the two stolen loads of ore had mysteriously been dumped, but no one knew anything about that particular business. Some serious research needed to be done.

Later, Roy spoke to Rhonda, who had just returned from delivering Alma in San Francisco. When he told her the news about Sorensen, she broke down crying.

The next morning, Charley, Roy, and Dean were on board the Citation jet, looking down at the Arizona Desert from twenty-five thousand feet. The trip to Silver City, New Mexico, would take less than an hour, during which the men lounged on the deep leather seats and sipped flavored water from crystal glasses. It was Dean and Charley's first flight in a private plane, and though there were bigger and fancier jets, the men looked like they had more than adequate room to stretch out and relax.

Rhonda was exhausted from getting Alma Ziegler packed, groomed, and bundled off to her new temporary home aboard Oceania's Regatta cruise ship. She had been home from San Francisco less than an hour when Roy called with the bad news about Sorensen. Roy had come over later that night and fixed her a bachelor's soufflé of three eggs, scrambled with sharp cheddar cheese and half a cup of Pace picante salsa. During the dinner, which was washed down with a vintage bottle of Diet Dr. Pepper, they had discussed the problem of getting their ore refined. She had offered her jet to get them to New Mexico and up to Colorado to organize the continuation of the all-important refining. "Rhonda said that Alma was so eager to get away from all the confusion here that she forgot her purse in the town car when they got to the ship's dock. Rhonda also had to have the driver fish around under the seat for Azi's walking stick which she insisted on bringing," Roy told the men.

"I'll bet Brighton would love to get his hands on that stick. He still has a walnut-sized knot on his shin where she walloped him with it the first time he encountered the nutcase," Charley added.

"Maybe we'll be lucky, and she will fall in love with some lonely captain of industry, and they will elope to Costa Rica, and we'll only see her in the news clips," Roy said, daydreaming. "I've certainly had enough face-to-face time with the woman to fill my barrel of laughs. I can't even imagine how she is going to react when it comes to deciding on the final touches on her new house. Remind me to take a long cruise of my own when she gets back."

❊❊❊

The sleek plane glided to a gentle touchdown on the narrow strip of asphalt, which from the air approach pattern didn't look wide enough to accommodate a tricycle. The tiny terminal was nothing more than a metal building and a fuel truck. It was a huge contrast to the luxurious general aviation terminal at the Scottsdale air park with its marble floors and Hooter look-alike assistants greeting the private passengers.

A dusty Suburban met them at the side of the plane. No TSA fatties here. The driver took their briefcases and put them in the back on top of a layer of dust and assorted tools scattered on the stained carpet. The driver was a friendly young fellow in his mid-twenties who introduced himself as the son-in-law of the owner of the refinery.

"Carl Stokes, my wife's dad, said to take you by Jenny's place and to see that you get a good lunch. The drive to the mill is only fifteen miles, but it takes close to an hour to get there. The road washed out in August when we had that gigantic monsoon that flooded the casino in Las Cruces. I'm sure you heard all about it."

None of them had paid any attention to the travails of New Mexico.

They ate greasy cheeseburgers and homemade fries, which they dipped in the local version of "fry sauce," a combination of ketchup, mustard, and jalapeño puree. The men each bought a roll of Tums on the way out and promised that they would be back for dinner if they were still in town.

The ride out to the refinery was rough. The paved road was full of potholes, which the driver seemed to take great pleasure in hitting at full speed. The last five miles of dirt road was as corrugated as a washboard, threatening to loosen the fillings of all three men's teeth.

"Can you imagine if Brighton had come?" commented Charley, after an unusually deep rut had nearly bottomed out the Suburban.

"At least he would be here to tighten my fillings," mumbled Roy, bringing his mind back from daydreaming about the night before, consoling the worried Rhonda.

Finally, they came to a stop in front of a steel-piped cattle guard. The driver honked his horn three distinct times, and suddenly a red light on a pole near the gate flashed green.

"That's the laser alarm system," the driver explained in a voice that had suddenly graduated to a master's degree level of sophistication from his previous country bumpkin accent. "If it isn't deactivated, two out of every three rails below us drop down, effectively trapping the tires of the car or truck in the cattle guard. The next security system is really high tech."

The SUV came around the corner of a small bluff, straight toward the figure of a 6'8" Apache Indian wearing a weathered cowboy hat and a leather jacket with tassels, while holding a small Israeli-made machine pistol. Behind the man stretched the compound of modern buildings with multiple conveyors, smokestacks, and loading docks. The central office building was bristling with antennas and surveillance cameras.

The meeting with the management of the small refinery went well, and although the price of refining was a bit steeper than in Colorado, an agreement was quickly reached, and a multiple-page contract was signed. Driving back to the airport in the dwindling light of dusk, two truckloads of ore dumped alongside the road outside the refiner's gate caught Roy's eye.

"Any idea where those loads came from?" he asked the driver.

"Somebody's worthless landfill, I guess."

"How about if you guys load it up and run with the rest of our truckloads?" Charley suggested to the son of the mill's owner.

"That's fine by me, but I'll have to check with Dad."

40

DEEP MISCHIEF

The Patel brothers had watched TV for half the day and were sick and tired of the house. Both of the parents were at work, and Harley needed to stretch his long legs. For the last couple of weeks he had been tied to a chain whenever he was outside. The fence still hadn't been repaired since the harvest of the ore in the backyard.

The boys ventured into the Steiners' backyards and soon were standing on the edge of the collapsed tunnel. They had been warned by their parents not to go down the sloping path into the tunnel.

Patrick and Tony looked down into the dark hole in the ground and looked at Harley, and then they smiled.

"You stay right here." Patrick, the older of the two, turned and went back toward the house. Less than a minute later, he was back carrying two Magnetite flashlights and a couple of extra batteries. Harley was on a ten-foot nylon leash and, at 130 pounds, was about to drag the leash holder across the threshold into the abyss.

"Should we take him?" Tony asked his brother.

"Heck yes. He can see and smell and hear things we will miss. Besides, if we leave him, he will bark until Mrs. Dunn gets worried and calls somebody."

With that settled, the boys and Harley slid, stumbled, and skidded their way to the bottom of the incline into the mouth of the ancient mining cavern. It had been almost two weeks since Brighton had been bitten by a snake and ten days since the boys had seen the blonde lady with the big boobs sneak her way into the Steiners' yards and disappear into the tunnel.

Already there were several weed-like desert plants sprouting at the bottom of the cave-in, and the one rain that came had settled the dust and defined the layered strata of the side wall of the caved-in area. A few animal footprints could be seen leading into the darkness, but the most obvious findings were spider webs. As far back as their lights would shine, they could see webs—new ones and old ones, some with their recent victims bound in endless threads of filamentous web like tiny Egyptian mummies. Some of the webs were empty, but others had glistening owners lurking in wait for a clueless fly, bee, or moth to happen into the sticky trap.

Tony scurried to the top of the incline and ran to the closest mesquite tree and broke off a branch. He stripped off the small leaves and twigs and headed back down the incline. "You hold onto Harley and shine the lights, and I'll clear the cobwebs," ordered Patrick, taking the branch and leaving no room for discussion. Though there was no one else around, and Harley was doing his best to wake the dead with growls and snarls, the boys communicated in whispers.

Slowly the boys worked their way deeper into the tunnel. Their lights seemed to get dimmer the further they went, though the cobwebs thinned out to almost nothing as they left the entrance behind. When they came to the first lateral in the tunnel, they had to make a decision. There were obvious footprints in the pulverized dirt on the floor of the cave. Some were the size of large men's boots while other smaller ones were probably from the woman. With the dog's four giant paws pulling and prancing, most of the prints were being obliterated before the boys could get a good look at them. Along the way they found several pieces of paper attached to old mine equipment and to some of the timbers. At one point they lit a small fire with the paper to clean the cobwebs off of their stick.

Reaching the fork in the tunnels, they decided on the path least traveled. Harley was insisting on the tunnel with no footprints. For several minutes they jigged and jagged and went up and down inclines. Suddenly, they found themselves at the end of the manmade portion of the tunnel facing a narrowed hole of a natural cavern. Harley jerked away from Tony, whose hand was getting raw from the constant yanking on the leash. The last they saw of him was the white tip of his long tail disappearing into the three-foot-high elliptical opening.

"Why did you let go?" scolded Patrick.

"I didn't let go; he jerked away. He weighs more than I do. Why didn't you hold him? You are the one who wanted to bring him along," whined Tony, rubbing his raw hand.

"Harley, get back here right now!" both boys yelled into the cave opening. Echoes were their only answer.

Patrick went first, slithering along on his hands and knees and at times his belly, shining his light ahead. He couldn't see the dog, but after twenty or so feet, the cave opened into a larger area. The boys had forgotten about spiders and had long since dismissed snakes from their minds. They needed to get the dog and find their way out of the place. The thrill of an adventure was gone, replaced with adrenalin-fueled anxiety and fear.

Patrick froze in place as his field of light expanded, revealing a giant cavern. It was a natural room, at least twenty feet high, forty feet wide, and fifty feet long. His bright light reflected off of the glistening wet walls with their stalactites and stalagmites, some reaching the full height of the room. At the far end, he could hear Harley lapping up water.

"I wouldn't mind it if you would keep moving," protested Tony sarcastically from behind, still scrunched in the claustrophobic tunnel on all fours. "I'm smothering back here."

Both boys inched into the huge room. They brushed the dirt and grit from their shirts and pants. The dust quickly disappeared into the dank, humid air of the space.

"What is this place?" Tony asked as he slowly and methodically moved the beam of his light around the cavern. They could hear Harley at their side now slobbering on their pant legs and shoes.

"Hey boy, what have you been drinking? Man oh man, you stink!"

It didn't take them long to discover the source of the putrid smell. A human-appearing body was in the far corner of the cave, lying in a small natural concavity. Even Harley didn't want to get too close, though after a few cautious sniffs he stuck his nose up close to what appeared to be a foot. He suddenly gave out a loud, deep bark that echoed through the cavern, making both boys jump away from the desiccated and creepy object. Harley became more aggressive and grabbed onto the heel of the old cracked leather boot and started to tug on it as though he were playing a game with him.

"Stop it!" commanded Tony. Patrick gave the dog's nose a quick kick with the toe of his tennis shoe. The dog backed off with a snarl and started sniffing around the rest of the room.

"How old do you think it is?" Tony asked.

"How long have you been dead?" Patrick posed his question to the mummified person, causing the boys to laugh. They both immediately realized that the joke was in worse than poor taste.

Again, Harley was in action, this time digging furiously at a space on the floor several feet to the right of the body. The boys heard the dog's claws scraping on something metallic and turned their flashlights on what looked like a small suitcase made of metal buried six or eight inches below the dirt floor. While Tony held the dog, Patrick brushed the loose dirt and rocks away. The pea-green, two-by-three-foot case was weathered and discolored, but the stamp-printed lettering was crystal clear: "U.S. ARMY MAIL."

Testifying to product consistency, the batteries in both flashlights failed at once. There is nothing on earth as dark as the inside of a natural cavern. Not being able to see one's own hand waving in front of the face is a frightening experience, but adding to it a mummified body and the reality that no one outside the tunnel and cavern knew where the boys were intensified the equation of fear. Patrick stood up straight, hitting his head hard on an overhanging stalactite. He let out a yelp and grabbed his head, immediately feeling something warm and wet. Tony dropped Harley's leash and groped in his back pocket for the extra batteries he had packed.

With his hands shaking and no visual cues, it was nearly impossible to slide out the three old batteries, discard them and add new ones. Harley had started barking again, and Patrick was whining and yelling for light. The batteries fell to the ground.

"Quiet!" screamed Tony, receiving a surprising compliance from his dog and brother. Listening as his hand searched the ground, he found one of the batteries. *Was it the good one or the bad?* With crunching and grinding, the metal flashlight lid screwed back into place, and with a hope and a prayer Tony pressed the on button.

Blood was the first thing he saw as the light shined on Patrick's head and face.

"You are very bloody," Tony said in a controlled voice.

Patrick wiped the spot on his head where he felt the most pain and looked at his blood-covered hand. "I can see that you tell the truth, White Man," Patrick responded in an out-of-place stab at humor. "Please take me to your leader."

The comic relief was just what the boys needed to reassess the situation and to make a plan to get out of the cave. They tied Harley to a stalagmite and carefully covered the three-by-two-foot rectangular mail case with dirt, even taking time to roll a few rocks on top of it. Then worrying that the light was getting even dimmer, they picked up the dropped batteries and headed for the narrowed entrance back into the mine tunnel.

The flashlight kept working until the end, when its light became dimmer with each step. Harley probably would have led them out without a light as long as they could hang onto his leash. He had enough of the dark cave and tunnel and the smell of the ancient dead.

As the three of them emerged from the darkness, the Arizona sunshine blinded them. Harley broke loose from Tony's grip and bounded up the steep dirt slope. Patrick couldn't go bounding up anywhere; he was dizzy and barely putting one foot in front of the other. The boys had left behind a sealed mystery, but also left behind a trail of Patrick Patel's blood.

***

Brighton Dunn sat in his operative chair staring into the mouth of a twenty-one-year-old ASU coed. She was a talker, and in spite of having her mouth full of cotton wads, metal dental instruments, and Brighton's fingers, she still tried to ask questions and tell stories.

It was a common annoying symptom of anxiety in the dental chair. His annoyance wasn't confined to the patient; his leg was killing him and his toes, though back to near-normal size, still throbbed. This was his first day trying to work all day, and the morning had been okay, but even after an hour of elevating his leg during lunch, the toes started to throb. He was so far behind in his patient load that canceling the afternoon was out of the question. Taking anything stronger than Advil was likewise unacceptable. He would just have to tough it out.

The office policy was strict regarding incoming phone calls. He wasn't supposed to be interrupted while he was actively working on a patient in the chair.

He felt the tap on the shoulder and turned his attention away from the girl's mouth just enough that he poked her in the non-anesthetized gum with a sharp probe, making her grab his wrist. Her eyes were about to bug out of her head.

"What?" he said to the secretary with less than cordiality in his voice.

The older woman gave him a glare over the edge of her half glasses that told him to behave and to come with her. He put down the instruments and excused himself. Ripping off his gloves, he followed her into his consultation office. Standing in the small office were Gina, Mrs. Patel, and Tony Patel. Brighton was immediately both confused and frightened.

"What is going on? What are you doing here? Is everything okay?" The string of questions didn't give time for answers. Gina put two fingers on his lips and closed the door to the hallway.

"Sit down and listen to this story," she ordered in a calm voice that included a hint of a secret to be heard. She nodded toward Mrs. Patel to begin.

Brighton sat down in his tufted leather chair and waited for one of them to begin.

"My sons, Tony here and Patrick, are very smart and curious boys. They had been told not to go down into the tunnel in our neighbors' backyards, but their curiosity overcame them." She spoke in a staccato Hindi accent using perfect syntax.

"Today the boys followed our unruly dog into the tunnel behind the Steiners' houses and found a hidden cavern. Patrick injured his head and is at the hospital with my husband. He lost a lot of blood, but we think he will be all right. What they found though needs to be explained, and I thought you would be the best one to talk to. Your sweet wife answered the telephone and was so kind to bring us here. I will now let Tony tell you the events of his afternoon." She turned to her son.

"Thank you, Mother," Tony began. He turned to Brighton, who was already getting anxious about leaving his patient alone in the dental chair. "My brother and I found a cave that extended off of one of the mine tunnels. Inside the big cave there is a dead person. I watch the Discovery Channel, so I am sure he has been dead a long time. Alongside the dead body was a buried metal case that said, "U.S. ARMY MAIL." Our dog Harley dug it up. I thought that since you were the one who was bitten by the rattlesnake, you should know what is still down there."

Brighton listened with interest and then renewed fear. A dead body, a buried treasure, snakes, and a vein of precious metal. *What had they gotten themselves into?*

"Is your other son going to be all right? Is there anything I can do to help?" Brighton asked.

Bavana Patel just shook her head no, and Gina decided it was time to get out of Brighton's hair. "I'm sure he'll be fine. We are going to the hospital now. Call me when you are done with patients."

The three visitors stood and quietly walked out of the room leaving Brighton sitting in his office, staring at the wall and wondering what train had just run over him.

Later, when he finished up with the last patient, he swallowed a handful of Advil and grabbed a can of Coke to drink on the way to the airport. He had called Charley and Dean to meet him at the control tower, where they would meet Roy during his dinner break.

✳✳✳

The meeting of the Executive Committee of Hidden Gravel LLC took place in the twilight glow of a golden Arizona sun, setting behind a few cirrus clouds in the west. The roar and drone of arriving and departing 737s required the meeting to look more like a football huddle. None of the men wanted to miss a single word being exchanged.

Brighton brought the three men up to date on the Patel broth-ers' incredible story of finding a body and a buried "treasure chest" in a cavern off one of the lateral mine tunnels.

"I don't recall seeing anything like that," said Roy, "but our flashlights were very inadequate for what we were doing down there."

They discussed the possibilities, which without any firsthand knowledge, were infinite. Obtaining more facts and thus more exploration was essential.

"What is the latest from Colorado?" Dean asked, not knowing who was getting what information anymore. He always seemed to be just a step behind the other three when it came to pertinent knowledge about the affairs of the group.

All eyes turned to Roy. "I spoke with Sheriff Brice, who in turn spoke to the Colorado Springs police, and they think Sorensen was bludgeoned by a big, tall man named Bill who had worked for the refinery for a couple of weeks ... sound familiar? Until Sorensen wakes up—if he ever does—no one will know for sure."

"It's got to be him, but where is he now? The other problem is Lori. Someone at the motel in Colorado where Bill was living reported seeing her with the man."

At the sound of her name, a shock surged through Dean. *Shar-ron's Lori?*

Charley started to talk just as a 747 rattled the windows around them. When it was gone, he started over. "We know that this Lori has been in the mine, and we know that there are lots of mysteries down there. The chance of us doing any successful mining in the tunnel is looking less and less likely. Maybe our best plan would be to continue the digging on Lot #29 until it is played out and then start excavating over at Alma's burned-out home site."

"What about the caved-in site at the Steiners'?" Dean asked. "Don't you think we should refill it as soon as possible and then approach the tunnel from the east end?"

"We have got to find out what else is in there before we do anything. What if the body is a recent murder victim or a miss-ing person whom somebody's family is waiting to hear about?" Brighton insisted.

The other three looked at him as though he just sprouted

horns or an elephant's trunk. The man could still barely walk on his traumatized leg.

"You want to go down into the cave again?" Roy asked Brighton. "Maybe you are still on too much Percocet?"

"Can't you see? We've got to know what's down there, and then we can report it to the sheriff. What if ... just think ... what if the body is the Lost Dutchman or someone he murdered? Just think about it. It's not out of the realm of possibilities. Or it could be one of the earlier Peraltas' or Gonzales' mines? Both of those families had mines that were never reported to be played out. There is a lot more hypothetical history of this area than there are hard facts," Brighton said.

"We could be sitting on a historical cash cow. We could set up a concession and charge to see the mine and cave just like they do at those diamond caves in Kentucky," Brighton continued. "My vote is that we assemble the right equipment and check out the entire network of caves and tunnels and then figure out how to open the east end for access. Next, we fill the Steiner cave-in. Then, we can call in the cavalry and archeologist and the press and not worry about the guy Bill or Lori or any of the tree huggers." Brighton finished just in time for another sound eruption from a departing jet.

"What about getting the rest of our ore processed and any new ore we get from Alma's property? We need to keep the trucks rolling." Dean the pragmatist already had accepted Brighton's suggestion and was moving on to the next unanswered questions.

"Let's do this," Charley said. "We can file a claim, not as a mine, but as a valuable historical site. We'll say it is probable that the body is that of the Lost Dutchman, Jacob Waltz. It probably isn't, but until all the testing is done, who knows? Next, we separate the ancient mine property and its entrance from the mineral rights property."

The men were each straining to hear over the din of the departing jets.

"How about donating the mine and an access road with an adequate parking area to the National Park Service? You know, just like the Kartchners did with the Kartchner Caverns near Tucson?" Brighton asked, directing his question to Charley.

"What an enormous tax shelter that would be!"

More questions were raised and suggestions exchanged. A game plan was laid out, and assignments were made. Brighton would check with the refineries to get the ore already in Colorado processed there at Pikes Peak Minerals if they were still operating after the loss of their boss, or in the new plant in New Mexico.

***

Rhonda listened patiently to Roy's entire story as they ate a midnight dinner of waffles and scrambled eggs. Roy hadn't finished his shift until eleven and had called to ask her if he could come by her house for a few minutes. Rhonda suspected romance as his motive. Little did she know.

"You want me to come down into the mine shaft with you? You can't be serious. Honey, I'm afraid of snakes and cobwebs and especially deep, dark places. Oh yeah, I almost forgot, I'm afraid of dead bodies as well, especially when they have been dead a long time ... in deep, dark places." She was standing with her hands on her shapely hips, feet planted wide apart, staring at him in disbelief. With a pair of six-shooters and a ten-gallon hat on her head, she could have been a stand-in for Gary Cooper in *High Noon*, ready for the first move of the gunslinger.

"That's fantastic that you have all of those fears," Roy said with a huge grin on his face. "We are so alike. I have the very same fears ... with the exception, of course, that I love dead bodies, especially real old ones." He took her hands from her hips, and when he gave her hands a tight squeeze, their noses were only inches apart. "But even more than dead bodies, I like live, frightened redhead female bodies, so you see, we'll be a perfect team."

She came into his arms, laughing at him and his warped sense of humor. They held one another tightly for several moments before he whispered in her ear. "If you come with me and hold the lights, I promise I'll let you be the one to open the mystery mail trunk. We could even have a film crew there to record it for posterity ... you know like Geraldo and Al Capone's secret crypt?" he said, stepping away and ducking a faked left hook.

They walked hand in hand out onto the patio. There was a harvest moon arising over the peaks of the mountains to the east, and the air was just chilly enough that his arms around her shoulders felt warm as well as reassuring.

"I'll do it," she whispered, "on the condition that when this tunnel mystery is finished and the mining is on cruise control, you will take a leave of absence from work and fly to Hawaii with me. I know that the guy is supposed to do the asking, but I can't wait for you to have time in your busy schedule. I want to be your wife. Will you please ask me to marry you?"

To any eavesdropper, it would have sounded like a line from a movie script, and maybe for Rhonda it was an old rehearsed line, but to the shy and unpretentious Roy it was like someone had just slapped defibrillator paddles on his naked chest with an extra dose of contact gel and hit the discharge button.

He nearly jumped off of the porch in surprise. "Did I just hear what I thought I heard?" he asked in a gasping voice, unable to register the magnitude of the circumstance.

She took two steps, which brought her closer to him again. She slid her arms around his waist and rested her head on his solid chest where she could hear his heart thumping. Slowly, he brought his sweaty palms up to her shoulders and pulled her even closer to him.

"Roy, you are everything I want and need. You are your own man. You don't ever try to impress anyone, and yet you impress everyone. You wear a countenance of knowing and caring about little, where in reality you know everything and care deeply about everyone. Yes, you heard the words correctly. I love you and want to be your wife."

His head was spinning. How could a simple, small-town boy marry a woman whose picture was on the cover of magazines in every bookstore, magazine counter, and doctor's waiting room in the country?

The last few months of this close relationship with her had been like a dream. Laughing and joking with her. Planning and traveling and enjoying her wealthy lifestyle. Looking at her beauty and listening to the tales of world tours and movie sets in faraway places. All that had seemed a temporary thing, like riding in the convertible around the football field on homecoming night, knowing that the next day he would be at work at the Chevron station, pumping gas and cleaning smashed bugs off of the windshields of the town's wealthy. Now he was being asked to continue living the dream, and not just with the homecoming queen, but with a genuine entertainment icon.

Roy held her silently for what seemed to be hours before he let go of everything but her right hand. He dropped to one knee and, without so much as a single lost motion, slipped his Sigma Chi fraternity ring, the only piece of jewelry he owned or wore, off his left little finger. Kissing her hand, he held the shiny ring so she could see only the smooth underside of it. Looking in her moist blue eyes, he said, "Rhonda Tucker, I offer you this ring as a temporary token of a permanent love. Would you honor me and my family's name by becoming my wife?" He slid the ring, Greek letters down, onto her left ring finger and then kissed her hand. Their eyes were locked as he waited for an answer, not sure even after all that had been said, whether she would say yes.

Rhonda dropped to both knees and, taking his face in her hands, kissed him and then, pulling his head close to her, whispered, "Yes, I will marry you."

41

CRUISING

The purser of the luxury cruise ship Regatta knocked on the door of the penthouse suite and waited for a response. The woman inside had seldom been seen on deck and, according to the census computer that monitored the passengers' activities, she had not gone ashore at any of the last four ports of call. She had often called for room service and, when she did eat in the main dining room, insisted on a table for one. A real loner.

He held a large FedEx envelope stamped URGENT. It had arrived at the last minute before the ship cast off from Sorrento, Italy, and was preceded by a fax addressed to the purser himself, instructing him to hand deliver the document and witness the required signatures. He was then to FedEx it back to Mr. Charley Banks at the given address. Included in the package was an American Express check for two hundred dollars for the purser's trouble.

The door to the suite opened, and the frail-looking woman with no makeup and graying roots of her barely combed hair stood at the door. The suite behind her was dark from drawn curtains. The smell of stale food and wet towels made him wonder when the room had last been cleaned and the food trays removed. In spite of the "Do Not Disturb" sign, he would have strong words with the butler and cabin maid.

"Madame, you have received important documents from Arizona in the United States. There is a request that they be read, signed, and returned as soon as possible. May I please come in?" he asked in his most formal British accent.

He didn't wait for her answer but stepped forward into her room, requiring her to move aside. The relative disorder of the room was despicable. He went immediately to the curtains and threw them back then opened the sliding glass door onto the spacious veranda, letting in a lifesaving burst of fresh sea air. The weather outside made for a perfect Mediterranean evening. He detested it when staff allowed the guests to let their rooms get in such a state.

"My, but it is a glorious evening outside, Ms. Ziegler. Why don't we take a stroll down the hall to the library where we can sit at a desk? While we are gone, the attendants can freshen your suite." It wasn't a question but a direct order, which confused Alma. She was in the middle of watching *Star Wars Episode VI: Return of the Jedi*, for the second time, and couldn't remember the ending.

The nice man from the ship put her red sweater over her shoulders and guided her into the narrow hallway. She didn't like walking down the long hallways with their rocking back and forth and having to pass so closely to the other passengers. The man stopped at a phone in the hallway and spoke softly into the receiver. He then led her to a large, well-lit room lined with leather-bound books and new magazines. It smelled like her daddy's study in Denver. Alma walked around, looking at the titles and remembering when she was a young girl, seeing the same titles and authors in her family room bookshelves.

Alma picked up a copy of *People* magazine and showed it to the purser. "This is my neighbor, Rhonda."

The purser knew the face and looked at the headline, which asked, "When will R.T. come out of the desert?" Even he knew that the beautiful redhead had dropped off the face of the planet to renew herself.

"Does she live near you?" he asked Alma politely, doubting her claim.

"When my new house is built, I will be living right across the street from her."

The purser rolled his eyes and pulled the stack of papers out of the envelope and directed Alma to an inlaid Italian desk. He spread the papers out and scanned them to see where the signatures were needed. It wasn't the first time he had had to assist a scatterbrained heiress or an incapacitated elderly person with legal documents. As they worked their way from the first page on down, he couldn't help but notice that there were some high dollar figures on the pages, and then on the final signature page he saw what he couldn't believe. There, along with several other names, was the typed name and personal signature, in a bold flowing pen, of Rhonda Tucker.

He gathered up the pages and took a different look at the disheveled woman. Maybe she really was someone important. He would have to take personal care of this one. With the task completed, he ordered a light snack for her to be served there in the library. While she ate, he made several calls.

By the time they returned to Alma's suite, the rooms were immaculate, and fresh fruit and flowers in colorful baskets had been placed on tabletops. There was a note on the bed that the beauty salon had a reserved time for her that afternoon, and there was an invitation to sit at the captain's table at dinner that evening. Although Alma was impressed with the service, she spent most of the time wondering when she was going to finish watching her *Star Wars* movie.

42

COUSINS

Dean and Sharron Shutter sat on a pile of wood flooring and admired the herringbone pattern in the oversize fireplace tiles in their new family room. The surrounding mantel would be of carved travertine. Their house had progressed with lightning speed once Dean warned his subcontractors that there was another house to be built across the street if and only if his own house was completed quickly. So far, it was working. The walls and woodwork were painted, and the appliances were sitting in the garage, waiting for the electrician. The granite man was working quickly, and the others were going to be right on his tail.

"So what was the big meeting about last night?" Sharron asked her husband. Dean had built a real fire in the fireplace using a few scraps of lumber. Sharron was in the best mood Dean had seen in months. He was falling in love with her again. They were spending more time together in the evenings, and with their daughter off to college in La Jolla, there was a lot less to argue about.

Since the emergence of cousin Lori and her involvement with the ancient mine tunnel claims, he had sworn to the other three partners that he wouldn't talk to Sharron about any of the mining business. It didn't take a calculus professor to figure out that most of the troubles of the Hidden Gravel LLC would disappear if Lori Pederson would disappear. It was rumored that the police were looking for a tall loudmouth named Bill. The bottom line for Dean was that he couldn't trust his wife to not slip up and unknowingly give confidential information to her cousin.

"At the meeting we had to discuss the plans for the house for Ms. Ziegler," Dean answered Sharron, not really lying to her but revealing just a fraction of the truth.

"For two hours? I waited up for you but finally couldn't keep my eyes open any longer."

"Thanks, sweetheart," Dean said, snaking his arm around her and pulling her close. "I know it's been hard on you the last couple of years, living in an apartment and not knowing how the finances of the project would play out. Maybe you should have married that redhead lawyer with the soft belly and his daddy's freebie practice to take over."

She gave a shoulder shrug. "And maybe you should have married the five-foot-tall redhead with the gigantic boobs whose hips and rear end have now caught up with her chest. After all, she is now twice the woman I am."

This was a recurrent verbal duel that the two carried out. It was usually healthy for both of them to realize that they had it pretty good being married to one another. Dean brought her around into his arms and held her. The crackling fire added to the romantic moment and almost dissuaded her from asking more questions.

"Are we really going to move into this house, or is it like the others that we put our heart and soul into, only to walk away from to have enough money to live?" Sharron asked.

"Not only are we going to move in, but it is time for you to hit the furniture stores and start replacing all the junk we have been dragging around for years. I'll transfer fifty grand into your checking account tomorrow morning … or should I make it a hundred grand?"

She looked up, grinning at him before she slipped a hand under his shirt and rubbed his back. "I really do love this guy," she thought.

"What about the mine tunnel?" Sharron asked. "Are you going to go ahead and work it or seal it off and hope the snakes stay inside? I for sure don't want the slimy things getting close to my house."

"The plan is for me to seal off the collapsed part of the tunnel, but first we have to identify the original entrance. Then I'll seal it to keep the snakes in."

He led her through the rest of the house, making decisions about tile and light fixtures and window coverings.

She was far from being a trained decorator. He suggested that she invite Kara and Gina to help her with colors and fabrics.

"He must be blind," she thought. "Those women hate me and

look at me like I am dirt. They have never included me in anything and never will. They would probably pick out something atrocious for my house just so they could have a good laugh." She knew who she could trust to help her do the decorating. Before she became interested in geology, her cousin had been majoring in home decorating. She would call Lori.

✳✳✳

Lori Pederson returned to Arizona scared to death. Though she didn't know it for a fact, she was almost certain that her previous partner Bill had attacked Mr. Sorensen. *What would he do next?*

She arrived home just before midnight, having driven for ten straight hours. She had rented the car at the Colorado Springs airport and hadn't let them know she would need to drop it in Phoenix. That would cost her a pretty penny. The drive back was not just long, but nerve-wracking.

The local radio stations had given frequent news updates on the murder attempt of one of the state's leading citizens. "Funny how most people don't become a "leading citizen" until they almost die or molest a child," Lori thought.

There was even a vague description of Bill, mentioning his being in the company of a blonde woman. Every cop she passed, she suspected, was looking at her with suspicion. At the gas station in Gallup, one had written down her license plate number while she bought a doughnut and coffee. She had waited in the restroom for ten minutes just to be sure the guy wasn't calling in the car ID.

Finally, back in town, she opened the door to her condo expecting to be met by her cat. Instead, she was accosted with the unmistakable smell of cigarettes and body odor. Bill's body odor.

Lori felt like she was having a heart attack. She could hardly catch her breath, and her hands were shaking so much that she couldn't press the alarm buttons to disarm the thing. *How did he get in and reset the alarm?* Then she remembered giving him a key and the code several months ago so he could feed her cat while she was in Toronto at the mineralogy meeting.

She disarmed the beeping security system before it could fire off a signal to the local police station and then turned on the hall light. There he was, asleep on the leather recliner, snoring away with her cat curled up on his lap, ignoring her completely. The hallway light's shadow was just dark enough that it didn't strike his face.

At first, she thought about running, but she really needed to pee, and the shock of seeing Bill in her house wasn't helping her control. She turned off the hall light and tiptoed into the master bedroom, locking the door behind her. Her bedside alarm clock's dim nightlight helped her negotiate the path to the bathroom. She closed and locked the bathroom door. Two barriers.

Relief was followed by a new wave of anxiety. What was she going to do now? If she called the police, they would connect her with Bill and the attack in Colorado. There was no way she could explain away the rental car and the credit card trail she had left. If she let him sleep and snuck back outside, she could—what? She was too tired to think. Letting him stay here was aiding and abetting a wanted criminal. She was toast. The only people she could think of to ask for help were her family, and the only family she had close by was her childhood buddy—cousin Sharron Shutter.

***

Dean had just gone to sleep when the phone rang. It was rare for him to get a late-night call and when he did, it was usually bad news. He rolled over to reach the phone and then sat straight up in bed when he heard the voice. Lori was whispering into the phone at a jabbering rate, which he couldn't understand. Sharron normally slept like a hibernating mama bear, but she had rolled over and had her hand on his back to let him know she was awake.

"I'm having trouble understanding you, Lori. Could you speak a little louder and slow down? I'm putting the phone on speaker so Sharron can hear," Dean instructed the frantic woman.

"I'm sorry to call and wake you up, but I don't have anyone else to help me. I have an emergency at my apartment and need help really bad. You know I wouldn't call if I wasn't desperate." Lori spoke in a slow cadence but in an almost spooky whisper. "I just arrived home from a business trip to find an old boyfriend asleep in my front room. He has a history of violence. Talking to him will make it worse. Maybe I could just come over to your place for the night? If I go to a hotel, he will find me and hurt me."

"You need to call the police. Do you want me to call them for you?" Dean was trying to sound helpful rather than angry.

"Just come over here, and we'll take care of you," Sharron said, now sitting beside her husband, half holding the phone. "I'll make up the couch and leave the porch light on for you. How long will it take you to get here?"

"I can be there in fifteen minutes. Are you sure it's okay?" The question was immediately followed by a panicked "Oh no!" and then the line was dead.

"What happened?" Sharron asked in a panic. "Call her back, Dean! She sounded desperate!"

Dean turned on the nightstand light and looked at the caller ID. He copied down the number and dialed it, keeping the phone on speaker. A ringing tone was followed by an immediate voice message greeting. Dean hung up the phone and tried the number again with the same results.

"You've got to go help her. The man is probably hurting her while we sit here doing nothing."

"Do you have any idea where she lives?" Dean asked, more irritated than worried.

"She never mentioned where she lives, just that she lives alone. Maybe we should call the police and give them the number."

"She didn't sound like she wanted the police involved. I'll try her number again."

This time the phone rang six or seven times before a man's voice came on the other end. "You've got the wrong number. Don't call back."

Dean hung up the phone and dialed 911.

The 911 call was getting them nowhere. Without an address, Dean couldn't get any action out of the operator until he played an ace card: his new best buddy, Sheriff Brice. When they finally got Brice awake and on the line, he was polite and took the information. He told them to hang up and said he would get back to them in ten minutes.

Eleven minutes later, Brice called Dean to report that there was no one at that home address and that the lights were out. The Scottsdale police had no probable cause to enter the house, and therefore left a notice for the occupant to notify the police when they returned.

"Now, Mr. Shutter, I need to inform you that when we put Ms. Pederson's name in the computer, the national computer showed that she has a rental car signed out. It is still under contract in her name. She rented it in Colorado, so maybe she is there and you've made some kind of mistake. If I push a button on the federal computer, then an all-points bulletin goes out to every state and local police department. If somebody finds her or the car, she will be treated as a wanted criminal until proven otherwise. You know the drill: guns drawn, spread eagle, handcuffs. Is that really what you want for the lady?"

Dean thanked the sheriff, apologizing for the waste of his time and promising to take him out golfing at the Phoenician when the winter grass was ready for play.

"Did you hear that? 'An all-points bulletin,'" Sharron said, having listened to the conversation on the speaker phone. "That guy has watched too many old Highway Patrol episodes. Now what are we going to do?" She looked at Dean, waiting for a solution. He always had a solution.

"He is right about us looking for her ourselves. We don't even know what kind of a car she is driving.

"What if she's at the house and is locked inside and hurt or murdered?"

"Now it's you who have seen too many TV shows," Dean answered. He was so tired; he could barely continue sitting upright. "Let's get some sleep, and we'll try the phone number in the morning. If she still doesn't answer, I promise I will drive over to the apartment and check it out."

Sharron was up and pacing the bedroom floor and in no mood to go to sleep, but she could see the wisdom of her husband's logic. Finally, Sharron crawled back under the covers and snuggled up against her husband. It would be a long night waiting for daylight.

43

REAL EXPLORING

The newest tunnel exploration party was ready. Roy, Brighton, and the Patel brothers assembled their equipment on the Patels' patio and were waiting for sunrise. In reality, it was a bit absurd to wait for the sun, since they would be entering a pitch-black cave, but it just seemed better to wait for daylight. The flashlights, cameras, and guns—two of them, both loaded with .22 caliber snake shot—were ready; along with water, power bars, and a two-hundred-foot length of polyester climbing rope. They hadn't forgotten the batteries either. They had enough, they thought, to power a small city.

Each of the would-be spelunkers wore leather gloves, and each had a knife in a scabbard on his hip. The teenage boys had their parents' hesitant permission. They were ready for an adventure, and it was ready for them. Each felt he had earned the right to get a thorough look at the secrets the caverns held.

Roy had tried in vain to dissuade Brighton from going with them, but the shortage of manpower was blatant. He had insisted that his leg and foot were fine, and he had even found a pair of hiking boots to wear. Emotionally, he was afraid to go back and face another physical injury, but his ego wouldn't let him say no.

Rhonda, although promising her new fiancé that she would go, complained enough about her fear of spiders and snakes—and snails and puppy dog tails—that Roy tactfully uninvited her.

The opening of the caverns, since the cave-in, had exposed the subterranean world to a whole new population of creepy, crawling critters. In the short time since the cave was last entered, cobwebs had been built again, eggs had been laid, and minions of baby spiders had hatched, scattering themselves into the far corners of the caves and tunnels. Black widows and the nasty brown recluse loved caves and tunnels, especially the corners made by the wooden support timbers. The brown recluse bite could leave an area of dead flesh the size of an apple.

Coyotes had come into the tunnel to investigate the new un-scented territory. With a new and bigger opening into the cavern, an entire bat colony had moved from one of the distant caves into the ancient mine shafts and tunnels. Even a ringtail cat had left its tracks in the powdery dust of the cavern's floor.

"Keep an eye out for snakes," Brighton said more to himself than to the others.

"I'll be watching for sharp rock outcroppings," Tony said, looking at the bandage on his brother's head.

Roy had brought a hard hat complete with a xenon headlamp that had enough candlepower to light a visible path for everyone. The others had eyed it with envy. He was feeling a little guilty about not offering it to Brighton or one of the boys, but finally decided that self-preservation was the key to preserving everyone.

Charley had agreed to come along with the group and had his gear all ready to go, but had received an email late in the evening that required a response first thing in the morning. It appeared to be a critical document for the final closing of the Ziegler ranch, making it property of the Hidden Gravel LLC.

Dean's equipment was in a pile on the Patels' patio, but he too had begged off with an early predawn call to Roy. "Something extremely urgent having to do with Sharron's family," was all he said.

"Dean hates spiders," said Brighton when he heard the news.

The expedition of four stayed together and made good progress. Brighton was in charge of photography and had his new Nikon D80 fully charged and dangling from around his neck. He started with pictures of the mine tunnel with its hand-hewn timbers and the mine cart rails running along the floor of the tunnel. Patrick and Tony were leading the group, clearing cobwebs with broom handles confiscated from their maid's cleaning closet. The cobwebs, once cleared, seemed to reappear behind the group within minutes, backlit by the diminishing daylight from the end of the tunnel.

Roy's headlamp was the first to pick up the new footprints, which were clearly more recent than the ones left by the men at the time of the snakebite and the prints made by the Patel brothers with their skater shoes. Even the various animal tracks looked old and trampled next to the new prints. Two sets of footprints were obvious: one set a boy's or woman's, having a flat tread like a street shoe, and the other huge and deeply imprinted with the waffle-sole pattern of a hiking or work boot. Brighton took photos of the tracks. He didn't like what he saw. Something about the boot print gave him a sense of having seen it before.

The party spoke in soft, almost reverent voices when they came to the spot where Brighton had encountered the rattlesnake. Carefully shining their lights around the area, they could make out the trampled footprints of a dog or coyote but no snakes. They took short forays into side tunnels, most of which extended less than ten or twelve feet from the main shaft. The side tunnels held only a few footprints, and none of the human variety.

A screeching and explosion of wings brought all four men to their knees as a swarm of mouse-size bats fought their way out of the tunnel, away from the human intruders. The men stopped to drink water from their bottles. They were discussing the bats when Roy saw a tiny beam of light coming from what seemed to be the far eastern end of the tunnel. He produced a pocket compass from his backpack, but the dial promptly began turning this way and that in a useless rotation, refusing to come to rest on a specific direction.

"Too much metal in the walls of the tunnel," he said.

They followed the distant beam of light, which seemed to stay just out of reach. Eventually, they were at what they believed was the original entrance. Whoever had closed off the entrance had done a great job. Boulders the size of truck tires filled the space with fist-size rocks fitted into the smaller spaces. At certain angles, they could make out sunbeams sneaking through from the outside. Tony started to attempt rolling one of the rocks back into the tunnel, but it didn't budge. They did notice something strange on the floor of the cave. Small firework-like casings were scattered near the boulders. The smaller footprints were there in abundance.

"Show us the entrance to the big cave," Brighton asked the Patel boys.

Agreeing, they turned, heading back into the depths of the tunnel, stopping here and there to take pictures of stacks of ancient equipment or to point out the veins of glittering mineral in the walls of the tunnel. Close to the narrowing side cave entrance, Roy noticed the waffle-like footprints again, clearly more recent than the boys' tennis shoe prints. The four stopped to listen, but heard nothing except the distant dripping of water. "That's strange," thought Roy. He had been in many dry caves and had never encountered water.

Down on hands and knees, the four crawled into the low, narrow, twenty-foot opening, which seemed to descend as they progressed forward. Brighton was the first to emerge into the cathedral-like room. Still on his hands and knees, he shined his bright flashlight around the cavity. The cavern was the size of a small high school basketball gym. This enormous cavern and the mine tunnels were less than three hundred yards from his bedroom where Gina was still asleep. He glanced around briefly and, groaning as he stood up straight, stretched his throbbing legs.

When Brighton saw the snake, he screamed and jumped away, banging his head on the rock outcropping overhead. The snake did not see him. Not only was it clearly dead, but it was missing part of its head and had rodent gnaw marks along the length of its body.

"Careful!" he warned as the others emerged, struggling with all their gear. The .22 rifle had been awkward to handle in the tight cave entrance, so Tony had leaned it against the tunnel wall. Roy had his pistol in his fanny pack. The four stretched and dusted themselves off, shining their individual lights around the huge cavern, producing a weird light and shadow show.

"Where is the body?" Roy asked.

They focused their lights on the ground in the side chapels, searching for the box and body. In the back of one of the side chambers, staring back at them was a body, but not the ancient miner Harley and the Patel boys had found.

Bound with shiny silver duct tape was a woman lying on her side. Not mummified. She was very much alive. Her eyes were staring into the four bright lights. She could make only primitive guttural sounds since duct tape had been stretched over her mouth and around her neck. Her legs were bare to above her knees, and her ankles were bound together with a man's wide black belt. Her hands were taped together in front, and she was covered with dust. Tracts of tears ran down her cheeks. Her long blonde hair was a tangle of snarls partially covered with a baseball cap pulled low over the top of her eyes. Every visible inch of her tan skin was covered with goose bumps as she shivered in the cool, damp air of the cave. It was Lori Pederson.

Roy diverted his light away from her eyes. He bent down and gently removed the cap and then the tape from her face and mouth. Not knowing exactly what to say, the men spoke softly to her, trying to reassure her that everything would be okay and that they were going to free her. Brighton pulled out his knife and was about to cut the tape from her hands when she screamed.

"Don't cut me! I'll help you or do anything you want!" She screamed, clearly not recognizing who they were. "Please don't cut the tape on my hands. He told me he had wired my hands to a trigger that would set off a load of dynamite!" she blurted out breathlessly. "I couldn't see what he did. It's so dark in here. Who are you?"

Doing first things first, Roy examined the constraints on the woman's hands and feet and then all around her. There were no wires or sign of any explosives.

"There are no explosives. He told you that to scare you," Roy said in a confident tone. He sensed immediately that Lori knew who he was. "We are going to free your hands and feet and help you sit up."

"Who is the "he" who left you here?" Brighton asked as he worked on the tape on her ankles and wrists. "And who are you? What are you doing here?"

"My old partner, Bill—we called him Big Bill. He dragged me here from my house and forced me to show him the tunnel and mine."

She was sitting up by now and leaning against the cavern wall, rubbing her hands and ankles.

"He saw the entrance to this cave and then forced me to come in here. There is a body further back in the cave, and there was a leather case of some sort. I didn't see it very well. When I saw the body and screamed, he slapped me. I hit him with a shovel handle, and that's when he got mad and tied me up and told me he was going to bury me alive."

"Did he take the metal box?" Tony Patel asked the sobbing

woman as he walked away toward the location where he and his brother had found the body and the mail case.

"I don't know what he did. It was too dark. I could only see the reflections of his flashlight. This whole thing is so crazy. I'm so scared and freezing. I just want to go home." She covered her face and began sobbing.

Roy helped her to her feet then left her in the shadows while he started to check out the rest of the cave with the other three men. They briefly examined the mummified body and could see where there was a depression in the ground, supposedly from the mailbox. It was no longer there, but it confirmed the story the Patel brothers had told. Next, Roy shined his light all around the spacious cavity and looked for another way out of the room. When he looked back toward the entrance and the last location of the Pederson woman, she had disappeared. Now the box, Big Bill, and the woman were gone.

The four explorers split up, yelling and searching until they were positive that every inch of the cavern had been explored. Lori could not be found. They decided to work their way back to the narrow cave entrance, but still couldn't find the assay specialist.

Brighton was the first to hear the new voices echoing down the tunnel into the cavern. He walked closer to the narrow entrance and listened intently, trying to recognize a voice, presuming it was Ms. Pederson.

"Hello? Can you hear me?" A woman's voice came through the small opening. Several minutes of suspense were followed by the appearance of Kara and then Charley and then Gina, each crawling on hands and knees through the mouth of the cavern. Each held simple flashlights. They stood upright, scanning the spacious cavern.

"What are you doing here?" Brighton asked his wife. The Patels and Roy had gathered around. "You shouldn't be crawling around pregnant, and I thought you still needed crutches to walk," he said to Kara, who was leaning on the shoulder of her husband, rubbing her ankle.

"We got worried about you after Dean called and said that Clyde had reported a truck with Colorado plates abandoned outside the gate. The police came immediately and said it had been stolen from the scene of the attempted murder in Colorado Springs. We were worried that that guy Bill might have come back," Charley said.

"He's back, all right, and his partner is here with him." Brighton explained the events of the last several minutes. The two women had wandered over to the ancient miner's dusty body and were inspecting it and the area nearby. Kara was still limping and nearly fell down trying to walk on the irregular cave surface.

"Where was the mail case buried?" Kara asked, her voice echoing in the cavern.

Tony pointed out the site to the two women. Gina walked around the area, moving the dirt around with the toe of her shoe when she struck the corner of something sharp. There under her foot was the corner of another square case.

Moments later, the whole group was gathered around as Roy, using his hunting knife, dug down around the sides of an eighteen-by-twenty-four-inch metal box. It took three of them to lift the box out of the ground. The box was rusted metal and painted a dull green color, but unlike the Army mail case the Patel boys had seen, this one displayed no writing. The box appeared to be made of hammered tin. The lid was hinged with three heavy brass hinges. On the opposite side of the box was a bolted clasp with a heavy brass padlock.

Charley was the first to speak. "Whatever it is, it looks important. We probably shouldn't have moved it."

"That has got to be at least a hundred years old," Gina said, pointing at the padlock.

"Probably more than a hundred and fifty," said Patrick Patel. "How much does it weigh?"

"I'd guess over eighty or ninety pounds," said Roy. "It's got something solid inside. I felt it shift when we moved the box. We'll need a dolly to get the thing out of here without breaking our backs."

"We really must leave it where it is and not try to open it or move it further," Charley said. "Whoever the rightful owners are will insist that we not tamper with it."

"You've had one too many days of legal training," chided Roy. "Can't you just once have normal greed and avarice like the rest of us?"

"Why aren't we the owners?" questioned Tony.

"There are hundreds of questions that need to be answered, but the first and most immediate one is, where is Lori?" said Roy. "You didn't see any sign of her when you came into the tunnel?"

"No," Charley said, answering for all three. The women both shrugged their shoulders and looked at Roy with worried expressions.

"Don't you think we should go and let the police or the sheriff investigate whatever is going on here?" Kara asked. She had seen all she wanted to see for this trip. Charley's and the women's flashlights were already starting to dim. Everyone was eager to see the sun and breathe some fresh air.

The Patel boys had headed off in another part of the tunnel, looking for something to break the lock on the strongbox. This was by far the biggest adventure they had ever been on. They didn't want to let a little legal question ruin their day. Luckily for everyone, they found nothing of possible use and returned to the group empty handed.

Brighton wished he had insisted that Dean come along as originally planned. It was obvious to him that they would have to return again with different equipment and possibly more help. Dean and Roy were strong enough that they might be able to drag the metal box out of the narrow cave opening, and from there it would be easy to load onto a mover's dolly to get it the rest of the way out of the tunnel. The problem of taking it right now was moot. However, if they left it, then the problem of possession of the metal box and the missing U.S. Army Mail case, should they find it, would become more of a battle. The Patel boys had found the cave and the body and the case. Kara had been the first to kick the dirt off the metal box. Many questions of ownership were beginning to present themselves.

"Let's all get out of here," Brighton said.

"We need to regroup outside and get more experienced help," Gina said. "Besides, I think I'm having contractions."

"Is your light still working?" Roy asked Gina, who nodded yes.

"How are you doing, Kara?" Charley slipped his arm around her waist so she could lean against him.

"I'm fine, but you'd better keep an eye on those boys." She nodded in the direction of lights in the far end of the cavern. The boys had wandered off again.

"Hey Tony and Patrick, you guys come on over here, and let's all leave together."

The brothers mumbled answers from the distance, and their lights started toward the main group. Suddenly, they each froze in place, listening to a loud mechanical noise roaring through the tunnel.

✳✳✳

The sound at first was like that of a distant jet airplane approaching an airport—faint, then loud, then louder. Suddenly there came the frightening rumble of the tracks of a Caterpillar tractor, echoing down the tunnels and into the cave. Roy was the first to react.

"I'm not sure what or who that is, but we need to get out of here now." There was no complaining or discussion. "Brighton, you lead the way, and I'll follow up the rear. Go, go, and go!"

Everyone lined up, giving the person in front just enough room to crawl through the narrow entrance, stooping over at first, then crawling on their hands and knees. Gina struggled behind Brighton, trying to keep her balance and not skin her knees. Next came Kara, whose injured ankle did not like the unusual angles and irregular surfaces. There was the expected groaning and grumbling, but most of the emotion was a mixture of fear of being trapped and disappointment that they were leaving many unknowns behind.

Midway through the tunnel, Brighton screamed out in pain. He had dragged his healing ankle across a long, jagged rock, scraping away the thin skin covering the site of his snakebite. Everyone froze in place again, listening intently to Brighton's cursing and the loud roar still echoing through the mouth of the cave.

In the relative darkness, Roy called out to the Patel brothers to go through next.

"Tony, Patrick, both of you follow Mr. Banks. Go through now." No answer followed, and a chill of panic went up Roy's spine. "Hey, you guys. Quit screwing around and get into the exit cave. We need to get out of here."

Roy shined his light around the vaulted room but saw nothing. *Did I miss them?* He had been taking one last look around for the Pederson woman while the girls and Charley were struggling into the narrow cave. He thought the boys were right there in front of him in the pitch-dark entryway.

"Tony, Patrick, I'm not kidding, get your butts over here now!"

No sounds followed the dimming echo of his voice.

He put his head into the cavern entrance and listened but could only hear scraping and crunching of underfoot rocks from those on the tunnel side of the cave. Just when Roy was giving in to his panic and getting on his hands and knees to crawl into the narrow opening, he heard voices behind him.

"We found her, we found her!" Patrick hollered from the darkness behind Roy.

Roy stood straight up, banging his head on the low ceiling of the cave entrance. He grabbed the back of his head and turned in the direction of Patrick's voice. He could see the reflections of the flashlights on the cave walls as they came closer to him.

"You found the blonde? Where is she?" Roy asked as he walked briskly toward the two boys. When they were just a few feet apart, he saw that they were alone.

"Not the woman," said Tony. "We found the back entrance to the cavern, and we found the gold mine—the real gold mine!"

"What are you talking about … the real gold mine?" Roy asked, not knowing whether to be upset or excited.

"There's a back entrance to this cavern, and just inside it is a flat wall with a bunch of writing chiseled on it," Patrick explained. "It says something about how he hopes some woman can live a life of riches when she cashes in her gold nugget. It is signed "J. W." You know? Jacob Waltz. From that wall there's a tunnel going back another fifty or hundred feet. We heard you yelling, so we came back instead of looking deeper into the mine. Where did the others go?"

Roy's answer was interrupted by the renewal of the sound of an engine roaring and metal grating on rock. Roy dove into the cavern entrance and scrambled the twenty feet through the narrow space into the main tunnel. The Patel boys were right behind him.

44

TRAPPED

The telephone rang five times and was about to go to voicemail when Rhonda finally pulled her satin, down-filled duvet away from her face and reached for the telephone.

"Hello," she whispered in a hoarse voice. She had practiced a new rendition of "Jingle Bell Rock" in her home recording studio late into the night. The repetitious singing always left her vocal cords swollen and her voice scratchy.

"Rhonda? It's Dean Shutter. I'm sorry to bother you so early, but I have been trying to reach Roy. It's an emergency. Do you have any idea where he might have gone?"

"Let me think," she said, glancing at the clock. It was 7:15 a.m. The sun had been up for a couple of hours, but her room was pitch black. She pressed the control button to raise the blackout curtains. "Wasn't it this morning that you all were going back into the cave with the Patel boys?"

"Oh crap, now I remember. We had a family emergency, and I had to miss it. I've been up all night and am not thinking straight. Sharron has not been herself ... I'm sorry to bother you. I called the Dunns and the Banks, and no one answered except the Banks girls who said something about their Mom leaving in a hurry. I guess I'll go to the Steiners' houses and see if I can find them."

"Give me five minutes, and I'll go with you. Are you at home or in your car?" Rhonda asked, sitting up on the bed and stretching her back and legs.

"I'm walking out the door of our rental as we speak. Take your time. I've got to stop and get some new batteries for the flashlights. I'll honk when I pull under your portico. Figure twenty minutes. Will that work for you?"

"I'll be waiting outside when you get here," Rhonda answered.

Dean hung up without responding. Rhonda stared at the phone and then hung it up and headed for the bathroom. This recent life she was living sure wasn't like her prior celebrity lifestyle. It was crazy and full of surprises. More surprises than any movie script, and to top it all off, it was real—very real.

Twenty minutes later, Rhonda pulled herself up into the Hummer. Dean gave her a friendly smile, his first of the day. He still wasn't used to the idea of living in the cul-de-sac with a living legend. The Hummer pulled around the corner of the street and drove straight up the dusty side drive of the Steiners' houses.

The mining operation with all of its truck and tractor traffic had essentially destroyed the once pristine landscaping. As the Hummer turned the corner at the back gate, Dean slammed on the brakes with a sudden force that threw the unbuckled Rhonda into the dashboard. Skidding on the grass and dirt, they came to a stop only after crunching into the rear bumper of a beat-up Ford pickup.

"What the heck is going on?" exclaimed Dean as Rhonda pulled herself back up onto the car seat.

***

Lori Pederson had crawled through the cavern exit into the mine tunnel and had then rushed blindly toward the exit. The absolute darkness had been nearly overpowering. Pure luck and a keen sense of smell made her take a critical turn. The alternative would have led her to one of the vertical shafts and a fall to her death. The diesel exhaust fumes that hung faintly in the stale air gave her direction, and then she heard the sound of the turbo-diesel engine.

The last fifty feet toward the dim light at the end of the tunnel had been a footrace. Bill had told her he was going to bury her alive, and she hadn't doubted him. The reality of his intent shot a new burst of adrenalin through her body and mind. Finally in the opening to the tunnel, the bright morning sunlight burned her eyes. The sound of the Caterpillar tractor rattling toward her produced an extra burst of energy. Her chest burned for air, and a catch in her side brought tears to her eyes.

She scurried on all fours up loose dirt of the cave-in ramp; a path that had become well-traveled. Near the top she stopped and peeked over the edge, where she came face to blade with the ten-foot-wide by six-foot-high scoop on the front of a huge Caterpillar tractor. It was pushing a full load of dirt and rock toward her and the sunken hole. She couldn't see the driver, nor could he see her. She knew it had to be Bill. Grabbing the protruding edge of a transected, black, plastic drip-line hose, she yanked hard enough to propel herself over the edge of the ramp. The forward-moving blade missed her arm by inches. Rolling into the edge of an oleander shrub, she hid herself long enough to avoid Bill's attention.

He sat atop the yellow, twelve-foot-high machine he had driven up from Lot #29. He was obviously on the verge of backfilling the caved-in tunnel. She squirmed along the ground on her belly, hands, and knees like a GI Jane under training fire. Finally, reaching Otto Steiner's back porch, Lori concealed herself behind a barbeque grill.

Catching her breath, she started to shake and knew it was the aftermath of extreme fear, partnered with a lack of sleep or fluids. She realized she had to stop Bill or he would trap the other men in the cave. There wasn't time to call the police, though breaking into the Steiner's house was a tempting but fleeting thought. She had to stop Bill.

She watched as he made a turn with the Caterpillar and scooped up several table-size boulders. He raised the giant scoop high in the air then rolled forward to dump the contents into the abyss, when the inconceivable happened. He had driven unknowingly over the intact but weakened roof of the old mine's tunnel below. With a groan and a rumble, the whole area began to tremble as the ground began to crack. With a skyward rush of air, the roof of the tunnel beneath the huge machine collapsed, sucking the Caterpillar and Bill straight down. The noise was accompanied by a billowing cloud of dust and then silence.

From Lori's view, one second the giant yellow machine was there, and the next second it was gone. The breeze carried away the dense dust cloud, revealing only a few inches of the tractor's roll cage. The entire rest of the machine was surrounded with dirt and rock as though it had been placed in the ground and intentionally buried. Bill was nowhere to be seen, nor was the previous opening to the tunnel. The burial was complete.

Lori was so exhausted and emotionally spent that she simply staggered toward a patio chair. She was just sinking into the padded fabric when Dean's accelerating Humvee rolled up the access drive to the backyard and then came to a crunching halt, crashing into the rear bumper of the old pickup truck, which Lori hadn't even noticed. She tried to get up from the chair, but her leg muscles were jelly. She saw Dean jump out of his truck and stop to stare at the hole where the opening to the tunnel had been. A woman appeared from the other door and stood frozen, taking in the scene.

Lori tried again to get up from the chair but couldn't move. Her wrists and ankles were burning from the restraints Bill had used to bind her. Her throat could barely utter a sound because it was so sore from screaming. She hid in the shadow of the patio cover, watching the two inspect the scene of the collapse.

Dean bent down and started digging furiously with his hands around the middle part of the twisted roll cage. She heard the woman ask in a panicked voice if he could find anyone. Suddenly, he yelled for the woman to find a shovel or something to dig with. Dust flew as the two of them threw dirt away from the hole near the roll cage. She saw the woman pull a green John Deere hat out of the new shallow hole, and then the digging stopped. The woman shook the dirt off of the green hat and then carefully placed it on top of the freshly dug hole. Lori could see through the bushes well enough to tell that the hat now sat on the crown of a head. It was when she heard Dean pronounce Bill's death that she struggled to her feet and ran for the side gate where Bill's old battered Ford truck was parked.

❋❋❋

The dust filling the interior tunnels of the old mine shafts was incredible. Not only was it difficult for the newly trapped Hidden Gravel HOA members to get a full breath of air, but it refracted the light beams from their flashlights so they could see only a few inches in front of them.

The group bumped into rock walls and vertical timbers as they rushed toward what they thought would be the exit. Brighton was leading the pack, limping severely. When they passed the site that he recognized as the place where the rattlesnake had struck him, he supposed they were in the correct tunnel, but knew he also should have been able to see a patch of light from the entrance. Instead, all he saw was the settling dust and what appeared to be a jumbled pile of dirt and rock.

"There has been a cave-in!" he yelled to the others.

Everyone was coughing and choking. Charley, a lifelong asthmatic, was in even worse shape. He was in the early stages of a full-blown asthma attack, and hadn't brought his inhaler.

When Roy and the Patel brothers caught up with the group, Brighton filled them in on what he guessed had happened when the tractor noise was followed by the tunnel filling with dirt and rock. Roy had the brightest light, so he crept up close to the new obstruction in the tunnel. Realizing that it could cave in more at any second, he was on tiptoes as he inspected the debris. He returned to report.

"It looks like the Steiner's whole backyard is down in the tunnel. I can see strands of black plastic drip lines and even a broken clay pot that was by the pool fence," Roy said.

"I hope the pool doesn't collapse and flood us. Their pool is enormous," said Tony with a quiver in his voice.

"How are we going to get out of here?" Kara asked the three men. Charley was doing his best to control his breathing without letting panic add to the problem.

It was Patrick who stepped forward with confidence in his voice. "We know that there is the original entrance to the mine shafts back the other way. Tony and I saw it, and you can see light between the rocks. We won't suffocate. Also, we think we saw another entrance at the back of the big cavern near where the writing is on the wall. Maybe it is big enough for someone to crawl through."

"We need to get away from the dusty air and get Charley where he can lie down," Gina insisted.

"Honey, you aren't in any shape to deal with all this stress. Is the baby moving?" Brighton asked, putting his hand on her protuberant belly. "I saw you rubbing it. Are you going to be okay?"

"I'm fine. Let's get away from this dust before all of our flashlights are out and we have to grovel along in the dark." Gina's determined voice, perhaps motivated by her maternal instinct of preservation, allowed for no arguments. "Brighton, why did you scream back there?"

He didn't answer, but it was impossible to miss his significant new limp.

"Only the leader and the tail need lights," Roy insisted. "We have to conserve every ounce of battery power. Charley, you and Tony lead the way."

"What about the cave entrance Tony and I found?" Patrick asked Brighton.

"Let's get everyone to the old main entrance where the air is good, and then we can plan new strategies. Maybe someone heard all the noise and reported it."

"Who even knows that we are down here?" asked Kara, choking back the emotion and fear she was feeling. She was worried about her husband, and her ankle was hurting more. "I told my girls we were going to breakfast with the Dunns. No one will even be looking for us."

45

Help!!!

Otto Steiner heard the crashing and scraping echo off the hills behind his house. The Caterpillar tractor noise had awakened him from an inebriated coma. He put on a tank top and headed for the back porch to take a look. When he opened the back door, he saw a cloud of dust still hanging in the air. Now, he remembered thinking for just a second that he had heard a man scream at about the time of the crashing and scraping, but he wasn't quite sure. The sun hurt his eyes, so he turned back into the house and phoned Heinz.

"Komm' mit," he said, asking his brother to come with him to check out what had happened. Lately, there were lots of strange things in the neighborhood, but he had followed the advice of Mr. Charley and kept his nose out of it, with the promise that all the neighbors were going to get a lot of money if they were patient.

The brothers met in front and walked around the house and up the long, dusty driveway. Out of nowhere, Mr. Shutter's black Humvee flew up the driveway, almost running them over. When it went around the corner of the garage, they heard a loud crunch of metal on metal. They were both winded by the time they reached the backyard.

At the top of the driveway, they saw the smashed trucks and then turned the corner to see an unlikely pair standing at the edge of a huge hole in the yard with the back of a yellow tractor's roll cage protruding from the hole.

At that instant a blonde woman came stumbling around the corner of the house, not watching where she was going but looking back over her shoulder. The two hefty brothers made a wide barrier and were too slow to step aside in time.

"Pas auf!" Otto yelled, but it was too late. The woman slammed directly into Heinz's keg-size belly, knocking him flat on the ground as the stunned woman rolled off to the side in the trampled dust and dirt. She looked like a tattered rag doll, conscious but too exhausted and defeated to move.

Dean and Rhonda, hearing Otto's yell, turned and watched the collision occur as though in slow motion. Otto, being the chauvinist pig he was, bent over to help his brother to his feet before offering the tattered woman his hand.

Rhonda on the other hand, rushed to the woman's side, stooping over her and trying to assist. Dean was in the middle of calling for the sheriff with Rhonda's cell phone.

Otto and Heinz stared at the site of the cave-in, now clearly seeing the yellow Caterpillar's roll cage and the unmistakable green John Deere baseball cap. Surrounding the edges of the hat was a flesh-colored head with one ear exposed.

"Idiots! Your whole neighborhood is full of idiots!" hollered the sheriff into the phone. "I'll take a barrio full of drug lords and hookers any day compared to the idiots in Hidden Canyon."

Dean tried to explain the situation, though he doubted that much was sinking in. When the sheriff kept going on about all the problems in the development, some of which Dean hadn't even heard about, he began to lose his temper. He was standing in front of a dead man who was 98 percent buried in the cab of a stolen tractor, standing beside a kidnap victim who sat on the ground sobbing, along with two babbling bewildered Germans who barely understood English, and beneath the earth, not far from his feet, was a buried mine tunnel holding an unknown number of victims, all of whom were his friends and neighbors.

"Why don't you get off your high hobby horse and get your butt out here with some excavation equipment? Maybe you can save somebody's life today."

Dean snapped the cell phone shut and turned his attention to Lori. She was covered in dirt and grime. Rhonda again offered to help her stand up, but she shook her head no and stayed sitting with her knees pulled up to her chest. She was audibly sobbing.

"Lori, we've been looking for you since you called last night. What in the world happened?" Dean knelt beside her and put an arm around her shoulder to console her.

Lori didn't look at him nor speak at first but kept looking toward the buried tractor and the green cap. Finally, between sobs she murmured to Dean, "There are people trapped in the tunnel. I've looked, and there is no other way out. They are all going to die."

"How many are in there?" he demanded.

"I don't know for sure. I saw two teenage boys and the dentist and the guy who brought me some assays to do a few months ago. But I heard other voices—a man and two women, I think—but I didn't see them, I just heard their voices." Lori was starting to come out of her state of shock and finally extended her hand to Rhonda and Heinz, who assisted her to her feet.

Heinz had dusted off his baggy pants and walked over to the cave-in. He bent down and brushed the dirt away from the dead man's face and knelt down to look straight into his face. "Er ist tot," is all he said and then walked over to the garden hose by the house, where he turned it on and washed off his hands.

Rhonda turned to Dean. "I knew they were going in there this morning, and I thought you were going with them. What happened?"

"It's a long story, and I'll be happy to share it with you, but first we need to open the tunnel some way."

Lori had sat down again, this time on a low retaining wall, gradually regaining her senses. She would incriminate herself with the next statement, but her basic Christian upbringing wouldn't allow her to stay quiet.

"I said there isn't a way out of there, but I was in that mine a few days ago and found the original entrance. It's covered with rock and overgrowth, but I'm pretty sure you can find it."

Before Rhonda or Dean could respond to Lori's admission, they heard the sirens of both the police and the paramedics. The ambulance roared up the side drive of the Steiner's house, turning the blind corner and smashing straight into the back of Dean's new Humvee, which in turn crunched again into the old Ford pickup.

✳✳✳

It didn't take long before the noisy morning invasion of Hidden Canyon by the police, fire, and rescue teams brought out all the neighbors. Dr. Patel heard from a nurse about there being an accidental cave-in, and he immediately left the hospital to return home and check on his boys. Within an hour, the news helicopters were circling the area and the satellite broadcast trucks were ascending on the development. By noon the collapse of a historic mining tunnel with the self-burial of a tractor driver and the subsequent entombment of seven people was on the Internet, CNN, and Fox News. The story even broke into a CBS network's soap opera. The word was out that a Fox News anchorman was already in a private jet on his way to investigate.

One of the first local newshounds to arrive had been unceremoniously kicked off the property months before while trying to get a scoop on Rhonda Tucker. He knew that Rhonda's house was just a few doors away, and he had his radar out for her. It took a while, because the Diamondback cap and oversize sunglasses she was wearing threw him for a few minutes, but he finally recognized her. She appeared to be in the middle of the action.

The sheriff's deputies had cordoned off the area, but the Clark Kent wannabe jumped the fence at the Dunns' and ducked into the group of neighbors and rescue people trying to get closer to Ms. Tucker. He had a small digital camera; his big Nikon would have been too conspicuous, and the point-and-shoot would do. A close-up of the Rockabilly Diva at a death scene should score a big paycheck with one of the movie gossip rags.

Dean had shaken off the bad phone call with Sheriff Brice and hadn't thought twice about the crushed rear and front ends of his Humvee. He was focused on developing a plan with the sheriff to rescue his entombed friends. Rhonda had stayed right at his side after the paramedics had taken over the care of Lori Pederson. Dean had tried to cover for Lori, but Brice had put her name and face together with the stolen Mustang and the death of the driver. He told one of the female deputies to go to the emergency room with the ambulance and to hold Lori for questioning.

Dean had called Sharron and asked her to round up a few of the neighbors to help control the crowds. He told her he had found Lori.

Rhonda had been afraid to frighten the Banks' twin girls, but it was essential that the rescue team knew who was in the tunnel. The girls confirmed that their mom had left in a hurry and was going to pick up Mrs. Dunn and meet their dad somewhere in the neighborhood. Rhonda told them to stay in the house and find a movie to watch. She gave them her cell phone number and ran back to the Steiners.

The Steiner brothers had made the lame suggestion that everyone in the neighborhood could bring shovels and dig the tractor and the dead guy out of the collapsed tunnel.

Dean now noticed another problem. The water level in the Steiner's swimming pool seemed to be receding slowly, with no explanation as to where the water was going. He could only guess. He called one of the civil engineers who lived in the project area near the main entrance. The man listened then left work immediately to help.

✳✳✳

Thus far, no one had a good answer for how to dig into the tunnel. Lori and Dean had been the only ones topside who had previously been inside, and Lori was now at the hospital. At the time, Dean had been so anxious helping Brighton after the rattlesnake bite that he had lost all sense of direction underground. Everyone who was consulted agreed that the worst thing they could do would be to collapse more of the tunnel on top of those inside. Rhonda reminded them of Lori's comment about an original entrance somewhere in the desert toward Alma's property.

The sheriff plucked his radio off his uniform sleeve and directed the Channel 4 news helicopters to land on the open lot across the street so that he and Dean and the engineer could get a close air survey of the hillside in hopes of spotting the entrance. Dean gave Rhonda, with whom he was becoming more comfortable, a hug of thanks for her suggestion, when the local news guy stuck a flashing camera nearly in their faces and clicked off a dozen or so pictures. "Great," thought Dean, "just what my wife will love to see."

The reporter then stepped closer and asked Dean, "What does it feel like to have those world-famous breasts pressed up against your side?" Dean lost it. He grabbed the camera that was still attached to the strap around the newshound's neck and dragged the panicked man to the edge of the swimming pool where he gave a final yank, projecting the camera and its owner into the water.

Sheriff Brice was standing right next to Dean and turned to him in surprise.

"That was uncalled for, Mr. Shutter," Brice said. "You should have just hit him in the mouth."

Rhonda gave Dean's arm a tight squeeze of thanks, and the three of them headed through the crowd past the emergency vehicles, and down the driveway toward the hovering chopper with its cloud of dust.

"What's the weird yellow contraption at the end of the lot?" Sheriff Brice asked Dean. That's when the idea struck him.

46

ENTOMBED

Roy was a master of self-control. Having worked daily in an environment where death or mayhem was always just a single mistake away, he was not, under any circumstances, going to allow the trapped group to do anything that wasn't thought out and discussed. He trusted Brighton with his life, but now the dentist's judgment was compromised. The healing area of his ankle was so vascular that the surface skin tore away under the bandages. That new injury, combined with the Coumadin he was on to prevent blood clots, potentiated active bleeding from his leg.

Roy insisted that the pregnant Gina stay with her husband and keep pressure on the wound. He situated them at a junction in the tunnels a good fifty feet back from the new cave-in. They were left with the small flashlight that Gina had grabbed off her utility room counter as she ran out the door just an hour before. By now it seemed like days.

Next, Roy assigned the Patel brothers to search the opening that they thought might lead out of the other end of the caverns. This was several hundred feet away. Roy worried about risking their safety, but felt they were the most experienced in this subterranean world. He gave them the best flashlights and a supply of new batteries.

That left Charley and Kara alone while he was getting the others organized. He returned to find trouble. Though Charley was a great attorney and a good guy, he was a lousy person to be stuck with in an emergency. When Roy finally had time to shine his headlamp on the couple, they were sitting against the wall of the tunnel not far from where the rattlesnake had bitten Brighton. Kara had her arm around Charley and was talking softly and slowly to him. He had his arms clutched around his knees and was shaking. His breathing was emitting an audible wheezing sound as his chest and back heaved up and down, struggling to move air through his lungs' narrowed airways. He glanced up at Roy and said, "You have got to get me out of this cave or I am going to die!"

Roy couldn't believe his ears. The immediate personality change was a study of legend in the Roy's profession: air traffic controllers under the stress of managing an airplane in mechanical trouble or facing potential lethal weather would freeze up, and even get up from their transmitting stations and run from the room. Roy's training bulled its way to the forefront of his consciousness. He took Kara by the arm and pulled her away from Charley and confirmed from her in low whispers that Charley was not just asthmatic but also claustrophobic. Once he knew the problem, he got on his knees in front of Charley, and with a quick swing slapped Charley across the face. Charley, who was visibly crying, jumped to his feet and screamed at Roy.

"What the hell are you doing? Have you gone insane?" Charley's wheezing stopped, and he was ready to fight, the adrenaline produced by his anger working wonders on his bronchial spasm.

"I need you to save Kara's and Gina's lives!" Roy shouted, taking him by both arms. "Take the best flashlights and go to the old entrance of the cave where we saw the light rays coming through the rocks and start a small fire. The air is blowing out that direction and will carry the smoke out so someone might see it. Here's a lighter. Take these and Kara with you." Roy handed the last of the batteries and his xenon headlamp to Kara.

"What do we start a fire with?" Charley asked, his face and pride still burning.

Roy angled the light so that both of their faces were visible. He looked Charley straight in the eyes and said, "Use whatever you can find—your clothes if you have to. But Charley, we all need to get out of here. You can make it happen. I trust you."

Roy was left standing alone in the black tunnel listening to footsteps filtering through the various passageways. He left his small light turned off for the time being and tried to organize his thoughts. He was standing in the middle of what could be the coolest historical find in a hundred years, worth millions of dollars to the LLC. On the other hand, if they couldn't get everyone out in a reasonable amount of time, it could become a deathtrap for all seven of them.

He walked toward the caved-in end of the tunnel. Shining his small light on the supporting timbers, he could clearly see that some were now at odd angles or had recently shifted in relationship to the supporting beams crossing the roof of the tunnel. There also were occasional large fallen rocks on the tunnel floor, which he had definitely not seen before. Once the Mole had originally collapsed with the first part of the tunnel, the entire branch had been weakened. He doubted that any of the tunnels close to the Steiners' houses was safe. It was as he was walking away from the cave-in that he heard the water. He pointed his light at ground level where he could see a fresh trickle leaking through the loosened dirt.

***

The helicopter created a tremendous cloud of dirt and dust as it lifted into the sky above Cactus Wren Circle. Dean, Rhonda, the engineer, and Sheriff Brice directed the pilot to hover over the Steiners' houses for a minute to get a lay of the land. Dean, having been in the tunnels below the visible surface, got a slightly clearer picture of which direction to fly and directed the chopper toward the east.

Outside the Hidden Canyon property line, the surface was one of small hills strewn with rocks and boulders, some the size of motor homes. The vegetation was virgin cactus and small trees with low bushes hiding a good part of the terrain. Trying to find the original opening to the mine, they flew toward the opposite side of the more prominent hills, toward Alma Ziegler's burned-out home site. Nowhere could they see any hint of removed vegetation or of mine tailings or man-made trails, nor could they make out any natural area where one would start digging a tunnel. Time and the weather had erased all hints of man's previous intrusion.

They had circled about twenty minutes when the helicopter pilot pointed to his fuel gauge and waved, indicating his intention of returning them to the neighborhood. Rhonda was becoming frantic, worrying about Roy and the others, but especially about

Roy. She tugged on the pilot's arm and, getting his attention, begged him to circle one more time. That's when they saw the tiny curl of smoke. At first it looked like a small dust devil wiggling and moving in the wind, like the hips of an exotic belly dancer dressed in white. Then there was an unmistakable poof of smoke, which reminded Dean of the Indian smoke signals in old John Wayne movies. Rhonda shouted as Dean directed the flight to a spot directly over the smoke. In the few seconds it took to get to the origin of the cloud, they saw another poof, this time more like the spouting of a humpback whale. Then the smoke was gone, the downdraft of the chopper scattering any hint of it.

Each of the four studied the area, and only then could Dean be pretty sure it was the ancient cleared trail that led from near the county's gravel road into the hills toward the apparent mine entrance. The sheriff wanted to mark the site but couldn't find anything suitable in the helicopter. In frustration, and much to the aggravation of the pilot, Brice opened the chopper door and dropped the headphone set he had been wearing. It fell straight to the ground, trailing its tethered cord as it fell.

✳✳✳

The Patel brothers were the first of those trapped in the caverns to hear the helicopter. They had crossed the cathedral part of the cave and tried three different tangential arms of small caverns only to find dead ends. The tunnel where they had seen the writing also proved to be a dead end. One tangential tunnel was literally dead, with a pile of bones appearing to be those of a large, furry animal or two. On a fourth try they found signs of where someone had chiseled out a narrow opening. This passage led them into yet another cathedral of smaller size than the first, but still with only one exit.

They crawled on an upwardly inclined ledge to what appeared to be a vent. There they could see sunlight. The fresh, dry air was invigorating, causing a spontaneous shout of joy from the brothers, but the opening was small and lined with solid rock. Tony crawled up, pressing his face into the opening, which allowed a view, but in only one narrow direction—upward. They tried to widen the opening with their hands, but needed proper digging tools. They had seen some antique tools—a pick and an old railroad spike—back in the mine tunnel, so they agreed to first find Roy and then bring the tools back to the opening.

✳✳✳

Kara led Charley through the tunnels like a mom leading her toddler. Her entire leg was extremely pained after all the unaccustomed walking and crawling, but she ignored the discomfort, pressing forward with intense determination. She had to keep reassuring Charley that they were going in the direction of the exit, not deeper into the abyss. She was consciously using her light sparingly, which made Charley even more anxious. Once they rounded the corner leading to the old entrance, they could see the beams of sunlight illuminating motes of dust.

Kara searched the floor of the tunnel and found some pieces of brush and a broken wooden lid. She found a level place against the pile of rocks that covered the entrance and smoothed out the dirt floor. She made a tiny pyramid of the brush and scraps of wood. She searched her pockets and found her grocery list. This she tore into small fragments, which she placed under the scraps of wood. She had never been a camper or even a Girl Scout, but with a prayer and a few false starts, she finally got a tiny fire started.

"Can you hear it?" Charley asked his wife. He was leaning on one of the bigger rocks blocking the entrance. "Listen, I hear a motor!"

"I think it's a helicopter. Help me find something else to burn."

So far, the smoke from the fire was starting to fill the tunnel. As they added more scraps to the pile, the fire took hold in the dry wood and gave off light and smoke. The smoke was starting to worry Kara. Both she and Charley started coughing, but then just as Roy had promised, she saw the venting begin. Like a big vacuum on the other end, the smoky air was being sucked out of the tunnel through the small cracks between the rocks. The sound of the chopper was getting closer.

"We need a bigger fire!" Charley shouted, exuberant over the prospect of rescue. Finding nothing close at hand, he peeled off his turtleneck and dangled it over the flames until it caught fire, sending off a larger white plume of smoke that was quickly sucked out of the tunnel. They both shouted for help a few times before realizing how inconceivable it was that anyone would hear them. The fire was burning down to small blue flames. Following her husband's example, Kara unbuttoned her blouse, laying the silk fabric carefully on the corner of the remaining flames. With a near flash of fire, another burst of smoke rose into the tunnel and was sucked out through the cracks in the rock barrier. In just seconds, the flames died into a pile of embers.

✳✳✳

From the distance, through the echoing tunnels, Brighton and Gina could hear shouts and then the laughing. If something good was happening, it needed to happen quickly. Brighton was sitting in a small pool of his own blood, and Gina's bottom was getting wet from a slow trickle of water dripping into the tunnel. She got up from the ground with a groan, feeling the baby kick in the process. Extending a hand in the pitch darkness, she clasped Brighton's hand and helped him stand. Carefully, they moved a few yards deeper into the tunnel to higher, drier ground.

Roy had left the couple with instructions to listen for the Patel brothers and to make the boys stay with them. He then headed in the direction of the shouts, and hopefully, the escape route. Once away from his injured friend and his pregnant wife, he muttered a secret prayer. He felt like his perception of direction in the darkness was improving, so he kept his light off until he walked face first into a solid wall. He took two steps back then turned on his flashlight, finding himself in a twenty-foot dead-end branch of the main tunnel. Four inches from his left foot was a downward shaft. Startled, he drew away from it then kicked a grapefruit-size rock down the shaft. The shaft was deep—too deep to have survived a fall into it.

The intrinsic danger of the place was reinforced in his mind. He had a moment of guilt for allowing his malignant curiosity to start the entire adventure. *They all had made a lot of money, but would they even live to spend any of it?* He snapped out of it and headed back to the main tunnel.

***

Once the helicopter was back on the ground, Dean and Rhonda joined a circle of the Hidden Canyon neighbors and filled them in on the sighting of smoke extruding through the large rocks. The sheriff went to his car and made a call requesting the county roads superintendent send out a crew with heavy equipment to dig open the mouth of the tunnel. The response he received back was that without the written permission of the landowner, the county highway department could not go onto the property. When told that the homeowner was unavailable, the superintendent simply told the sheriff he would have to get a court order. This initiated a long argument over the phone that ended when Brice looked out through his rearview mirror to see the large, strange, yellow machine pulling out slowly onto the paved road. He got out of his Yukon and recognized Dean Shutter in the driver's seat with Rhonda Tucker and several of the other neighbors, armed with shovels and picks and fence cutters, walking behind it.

There was a small path between the homes on the upper cul-de-sacs of Hidden Canyon and those of the homes closer to the entrance and HOA pool and clubhouse. Originally, the path had been created by the desert animals, especially the coyotes with their constant late-night prowling. Over the years, weekend hikers and mountain bikers had widened the trail. It led in a somewhat circuitous way to the county road on the other side of the hill. It had been Alma's path to spy on the development and had probably once been the trail that led the ancient prospectors to and from their mines into the town.

It was a difficult and uneven path for the Mole to trek, but with the pack of eager helpers moving larger rocks and scouting ahead, Dean was able to make good progress toward the mine's probable entrance. Arriving at the barbed wire fence that delineated Alma's property line, Otto and Heinz did the honors with the wire cutters, and the Mole proceeded along the trail. "Maybe this is all of our property," thought Dean, wondering if Charley had finalized the paperwork with Alma for the transfer of ownership.

A growing number of people from the city and surrounding neighborhoods joined the action, following the Mole in a single-file line, which eventually stretched out for half a mile. The helicopter pilot had returned to his home base for fuel and was back in the air with a camera crew and the channel's star reporter, a skinny blonde with big eyes, big teeth, and a pronounced profile. She was smiling into the camera and giving live feed to the station and the nation, reporting on the progression of the mechanical Mole, its human lemmings, and the entombed victims of the homicidal—and now dead—Caterpillar driver.

The neighbors and onlookers were filling the ears of the ground-based reporters with rumors that were growing in size and intrigue. The reporter whom Dean had thrown into the swimming pool was looking like a wet hen and spewing rubbish to anyone who would listen. The dead tractor driver, presumed to be the missing attempted murderer Big Bill, was still buried up to his nose with the Caterpillar tractor. Ribbons of crime scene tape surrounded the back of the Steiners' houses, but it was generally ignored by anyone who wanted to get a close look at the dead man's head.

"Hundreds of people rush to save neighbors trapped in the Lost Dutchman's Gold Mine," read the trailer running across the bottom of every news and network channel.

"Bones of the Lost Dutchman found in buried gold mine," read another one.

"Dozens of people are buried in historic gold mine collapse in Arizona. It may be too late to save them," began the anchorman for the national noon CBS News broadcast. "A secret gold mining operation in the exclusive neighborhood of movie and singing star Rhonda Tucker has led to a disaster of epic proportions. At this moment, the actress herself is leading a rescue operation to save the lives of dozens of her neighbors, including her boyfriend and a pregnant woman."

47

COMING UP NEXT

When Sheriff Brice checked on the scene at the Caterpillar cave-in and found that the cordoned-off crime scene had been breached by rubberneckers, he nearly had a stroke. After screaming at one of the deputies, he ordered the shaken officer to arrest four random trespassing adults and handcuff them to the metal swimming pool fence.

"They are trespassing and interfering with a crime scene investigation," he told a reporter for ABC News. "If and when we rescue the trapped folks from the tunnel, then—and only then—will I release these four ghoul seekers. Tell the rest of your enthralled audience that unless they want to spend their night on a metal cot at Tent City, they had better stay home and follow the excitement on TV."

Dr. Patel helped the officers clear most of the crowd from the Steiners' properties. He walked among the onlookers spreading the rumor that the collapsed tunnel had allowed the escape of poisonous gas, and that the gas might contain a form of nineteenth century hemorrhagic fever virus ... Embolus Superstitious, he called it. The rumor spread like a hive of enraged Africanized bees, and so did the crowd.

Sheriff Brice left the crime scene in the hands of his deputies and drove his Yukon out of Hidden Canyon's entrance gate and around to the county road near Alma Ziegler's. As he drove over the dusty gravel road past the woman's burned-down house, Brice could see the trail of dust the Mole and its entourage was kicking up. It was then that he noticed a black Mercury Marquis parked along the road just past the Ziegler woman's burned house. It was definitely not a local. Because of its three-digit license plate, he knew it had to be from some shadow agency of the federal government—but which one, and what were they doing there? As his Yukon drove over the next rise, the sheriff slammed on his brakes, locking up all four wheels. He skidded a good hundred feet on the gravel surface before he came to a stop just short of a gray helicopter sitting in the middle of the road with its rotor blades spinning idly.

The chopper was completely blocking the narrow road. The bar pit on each side was way too deep to go around. At first Brice presumed it was one of the news channel's birds, but he couldn't see any markings or even a pilot. He honked his horn repeatedly then turned on his siren, but no one appeared. Frustrated, he jumped out of his vehicle and ran up to the chopper.

A sharp whistle pierced the air, and Brice looked up the side of a nearby hill toward the sound. Standing on a boulder holding very large binoculars were three men. Two were dressed in dark suits, white shirts, and ties; the third wore a military-like jumpsuit. Brice waved and yelled for someone to move the chopper so he could get by, but the men just stood there looking at him. It was only when he got back in the Tahoe and drove right up to the side of the helicopter, putting the SUV's front bumper against the side of the chopper and revving the engine that the action began.

Two of the men in suits drew concealed pistols while running toward Brice and taking aim at the sheriff's Yukon. Brice butted his bumper against the helicopter and pushed on the gas. He had drawn his own pistol and had it on the seat beside him, but was using both hands to guide the SUV. With crunching of gravel and some metallic complaining, the chopper began moving sideways, tilting and shaking.

Brice could see the men now running down the hill. He had pushed the helicopter about twelve feet when he thought he had enough room to get by. He put his car in reverse and punched the gas, backing up twenty feet or so. Just as the men ran up behind him, he stomped on the gas, spinning his wheels and spraying a double rooster tail of gravel in their direction.

"Screw you!" he yelled out the window as they tried to catch up to him. He had a job to do and didn't care if J. Edgar Hoover himself was reincarnated and standing in the road; Brice wasn't going to let anyone stop him. Moments later, the stealth chopper and the black sedan were gone.

***

Patrick and Tony Patel were getting tired and thirsty. They had left their backpacks somewhere in the mine tunnels, but hadn't come across them again. They had now made three trips back and forth from the mine tunnel into the caverns. Each time, they had used only a minimum of battery power but would soon need new batteries. They had heard all the echoes and could now hear an engine's throbbing sounds. They had looked in vain for adequate tools to expand the small vent hole at the far end of the cavern but had only found an old pick. Its handle had broken on the third swing, leaving them to chip away holding the jagged, rusted tool in their bare hands. Within a couple of minutes, even taking turns, both of their hands were blistered and bleeding. The potential escape hole appeared to be getting smaller instead of larger.

"This isn't working!" blurted Tony, picking a rock chip out of his tearing eye. Patrick had concluded the same thing several minutes earlier, but Tony had insisted on still trying longer.

"Let's go back and find Roy. I can hear a helicopter and some other motors running. Maybe the rescue people are here."

"No one knows for sure that we're even in here," insisted Tony. "What if they rescue the others and forget about us?"

He shook his flashlight again, but this time the beam didn't brighten. He picked up the metal pickax head, and with his near useless light in the other hand, he stumbled along behind his brother back toward the mine tunnel.

***

Gina had mustered every bit of courage she could to help her husband. She had ripped off her sequined T-shirt top and tied it around the bleeding leg wound as tightly as Brighton could tolerate. It appeared to slow the bleeding a little but, with no light source, she wasn't sure. She feared that Brighton had gone into a mild state of shock. He was still able to communicate but only in a voice that sounded drugged. She had wanted him to lie flat and elevate his legs, but by now there was an inch layer of cold, muddy water surrounding them. She had searched in the dark for a drier place only to find the water deeper elsewhere. Something in her jeans was pinching her thigh. When she tried to adjust it, she was surprised by the car keys in her front pocket. She dug them out with some difficulty, as Brighton's head rested on her lap.

"I've got a light, Brighton! I've got a tiny flashlight on my key. Remember the little keychain light the salesman gave me when I got my new car?"

"Be careful not to drop it in the water," he whispered. His voice had a ghost-like quality as it echoed in the dark, narrow tunnel.

She pressed the tiny button then smiled as the light's narrow but powerful beam lit up the tunnel. Gina inspected Brighton's leg and had to suppress a shriek when she saw the pool of blood that had soaked his pant leg and diluted into the surrounding water. Brighton's eyes were closed, and his head was getting heavier as his muscles lost their tone. She wanted to yell out for Roy or Charley or anyone, but for some strange reason she hesitated. She didn't want to startle Brighton. She could feel her baby move beside its father's head and could feel the sting of the sharp rocks and water irritating her bottom. She felt helpless, and yet she was the only help there for her husband and her unborn child. For some unknown reason, she started to whistle.

✳✳✳

Roy was looking for the Patel brothers, but his light was now out. He remembered the backpacks the boys brought into the tunnel but was too disoriented by now to remember where they had left them. It was so dark that each time he made the slightest turn, he felt like his face would hit a rock wall or a protruding piece of timber. He had left the two tough women with their husbands and was most worried now about the boys. Suddenly, he thought he heard someone whistling and turned in the direction of the sound. He knew there were places where one could fall into vertical shafts, though he was sure those were in the other direction. At least he thought they were. He found out differently.

It was like stepping off the end of a swimming pool diving board. One second he was on solid ground and the next, he was descending, gravity jerking him toward the center of the earth. He hit the bottom. Luckily for Roy, that happened only eight feet below the path he had been blindly following. When he hit the uneven bottom of the aborted vertical shaft, his right ankle took his full weight, giving off an audible snap and shooting bright lights of pain to his brain. What the rest of his body felt he couldn't tell or care. He let out an involuntary scream, his ankle screaming back at him.

Gina heard the scream and thought how out of character it was for Roy. She was sure it was his voice. It was a scream of surprise, pain, and helplessness, and it wasn't far away.

She couldn't just sit there in the water, listening and waiting for her husband's breathing to stop. She turned on her tiny light and searched again. Further down the tunnel she thought she saw the shadow of something round. She eased Brighton's head off of her lap and slid her body out from under it. As much as she hated to do it, she gently settled his head onto the ground, submersing him into an inch of cold, muddy water. He stirred but didn't say anything. Her body was sore, stiff, and shivering from the cold and dry air, and she had to pee so bad she could hardly walk.

Next to the tunnel wall, twenty feet down the tunnel and half-hidden by a large vertical timber, she saw the backpacks. Using her tiny keychain light, she examined the area around the bags for snakes or spiders. There were none. Tears welled up in her eyes as she rummaged through the two blue Northface packs and found new flashlights, batteries, a camera, a sweatshirt, a first-aid kit, snack food, a small bottle of Advil, red Gatorade and, best of all, a cell phone.

Excited by the find, she went into action. She found the brightest flashlight and an extra pair of C-size batteries for it and dumped the rest of the contents out on the dry ground. She put on the ASU sweatshirt, feeling no disloyalty to Stanford. The gold-colored shirt was warm and dry and gave her a renewed sense of confidence. She found an out-of-the-way corner and emptied her bladder. Now she could go to work.

She quickly stuffed one backpack into the other, and taking the first-aid kit and a bottle of water with her, she went back to Brighton. With the bright light she was able to find an area of high ground five yards into one of the side tunnels. She laid her newfound treasures down, and with the light on the ground reflecting off the rock walls, she approached Brighton.

"Sweetheart? I know you can hear me. I am going to move you

out of the water to a dry spot and get you something for the pain and something to drink," she said in a gentle, assuring voice.

She could feel him move a little in response to her voice. She pushed up the sleeves of the sweatshirt to keep herself as dry as possible and slid her arms under his shoulders. It was an awkward angle, but she was able to lift his head and torso enough to drag him to the higher ground. She repositioned his arms and legs and with the bright light reexamined his bloody leg. Her shredded shirt had slowed the bleeding to an ooze. The leg, though cold from the water, was pink and elicited a response from Brighton when touched. Gina considered these good signs.

She propped his head up and offered him a drink of the red liquid, which he spilled a significant part down the side of his cheeks. She tucked some Advil into the corner of his mouth, and he drank and swallowed again. Next, she cleared a smooth spot on the ground for his head and, using the stuffed backpack, propped up his bloody leg. She stood up and examined the area again for critters and, satisfied he would be safe, turned her attention to the cell phone.

The only people she knew phone numbers for were with her in the cave, so she dialed 911 and waited. She hadn't considered that the signal would be blocked by the surrounding wall of the tunnel, probably made worse by the high metal content of the walls. In frustration, she almost threw the phone at the wall but instead slid it into her front pants pocket. She took a long, deep breath and then turned toward the direction of Roy's scream.

***

The Patel brothers also had heard the scream, but it was a just an echo through lengths of tunnels when it finally reached their ears. Sensing the direction to the sound was useless. Tony's light had just enough candlepower left to keep them from bumping into walls, thus the going was slow and met with several U-turns out of blind work tunnels. The first hint that they were close to the main tunnel and the cave-in, was the splash of water under their feet. Reassuring as this was, it entered a new equation into the boys' overactive brains. Were they all going to drown from some underwater river that had been disrupted?

They began calling out for Roy or Brighton. And once they

realized that they had to listen several seconds after each shout until their own echoes dissipated, they finally heard a reply.

"Hey, you made it!" the woman's voice said from behind, causing them to both jump. With the light in their eyes, they were temporarily blinded, but then could see Mrs. Dunn standing near a small pile of their equipment. She gave them a quick update on Brighton and the others and helped them reload their flashlights. All three of them had a quick drink of juice. After checking on the sleeping Brighton, they set out toward the direction of Roy's voice—not screaming for help, but instead giving a beacon-like shout every minute or so. They soon found him. Their injured leader was sitting against the wall of an aborted vertical shaft, eight feet below the main floor. Next to him was the desiccated body of a dead coyote that had wandered into the same hole and not been able to crawl out either.

"Hey, you up there," Roy said in a casual voice, "you wouldn't happen to have a cheeseburger and a Coke, would you?" In spite of the seriousness of the moment, all four of them broke out in laughter.

Tony found a broken piece of timber and slid it down into the hole for Roy to stand on. Roy now had enough of a height elevation that the boys, lying flat on their bellies, could reach toward his extended arms. The pain in his ankle was intense, and to reach their hands, he had to push up on his tiptoes. Finally, with some grunting and groaning, the boys extricated Roy from the hole. He lay on the ground, gasping for a few moments, and then got to his feet. Leaning on Tony's shoulder, he tried to walk toward the original mine entrance where he sent Charley and Kara.

"We're going the wrong direction," said Patrick. "All we need are some tools and then we can widen a small air vent at the far end of the cavern. I think we can get out that way."

"Where are Kara and Brighton?" asked Gina, shining her light on Roy's face.

"They are at the original mine entrance. If we are going to get out of here soon, it will be through the old entrance. Trying to chisel through rock would take hours if not days," Roy said.

"We heard a tractor or something outside the cave. They are probably trying to get to us that way," Patrick said.

"I've got to go back and check on Brighton," Gina said, tugging on Roy's shirtsleeve. "Can you walk well enough to make it to the entrance?"

"Roy is tough; he's the man. I'll get him to the front, and you go with Mrs. Dunn," Tony said in an authoritarian voice to his brother. "When I get Mr. Richards squared away, I'll come back and the three of us can carry Dr. Dunn to the front with the others. Is that okay with you?" he asked the two adults, illuminating their faces with his newly recharged light.

The plan was agreed upon, and the two groups set out in opposite directions. Keeping their eyes on the trail and making good speed, Gina was soon back at Brighton's side. He was awakened by the motion around him and mumbled a few words that neither Gina nor Patrick could understand; something about the ground and a shake. Gina could see that the bleeding had responded to the pressure of her shirt wrapped around his leg and the elevation of his foot. She checked his pulse and found it to be stronger than it was twenty minutes before.

"How do you want to do this?" Patrick asked.

"Let's not wait for your brother. Let's see if we can carry him ourselves," Gina responded.

"Maybe we can make a sling out of the backpack straps—you know, put them under his shoulders and legs and each take a side."

"How can we see if we both have to hold the straps?" Gina asked. "We can't hold the flashlights."

Patrick reached up to his head and flipped on the switch of the xenon headlamp, newly fitted with fresh batteries.

"Voilà!" he said with the sound of triumph in his voice.

They adjusted the straps with the backpacks under Brighton's limp body and, with the straps at full length, pulled them out on each side of his hips and arm. Patrick was surprised at the weight of the man, but was even more surprised at the strength of his wife.

The makeshift gurney worked pretty well for the first twenty yards, and then there was a glitch. Brighton heard it first and jerked his dangling head up. Gina's reflexes weren't far behind. The "ground-shake" Brighton had mumbled about earlier was now clearly the word snake.

There was no question what the buzzing was. Though Gina

had never really heard that sound before, her sense of awareness was so heightened that a new chill went up her spine. She started to drop Brighton, but at the last millisecond controlled herself. Patrick was oblivious to the buzzing. He was having a struggle trying to shine the awkward headlight in the correct direction and carry the bleeding dentist at the same time. When Gina yelled, "Rattlesnake!" he first froze for a few seconds and then panicked. "Where? Where? Where?" he screamed, darting his headlight this way and that in such a random manner that he wouldn't have seen a hippo next to him.

"It's behind us!" yelled Gina, not really knowing where it was. "Just keep moving!"

When they started to walk again, Brighton had twisted his body trying to see the snake, just enough that the strap around Gina's hand also twisted, cutting into her left ring finger and squeezing the ring at an angle. It felt like her finger was being severed. She tried to untwist the strap, but it only made it worse. It was bizarre that with all the insane things happening around her, her ring finger became her only focus.

"Stop! Stop! We have to set him down for a minute!" Gina yelled.

"No way!" demanded Patrick in a tone of voice she hadn't heard him use before. "The snake might be right under our feet. We have got to keep moving."

"My finger is twisted. I have to stop!" She bent down, laying her side of Brighton's body on the uneven rocky floor of the tunnel. Patrick, however, was still moving, thus the straps of the backpacks jerked out of his right hand, but his left hand was twisted in the strap pulling toward the ground. He tripped and fell, hitting the brow of his forehead on a jagged rock and knocking the headlamp off his head onto the ground. The light was out, and again the world was absolute blackness.

Brighton let out a groan as his body skidded on the ground, coming to a stop at an odd angle with his face smashed against Patrick's knee and his arms pinned against his sides by the backpacks. Gina extricated her finger from the twisted canvas strap and rubbed it until the feeling returned. She pulled the flashlight from her front pocket and helped Patrick find his headlamp. She then adjusted the backpacks and Brighton's arms. Patrick got to his feet without a word. He grabbed his side of the straps, and they heaved the shaken Brighton up off the ground and proceeded down the tunnel.

✳✳✳

The craziness of the scene outside the tunnel grew exponentially. Not only were there three network helicopters circling the area, but independent photo hounds were making low-level passes in small, single-engine airplanes. Sheriff Brice's deputies were doing their best to hold back the crowds, but there was just too big of a perimeter to cordon off and enforce. Dirt bikes and off-road buggies were heard close by with their high-revving engines. Trails of dust were seen in multiple directions as the curious converged on Alma Ziegler's ranch and its hidden mine tunnel.

The Mole, with Dean at the helm, bounced its way to the area where the helicopter's dropped headphones lay wedged among the boulders, marking the entrance site. Dean was able to position the Mole at such an angle into a steep hillside that he felt he could bore through the side of the tunnel at an angle thirty feet back from the blocked entrance.

The hillside angle approach to drilling into the cave still required several La-Z-Boy-sized boulders to be rolled out of the way. This was done quickly by the force of eight or ten men, Otto and Heinz leading the team, and Rhonda standing atop a nearby boulder shouting directions. When the Mole finally nosed up against the side of the steep hill and Dean engaged the clutch on the rotating jaws, the crowd gave a lusty cheer. The Mole began to work its way into the side of the hill, Dean hoping a hole about fifteen or twenty feet in length would likely intersect the old mine shaft and free those trapped inside.

A broadcasting van with its extended satellite dish had tried to follow a jeep trail off of the county road toward where the Mole had begun digging. About twenty yards into the desert, the driver's side front tire had climbed the side of a rock, tipping the van enough that, with its extended dish, the center of gravity was too high and it had fallen over on its side among the rocks and cactus. This angered the other newsmen who were about to follow in the path, and found no location for the news helicopters to land. The newsmen were stuck with hiking into the scene and using handheld mobile equipment, most of the teams hitching their gear on their backs and trudging off through the dust and cactus. Nerves were on edge; this news story was the biggest to hit the Phoenix area in years.

***

Alma Ziegler's ship was sitting in the Port of Livorno, Italy. Alma had finally, with the encouragement of her new butler Dorvac, mustered the courage to take a taxi into the little town of Pisa to visit the Leaning Tower. She would not have dared to climb to the top of the structure, but she did find the long row of tourist shops interesting. They had statues of the tower in every imaginable form, from tiny key chains and miniature chess sets to thousand-pound brass models. She settled on one made of alabaster, about the size of a football. She was going to give it to Gina as a baby gift and thank-you gift for letting her stay at her house, and probably saving her life from that nasty Hicks man. She had already bought Rhonda a two-foot gondola in Venice. It was carved out of real wood and had a little man in a striped shirt and a bowler hat at its rudder. Now she wished she would have bought one for herself.

She had just returned to the ship and had stripped off her soggy clothes to take a refreshing shower. The muggy Italian air was nothing like Arizona's. As she dried off in front of the bed in her cozy stateroom, the door flew open and her Greek butler walked in carrying a tray of hors d'oeuvres and rattling off something about the news in Arizona. Oblivious to her nakedness—he had burst in on much stranger situations before—he set down the tray and turned on her television. Immediately, the live picture from CNN lit up the screen with an aerial view of that weird yellow digging machine Alma had seen in Hidden Canyon. A zoomed-in view showed a man sitting at its controls. "That's Mr. Dean Shutter!" she shouted. Even more of a surprise was the woman standing alongside the machine holding a shovel. "That's my best friend, Rhonda Tucker. They're my friends!" she screamed again. Alma couldn't believe her eyes, and oblivious to her state of undress, she hugged the butler. Her exuberance was so out of character that he joined in the celebration, though he didn't understand what was going on.

Alma finally settled down and, wrapping the towel around her skin-and-bone frame, she sat down on the edge of the bed and stared at the TV, trying to figure out what really was going on and why her neighbors were on international television.

As she watched and listened to the reporters, she finally began to understand the whole fuss. She had seen at least six familiar faces, including that of Sheriff Brice. Dorvac stood beside her for several minutes, confused about his patron's connection to the television story. When his beeper vibrated, he reluctantly left, still confused. He did, however, have an enhanced appreciation for the American woman's body. And here he had thought she was old.

Alma saw aerial photos of her burned house and pictures of the backyards of the residents of Hidden Canyon. Then with shock and a bit of thrill, she saw a picture of herself—her old driver's license photo. The voice said that she was the owner of the land and that there was a hidden gold mine on the property and skeletons inside the tunnels. The reporter said that the police were looking for an Alma Ziegler for questioning in connection with the possible murder of a Caterpillar tractor driver and the burying alive of several of her neighbors. She felt a wave of nausea, and the room began spin. She opened her door and entering the hallway hollering for Dorvac.

"Where is the nearest airport?" she shouted as he popped his head out of the galley. "I need to fly home to Arizona. Where is the airport?"

The butler gently guided Alma back into her stateroom and tried to calm her frazzled nerves. "Madame, the ship has already lifted anchor. Can you feel the motion of the sea? It would be impossible to leave the ship at this time. Perhaps I could get you something to settle your nerves. Perhaps a brandy or. . . ."

"I've got to get off the ship and fly to Arizona. The police are looking for me, can't you see?" she said, pointing to the television.

Dorvac looked at the TV but saw only an advertisement for a weight-loss pill. This time he sat her down on the edge of the bed and, grabbing another large towel from the nearby bath, wrapped it around Alma's shoulders to cover her chilled body. Next, he called the infirmary. Alma stared at the flickering screen, which had scrolled to a European weather map.

The ship's doctor arrived with her medical bag and examined Alma briefly. "Ms. Ziegler, it is for the better if you come with me to deck five. We have a tiny infirmary there. I think it is good for you that I give you something for your blood pressure and let you rest there for a few hours."

Alma started to protest, but Dorvac put his finger to her lips, so she said no more. Everything is going to be all right," he said. "I am going to step into the hall while you put on some clothes. Come out when you are ready, and I will walk you down to the infirmary." He nodded to the doctor that she could leave, and the two of them stepped out into the narrow hallway.

Alma turned back to the television, staring at it and willing the familiar pictures and the story about home to come back on. She curled up on the bed and sobbed.

Dorvac waited for ten minutes, and when she didn't come out, he knocked. When he finally opened the door to check on her, she was sleeping like a baby. He closed the door behind him and went to her side. She was such a fragile and yet beautiful woman. He moved the wet lock of hair away from her eyes and removed the damp towels. Carefully he draped a soft blanket over her white skin. Though time to leave, he hesitated, studying the face. He was developing affection for this strange woman.

48
Dig It

Sharron Shutter saw her husband on the television. She had sent Dean off to find her cousin Lori and had been nearly frantic waiting for a phone call. She had tried his cell a dozen times but only got voicemail. She was afraid to leave the apartment for fear that she would miss a call. At first she couldn't believe her eyes, but sure as the desert is dry, there was her husband sitting on the stupid yellow digging machine that the neighbors had named the "Mole."

She picked up Dean's business phone and looked at his speed dial contact list. She tried the dentist and then the lawyer with no answer. Next, she tried the mysterious air traffic control guy but got only voicemail. She hung up the phone in frustration and grabbed her purse and car keys. On the way out the door, she stopped and stared. There on her TV screen was her cousin Lori, being loaded into the back of an ambulance. She looked like crap. Sharron heard the updated report stating that the woman was being admitted to Scottsdale East Hospital for observation, but was in stable condition. "Dean can take care of himself," she thought. "I'm going to take care of Lori."

✳✳✳

Gina was sure that her hand would never be the same. The twisted strap of the backpack had cut a deep ridge into the skin and tendons of her left ring finger without even breaking the skin. For the last fifty yards that she and the Patel boy carried Brighton, it was all she could do not to scream. Kara and Tony Patel heard them coming and met them part way. The group was finally all together.

Brighton was barely conscious with a new trickle of blood oozing out of the makeshift bandage. Roy was lying on his back with his foot elevated, his ankle the size of a volleyball and a grimace of pain on his face. Patrick had a deep cut on his forehead and multiple scrapes. Charley had withdrawn all emotion, sitting with a blank stare on his face. His breathing was better, but his claustrophobia had gotten the upper hand.

"Turn off the light!" yelled someone from the shadows of the tunnel entrance. Batteries were at a premium and every time anyone turned on a light, someone else complained that they were wasting power. The seemingly generous supply of spare batteries was practically gone. They sat in the dark, unable to see the person next to them, but with their other senses enhanced. They were more than able to hear each other breathe and to smell the potpourri of dirt, mold, and body odor mixed with blood, sweat, and fear. A whiff of Gina or Kara's perfume added a rare sense of hope.

"What should we do next?" Tony asked the group. He was uninjured and in the best physical shape of the group.

At first there was no answer, and then Roy said, "We all need to sit quietly and conserve our energy. People know we are in here and will be coming to get us out. Our best bet is to be patient and not get ourselves in worse shape. Patrick, are you keeping enough pressure on your cut?"

"It stopped bleeding, Mr. Richards. It still hurts like heck, but I'm okay. Is there any more Advil in the first-aid kit?"

"Gina? Are you all right?"

"I'm fine. Brighton's leg is still bleeding, and his pulse is getting faster. I think that's a bad sign. His heart is trying to compensate for the blood loss, and that just pumps more blood to the wound. Does anyone have any ideas?"

"You have to hold more pressure on the bleeding area. Let's put another bandage on it," said Kara. "Tony, do you still have any Gatorade left? He needs fluids to offset the blood loss. Gina, let's try an extra-pressure bandage."

Tony handed her a bandana that had been in his back pocket.

With Tony shining the dimming light, the two women removed Gina's blood-soaked shirt and cut away the leg of Brighton's Levis. The long, raw wound on Brighton's calf and shin had no single bleeding point but oozed from an area the size of a potato. The tissue damage from the snakebite had been extensive but had been healing until a jagged rock had dragged across the surface, leaving deep furrows. Gina cut the bandana in strips and wound them around the leg. There was no tape to secure the bandage, but one of the backpacks had a drawstring that Gina deftly tied around the leg.

"Talk to me, Charley," Roy said in a conversational voice, trying to redirect the conversation. "What do you think our chances are to get control of the mine and the contents? That metal box and the mailbox the boys saw earlier could contain some pretty valuable items."

Charley didn't answer at first, but after a minute or two, everyone could hear him shuffling in his little corner. He cleared his throat a few times and then began to answer Roy's questions, giving a long legal diatribe about the rights of eminent domain and the difference between surface and subsurface salvaging. His voice grew stronger. Most of the group gave up listening after a few minutes, but all were relieved that the real Charley Banks was back.

An earsplitting noise sounded inside the mine. Kara screamed and everyone jumped, some to their feet. On the other side of the collapsed tunnel entrance, something important was finally happening.

✳✳✳

Big rocks, little rocks, dust, ground-up plants, and smoke all poured out of the conveyor belt behind the rotating jaws of the Mole. It had taken major manpower to move away enough of the bigger boulders for the Mole to dig into the side of the mountain. The noise from the Mole alone had made most of the onlookers back off the scene. Several had climbed to higher vantage points. Rhonda and the HOA gang had cotton or Kleenex stuffed in their ears to mute the noise and were standing by, ready to widen the hole once the tunnel was breached. They were all covered from head to toe with dust, their mouths and eyes staring out of blackened faces, looking like raccoons.

A young cowboy in a two-ton Dodge Power Wagon had noticed the overturned broadcast van blocking the Mole's trail, so he hooked a chain to its bumper and dragged the van off the side of the trail. This act was sincerely appreciated by the paramedics, allowing their rescue trucks to get closer to the digging Mole.

The TV crew with the van, however, had nearly killed the guy since he had collapsed the antenna frame and shredded the inch-thick harness of wires leading into the van. The side of the van itself was reduced to shredded scraps of sheet metal.

Dean was getting optimistic about their progress and felt that another hour or so of digging would allow them to enter the tunnel. Like all emergencies, the plan had to be altered and tweaked to meet the unexpected. In this case, the unexpected was the failure to calculate the amount of fuel used to drive the Mole out of Hidden Canyon and around the mountain to the other side. Dean had stopped twice to check the oil and to lubricate the rotating jaw bearings, not bothering to check the fuel stick. He "knew" that he had enough fuel, until then the engine just quit.

"What happened?" Rhonda had shouted, though her raised voice was unnecessary with the engine dead.

"I have no idea. It isn't overheated, and the oil pressure was fine," he said in disgust.

"What about gas?" she asked in a teasing voice.

"It doesn't use gas. It burns diesel, and I filled it up right after the last time I used it."

"Would it hurt to check?" Rhonda asked, not willing to give up easily. She hadn't reached stardom by accepting patent negative answers from know-it-all men.

By now there were at least a hundred people crowding closer to the Mole, all wondering why it had stopped running and when the scene was going to progress to something more exciting.

Dean walked around to the other side of the machine and unscrewed the fuel tank lid. The wooden dipstick used to check the fuel level was in a clip at the side. With the starlet looking over his shoulder and everyone holding their breath, he dipped the wooden stick deep into the tank and pulled it out. The look on his face was one of pure astonishment. The tank was drier than a dust devil in Death Valley.

Gasps went through the crowd, and multiple suggestions were shouted. One of the paramedics stepped forward with a solution. "That cowboy who pulled the TV van out of the way had an auxiliary tank onboard his turbo diesel truck."

It took over twenty minutes before the Dodge owner could be found and the truck driven up close enough to the Mole for a transfer of fuel to take place. When the Dodge backed away from the Mole, the crowd gave a round of grateful applause. The Mole's diesel engine then had to be re-primed and restarted. When a black cloud of smoke shot out of the exhaust stack and the engine came to a clattering roar, the crowd let out an even louder round of cheers and applause.

✻✻✻

"The noise stopped," murmured Brighton. The trapped group had been huddled on the far side of the tunnel ever since the vibration and noise had begun. Their adrenalin levels had been on high for so long that when they finally settled away from the noise, each one of them relaxed. The Patel brothers had even fallen asleep. They weren't normally early risers, and the 4:00 a.m. alarm clock had cut deeply into their morning dreams. The resonating noise had made a few small rocks and some dirt fall from the tunnel ceiling, thus the group had withdrawn a few more yards back into the tunnel just to be safe. Now the noise had indeed stopped.

Gina shined the light on her husband's leg and found only a small amount of seepage through the makeshift bandage. "How are you doing?" she whispered in Brighton's ears, trying not to disturb the others. She needn't have bothered, for the silence had brought them all back on full alert.

Roy had guessed what was going on outside the tunnel. The Mole's engine had a distinct sound produced by the extra-large camshaft. That low base sound had carried into the tunnel. The big question in his mind was: *Why wasn't the digging at the entrance itself and now, why had it stopped?*

Only two of the many flashlights still worked, and they were getting very dim. Try as they did to be conservative with the use, the Eveready bunnies had all hopped away.

Charley, with renewed confidence and not wanting to relapse into his claustrophobic panic, decided to entertain the group by telling his captive audience stories of lost miners, stranded mountain climbers, and refreshing stories of small boats lost at sea. He of course told only the stories where the outcome was happy. Not mentioned were the frostbitten fingers, toes, and noses or the companions left behind. Charley recounted as much as he could remember of the story of the Lost Dutchman and how the man himself wasn't lost—just the mine itself. He told how prospectors had found the mine of a wealthy Mexican family and had promptly let it become lost again. The exhausted group rallied to the optimism of the stories and even laughed when Charley suggested that they had possibly found the Dutchman's actual mine.

The silence outside the tunnel persisted.

"Maybe they took a break for lunch," suggested Tony. "What time is it, anyway? I'm famished. I could eat one of those dead rattlesnakes or even that scruffy coyote you found, Mr. Richards."

The others tried not to laugh, sensitive to Brighton and his life-threatening injury, but Kara couldn't suppress her giggle, and soon they all were laughing and adding their sick versions of what they could eat.

"Not me, I hate snakes," Brighton whispered, "but one of those bats we flushed out of here earlier would taste pretty good on a bed of steamed rice with some A-1 Steak Sauce basted in. I hear in the Pacific Islands they eat the fruit bats with rice and melons." It was the first full sentence Brighton had composed.

"That dead coyote in the hole I fell into smelled pretty ripe. It made me hungry for the cafeteria food they used to feed us back in grade school," Roy added.

Laughs were followed by what seemed to be an even more profound silence.

Time in the tunnel passed slowly. Thirst, hunger, pain, and discomfort added to the delay. The cave seemed to be getting colder and the rocky ground harder. It was hard to stay optimistic, but every once in a while a sound would filter into the cave, and heads lifted and ears pricked up with hope.

Then the loud rescue sound started again.

When the roar of the Mole's engine and grinding teeth echoed again through the cave, a spontaneous cheer came from the dry mouths of the trapped neighbors. They couldn't hear the even louder cheers of those outside, but knew in their minds and hearts that there really were people out there that cared about them. Gina started to cry, not just tears of joy, which no one could see anyway, but deep sobs of relief. Dealing with death was an unfamiliar event in her life. No one tried to shush her; they just listened and let her work it all out.

"I knew they would get it started again," Patrick whispered to Roy. "I'll bet your girlfriend Rhonda is out there cracking the whip to keep them working."

Roy chuckled at the thought, first of Rhonda being his girlfriend, then of her cracking a whip. The realization that his relationship with Rhonda was such common knowledge that a teenager he hardly knew was keeping track of his love life gave him a renewed sense of confidence.

✳✳✳

Rhonda was on the cell phone ordering food and drinks for the mob of emergency workers and for the onlookers as well. She didn't count heads but just told the Bashas' grocery manager to send enough cold water, cold sodas, and sandwiches for a 150 people. She promised to send someone to pick it up, but Preston Rose, the manager, told Rhonda he would ask one of the news helicopters to fly it over and lower it down to the scene.

By the time the chopper showed up thirty minutes later, the sun was getting low in the sky, and the lack of food and hydration had become a problem. When Rhonda, the Steiner brothers, their kids, and Dr. and Mrs. Patel started passing out the food, there was another big round of applause.

Dean was beyond exhaustion. Without anyone to relieve him at the controls of the Mole and nothing much to eat or drink until now, he was starting to hallucinate. He imagined the Mole breaking through the wall only to have it create a gigantic cave-in, smashing all those inside. The constant drone of the engine and the grinding of the drill bits pushed his brain into imagining the Mole coming through the tunnel wall exactly where the seven people were passed out, sucking them up into the grinding jaws and spewing them out on the conveyor belt as bloody chunks of meat and bones.

Dean was about to shut the machine down when Rhonda moved up and held out a two-liter bottle of cold water, motioning that she was offering to pour it over his head. Without wearing his usual hat all day long, his head was beet red with sunburn. When he nodded consent, the cold water sloshed down over his head and face and ran down onto his chest and back. He felt ecstatic. The weird visions of mishaps vanished from his mind, and he had a renewed sense of confidence that Rhonda and his plan were going to succeed. He ate a sandwich with one hand and chugged a Dr. Pepper to wash it down. With his drenched frozen head, the caffeine, and a carbohydrate boost, he moved the throttle up another notch and continued digging.

Rhonda had lost herself in the service of those around her. People whose faces she had seen driving through Hidden Canyon had shown up with picks and shovels and work gloves. The ground-up rock and gravel spewing out of the end of the Mole's conveyor belt was being shoveled away from the path it cut by strangers. She hadn't thought of it before, but without clearing the path behind the Mole, there would be no way for it to back out of the way once the tunnel was entered. Clearing the path also would make room for the emergency vehicles, though she hoped that they wouldn't be needed. She walked up close to each of those wielding tools, and over the racket of the grinding, growling Mole, she hollered appreciation in their ears.

Another hour and then another went by. They refilled the fuel tank and Dean dug some more. The sunlight had faded, and the Steiners, with Clyde's help, brought a huge floodlight from the clubhouse with a gasoline generator. Someone even showed up with a camping Porta-John complete with a canvas curtain and aluminum poles to mount it on. The women in the group lined up, offering thanks.

✳✳✳

Inside the tunnel, no one was worried about Porta-Johns. Kara was the first to think about the fact that she hadn't needed to go all day. Dehydration could kill, and she knew it. *How long had it been?* The good thing was that the temperature of the tunnel had stabilized. Brighton's pulse rate was still fast, but the bleeding had apparently stopped. The previous worry about the water leaking into the other end of the tunnel had been forgotten. The Steiner's swimming pool was long since empty.

The only instructions or commands came from Roy. Kara knew that in spite of the severe pain he had in his ankle, he was still thinking clearly and in the best interest of the group. Brighton was the only one who was allowed to drink from the remaining Gatorade bottle. Brighton was now covered with the shirts of the men. Even the emptied backpacks were used to cover and help warm their critically injured friend. By warming Brighton, his pulse had become stronger. Not surprisingly, the sacrifice of the others in the group had given a sense of solidarity and determination to everyone.

Gina had been able to relax for the last hour, and the uterine contractions she had experienced while they were running and lugging Brighton—worrying every second that they were all going to die—settled down to an occasional mild episode of uterine irritability. Kara had been an immense source of comfort to her, holding her hand and stroking her head and whispering that everything would be fine. She had even made little jokes about what her girls were doing with their parents missing and no grown-ups around the house to control them.

"If we come home and they are having a party, I'm going to ground them for a month. Or maybe I'll just join in the fun," said Kara.

"Give me a call, and I'll join you," Gina whispered. "Brighton and I haven't had many parties lately."

The grinding noise was getting much louder inside the tunnel, and the ground was beginning to vibrate. An occasional rock could be heard falling from the tunnel walls or ceiling and clattering to the rocky floor. At first those inside had flinched or looked up in fear of the falling rocks. Later they became oblivious to whatever was raining down. Fatigue from the stress was overcoming their senses.

"Patrick, do you have any power left in the headlamp?" Roy asked in a voice of sudden concern.

"It was about to go out a couple of hours ago, but you told me to shut it off."

"I think we all need to move further back into the tunnel. They must be drilling in from an angle, and we are too close to where I think they could enter. Point the light down the direction you think we came in from and turn on the light for just a second—and I mean one second—and then leave it off until I direct you further," Roy said.

"By the noise they're making, they may be directing a Southwest jetliner in here for a landing," commented Charley. It was his first statement for over an hour. The sentence didn't make much sense and was ignored by Roy and the boys.

"Get into position, Patrick, and when you are ready, let me know and I'll say 'on.'"

Patrick did as he was instructed, and at the 'on' command, turned on the headlamp. The light was so dim that it barely illuminated the opposite wall of the tunnel.

"Turn it off now," Roy said. "I want everyone to reach out and grasp the hand of the person next to you and then hum softly."

It took some shuffling and a question or two, but soon the six of them were humming. Roy, limping badly, led them slowly deeper into the tunnel, away from the outside wall for a distance of twenty feet and then stopped.

"Everyone sit down and make yourselves comfortable. Tony, will you try to follow me back to pick up Dr. Dunn?"

"I can't see a thing," Tony replied. "Maybe I've gone blind."

"I'll start humming, and you follow the sound. Patrick, when I give you the word, shine the light toward us so we can pick up Dr. Dunn without hurting his leg. Are you ready?"

Call it divine intervention or a quirk of electrochemistry, but when Roy and Tony had walked the distance back to the recumbent dentist and Roy gave the command to let there be light, there was light. Not just a wimpy, dull casting but a bright, full beam that lit up the tunnel, allowing Roy to find Brighton, examine his leg wound and to safely carry him back to the waiting group. Tony took the head and Roy the legs. It was about all Roy could do to hobble and endure the pain in his ankle. By the time he was finally able to sit down, the throbbing and sharp needles shooting up and down his leg were merciless.

Gina and Kara took over Brighton's care; resting his head on Gina's lap and elevating the bloody leg onto a dusty old wooden crate they found in the now dimming light. Kara was being ever so careful with the leg, kneeling on the sharp rocks of the tunnel floor and sliding the box underneath the ankle. At that moment, a scorpion scampered out of its wooden home and struck.

For the first second, Kara thought she had poked her finger with a wood sliver, but then the sensation of electricity shooting from her middle finger, up her arm and into her armpit was excruciating. As Patrick's headlamp dimmed to zero light, Kara had the distinct impression that her eye had picked up the movement of the arachnid, but then it was dark again.

"Crap, oh crap!" Kara screamed, dropping Brighton's leg the last few inches onto the wooden crate.

"What's the matter?" Charley asked.

"I'm pretty sure I've been stung by a scorpion. I'm sorry I dropped your foot," she said to Brighton. She had jumped to her feet, shaking her hand and frantically brushing off her knee-length shorts and her sports bra to rid herself of the creepy scorpion. Her whole arm and hand now gave the intense sensation one gets by hitting the "crazy bone" on the inner elbow. No amount of rubbing or moving made it any better. For the second time in a month, Kara was crying with indescribable pain.

"You need ice on it," said Tony in a confident voice. He was correct, but under the circumstances it sounded outrageously stupid.

No one else had the chance to render an opinion. With an explosive sound and flying rocks and dust, the spinning jaws of the Mole broke through the tunnel wall, exactly where the seven entrapped neighbors had been sitting less than ten minutes prior.

✳✳✳

The Mole's engine had run like the proverbial charm. Except for when it ran out of fuel earlier in the day, it had never stalled, overheated, or given even a hiccup. Suddenly, the drilling jaws began to spin faster, and then the tachometer needle swung over into the redline area. Before Dean could react and pull the throttle back to idle, the engine threw a rod and quit. There was a screeching mechanical noise from the transmission and the rotating heads as they came to a halt. Black smoke poured out of the sides of the diesel block, and then there was silence.

The floodlight surrounded by smoke created an almost haunting aura as the spectators and workers alike processed their individual thoughts. The silence was absolute, and lasted for what seemed like hours. A distant cry of a lonely coyote added to the mood. And then they heard the voices from inside the tunnel.

Dean jumped out of the driver's seat and ran around to the front. Not entirely sure whether the tunnel had been breached, he stuck his head right up next to the drill heads and yelled, "Hello in the tunnel! Can you hear me? Brighton, Roy, Charley; are you in there?"

Rhonda quickly joined him, yelling, "Roy, Gina, Roy, Gina, are you in there? Answer us! It's Rhonda and Dean."

The voice that returned made them both jump. Rhonda hit her head on the roof of the freshly dug tunnel. The voice was Kara's, and her face was less than five feet from Dean's.

"We're right here. Don't leave us! We need help! Don't leave us alone, please!"

"They're in there, they're in there!" went out the chanted wave of information through the crowd. It was followed by cheers and applause and then a new chant. "Back it out! Back it out!"

The problem was that the Mole weighed over twenty-five thousand pounds, and its engine was trashed. It couldn't move an inch on its own.

Otto Steiner nudged Dean and Rhonda out of the way. Otto had a crowbar in his hands, and Heinz was beside him with a pickax. Dean had been getting a status report from Kara through a four-by-six-inch hole in the tunnel wall between the rock and the drill heads of the Mole.

"They are all alive and will be okay for a few minutes more. We need to pull this thing out of the way!" Rhonda shouted, looking at the Patels and then at the fire and rescue team. "Get your strongest trucks and chains up here close, and pull the Mole backward. Just a few feet are all we need."

Otto had already started whaling away at the solid rock wall only to be screamed at by Roy to stop. His strokes were spraying rocks into the tunnel like bullets from a rifle.

It took twenty agonizing minutes for three trucks to be lined up on the makeshift trail and connected in a series, bumper to bumper, with chains like diesel train engines. A team of the Hidden Canyon neighbors shoveled away as much of the loose rock as possible from behind the Mole, creating a slight downhill grade. When the last chain was attached to the Mole, the truck engines revved up. Dean gave the signal, and with twelve huge tires spinning and spraying rocks and gravel, the Mole began to move. Inch by inch the giant lifesaver retracted its silent drill bits out from the newly dug tunnel. Dean gave the drivers the stop sign, and all three shut off their engines at once.

The cloud of dust was stifling. Amid coughs and sneezes, the desert breeze slowly moved the dust cloud away from the opening, and out walked, limped, stumbled, or were carried seven exhausted, yet happy survivors. They were met with cheers from the crowd and stretchers by the paramedics. Charley, his near psychotic episode now forgotten by the others, led a stretcher-bearing paramedic team back into the tunnel to retrieve Brighton.

Sharron Shutter had joined the expectant crowd only when she could reasonably expect that the end of the vigil was near. She rushed up to Dean and embraced him.

Rhonda personally inspected each of the seven survivors, saving Roy for last. She took hold of his arm and walked around him, looking him over like he was a steer at a livestock auction, and then she pronounced, "You will do. I'm keeping you for myself."

Roy laughed and took her in his filthy, scuffed, and bruised arms and gave her a long, tender, and very dry kiss. He was then loaded onto a stretcher and carried to one of the waiting ambulances. There he joined Kara, whose right hand and arm were hanging at her side, still burning and now a little swollen from the scorpion sting. Charley was close at her side, and the way he was giving instructions, one would guess he was an attending physician. He had refused any medical assistance and took a drink of water only after he was sure his wife was being treated.

Tony was reluctantly loaded onto a stretcher, but once he realized his parents were there, he jumped off of it and ran over to his Mom. Dr. Patel was helping the paramedic treat Patrick. When the paramedics cleaned his head laceration and wiped away the protecting blood clot, the wound was revealed to be deeper than it had originally appeared.

The second Brighton was put in the ambulance, an IV was started, and a dose of morphine was given. An Air Evac helicopter was hovering out near the gravel county road waiting for him. The ambulance headed out of the dusty confusion to meet the helicopter. Brighton had not spoken for over an hour, and Gina was upset when the nurse refused to let her ride in the helicopter with her husband. Her baby was kicking up a storm of its own and after one look at her clutching her belly, the pilot said, "The flight would be too strenuous on someone in your condition."

The three ambulances followed one another over the makeshift road. Within fifteen minutes of the rescue, all seven survivors were gone from the scene and so were most of the rescuers.

The Steiner brothers took immediate control of the newly dug tunnel entrance. Roy had whispered instructions to them on his way to the ambulance. They borrowed yellow crime scene tape from the sheriff and strung it across and around the mine's entrance area, creating a yellow DO NOT ENTER zone. One aggressive reporter tried crawling up onto the top of the Mole, brazenly straddling the tallest part of the machine, to give his report live. When Heinz saw him, the sweaty German slipped behind the crippled Mole and released the parking brake, causing it to roll backward for four or five feet. This sent the man and his microphone flying toward the lattice of crime scene tape.

It took over an hour for the last of the crowd of spectators to vanish from the desert. Otto and Heinz sat on a rock with a cold beer that the hero cowboy with the Dodge Power Wagon had handed him. They tried visiting for a few minutes, but the cowboy spoke only Texan, and the German brothers couldn't understand a word he said. They ended up just sitting there listening to the sounds of cars and onlookers fade into the night.

The crowd had trampled and littered at least ten acres of Alma Ziegler's ranch. The yellow crime scene ribbon covering the mine shaft's new entrance wafted in the late evening breeze. Within an hour, a pack of coyotes was sneaking about, cleaning up anything edible left behind and marking their territories again. Later, the brothers flipped a coin to see which of the two would stay behind to keep an eye on the tunnel. Everyone, they feared, would be trying to sneak into the mysterious and now-famous excavation.

49

PICKING UP THE PIECES

The Patels were allowed to take their sons home from the hospital soon after midnight. The boys had been thoroughly examined. Patrick had sixteen tiny stitches carefully placed, closing the deep laceration in his forehead. Since Patrick's father was a physician, an overnight observation for possible concussion complication wasn't deemed necessary. Both boys were given tetanus boosters and a ream of informed consent forms warning them about everything from rabies—there were bats in the cavern—to psychotic nightmares. The four were exhausted and looking forward to showers and the comfort of their beds.

What they found at home was another circus. Police cars with flashing lights lined the road in front of the Patel and Steiner homes. A large white coroner's van was parked in the Steiner's driveway, and two unmarked sedans with flashing lights were in the Patels' driveway. Many observers had moved back into the neighborhood from the desert.

"What is it now that these crazy Americans are doing to our private home?" Dr. Patel exclaimed, not expecting an answer. "Do they not have enough to do at the Steiner's house?"

"You go, all three of you, into the house, and I will discover what it is that the police are still doing on our property," Doctor Patel said in a weary but responsible voice.

When he climbed the Steiner's driveway, he found a team of four large men all in gray jumpsuits with "FORENSICS" printed across the back. They had set up camp in the Patels' yard, not wanting to disturb anything of the crime scene next door. Each of the men had shovels and was standing in a deep and dusty depression. Illuminated by several tripod-mounted flood lamps, they were digging around the tractor in an attempt to extricate the dead man who was still seated upright at the tractor's steering wheel. They had worked themselves down to the man's knees, well below the level of the tractor seat but hadn't removed the body. Instead, they had tied his torso to the seatback with a length of orange extension cord. The shadows cast by the upright body gave Kashmir a shiver. One of the men had dropped to his knees and began brushing dirt and rocks away from the top of a square case wedged up against the dead man's knees.

"It's Big Bill, the mineral assay man," came a voice from the shadows of the patio.

Dr. Patel's body jerked at the startling sound of the voice. He turned and saw Roy Richards and Dean Shutter sitting in the cushioned chairs on the Steiner's patio, taking in the investigative scene.

Patel composed himself and asked, "Why did he want to murder my sons?"

"I doubt he knew they were in there. He just wanted to hide the evidence of his and his partner's messed-up attempts to take over the mining operation and get rid of his partner in the meantime. The investigators here just found the U.S. Army Mail container that Patrick and Tony described. That's what is buried beside the guy's leg."

"How is your ankle, Mr. Richards?" Patel asked, pointing to the cast on Roy's leg.

"It's broken and hurts like heck, but I don't have to run any races tomorrow, and I have plenty of pain pills. Thanks for asking. How are your boys?"

"They are doing quite well, thank you. Patrick has a new haircut about which he is not happy camping. The boys tell a fascinating story about what they witnessed and the heroic activities all of you performed."

"They were the heroes. You can be proud to be their father. There isn't anything you can do out here now, Dr. Patel. You might as well go home and get your family settled and go to bed."

"We will keep an eye on these guys," Dean said, motioning toward the crime scene investigators.

"Dr. Patel?" Roy said, as the petite man was walking away.

"What, Mr. Richards?"

"The next time your neighbors want to use your backyard for an HOA activity, I would strongly advise you to just say no."

A staccato chuckle was heard echoing off of the rocks of the canyon beyond.

***

Rhonda received an email from the Oceania cruise ship in Barcelona. At first she put a check in the delete box, assuming it to be just another ad for a gimmicky deal. At the last second she paused, curiosity winning, and opened the message:

Dear Sirs:
I am sending this message at the request of a Miss Alma Ziegler, a recent passenger on our ship. She has asked me to inform you that she has met a young man. He is a resident of the island of Santorini, Greece. Miss Alma has de-boarded the ship and plans to travel to Santorini accompanied by the young man. She seems much happier than when she arrived. I am mailing a package giving more information and a power of attorney to a Ms. Rhonda Tucker to manage all of Ms. Ziegler's affairs in her absence. It was witnessed by the ship's captain and is quite legal. Ms. Ziegler sends her best regards and wants to thank all of her neighbors for rescuing her from her former life.

Sincerely, Dorvac
Assistant Head Butler
Oceania Cruise Lines

***

Brighton Dunn spent the next ten days in the hospital. He was back in his previous room and was beginning to feel like one of the staff. His doctors would not release him for fear that he would injure his leg again, but they did allow him to wheel down to the indigent dental clinic for a couple of hours a day. There he checked the work of the dental students. Gina visited twice a day and brought him home-cooked meals and updates from the neighborhood. It seemed everyone wanted to be friends with the residents of Cactus Wren Circle. She had a run of premature contractions the day after they were freed from the mine tunnel, and was given a terbutaline pump to reduce their frequency. She hated the fast heart rate it gave her, and so she stopped it after two days and hadn't had any contractions since. She still bore the residual scrapes and scratches incurred in the tunnels and caves.

Brighton's leg was healing quickly, thanks to daily treatments in the hyperbaric oxygen chamber and two skin grafts from a new and very expensive cultured graft material. He was told it cost thousands of dollars per square inch.

In his previous life he might have worried about money and the reality that his newly built dental practice had all but up dried up and disappeared. His dental assistant had taken another job, and his secretary promised to stay on the job only if she could study for her night classes at work and stop lying to the patients when they asked when he would be back at the office. She now told them, "Try again next month." He did not, however, worry about the money. Just as in the legendary Argentinean song about Evita Perón, "The money kept rolling in."

✳✳✳

Charley and Roy had become very busy after the rescue. Roy had undergone X-rays and hobbled with a non-weight-bearing cast. He was required to take several weeks off of work. Charley had also seen a doctor and was told to rest in a non-enclosed area for several days. Within 24 hours they were both going stir-crazy.

Sitting at home or in Charley's home office, they had made many conference phone calls. Eventually, they had cut a new deal with the New Mexico mining company. The company had taken a close look at the receipts and the assays of the previous months' mining on the home sites of Hidden Canyon and had sent a team of geological experts onto Alma's property, where they took several core samples.

After just two days of number crunching, they had agreed to mine the entire area except the old tunnel and caverns. White Sands would take all the risks and pay an upfront fee of twenty million dollars plus 40 percent of the net profits. When the mining was completed, they would be responsible for the re-vegetation and any other environmental costs. They estimated that the project would net the Hidden Gravel LLC about two hundred million dollars over the next three years. All the final product from the refining of the Hidden Canyon HOA gold and platinum group metals—particularly the rhodium—would be shipped, under military guard, directly to Los Alamos Proving

Grounds, just north of Santa Fe. The men in a black car and with a slightly damaged helicopter, had seen to that.

Roads were to be built to the entrance of the old mine tunnel. With a little public relations work by Rhonda Tucker, in conjunction with the National Parks Service, an agreement was reached accepting the mine and the adjacent caverns to develop as a historic park.

When the mining was completed, the restored land would be turned into a desert botanical garden and eventually would be part of a protected wildlife habitat with trails and riparian areas.

The agreement Roy and Charley cut to donate the land and tunnels would create a substantial tax deduction for the Hidden Gravel LLC. Preliminary letters of IRS agreement had been obtained. It took only a few days to get everyone's signature on the deal, except Alma's. The Arizona courts would not recognize a power of attorney witnessed by a Greek ship captain anchored off the coast of Spain.

Tracking down the missing Alma had been a bit of a task. Rhonda, however, knew a senator in Tennessee who called the head of the Immigration and Naturalization Service. He in turn traced the passport trail left by Ms. Ziegler when she disembarked the ship in Barcelona. A computer search of the European Union yielded results. Within forty-eight hours, Rhonda had found the address and telephone number of Alma's rented seaside cottage on Santorini. A round-trip to the island would be required. Rhonda, with very little friendly persuasion required, talked Roy into making the trip with her.

The trip to Greece took nearly two full days. Rhonda had at first thought of using her jet, but it was in the shop for its annual certification check by the FAA. First class on Virgin Atlantic out of L.A. was the next choice. The trip was wonderful except for the jet lag, something Roy was not used to. The commuter flight from Athens was hot and bouncy, and when they checked into their small hotel, Roy was exhausted. However, Rhonda had on her show face and was eager to get going. They both took quick showers and headed out the door to find Alma.

The narrow roads of Santorini ran along the steep ridge of the volcanic cliffs and eventually led them back down to sea level and a long white stretch of beach. After a few wrong turns, they made it to the door of a cute cottage with hanging flower pots and a sleepy porch cat. The afternoon was breezy and clear. Waves crashed in the distance, and far out to sea, a four-mast cruise ship was making its way across the horizon.

When Alma answered the door, she was tan, wearing makeup, and had trimmed her silver hair short. She was wearing a loose cover-up with a bikini underneath. Her smile was the first thing Roy noticed. He didn't realize that she ever had one.

She was excited to see Rhonda and Roy and insisted that they stay for lunch. She found a luncheon menu from a local taverna and phoned the order to the restaurant. Her new boyfriend, Dorvac, was a handsome and well spoken native of the island. He seemed very protective of Alma and friendly, but not solicitous to Rhonda and Roy. They ate out under a trellis with grapevines shading them from the sun. It was a wonderful meal of fresh goat cheese salad and moussaka washed down with ice-cold Coca-Cola. When it came time for the business of signing the papers, Alma asked Dorvac to run the dishes back to the taverna.

"I have read the paperwork you faxed to the American Express office," Alma said. "I actually had an American attorney who works for an import company read through them. Quite honestly, I am ashamed of the way they read. The terms are unacceptable the way you have written them. My share of the money is not what I had expected. In fact, it is way, way too much. I have asked the attorney here to change the percentage so that I receive an equal share with the rest of you. If it weren't for all of you, I would probably be in jail or in the mental hospital."

Roy glanced at Rhonda, not knowing what to say.

Alma brushed the silver hair away from her face. She opened a small drawer in a side table and took out an amended copy of the documents, handing it to Roy.

"I have already signed the addendum and have had it notarized by the U.S. consulate. He assured me that it would be perfectly legal this way."

Rhonda and Roy looked at each other and shrugged. The check they had for her was for a small partial payment, but for her increased share. They didn't know quite how to handle it. Even at a reduced percentage, she would still have a lot more coming to her in the months ahead.

"Take this check anyway, and we'll let Charley work out the details later," Roy said. He handed her a cashier's check for twelve million dollars and had her sign a receipt letter.

Rhonda watched as Alma read the check and lowered her head. When she looked up again, she was smiling as she blotted the tears from her eyes. When Roy's body language indicated it was time to leave, she took Alma's hand and gave it a tender squeeze. Hugs were exchanged at the doorway and vague promises were made to see one another soon. Dorvac had returned from the tavern just in time to offer them all a drink of some disgusting green liquor that smelled like paint remover. All three Americans politely refused.

The last time Roy and Rhonda saw Alma Ziegler, she was standing in the window waving goodbye and tucking the cashier's check into her bikini top, her silver hair now pulled back with a small black ribbon.

Future attempts to call or email her would never prove successful. The future checks she received were cashed, however. The endorsed signature on the back always read the same: Azi Z. Desert Lady."

✱✱✱

It was nearly two weeks before the County Attorney allowed the archeologist from the University of Arizona to enter the abandoned mine tunnels or the natural caverns in the hills of Hidden Canyon. The criminal forensic experts had to have the first look. They spent days in the tunnels under close observation of Hidden Gravel LLC's attorney. Charley made certain that nothing was disturbed or stolen. The desiccated human body the Patel brothers had found was carefully bagged and collected from the scene, and then the surrounding area was searched for clues to his identity. Numerous studies would be done in the lab. No other bodies were found, nor was there conclusive evidence of foul play. A total of seven live rattlesnakes were found and relocated.

When the archeologists entered the tunnel, it was again under the supervision of one of its present owners. The partially buried metal box was still in its original place. The observing attorney let there be no question that it was the property of the LLC, as were all the other removable contents of the caverns and tunnels. Replicas of any interesting items could be made when and if the area was opened to the public.

The U.S. Army Mail trunk was found wedged between the leg and the left brake of the dead Caterpillar driver. Accidental death had been the conclusion of the police inquiry. His body was identified as Big Bill by his previous female employer, and later his identity was confirmed by the owner of a Colorado refining company who was recovering at a Scottsdale Resort from a serious concussion. No one was shedding tears over the loss.

The U.S. Army Mail trunk was opened in the company of the television news crews and an Army major from the local recruiter's office. Patrick and Tony had done the honors of opening the lid. Special care was taken not to damage anything inside. There was nothing inside to damage. It apparently had been used by the miners to store food, and in the bottom corner was a tiny hole made by a mouse.

The media was not informed about the large metal box. It was removed from the cavern through the narrow opening by Dean and Roy ten days after the rescue. They had to use a mover's dolly to get it to the opening of the narrow cavern where they laid it on a piece of plywood and, with a rope attached, dragged it through the narrow opening into the tunnel. From there the heavy chest was taken early one morning to the Hidden Canyon clubhouse. The Hidden Gravel LLC members had voted unanimously that the metal box and its contents, whatever they were, would be shared in part with all the other resident members of Hidden Canyon HOA, thereby repaying the effort many of them had made to help during the long vigil of the tunnel rescue.

"Who is going to do the honors?" asked Clyde. It was assumed that Brighton would open the metal strongbox. Dean had a large bolt cutter handy to cut the padlock if it couldn't be picked. Brighton, however, stayed in his chair.

"I want to do it. I can open the lock without damaging it." The voice came from the back of the room. There standing next to Sharron Shutter was a tall, very attractive blonde woman. Most of the group had never seen her before. Lori Pederson stepped forward with Sharron and Dean at her side. Where she had been for the last few weeks no one was saying, and the look on Dean's face indicated that no one was to ask. She had yet to be arrested, and she looked fine, very fine. Though a faint murmur went through the crowd, no one questioned her right to be there or her offer to open the strongbox's padlock.

She produced a leather pouch and laid out a set of tools that looked like dental instruments. She took an optical loop from her jeans pocket then got down on her knees and studied the lock for a short time. Carefully, she selected the correct tools. With adeptness, the training of which one could only guess, Lori set to work and in less than five minutes had the lock open. She stepped away, carefully setting the valuable antique padlock on a flannel cloth on a nearby table.

A short applause erupted from the group. Who would be next? The Patel brothers stepped forward, hoping for better luck than the last time. As cameras flashed and the boys smiled, acting as though they had rehearsed the action, Tony lifted the latch and Patrick raised the two-foot by three-foot rectangular lid. The box didn't give up its secrets quietly. A creaking from the corroded hinges was accompanied by a thin cloud of dust as the lid swung back nearly 180 degrees. The same question was on everyone's mind. Was it empty like the mail container, or was the heaviness due to something valuable inside?

The boys stared into the bottom of the eighteen-inch-deep chest and, glancing at one another, started to laugh. As the others crowded around and peered inside, they too broke out laughing. High fives were shared around the group. Then when all was quiet again, Mrs. Bavana Patel stepped forward. With long, padded forceps used for her stamp collection, she carefully reached into the chest and retrieved one of the hundreds of pieces of folded woven material. As she laid it on the table next to the trunk, the fabric fell apart. Onto the table rolled an oblong, solid piece of metal about the size of a woman's thumb. A gasp ushered forth from the group as more of the pieces were removed. It became obvious as the doctor rolled them from side to side, the light shimmering from their surfaces, that the fantasies of the HOA neighbors were coming true. The entire bottom of the strongbox was full of shiny, solid-gold nuggets the size of which no one in the room had ever seen.

EPILOGUE

Little Braden Dunn arrived on schedule two days before Christmas and went home from the hospital with his mom and dad just in time to receive a visit from Santa. The Dunns weren't going to spend any more time in the hospital than absolutely necessary, afraid they might be assigned their own personal parking spot. Brighton had recently returned to his dental office, working for a flat fee of fifty dollars per visit, regardless of the procedure, and limiting his practice to patients who fell into the gap between being able to afford insurance and being so poor that they qualified for Medicaid. Most of his patients were starving students or hard-working single parents trying to raise a family on a very limited budget. Gina had helped out, working in the office right up to the day she went into labor.

Kara was in the waiting room with her twin girls when Gina delivered. Charley couldn't make it until later. He was on a conference call with the Director of the Smithsonian Institute, arranging for a traveling exhibit of the country's newest and largest collection of pure gold nuggets. Charley had become an expert in the tax advantages of donations, especially when those donations were made to the U.S. government. He had discovered that the half of the Hidden Canyon HOA's two 254 solid gold nuggets, belonging to the Hidden Gravel LLC, fell into a special class of value beyond estimation. Thus, the tax write-off was likewise beyond estimation.

Giving credence to his elation was a recent precedent-setting donation of Vincent Van Gogh's Irises painting to the National Museum. The IRS allowed it to shelter its benefactor to the tune of $400 million.

***

Roy and Rhonda were married on Thanksgiving Eve in a private backyard ceremony at her home, attended by a limited number of family and friends. No paparazzi were invited. She and Roy had several trips planned together for the coming year, she to perform several concerts and he to do on-site airport tower inspections for the FAA. Once his name hit the news media in the same sentence with Rhonda Tucker's, it became blatantly apparent to his FAA bosses in Washington that he possessed "executive-level skills" and was wasting his talents sitting in an ordinary control tower.

✳✳✳

The Patel family had taken their Christmas break at Rhonda's house in Hawaii while their house and yard were being put back together. The Steiner clan members were caring for Harley and keeping an eye on the mine tunnel. They were the LLC's official, self-appointed wacht hunde or watchdogs. They liked to march around the entire Hidden Gravel LLC property, picking up loose papers and chasing off the paparazzi.

✳✳✳

Dean and Sharron Shutter moved into their new house the week before Christmas. It was a beautiful home, truly a showcase of the best and newest of everything in home construction, design, and decorating. It even had voice recognition control panels that unlocked and opened the doors, controlled the entertainment system, and ran the glass elevator up and down merely by giving quiet, audible instructions. Sharron didn't tell anyone, but she and Dean had bought out Cousin Lori's assay business for a cool one million dollars and then taken Lori to the airport for her one-way flight to Argentina. "They've got lots of minerals there," Dean promised.

✳✳✳

By the following summer, Hidden Canyon was hot and dry and showed no apparent sign of the previous year's mining and murder exploits. The Hidden Canyon HOA had a new female president whose only campaign promise was to maintain healthy flowers in all the common flowerbeds. She had been elected by a landslide.

All the homes in Hidden Canyon were large and well designed with natural-looking desert landscaping in the front and a scattering of swimming pools, putting greens, and sizable patches of manicured play grass in the back. Every house was occupied with happy or wanting-to-be-happy families.

The only exception was the smaller but well-cared-for house on Lot #29 in Cactus Wren Circle. That house stood empty. Its natural desert backyard was open onto a wash that meandered through the Hidden Canyon neighborhoods. The house had no fences or automatic yard lights, just a half-buried rubber watering trough with float valve to keep it full for the desert animals. The property was frequented by any number of desert birds, coyotes, rabbits, javalina, and an occasional fox, looking for a drink of water or hoping for an old friend to return. Inside, in the front window, was a small lamp that burned night and day in case the gray-haired woman returned.

Acknowledgments

My family and friends are the fire that wakes me in the morning and keeps me going late into the night. Without their encouragement and constructive criticism this book would still be another boring dinner table conversation. Thanks to all, especially: Elyssa, Dave, Tasha, Derek, David, Andrea, Dalan, Margaret, Carl, Debbie, Julie Lassetter, Dennis Toleman, Lyn & John Glenn, Patty & Mike Pierson, and Mary & Mitch Platt.

In addition, many thanks to my terrific editor, Lisa Schleipfer, who picked up the ball at halftime and carried it into the end zone.

And to my fantastic publisher/agent/mentor/friend, Lisa Akoury-Ross, who has taught me everything I know about putting fanciful ideas into legible sentences and onto the printed page.

Most of all, I thank my wife Paula Peterson Dahl for 43 wonderful years of hard work, self-sacrifice, and loving patience. It can't be easy tolerating a mind that can't stop imagining.

About The Author

After thirty years of medical practice and raising five children, Dr. Steven I. Dahl and his wife Paula split their time between their homes in the Arizona desert and the mountain peaks of Utah. Humanitarian medical missions in third world countries, spending time with their seventeen grandchildren and writing fiction thrillers fill the retirement years. With his fourth novel penned, he and Paula are living in Europe, fulfilling a medical mission and working on his next adventure.

Order *HOA Gold* for Your Friends!

Or other books written by Steven I. Dahl, M.D.

Simply visit us at:

www.PublishAtSweetDreams.com and click on the book title to order online.

OR: Fill out the form below and mail your order to:

Sweet Dreams Publishing of MA
5 Federal Street
Weymouth, MA 02188
Attn: Lisa Akoury-Ross

Title: (check which title or both)
❑ HOA Gold: $14.95   Quantity: _____
❑ Chicken Fried Steak: $14.95   Quantity: _____
Total number of books: _____   Subtotal: _____
                                          Shipping and Handling: _____ $7.00

                                                                    Total: _____

Name: _____

Street: _____

City, State, Zip: _____

Phone or email: _____